Mystery of
PROPHECY

THE MYSTERY OF PROPHECY
VOLUME 1

The
Secret
of
Daniel

HARLAN LEGARE

ISBN: 978-1-961677-88-3 (Paperback)
ISBN: 978-1-961677-31-9 (Ebook)

Library of Congress Control Number: 2023915760

Printed in the United States of America

Published by:

info@thequippyquill.com
(302) 295-2278

CONTENTS

Remember the former things of old: for I am God, and there is none else; I am God, and there is none like me, declaring the end from the beginning, and from ancient times the things that are not yet done, saying, My counsel shall stand.

∽ Isaiah 46:9–10 ∾

But you, O Daniel, shut up the words, and seal the book, even to the time of the end.

∾ Daniel 12:4 ∾

CHAPTER ONE
The Secrets of Daniel

The apostle John was told that *"in the days of the voice of the seventh angel, when he shall begin to sound, the mystery of God should be finished, as he declared to his servants the prophets"* (Revelation 10:7). This *mystery of God* is thus the story that is told through the words of the prophets.

The Greek word *mystérion* used here speaks of knowledge with held by God. Further, it is knowledge that can only be revealed by God, and revealed only in his time. Such are the prophecies of Daniel: *"But you, O Daniel, Shut up the words, and seal the book, even to the time of the end"* (Daniel 12:4). While the mystery itself may have been declared to the prophet Daniel of old, the understanding of that mystery has yet to be revealed.

Amos was told of these prophecies, *"Surely the Lord God do nothing, but he reveal his secret unto his servants the prophets"* (Amos 3:7).

It's quite simple; until the secrets of that mystery concerning the time of the return of Jesus are revealed, rightly understood, and declared unto the world, the *Lord God will do nothing* toward completing the *mystery of God*.

Sealed Till the Time of the End
No one can correctly interpret most of the prophecies concerning the time of the return of Jesus without knowing the secrets that were hidden in the book of Daniel, for it is his words that hold the keys to the understanding of the words of many of the other prophets.

That is quite a bold statement for anyone to make, considering all the theories of prophetical interpretation expounded upon today. But think about this - Daniel was told of his prophecies, *"The words are closed up and sealed the time of the end"* (Daniel 12:9). That means that no matter how honest the effort, no matter how hard the try, no matter how Godly the man, the correct interpretation of Daniel's visions could not be obtained until the season of Christ's return. Simply put, the secrets of Daniel could not be correctly understood until this day when God chose to reveal His.

What Do We Really Know?

What effect does this have on what we think we know of events of the end of this age? Interpretations of Daniel's visions have abounded for centuries. And, essentially all that is taught today of his prophecies is based on those long-held theories, theories that were formed before Daniel's words could be rightly understood. So the question must be asked—since the words of Daniel were closed to our understanding, how valid are those interpretations?

Also, the words of Daniel are most often the key to the understanding of much that was written by other prophets concerning the events of the last days. This is especially true of the book of Revelation which records the completion of all these prophecies. Thus, if we could not know Daniel's words, what could we know of the words of the other prophets? What, then, is the validity of those theories? What truth do we really know of God's prophetic word for the end of this age?

Shut Up the Words

"But you, O Daniel, Shut up the and the book, to the time Of the end".

(Daniel 12:4)

What was meant when Daniel was told to *shut up the words?* After all, the words themselves have not been kept from us since they have been printed for centuries for all to read, It is not then the words themselves that were shut up, but the understanding of the words that has been hidden from us, and thus the understanding of the prophecies.

But Which Words?

Which words of Daniel could not be under stood? I can only speak to that which the Holy Spirit has revealed to me—after all, we cannot know what has been hidden until it is revealed. What is written in these pages is what God has taught me of His words written by Daniel. The credit is thus His, not mine,

Much of the book of Daniel is prophecy, and it has been primarily the prophetic word that was sealed. We could understand the stories of Daniel in the lion's den and of Belshazzar and the hand writing on the wall, but we could only catch a glimpse of Nebuchadnezzar's dream of a great and startling image made of many metals, of Daniel's vision of the conflict between the king of the north and the king of the south, of the vision of the seventy weeks that are determined upon the Jews and the city of Jerusalem, or of the vision of the daily sacrifice that is taken away. These are some of the "words" that had been *sealed till the time of the end.*

Why?

The next logical question is, why were the words of King Belshazzar and the hand writing on the wall that announced that this ungodly king was weighed in the balances of God's law and found to be wanting is another account of man's disobedience to God. These stories are told of the Gentiles,

The sum of these stories tells of the blessing and of the punishment of individuals as a consequence of their obedience, or lack thereof, to God Accounts are given of captives and of kings, of the Jew and of the Gentile, to show that all men are accounted to God for their obedience to him. The message of the book itself is therefore a message to each one of us that we are individually account able to God for our obedience.

The prophecies of the book of Daniel continue the theme of accountability to God However, his prophecies are an account of God's dealing with the disobedience of the nation of Israel—not of the disobedience of people individually but of the people collectively,

This can be stated no better than in Daniel 9:24: *"Seventy weeks are determined upon your people and upon your holy city, to finish the transgression, and to make an end of sins, and to make reconciliation for iniquity, and to bring in everlasting and to seal up the vision and prophecy, and to anoint the most*

Holy." It is a prophecy concerning the accountability of the Jews to God.

The prophecies of Daniel tell the story of seven Gentile kingdoms that God brings against Israel, These kingdoms are used in part as a rod of punishment for the nation's continuing disobedience and, in part, as a staff of correction to bring about the nation's return to God. Daniels prophecies identify those Gentile kingdoms and Israel's involvement with them throughout history, down to the battle of Armageddon and to the establishment of the government of the Messiah, their triumphant king. This means that Daniel describes the nations and the events of the last days of this age, When we see, and understand, what Daniel saw, we will know that Jesus is on his return to this earth to rule and to reign!

So why was this information kept from us throughout history? Every generation of Christians since the resurrection of Jesus has expected his imminent return because they saw something in the world around them of the signs spoken of in the Scriptures that foretold his return. This expectation that Jesus could return at any moment has moved untold numbers to seek God, and countless others to remain obedient to Him. If these generations had understood the words of Daniel, they would have known of that which Daniel had seen. Then, looking at the nations and events of their world and not seeing What must first be in place, they would have known that the return of Jesus was far off Not seeing what must first be, how many would have said "I have plenty of time to get right with God" and then been lost for eternity?

The expected imminent return of Jesus in past generations brought people to him Knowing what Daniel saw would have destroyed that expectation. That is why Daniel was told to *shut up the words* until the time of the return of Christ

Why Now?

So why are we now allowed to understand what Daniel saw? If we are now to know what Daniel saw, would not that knowledge destroy our expectation of a soon return of Christ? Certainly not! In fact, with the correct understanding of Daniel's prophecies, we can see today what Daniel saw. It is because of what we now see we know for certain that Jesus is on his way.

For What Purpose?

So, what is the purpose of the prophecies in the book of Daniel? Daniel's prophecies are to show the nation of Israel today the almighty hand of God and His love for them. It is as if Isaiah was speaking to today's Israel, when he said:

> *¹Hear you this, O house of Jacob, which are called by the name of Israel.... ³I have declared the former things from the beginning; and they went forth out of my mouth, and I showed them; I did them suddenly, and they came to pass. ⁴Because I knew that you are obstinate, and your neck is an iron sinew, and your brow brass; ⁵I have even from the beginning declared it to you; before it came to pass I showed you: lest you should say, My idol has done them, and my graven image, and my molten image, has commanded.*

> *(Isaiah 4811, 3-5)*

When the events of the last days of this age unfold, Israel will begin to understand that it was not man who has brought about these things by his own hand, but that they have been brought by the hand of God. Israel cannot yet see what God has *declared* through Daniel that is *to come* to pass for their nation. *"Blindness in part is happened to Israel"* *(Romans 11:25)* because of the corporate disobedience of the Jews. But at *the time of the end* spoken of by Daniel, this *blindness* will be lifted, and they shall understand Daniel's message of Obedience- They will recognize that God had told them that it was His hand that has been on these nations for their good and will again seek Him in their obedience. God said of this time, *"I will pour upon the house of David, and upon the inhabitants of Jerusalem, the spirit of grace and of supplications: and they shall look upon me whom they, have pierced"* *(Zechariah 12:10),* In their return to obedience, they will find their Messiah in Jesus.

What about Us?

If the prophecies of Daniel are for the nation of Israel, what have they to do with us today as Gentiles? We go back to *Arnos 3:7: "Surely the Lord God Will do nothing, but he reveal his secret unto his servants the prophets,"* We, as Christians, are yet the messengers of God's word, We are those prophets spoken of by Amos and, will remain so until the Rapture, So it is our responsibility to seek the truth word and tell it unto the world.

The church will not be raptured until the truth of God's prophecies is known.

What Secrets Are Now Revealed?

What secrets does the book of Daniel now reveal? What is written in these pages reveal many truths that, to my knowledge, have never been told. Some are blockbusters, such as the "time" of the Rapture, the identification of the head of the beast that was wounded to death and was healed, and the origin of the one we call the Antichrist. Others are less dramatic in their telling but are just as startling in their conclusions, such as the meaning of the symbols of the beasts, the heads, the horns, and the crowns that are used to describe the three beasts of the book of Revelation. The secrets that have been revealed to me are scattered throughout the chapters of *The Mystery of Prophecy*. Some are told of outright, but most are revealed by the understanding of the prophecies interpreted.

The Mystery of Prophecy tells the story of the disobedience of the nation of Israel and of their redemption to God. This story is told through Israel's involvement with a series of Gentile kingdoms that God brings against the nation of Israel. But that story is far more than just the conflict between a handful of countries, for it will consume every man, woman, and child on this earth, for man's disobedience of God has brought about a set of events that is leading the world to the battle of Armageddon and to an accounting of his disobedience.

For those who are watching for the return of Jesus Christ, *The Mystery of Prophecy* will bring into sharp focus the events that we will see on the horizon as we take flight into the heavens.

I saw three unclean spirits like frogs come out of the mouth of the and out of the mouth of the beast, and out of the mouth of the false prophet.

∽ Revelation 16:13 ∾

CHAPTER TWO
With Three Beast

We start our story in the book of Revelation and with three beasts seen by the apostle John. John describes the first of these beasts as a red dragon having seven heads and ten horns, confronting a woman clothed with the sun, with the moon under her feet, and crowned with twelve stars. The second beast John saw was rising out of the sea, appearing as a leopard, but with the feet of a bear and the mouth of a lion, The third beast, a beast with two horns. was seen coming up from the earth. We start with the identification of these three beasts because the understanding of their descriptive symbolism is the key to unlocking the interpretation of the prophecies for these last days, The official names of these three beasts, if they are to be titled, are the Dragon, the Beast, and the False Prophet. These are given to us in Revelation 16:13-14, where John states. *"¹³I saw three unclean spirits like frogs come out of the mouth of the dragon, and out of the beast, and out of the mouth of the false prophet. ¹⁴For the y are the spirits of devils, working world, to gather them to the battle of that great day of God Almighty."*

The Dragon

³There appeared another wonder in heaven; and behold a great red dragon, having seven heads and ten horns, and seven crowns upon his heads. ⁴And his tail drew the third part of the stars of heaven, and did cast them to the earth: and the dragon stood before the woman which was ready to be delivered, to devour her child as soon as it was born. ⁷And there was in heaven: Micheal and his angels fought against the dragon; and the dragon fought and his angels, ⁸and prevailed not; neither was their place found any more in heaven. ⁹And the great dragon was cast out, the old serpent, called the Devil, and Satan, which deceives the whole world: he was cast *out into the earth, and his angels were cast out with him…. ¹³And when the dragon saw that he was cast unto the earth, he persecuted the woman which brought forth the man.*

(Revelation 12:3-9, 13)

The Beast

¹I stood on the sand of the sea, and saw a beast rise up out of the sea, having seven heads and ten horns and upon his horns ten crowns and upon his heads the name of blasphemy. ²And the beast which I saw was like unto a leopard, and his feet were as the feet of a bear, and his mouth as the mouth of a lion: and the dragon gave him his power, and his seat, and great authority. ³And saw one of his heads as it were wounded to death; and his deadly wound was healed: and all the world wondered after the beast,

(Revelation 13:1-2)

The False Prophet

¹¹I beheld another beast coming up out of the earth; ¹²and he had two horns like a lamb, and he spoke as a dragon. And he exercises all the power of the first beast before him, and causes the earth and them which dwell therein to worship the first beast, whose deadly wound was healed. ¹³And he does great wonders, so that he makes fire come down from heaven on the earth in the sight of men, ¹⁴and deceives them that dwell on the earth by those miracles which he had power to do in the sight of the beast; saying to them that dwell on the earth, that they should make an image to the beast, which had the wound by a sword, and did live. ¹⁵And he had power to give life unto the image of the beast, that the image of the beast should both speak, and cause that as many as would not worship the image of the beast should be killed. ¹⁶And he causes all, both small and great, rich and poor, free and bond, to receive a mark in their right hand, or in their foreheads: ¹⁷and that no man might buy or sell, save he that had the mark, or the name of the beast, or the number of his name….¹⁸The number of the beast is a number of a man; and his number is six hundred threescore and six.

(Revelation 13:11-18)

The Symbols

These three beasts can be known by deciphering the meaning of the symbols used to describe them. The symbols *beast, head, horn,* and *crown* of these beasts are explained in the following pages, as these three beasts are at last revealed in truth. Only the explanation of the symbols and their application to the Red Dragon, the Beast, and the False Prophet are given in this chapter. The validity of the interpretation of the symbols themselves and of the beasts they portray is proved in following chapters as God reveals the secrets of the book of Daniel.

A Beast

The word beast that is used when speaking of the Dragon, the Beast, and the False Prophet is *therion,* meaning *a wild beast.* It is the same word that John would have used when speaking of the bear or the lion that was common to the Middle East in his day. There is nothing in the word *beast* itself that has prophetic relevance, but it is an apt symbol that can take many forms and yet be easily visualized by the reader. In the context of these three creatures, a beast is used to symbolize an *empire.* The beast that is the Red Dragon, with its seven heads and ten horns and with seven crowns on his heads, is thus an empire. The Beast that rises from the sea, which also has seven heads and ten horns but which has ten crowns upon its horns, is another empire. The False Prophet, the beast that comes up out of the earth, which has two horns like a lamb, is a third empire.

The word *empire* comes from the Latin *imperium,* meaning *absolute authority.* An *empire* is defined as *a major political unit having a territory of great extent.* It can also be defined as *a number of territories or peoples under a single sovereign authority.* But no matter the form, an empire always consists of two parts: *a ruler* and the *ruled.*

The ruler of an empire can be *a major political unit or a single sovereign authority,* while those ruled can be *a territory of great extent or a number of territories or peoples.* An empire therefore can take many forms. We think of empires most often in terms of kings and nations such as the Roman Empire of ancient times or of the British Empire of more recent times. But we also speak of political, economic, and social empires, which also have some form of the two components of *ruler* and the *ruled.*

Even though empires take many forms, one characteristic remains the same in each—the ruler has *absolute authority* over those ruled. This totalitarian relationship between the ruler and those ruled melds the two into one, making the ruled an extension of the ruler. This unity seen in an empire is often reflected in our use of language where the two parts are spoken of as if they were one, or are spoken of interchangeably as if the two were one and the same. An illustration of this is the political empire of the president of the United States and his administration. In this illustration, the president is the ruler of this empire, and his administration is the ruled. As ruler, the president sets forth his policy and appoints an administration to carry out that policy. Because the task of the administration is to carry out the president's policy, the administration could be viewed as those who are ruled. In the sense that those of the administration are there at the sole discretion of the president, the ruler has absolute authority over those who are ruled. This relationship of ruler to those ruled is established so as to speak with one voice, which is that of the president's, no matter who within the administration may be speaking. In this respect, the ruler and the ruled become one and the same. The effect of this absolute authority is seen in the press when it is reported, "The White House said today…" Whether the reported statement was spoken by the president or by a member of his administration, the statement stands as that of the president's.

When the White House is used to encompass both the president and his administration, it becomes the symbol of the empire. The Bible speaks of our three beasts in the same manner. In Revelation 12:3, John describes the first of these beasts as *a "great red dragon, having seven heads and ten horns, and seven crowns upon his heads."* In verse 9, John is told that *"the great dragon was cast out, that old serpent, called the Devil, and Satan, which deceives the whole world."* The Red Dragon is therefore said to be Satan. But is Satan really a red dragon with seven heads and ten horns? Not really. What we are shown by these verses are the two parts of an empire. The red dragon with *seven heads and ten horns and seven crowns* is that which is ruled. The red dragon which *deceives the whole world* is the ruler, Satan. Together they form an empire that is portrayed as a beast.

The Scripture uses the symbols of the Red Dragon, the Beast, and the False Prophet just as the press uses the symbol of the White

House to identify the source of authority by which an action is taken. We discern from the text whether the act was that of the ruler or was an act carried out by the ruled on behalf of the ruler.

A Head

A head of a beast symbolizes a kingdom. The kingdom is a literal parcel of real estate that has a people, a government, and a territorial boundary. These kingdoms are of three forms: a nation, an empire, and a confederacy.

A nation is a single sovereign state like modern Egypt or Israel. Their rulers could be a king, a president, a prime minister, or a dictator.

An empire is a group of nations under rule or tribute to a single sovereign ruler. The Roman Empire would be an example.

A confederacy is a group of nations that form a league or compact for mutual support or for common action. Although each of the nations in a confederacy is itself sovereign, they submit some of their authority to a common government by mutual consent. The European Union is an example of a confederacy.

A Horn

A *horn* represents a *man of authority*. The empire of the Red Dragon has ten horns as does the empire of the Beast. The empire of the False Prophet has just two horns.

A Crown

A *crown* is the symbol of *sovereignty*. A crown on a head signifies that the head of a beast is a sovereign kingdom. A crown on a horn of a beast signifies the sovereignty of that man; he is a king. In today's world, this king could be a man or a woman, a monarch, emperor, president, or dictator.

With the symbols *beast, head, horn,* and *crown* defined, we can now start to identify the empires that are the Red Dragon, the Beast, and the False Prophet.

The Empire of the Red Dragon

The Red Dragon is an empire ruled by Satan. Those who are ruled are represented by the seven crowned heads, which are kingdoms. The ten horns, seen without crowns, are men who will later be seen as kings. The first six kingdoms are the Assyrian, Egyptian, Babylonian, Medo Persian, Grecian, and Roman Empires of the distant past. The seventh kingdom is a confederacy yet to be formed that I call the League of Ten. These seven heads of the Red Dragon are crowned, showing that these seven are each a separate sovereign kingdom. The kingdom that is the League of Ten will be a confederacy of ten nations. These nations of the League are in turn represented by the ten horns, which are all on the seventh head of the beast. The empire of the Red Dragon is shown pictorially in figure 2.1.

Figure 2.1. The Red Dragon.

It is said by some that this entire world is presently the kingdom of Satan. That is in some ways true in that Satan is the current proprietor of this world, taking it from Adam when Adam disobeyed God. But Satan has only limited authority as proprietor; he does not have the absolute authority necessary to make it his empire.

It is also true that Satan has held sway over many of the world's empires other than these seven of the Red Dragon, yet they are not included here. Why is it then that just these seven make up the empire of the Red Dragon? The answer typically given is that only these seven of the Red Dragon rule the world.

But no empire has yet to rule the world. In ages past, and even in recent times, there were empires that ruled more territory than did Rome, and there were empires that ruled more people than did Rome. It was said of one of these greatest of empires, "the sun never sets on the British Empire." These empires ruled the world as much as did Egypt, or Babylon, or Rome; yet, they are not part of the Red Dragon. Why? The answer to why only seven of the world's empires make up the empire of the Red Dragon is found in the phrase "Judah, Israel, and Jerusalem" spoken by Zechariah in his vision of the four horns (Zechariah 1:19). God has brought many kingdoms against the Israelites, partly in wrath for their disobedience, and partly as a means to turn this disobedient nation back to Him in repentance. Many of these kingdoms came at a time before the city-state of Jerusalem became a part of the Israelite nation. Others, such as the British and Ottoman Empires possessed the land that was Israel, but the nation did not then exist. In Zechariah's vision, the four who were counted as having *scattered* the Israelites are those who had conquered Judah, Israel, and Jerusalem. It is thus from the time of the addition of the city-state of Jerusalem to the kingdoms of Judah and Israel that the story of the Red Dragon begins. The kingdoms that Zechariah counted were Assyria, Egypt, Babylon, and Medo-Persia, the first four of the seven Gentile empires that God brings against *Judah, Israel, and Jerusalem* in his plan to return this disobedient nation back to Him.

The first six of the seven Gentile empires of the Red Dragon made *Judah, Israel, and Jerusalem* subservient to them. Thus, in one way or another, the nation of Israel became a part of the invading empire. By the pattern thus established, the *Judah, Israel, and Jerusalem* of today, meaning the entire nation of Israel, must also become a part of the seventh kingdom. These seven heads of the Red Dragon are thus unique amongst the world's empires, having one thing in common that no others can claim—every one of these seven of the Red Dragon contains the nation of Israel!

The Red Dragon as seen by John has seven crowned heads, representing seven sovereign Gentile kingdoms that will rule over the nation of Israel, and ten horns, representing the yet-to-be-crowned kings of the seventh kingdom still to come. I have claimed that this beast is an empire, having a ruler and those who are ruled. It is interesting to note, then, that of the symbols used to describe the empire of the Red Dragon, we are shown only those who are ruled; there is no symbol that we can identify as the ruler of this empire.

Even though John tells us that this Red Dragon is Satan, so he is there somewhere, we need something more to show us how Satan is revealed as the ruler of this empire. That I will show shortly.

Revelation 12:4 states that the tail of the Red Dragon drew a third of the stars of heaven and cast them to the earth. These are the angels that are cast to the earth with Satan (v. 9). This depiction shows Satan's rule over those angels who rebelled against God, as did Satan. These angels are shown with the beast in figure 2.1. Thus, we are shown both the spiritual empire and political empire of Satan.

The Empire of the Beast

The beast that John saw *"rise up out of the sea" (Revelation 13:1)* has seven heads and ten horns as does the Red Dragon. But this beast has ten crowns rather than seven, and they are on its horns rather than its heads. The empire of the Beast is shown pictorially in figure 2.2. This is the empire of the Antichrist.

Figure 2.2. The Beast from the Sea.

The seventh head of the Red Dragon, the head with the ten horns, will first exist as a confederacy of ten sovereign nations that I identified as the League of Ten. That confederacy is represented here by their kings, the ten crowned horns of the Beast from the sea. This confederacy is formed at the time when *"the prince that shall come…shall confirm the covenant with many for one week" (Daniel 9:26–27). The many* in this verse are the nine other nations that also *confirm the covenant,* the agreement forming the confederacy.

The English word *confirm* is translated from the Hebrew verb *gabar,* meaning to *strengthen.* The form of this verb used in verse 27 is the Hiphill conjunction *he caused to strengthen.*

The signature of this *prince that shall come* adds strength to this covenant because it adds the assets and the support of his nation to this confederacy. *This prince that shall come* is thus only one of ten to confirm this covenant.

Shortly after the signing of this covenant that brings into existence the League of Ten, this *prince that shall come* will rise to the position of king of his nation. This prince, now a king, will then invade and conquer three other nations of this confederacy, absorbing them into his own nation; thus the four horns with crowns seen on the one head. This kingdom will still contain the ten nations, but it will appear as having only seven. These seven remaining nations are represented by the seven heads of the Beast. The other remaining six nations of the confederation will then give the sovereignty of their respective nations over totally to this new king. By these acts, the confederacy of ten nations will become an empire of seven nations. Thus, the Beast represents both the initial form of the kingdom as a confederacy and the final form as an empire.

As previously stated, the Red Dragon has seven heads, which represent seven kingdoms. The first six kingdoms to appear were the Assyrian, Egyptian, Medo Persian, Grecian, and Roman Empires. The seventh kingdom to appear, the one with the ten horns, will be the League of Ten that will in turn become the empire of the Antichrist. Therefore, the seventh head of the Red Dragon essentially represents both the confederacy of the League of Ten and the empire of the Beast.

The uniqueness of the seven heads of the Red Dragon is that these seven kingdoms each contain the nation of Israel. Just as Israel was part of the Assyrian or of the Roman Empire, Israel will be part of the seventh that contains the ten nations of the League of Ten. The nation of Israel is represented by a crowned horn of the Beast and not a head of the

Beast because Israel is a conquered nation in John's description of the Beast. Revelation 13:4 states of this beast from the sea that John *"saw one of his heads as it were wounded to death; and his deadly wound was healed."* Remember, a head of this beast must be a nation. This head that was *wounded to death* but whose *deadly wound was healed* must therefore be a nation. There has been only one nation in the history of this world that has died by the sword, was buried, and yet has come back to life—Israel. The head that was wounded to death but whose deadly wound was healed is the nation of Israel.[1]

In the symbols of this empire we see both the ruler and those who are ruled. The Antichrist will become the king of one of the nations of the League of Ten and thus is one of the ten crowned horns. Those who are ruled by the Antichrist are the ten nations of those kings, shown in their final configuration as seven heads.

The Empire of the False Prophet

John *"beheld another beast coming up out of the earth; and he had two horns like a lamb, and he spoke as a dragon"* (Revelation 13:11). This beast is also an empire, with a ruler (actually two rulers) and those who are ruled. This beast originates in religion. The empire of the False Prophet is shown pictorially in figure 2.3.

Figure 2.3. The False Prophet.

It is of utmost importance to the understanding of this beast to recognize that the title "False Prophet" applies to the beast, that is, to the empire. "False Prophet" is the name of the empire; it is not the name or title of either ruler of the empire.

This beast is described by John as a beast having two horns, but he makes no mention of it having a head. This beast thus has two horns but no head. But how can a beast have two horns without having a head? John may have actually seen a beast that had a head, and the two horns likely were on that head. However, what is important to our understanding of this beast is how John presents that beast to us. He describes it as having two horns. God is telling us through John's description of this beast just what He wants us to see—and we see no head. This tells us that this empire does not consist of nations.

This beast also has no crowns, telling us that this beast is not a sovereign entity. Therefore, this empire must answer to a higher authority. This beast has two horns *like a lamb*. This does not mean this beast appears as a lamb, but rather, the horns are like those of a lamb—small, without great stature. These horns also are seen without crowns, so these two horns are not sovereign; thus, they answer to a higher authority. These two horns are not kings, nor do they have great stature, but they still represent men of authority.

They are rulers in their own right but are rulers with limited authority. John tells us also that this beast *spoke as a dragon*. This beast not only receives its authority from Satan but is also under Satan's authority at some level.

The False Prophet is a bureaucratic empire within the government of the Antichrist. The two horns are two men of position who work for the Antichrist. The one man is the head of the Ministry of Religion. Although we know this man is a false prophet by his actions, we incorrectly give him the title of False Prophet, the name of the empire of which he is a part. His correct title is *"image of the beast" (Revelation 13:14)* since he is much like the Antichrist. The other man is the head of the Ministry of Finance. He institutes the *"mark of the beast" (Revelation 13:16)*. Both of these men will have control over people, but each will rule them by different means. The False Prophet is thus a beast, an empire with two rulers and those they rule.

Something's Missing

A beast here has been defined as an empire, consisting of a ruler and those who are ruled. The description in Revelation 12 of the Red Dragon as a beast having seven heads and ten horns, with seven crowns upon its heads, is thus an incomplete view of the empire in that it shows only the symbols of those who are ruled, that of the seven kingdoms and ten kings. There was no symbol given that would represent Satan, the ruler of this empire (Satan can not be represented by a horn with a crown, a king, as a horn can only represent a man). Yet, we know Satan is a part of this empire since Revelation 12:9 states, *"The great dragon was cast out, that old serpent, called the Devil, and Satan, which deceives the whole world: he was cast out into the earth."* From this verse alone it appears that the beast represents only Satan. But it applies to Satan only in that he is a part of the beast. This verse cannot apply to the whole of the beast because it is Satan that is *cast out into the earth*, not the kingdoms he rules. The seven heads of this beast cannot be cast out *[from heaven] into the earth* because they are literally kingdoms of this earth; they have never been a part of heaven. The Red Dragon is therefore not Satan but the empire of which Satan is a part. To get the complete picture of this beast we must go to Revelation 17.

In chapter 17 there is seen a beast having seven heads and ten horns that carries the woman identified as *Babylon the Great, the Mother of Harlots and Abominations of the Earth*. The mystery of this beast is revealed later in the chapter "Babylon the Great, A Mystery No Longer," so pertinent information revealed there of this beast is used here with no further explanation.

The scarlet-colored beast with seven heads and ten horns that carries this woman is the Red Dragon. The seven heads of the beast on which the woman sits are said to be seven mountains, which represent seven governments. This does not change our definition of a head of a beast as a kingdom but, rather, complements the definition with the use of a *mountain* to represent the *government* of the kingdom. The purpose for this is to focus our attention at this point on the kings of those kingdoms rather than on the kingdoms themselves, for there are also seven kings. Of these seven kings, five have fallen, one is, and the other is not yet come. And when he comes, he will rule only for a short time. We recognize these seven kings as the representative kings of the seven kingdoms of the Red Dragon.

With the scarlet-colored beast identified as the empire of the Red Dragon, our attention is now brought to the king of that empire. This beast *"was, and is not; and shall ascend out of the bottomless pit, and go into perdition: and they that dwell on the earth shall wonder, whose names were not written in the book of life from the foundation of the world, when they behold the beast that was, and is not, and yet is"* (Revelation 17:8). This is Satan, the king of the empire of the Red Dragon. *"The beast that was, and is not, even he is the eighth, and is of the seven, and goes into perdition"* (Revelation 17:11). These seven are the seven kings of the seven kingdoms of the Red Dragon. Satan is in turn king over these seven as the ruler of the empire. Satan is therefore *the eighth* king within this empire. With Satan identified as the eighth king of the scarlet-colored beast, all the parts of the empire that is the Red Dragon, having seven heads and ten horns, and seven crowns upon his heads, have been accounted for. (Satan is never depicted as a horn in the descriptions of these three beasts, as a *horn* represents a *man*.) In John's vision of the beast from the sea, both the ruler and those who are ruled are included. This beast also has seven heads and ten horns, but has ten crowns upon his horns. The Antichrist is the ruler of this empire, but he is also one of the ten horns. Those who are ruled are the seven heads and the other nine horns.

The vision of the False Prophet is similar to the vision of the Red Dragon in that only part of the empire is represented by symbols in the vision seen by John.

In the vision of the empire of the False Prophet, only the rulers of the empire are depicted: the two small horns. Those who are ruled are identified in the narration of the vision. Those who are under the authority of the Ministry of Religion are given in Revelation 13:12: *"And he [the one small horn] exercises all the power of the first beast before him, and causes the earth and them which dwell therein to worship the first beast, whose deadly wound was healed." Those under the authority of the Ministry of Finance are given in Revelation 13:16–17: "And he [the other small horn] causes all, small and great, rich and poor, free and bond, to receive a mark in their right hand, or in their foreheads: And that no man might buy or sell, save he that had the mark, or the name of the beast, or the number of his name."* With this, both the rulers of the empire of the False Prophet and those who are ruled by the empire are identified.

God's Role for These Three Beasts

Even though these three beasts are defined as empires whose ultimate ruler is Satan, they are yet a creation by God's hand. It's not that God is the source of this evil, but that at times He uses the godless for His purposes just as He uses the believers to do His good work. These three beasts are used to bring the wrath of the Lamb upon His chosen people, Israel.

I will show unto the king the interpretation.

—Daniel 2:24 1

Not only is Israel the only nation in history to come back to life when once dead; the language of the nation, Hebrew, is the only dead language that has ever been resurrected.

CHAPTER THREE
Breaking the Code

Now we go to the book of Daniel and to the revealing of some of those words that were *closed-up and sealed till the time of the end.* The three beasts of Revelation, the Red Dragon, the Beast, and the False Prophet have been presented to us in the symbols of beasts, heads, and horns. These symbols are defined for us in the book of Daniel, which we shall see in this chapter. In the defining of these symbols, we also see that we are given the outline of our story.

Daniel was a young man when Judah and Jerusalem came under the control of the Babylonian Empire in 605 BC. To assure the loyalty of the king of Judah to his new master, *"certain of the children of Israel…well favored, and skillful in all wisdom, and cunning in knowledge"* *(Daniel 1:3–4)* were taken hostage to Babylon. Daniel was among those taken. There he was trained for service in the Babylonian government and was appointed to a position of responsibility.

Babylonian society was a culture of magicians, astrologers, and sorcerers where dreams were believed to be messages from the gods, and interpretation of those dreams was of great importance. God used that culture of dreams and interpretations to tell us today what is about to come upon our world.

The Three Dreams

Daniel tells of a dream of Nebuchadnezzar, the Babylonian king, who saw a great statue of a man made of many different metals. Daniel also tells of two of his dreams. One is a dream of four beasts that arise from the sea: a lion, a bear, a leopard, and a beast that he said had teeth of iron and nails of brass. The other is a dream of a ram and a goat in mortal combat. These three dreams were all of a series of

Gentile empires that were to come to rule on the earth. Daniel not only tells us these dreams but also tells us their interpretation.

Although Daniel interprets these dreams, he did not understand all of what they told. And though they were written over 2,500 years ago for all to read, generation after generation could not understand all that they told. The time was not right for man to know of their secrets, until today.

The understanding of the meaning of the symbolisms in these dreams comes, in part, from the interpretation of each dream given in the book of Daniel itself. Since these three dreams are all dreams about the same entities, additional understanding of the symbols comes from comparison of their use from dream to dream. Comparing the dreams with historic events provides further understanding of the use of the symbols. That is the mechanical process used to begin the interpretation of the symbols. It is, however, truly the Holy Spirit who guides us in the application of this knowledge of the symbols to rightly interpret the words of Daniel, for it was God who had *closed up and sealed* our understanding of them.

Why are the answers scattered throughout three dreams? Part of that answer is that each dream gives information that cannot be conveyed by the nature of the other dreams. The other part of the answer is God's message to the one who desires to know the truth of these prophecies—take into account all of the Scripture! All text is there for a purpose; it is there to instruct us.

To select one verse because it supports an appealing theory and then ignore the next verse because it does not is folly. We must take into account all of God's word if we are to know the truth of what He has written to us. The following is the comparison of each of these three dreams to their respective given interpretation, the comparison of each dream with the other two dreams, and the comparison of the three dreams to history. This gives us the beginning of the understanding of the symbols of the dreams and of the secrets to be revealed in the book of Daniel.

Nebuchadnezzar's Dream of a Great Image

> *31You, O King, saw, and behold a great image. This great image, whose brightness was excellent, stood before you; and the form thereof was terrible.*

[32] This image's head was of fine gold, his breast and arms of silver, his belly and his thighs of brass, [33] his legs of iron, his feet part of iron and part of clay.

[34] You watched until a stone was cut out without hands, which smote the image upon his feet that were of iron and clay, and broke them to pieces. [35] Then was the iron, the clay, the brass, the silver, and the gold, broken to pieces together, and became like the chaff of the summer threshing floors; and the wind carried them away, that no place was found for them; and the stone that smote the image became a great mountain, and filled the whole earth.

(Daniel 2:31–35)

Nebuchadnezzar's Dream Interpreted

[33] You, O King, are a king of kings: for the God of heaven has given you a kingdom, power, and strength, and glory. [38] And wheresoever the children of men dwell, the beasts of the field and the fowls of the heaven has he given into your hand, and has made you ruler over them all. You are this head of gold.

[39] And after you shall arise another kingdom inferior to you, and another third kingdom of brass, which shall bear rule over all the earth.

[40] And the fourth kingdom shall be as strong as iron: forasmuch as iron breaks in pieces and subdues all things: and as iron breaks all these, shall it break in pieces and bruise.

[41] And whereas you saw the feet and toes, part of potter's clay, and part of iron, the kingdom shall be divided; but there shall be in it of the strength of the iron, forasmuch as you saw the iron mixed with miry clay. [42] And as the toes of the feet were part of iron, and part of clay, so the kingdom shall be partly strong, and partly broken. [43] And whereas you saw iron mixed with miry clay, they shall mingle themselves with the seed of men: but they shall not cleave one to another, even as iron is not mixed with clay.

[44] And in the days of these kings shall the God of heaven set up a kingdom, which shall never be destroyed; and the kingdom shall not be left to other people, but it shall break in pieces and consume all these kingdoms, and it shall stand for ever.

[45] Forasmuch as you saw that a stone was cut out of a mountain without hands, and that it broke in pieces the iron, the brass, the clay, the silver, and the gold; the great God has made known to the king what shall come to pass hereafter: and the dream is certain, and the interpretation thereof sure.

(Daniel 2:37–43)

Although Daniel did tell Nebuchadnezzar the meaning of his dream, he told only that part of the story that God had revealed to him. Within the narration of the dream, and within the narration of its interpretation, was hidden the rest of the story.

Nebuchadnezzar's dream told of a series of great kingdoms that were to come upon the earth. The Babylonian Empire was to be the first, and the most glorious. From history we know the empire of the Medes and Persians, then the empire of the Greeks, and then of the Romans, followed that of the Babylonians. But these four great empires have not yet fulfilled all of Nebuchadnezzar's dream. The empire of iron and clay is yet to come. God's empire is also yet to come.

The Head of Gold

Daniel told Nebuchadnezzar of his dream: *You, O King, saw, and behold a great image…. This image's head was of fine gold…. You, O king, are a king of kings…. You are this head of gold.* Nebuchadnezzar, at the time of his dream, was king of the Babylonian Empire, a great and glorious empire that ruled over much of the world known to the Jews of that day. And, Nebuchadnezzar was the king who had brought the greatness and the glory to this empire. He was "a king of kings," just as gold was the most precious of metals.

The breast and arms of Nebuchadnezzar's great image were of silver. Daniel told Nebuchadnezzar that this silver portion of the image meant that *after you shall arise another kingdom inferior to you.* But, *another kingdom* did not arise after Nebuchadnezzar.

Three kings were to follow Nebuchadnezzar to the throne of the Babylonian Empire before the empire fell to the Medes and Persians. Therefore, the kingdom that was to arise, was to arise at the fall of the Babylonian Empire, not at the death of King Nebuchadnezzar. What seems to be here a minor point in chronology is the start of the breaking the code of the symbols that define the three beasts of Revelation.

The head of gold was Nebuchadnezzar, the *king* of the Babylonian Empire. The breast and arms of silver was the Medo-Persian Empire, which was a *kingdom*, not a king. The belly and thighs of the image was brass, which, we are told, represented *another third kingdom.* This was the Grecian Empire, which conquered the Medes and Persians. And the legs of the image were of iron since *the fourth kingdom shall be strong as iron*. This fourth kingdom was the Roman Empire, which conquered the Greeks, and most everyone else.

The iron, the brass, and the silver each symbolized a *kingdom*. Yet the gold symbolized a *king*, not a *kingdom*. The significance of the first metal symbolizing a king and the following metals symbolizing kingdoms is to show that a king can represent a kingdom. That a *king* can represent a *kingdom* is reinforced by the words of Daniel—another kingdom would arise after Nebuchadnezzar, followed by *another third kingdom*, and yet still another, the *fourth* kingdom. *Another* kingdom means that Nebuchadnezzar must somehow be the first kingdom. Further, if there is a fourth kingdom of iron, a third kingdom of brass, a second kingdom of silver, there must logically be a first kingdom, and it must be of gold. But, what should be the first kingdom is described only in terms of a king. God said, *You, Nebuchadnezzar* are the head of gold. He also said that the coming kingdom will be inferior *to you*. There is no question that God is telling us that King Nebuchadnezzar represents the Babylonian Empire.

Conclusion Report 1

As we work our way through the analysis of these dreams and their interpretations, it can be quite easy to lose track of each concluding point. Thus, a report will be periodically given as conclusions are drawn. This will show the progression of the analysis and how the final conclusions were determined.

Thus far:

- A king can represent a kingdom. Depicts the absolute authority of the ruler over the ruled.

Daniel's Dream of Four Beasts from the Sea

There is yet much to interpret of Nebuchadnezzar's dream, but at this point it is necessary to introduce Daniel's dream of the four beasts that arise from the sea. The images seen in Daniel's dream are very different from the great statue seen by Nebuchadnezzar, but Daniel's dream parallels Nebuchadnezzar's dream in that both describe the same series of empires that were to come upon this earth.

> *[2]I saw in my vision by night, and, behold, the four winds of the heaven strove upon the great sea. [3]And four great beasts came up from the sea, diverse one from another.*
>
> *[4]The first was like a lion, and had eagle's wings; I beheld till the wings thereof were plucked, and it was lifted up from the earth, and made to stand upon the feet as a man, and a man's heart was given to it.*
>
> *[5]And behold another beast, a second, like to a bear, and it raised up itself on one side, and it had three ribs in the mouth of it between the teeth of it: and they said thus unto it, Arise, devour much flesh.*
>
> *[6]After this I beheld, and lo another, like a leopard, which had upon the back of it four wings of a fowl; the beast had also four heads; and dominion was given to it.*
>
> *[7]After this I saw in the night visions, and behold a fourth beast, dreadful and terrible, and strong exceedingly; and it had great iron teeth: it devoured and broke in pieces, and stamped the residue with the feet of it: and it was diverse from all the beasts that were before it; and it had ten horns.*
>
> *[8]I considered the horns, and, behold, there came up among them another little horn, before whom there were three of the first horns plucked up by the roots: and, behold, in this horn were eyes like the eyes of man, and a mouth speaking great things.*
>
> *[9]I beheld till the thrones were cast down, and the Ancient of days did sit, whose garment was white as snow, and the hair of his head like the pure wool: his throne was like the fiery flame, and his wheels as burning fire.*
>
> *[10]A fiery stream issued and came forth from before him: thousand thousands ministered unto him, and ten thousand times ten thousand stood before him: the judgment was set, and the books were opened.*
>
> *[11]I beheld then because of the voice of the great words which the horn spoke: I beheld till the beast was slain, and his body destroyed, and given to the burning flame.*
>
> *[12]As concerning the rest of the beasts, they had their dominion taken away: yet their lives were prolonged for a season and time.*

13I saw in the night visions, and behold, one like the Son of man came like the clouds of heaven, and came to the Ancient of days, and they brought him near before him. 14And there was given him dominion, and glory, and a kingdom, that all people, nations, and languages, should serve him: his dominion is an everlasting dominion, which shall not be destroyed.

(Daniel 7:2–14)

The Dream of the Four Beasts Interpreted

17These great beasts, which are four, are four kings, which shall arise out of the earth.

18But the saints of the most High shall take the kingdom, and possess the kingdom for ever, even for ever and ever.

19Then I would know the truth of the fourth beast, which was diverse from all the others, exceeding dreadful, whose teeth were of iron, and his nails of brass: which devoured, broke in pieces, and stamped the residue with his feet; 20and of the ten horns that were in his head, and of the other which came up, and before whom three fell; even of that horn that had eyes, and a mouth that spoke very great things, whose look was more stout than his fellows.

21I beheld, and the same horn made war with the saints, and prevailed against them; 22until the Ancient of days came, and judgment was given to the saints of the most High: and the time came that the saints possessed the kingdom.

23The fourth beast shall be the fourth kingdom upon the earth, which shall be diverse from all kingdoms, and shall devour the whole earth, and shall tread it down, and break it in pieces. 24And the ten horns out of this kingdom are ten kings that shall arise: and another shall rise after them: and he shall be diverse from the first, and shall subdue three kings. 25And he shall speak great words against the most High, and shall wear out the saints of the most High, and think to change times and laws: and they shall be given into his hand until a time and times and the dividing of time. 26But the judgment shall sit, and they shall take away his dominion, to consume and to destroy it unto the end. 27And the kingdom and dominion, and the greatness of the kingdom under the whole heaven, shall be given to the people of the saints of the most High, whose kingdom is an everlasting kingdom, and all dominions shall serve and obey him.

(Daniel 7:17–27)

In this dream, Daniel watched as *the four winds of the heaven strove upon the great sea. And four great beasts come up from the sea, diverse one from another. One of them that stood by* Daniel made known to him the *interpretation of these things. These great beasts, which are four, are four kings which shall arise out of the earth. A beast here is a king.*

We are told that the *"great sea"* is *"the earth"* (Daniel 7:3, 17). The *sea* may be visualized more as a sea of people on the earth, rather than the earth itself, because the kings arise from the people. This means that these kings are men, as opposed to spiritual beings, an important distinction.

Notice who it is that brings forth these kings—*the four winds of the heaven.* It is God that *"rules in the kingdom of men, and gives it to whomsoever he will"* (Daniel 4:32). Thus, it is God that brings forth these kings and their empires, and He brings them forth for His purpose. That purpose is to bring His chosen people, the Jews, back to Him in repentance from their disobedience.

These four great beasts that come up from the sea are *diverse one from another. Diverse, meaning different one from another,* has two meanings when applied to these beasts. The first is that these beasts are separate from one another; they are four individual kings. The second is that these beasts will be four different kinds of beasts. Just how each beast is different from the others will be shown after the beasts have been identified.

Conclusion Report 2

- A *king* can represent a *kingdom.* Depicts the absolute authority of the ruler over the ruled.
- *A beast* represents a *king.*

The Lion

The first beast that Daniel saw arise *was like a lion, and had eagle's wings.* As Daniel watched, *the wings thereof were plucked, and it was lifted up from the earth and made to stand upon the feet as a man, and a man's heart was given to it.* This, in a few short words, describes a significant event in the life of Nebuchadnezzar, which is recorded in the fourth chapter of Daniel.

The words emboldened in the following text are those which have been condensed into this description of the first beast:

> *[4]I Nebuchadnezzar was at rest in my house, and flourishing in my palace: [5]I saw a dream which made me afraid.... [10]Thus were the visions of my head in my bed: I saw, and behold a tree in the midst of the earth, and the height hereof was great. [11]The tree grew, and was strong, and the height thereof reached unto heaven, and the sight thereof to the end of all the earth...*
>
> *[13]I saw in the visions of my head upon my bed, and, behold a watcher and a holy one came down from heaven; [14]He cried aloud, and said thus, Hew down the tree, and cut off his branches, shake off his leaves, and scatter his fruit: let the beasts get away from under it, and the fowls from his branches: [15]Nevertheless leave the stump of his roots in the earth, even with a band of iron and brass, in the tender grass of the field: and let it be wet with the dew of heaven, and let his portion be with the beasts in the grass of the earth: [16]****Let his heart be changed from a man's, and let a beast's heart be given unto him:**** and let seven times pass over him.*

Then Daniel answered and said,

> *[20]The tree that you saw, which grew, and was strong, whose height reached unto the heaven, and the sight thereof to all the earth...[22]****It is you, O King****, that are grown and become strong: for your greatness is grown, and reached unto heaven, and your dominion to the end of the earth. [23]And whereas the king saw a watcher and a holy one coming down from heaven, and saying, Hew the tree down, and destroy it; yet leave the stump of the roots thereof in the earth, even with a band of iron and brass, in the tender grass of the field; and let it be wet with the dew of heaven, and let his portion be with the beasts of the field, till seven times pass over him.*
>
> *[24]This is the interpretation, O King, and this is the decree of the most High, which is come upon my lord the king: [25]That they shall drive you from men, and your dwelling shall be with the beasts of the field, and they shall make you to eat grass as the oxen, and they shall wet you with the dew of heaven, and seven times shall pass over you, till you know that the most High rules in the kingdom of men, and gives it to whomsoever he will, [26]And whereas they commanded to leave the stump of the tree roots; your kingdom shall be sure unto you, after that you shall have known that the heavens do rule.*

*[29] At the end of twelve months he walked in the place of the kingdom of Babylon. [30] The king spoke, and said, Is not this great Babylon, that I have built for the house of the kingdom by the might of my power, and for the honor of my majesty? [31] While the word was in the king's mouth, there fell a voice from heaven, saying, O King Nebuchadnezzar, to you it is spoken; The kingdom is departed from you. [32] And they shall drive you from men, and your dwelling shall be with the beasts of the field: And they shall make you to eat grass as oxen, and seven times shall pass over you, until you know that the most High rules in the kingdom of men, and gives it to whomsoever he will. [33] The same hour was the thing fulfilled upon Nebuchadnezzar: and he was driven from men, and did eat grass as oxen, and his body was wet with the dew of heaven, till **his hairs were grown like eagles', feathers,** and his nails like birds' claws.*

*[34] And at the end of the days I Nebuchadnezzar lifted up my eyes unto heaven, and **my understanding returned unto me,** and I blessed the most High, and I praised and honored him that lives for ever… [36] At the same time **my reason returned unto me;** and for the glory of my kingdom, my honor and brightness returned unto me; and my counselors and my lords sought unto me; and I was established in my kingdom, and excellent majesty was added unto me.*

(Daniel 4:4–36)

Nebuchadnezzar is described as a tree so great that it reached unto heaven, and its branches could be seen from the ends of the earth. It provided the needs of all creatures of his world. This describes the greatness of Nebuchadnezzar, "a king of kings." It is fitting then that this first beast *was like a lion,* which man has proclaimed to be "the king of beasts."

This great tree was cut down, but a stump remained; Nebuchadnezzar was humbled by God for his haughty pride. He was chained in the field like an animal, his hair growing till it appeared as eagle's feathers. When Nebuchadnezzar recognized that his great abilities were of God and not of himself, his sanity and his position were restored. Therefore, his eagle's wings were plucked, and he was *lifted up from the earth and made stand upon the feet as a man, and a man's heart was given it.* Thus, the first beast to rise out of the sea is King Nebuchadnezzar.

Daniel was told that the four beasts that were seen in his dream were four kings who were to arise from among the people of the earth. The first beast, which appeared like a lion, was King Nebuchadnezzar of the Babylonian Empire. It is clear thus far that a *beast* is a *king*, as verse 17 said they were to be.

The Bear

The king that was to arise after Nebuchadnezzar is then described: *"behold, another beast, a second, like to a bear, and it raised up itself on one side, and it had three ribs in the mouth of it between the teeth of it: and they said thus unto it, Arise, devour much flesh"* (Daniel 7:5). This, however, is not a description of a king, but of a kingdom. What is described as a bear is the Medo-Persian Empire, which was ruled by two major groups of Iranians, the Medes and the Persians. Therefore, a *beast* can also represent a *kingdom.*

The Median kingdom was established many years before the rise of the Persian kingdom. During much of this period, the Persians were under the control of the Medes. Cyrus II, called Cyrus the Great, king of the Persians, rebelled against the ruling Medes and in turn made the Medes subservient to the Persians. Thus, the Median Empire became the first Persian Empire. Although the Median kingdom became essentially a vassal state of the Persians, the Medes retained their kings, and at times, their kings ruled the Persian Empire.

Under Cyrus the Great, the two kingdoms acting together created the largest and most powerful empire the world had yet seen. It is therefore fitting that a bear, a large and powerful animal, represents this empire. Even though the two peoples became one empire, the Persians remained the more prominent and powerful of the two. Thus, a bear "raised up on one side" well represents the empire.

The bear was told to *"Arise, devour much flesh" and was seen* with *"three ribs in the mouth of it between the teeth of it"* (Daniel 7:5). These ribs represent those that the bear had devoured. The Medo-Persian Empire conquered the Babylonian Empire, and with it, the Assyrian Empire that Babylon had conquered. The Medes and Persians then conquered Egypt. These three, the Babylonian, Egyptian, and Assyrian Empires, are the three ribs in the mouth of the bear. But, the significance of the three ribs goes far beyond the mere identification of whom the Medo-Persian Empire conquered.

Conclusion Report 3

- A *king* can represent a *kingdom*. Depicts the absolute authority of the ruler over the ruled.
- A *beast* represents a *king*.
- A *beast* represents a *kingdom*.

The Seven Empires

The three ribs in the mouth of the bear bring together seven Gentile empires: the five empires we are discovering in the dreams of Nebuchadnezzar and Daniel, and two empires that arose before, the time of Daniel. These seven empires are the seven heads of the Red Dragon.

Daniel saw five of these seven empires looking forward in time. These are the Babylonian Empire, which was in existence at the time of the dreams, and the Medo-Persian, Grecian, and Roman Empires, and the confederation of the League of Ten out of which the
empire of the Antichrist will come, that were to follow.

Zechariah saw four of these seven looking back in time from the days of the Medo-Persian Empire in which he lived. He had a vision concerning Jerusalem and the states of Judah and Israel that God had punished by scattering the disobedient Israelites to the neighboring countries. Zechariah said that he, *"18lifted up my eyes, and saw, and behold four horns. 19And I said unto the angel that talked with me, What are these? And he answered me, These are the horns which have scattered Judah, Israel, and Jerusalem. 20And the Lord showed me four carpenters. 21Then said I, What come these to do? And he spoke, saying, These are the horns which have scattered Judah, so that no man did lift up his head: but these are come to fray them, to cast out the horns of the Gentiles, which lifted up their horn over the land of Judah to scatter it"* (Zechariah 1:18–21).

The four Gentile horns that had *scattered* the Israelites up to that time were the Medo-Persian, Babylonian, Egyptian, and Assyrian kings.

The apostle John saw all seven of these Gentile kingdoms together in a vision recorded in the book of Revelation: *"And there are seven kings: five are fallen, and one is, and the other is not yet come; and when he comes, he must continue a short space"* (Revelation 17:10). These seven kings represent the seven kingdoms of the Red Dragon, the same as the four horns of Zechariah's vision represented those four kingdoms.

From John's view, the five that had fallen were the Assyrian, Egyptian, Babylonian, Medo-Persian, and Grecian Empires. The one that is was the Roman Empire, the empire that ruled in John's day. The one *not yet come* is the League of Ten.

There have been many world-class empires that have come and gone through the ages, many more than just the seven we see here. However, what sets these seven apart from all others is that they are *the horns that have scattered Judah, Israel, and Jerusalem.*

Since the nation of Israel was a part of each of the first six empires of the Red Dragon, this tells us that Israel must also be a part of the seventh empire.

Back to Daniel's Dream of the Four Beasts

The second beast that came up from the sea was described as a bear, raised up on one side, with three ribs in its mouth. This bear is the kingdom of the Medo-Persian Empire.

Daniel had seen four beasts and was told that those four beasts were to be four kings. The first beast, the lion, was a king. However, the second beast that arose, the bear, was a kingdom, not a king. And, we shall see that the third and fourth beasts to arise will also represent kingdoms, not kings. If these beasts were to be kings, why are they described as kingdoms?

Look at the pattern of interpretation thus far: The different metals of Nebuchadnezzar's image were said to represent a series of kingdoms. But the gold represented a king, not a kingdom. Daniel's dream is just the reverse in that the four beasts were said to represent kings. Only the first was a king; the last three are kingdoms. What appears to be another discontinuity in the meaning of the symbols is really showing us that the king and his kingdom are viewed as one.

Up to this point, a beast symbolized a king, which we now see is only one part of the whole. From this point on, a beast will be seen to symbolize an empire, which has both a king and a kingdom. This is not a contradiction in the use of symbols but rather an expansion of the definition of a beast.

One conclusion, then, is that the various metals of Nebuchadnezzar's image represent various Gentile empires. The beasts of Daniel's dream also represent those same Gentile empires.

Conclusion Report 4

- A *king* can represent a *kingdom*. Depicts the absolute authority of the ruler over the ruled.
- A *beast* represents a *king*
- *A beast* represents a *kingdom*.
- A *king* and his *kingdom* can be seen as one.
- A *beast* therefore can represent both the *king* and his *kingdom*, either separately or as one depending on the context of the text.
- All the *kingdoms* of these visions are *empires*. Therefore, a *beast* can symbolize an *empire*.

Daniel's Dream of the Goat and the Ram

Before continuing to interpret either Nebuchadnezzar's dream of a great image or Daniel's dream of the four beasts, another of Daniel's dreams must be introduced. This dream is of a ram and a goat, two beasts that symbolize two of the seven empires we are discovering. This second dream of Daniel's is introduced because it adds to the interpretation of the four beasts that arise from the sea.

> *[2]I saw in a vision…and was by the river of Ulai. [3]Then I lifted up my eyes and saw, and, behold, there stood before the river a ram which had two horns: and the two horns were high; but one was higher than the other, and the higher came up last. [4]I saw the ram pushing westward, and northward, and southward; so that no beasts might stand before him, neither was there any that could deliver out of his hand; but did according to his will, and became great.*
>
> *[5]And as I was considering, behold, an he goat came from the west on the face of the whole earth, and touched not the ground: and the goat had a notable horn between his eyes. [6]And he came to the ram that had two horns, which I had seen standing before the river, and ran unto him in the fury of his power. [7]And I saw him come close unto the ram, and he was moved with choler against him, and smote the ram, and broke his two horns: and there was no power in the ram to stand before him, but he cast him down to the ground, and stamped upon him: and there was none that could deliver the ram out of his hand.*
>
> *[8]Therefore the he goat waxed very great: and when he was strong, the great horn was broken; and for it came up four notable ones toward the four winds of heaven.*

[9]And out of one of them came forth a little horn, which waxed exceeding great, toward the south, and toward the east, and toward the pleasant land. [10]And it waxed great, even to the host of heaven; and it cast down some of the host and of the stars to the ground, and stamped upon them. [11]Yea, he magnified himself even to the prince of the host, and by him the daily sacrifice was taken away, and the place of his sanctuary was cast down.

[12]And an host was given him against the daily sacrifice by reason of transgression, and it cast down the truth to the ground; and it practiced, and prospered.

[13]Then I heard one saint speaking, and another saint said unto that certain saint which spoke, How long shall be the vision concerning the daily sacrifice, and the transgression of desolation, to give both the sanctuary and the host to be trodden under foot? 1   [14]And he said unto me, Unto two thousand and three hundred evenings and mornings; then shall the sanctuary be cleansed.

(Daniel 8:2–14)

Daniel's Dream Interpreted

[20]The ram which you saw having two horns are the kings of Media and Persia. 21And the rough goat is the king of Grecia: and the great horn that is between his eyes is the first king.

[22]Now that being broken, whereas four stood up for it, four kingdoms shall stand up out of the nation, but not in his power.

[23]And in the latter time of their kingdom, when the transgressors are come to the full, a king of fierce countenance, and understanding dark sentences, shall stand up. [24]And his power shall be mighty, but not by his own power: and he shall destroy wonderfully, and shall prosper, and practice, and shall destroy the mighty and the holy people. [25]And through his policy also he shall cause craft to prosper in his hand; and he shall magnify himself in his heart, and by peace shall destroy many: he shall also stand up against the Prince of princes; but he shall be broken without hand.

(Daniel 8:20–25)

The river that Daniel saw in this dream symbolizes a dividing line, a change in the course of events. The change that Daniel saw was the rise of the Grecian Empire that would conquer the Medo-Persian Empire.

The ram on one side of this river had pushed *westward* conquering the Babylonian Empire, *northward* conquering the remnants of the Assyrian Empire, and *southward* conquering Egypt *so that no beasts might stand before him.*

The ram, by the description of its actions, symbolizes the empire of the Medes and Persians who, by their combined power, consumed more territory than had any empire before them. Note that the empires conquered by the Medo-Persian Empire are also spoken of as beasts. The goat on the other side of this river is the Grecian Empire. Again, a *beast* is an *empire.*

Daniel's vision of the ram and the goat introduces a new symbol, the horn. With the introduction of the horn as a symbol, there is the beginning of the identification of the kings apart from their empires.

The ram *had two horns, and the two horns were high, but one was higher than the other, and the higher came up last.* The two *horns* represent the two lines of *kings* who ruled the Medo-Persian Empire. Both horns *were high,* meaning that they both had stature as kings. However, one horn was *higher than the other,* meaning it had greater authority. That the *higher came up* last is an accurate description of the Persian kings who came to power after the Median kings but were the prominent kings of the dual empire.

One could possibly argue that the two horns represent the two kingdoms, not the two kings. However, in verse 21, Daniel states of the other beast, *the great horn* that is between the eyes of the goat is *the first king.* A consistent interpretation of the symbols would have the two horns on the ram representing kings, just as the horn on the goat represented a king. A *horn,* therefore, symbolizes a *king.*

Daniel declares in verse 20 that *the ram* that you saw are *the kings* of Media and Persia. But he also states in verse 3 that the ram *had two horns…but one was higher than the other, and the higher came up last,* meaning that the *horns* are the kings of Media and Persia. Both of these two statements cannot be correct unless it is understood that these two kings each represent their respective kingdoms. Therefore, "the horns are the kings of Media and Persia while the ram is the empire of the kings of Media and Persia."

The Scripture is again showing us of the close relationship of these kings to their kingdoms.

Conclusion Report 5

- A *king* can represent a *kingdom*.
- Depicts the absolute authority of the ruler over the ruled.
- A *beast* represents a *king*.
- A *beast* represents a *kingdom*.
- A *king* and his *kingdom* can be seen as one.
- A *beast*, therefore, can represent both the *king* and his *kingdom*, either separately or as one depending on the context of the text.
- All the *kingdoms* of these visions are *empires*. Therefore, a *beast* can symbolize an *empire*.
- A *horn* represents a *king*.

The Kingdom of Silver

All three dreams about Nebuchadnezzar's series of Gentile empires have now been introduced. The vision of the ram with the two horns of unequal length on its head parallels the vision of the bear that was raised up on one side. We were told in the Bible that the horns on the ram were the kings of Media and Persia. The ram is, therefore, the Medo-Persian Empire. It is reasonable to believe, then, that the bear also represents the Medo-Persian Empire. This in turn confirms without a doubt that the kingdom that was to follow Nebuchadnezzar, represented by the *breast and arms of silver,* was the Medo-Persian Empire, the second empire in the series depicted by the great statue seen by Nebuchadnezzar.

The Kingdom of Brass

"After you [Nebuchadnezzar] shall arise…another third kingdom of brass, which shall bear rule over all the earth" (Daniel 2:39). This introduces the *third kingdom of Nebuchadnezzar's great image,* which is the Grecian Empire. In Daniel's dream of the ram and the goat in combat, the goat symbolizes this same Grecian Empire.

As Daniel pondered over the ram with the two horns *"an he goat came from the west on the face of the whole earth, and touched not the ground: and the goat had a notable horn between his eyes. [6]And he came to the ram that had two horns, which I had seen standing before the river, and ran unto him in the fury of his power. [7]And I saw him come close unto the ram, and he was moved with choler against him, and smote the ram, and broke his two horns: and there was no power in the ram to stand before him, but he cast him to the ground, and stamped upon him: and there was none that could deliver the ram out of his hand. [8]Therefore the he goat waxed very great"* (Daniel 8:5–8).

This scene of the goat attacking the ram takes place *before the river,* telling us that this is a dividing line in history. The change is the goat rising to power by destroying the ram.

We are told that *"the rough goat is the king of Grecia"* (Daniel 8:21). This confirms that the Grecian Empire follows the Medo-Persian Empire in our series of kingdoms.

It is stated in verse 21 that *the rough goat is the king* of Grecia, but it also states in that same verse that *the great horn* that is between his eyes *is the first king.* Just as it was with the ram and its two horns, these two statements cannot both be correct unless it is understood that the king represents his kingdom. Therefore, "the great horn that is between his eyes is the king of Grecia while the rough goat is the empire of the king of Grecia." The Scripture is again showing us the integral relationship of these kings to their kingdoms.

The great horn that is between his eyes is the first king. This is Alexander the Great, the first king of the Grecian Empire. Again, a *horn* is used to symbolize a *king.*

The goat *"came from the west on the face of the whole earth"* (Daniel 8:5). Alexander came from Macedonia, which was at the far west reaches of the world common to the Medes and the Persians. Thus, to them, Alexander did cross *the face of the whole earth.* Alexander first conquered Greece, then quickly all of Asia Minor and Egypt, then was soon at the doorstep of the heart of the Medo-Persian Empire. By his military genius, he moved across the continents conquering nations with such speed that it was said he *touched not the ground.*

Upon his death, Alexander's great empire ceased to exist. The empire that he had so quickly built was in time divided among several of his generals. Thus, Alexander the Great and the Grecian Empire did exist as one. Alexander the Great is therefore the symbol of the Grecian Empire, just as Nebuchadnezzar is the symbol of the Babylonian Empire.

The two beasts, the ram and the goat, are shown by their actions to represent the Medo-Persian and the Grecian Empires.
Thus, again, a beast is used to symbolize an empire.

The dream of the ram and the goat follows the same pattern in the use of symbols as that used in the vision of the great image made of several metals. Just as silver was more valuable than brass, sheep (shown here as a ram) were more valuable than goats to the people of Daniel's day. Therefore, the Medo-Persian Empire, represented by the silver and the ram, preceded the Grecian Empire, represented by the brass and the goat.

The Division of the Grecian Empire
"Therefore the he goat waxed very great: and when he was strong, the great horn was broken; and for it came up four notable ones toward the four winds of heaven" *(Daniel 8:8)*. Alexander the Great died at the height of his power at the time when the Grecian Empire contained essentially the entire world known to the Jews. Upon his death, the empire was divided among several of his generals. Eventually, the territory that had been Alexander's empire was consolidated into four separate kingdoms. Since there were at first more than four vying for control of territory, the four that survived the struggle and established lasting kingdoms are called notable horns. Again, a horn is a king. The four horns coming up in place of the great horn represents a division of rule within the empire.

Conclusion Report 6
- A king can represent a kingdom.
- Depicts the absolute authority of the ruler over the ruled.
- A beast represents a king.
- A beast represents a kingdom.
- A king and his kingdom can be seen as one.
- A beast, therefore, can represent both the king and his kingdom, either separately or as one depending on the context of the text.
- All the kingdoms of these visions are empires. Therefore, a beast can symbolize an empire.
- A horn represents a king.
- The four horns coming up in place of the great horn represent a division of rule within the empire.

One Little Horn

⁸Therefore the he goat waxed very great: and when he was strong, the great horn was broken; and for it came up four notable ones toward the four winds of heaven. ⁹And out of one of them came forth a little horn"

(Daniel 8:8–9)

"And in the latter time of their kingdom, when the transgressors are come to the full, a king of fierce countenance, and understanding dark sentences, shall stand up".

(Daniel 8:23)

In his vision, Daniel saw a little horn come forth out of the line of one of these four notable horns of the he-goat.[2] This little *horn* is said to be a *king* in verse 23, just as the great horn and the four notable horns were shown to be kings. This little horn came *in the latter time of their kingdom*, which is a reference back to the kingdoms of the four notable horns that came in place of the great horn. This king therefore came on the scene in the later end of the reign of the Greek kings. This king *of fierce countenance* was Antiochus IV Epiphanes, an infamous king of the Seleucid Empire, one of the four kingdoms of the divided Grecian Empire. Again, a *horn* is a *king*.

The Leopard

The Grecian Empire that was symbolized by the he-goat with the great horn between his eyes was the third kingdom from the Babylonian Empire. In Daniel's vision of the four great beasts that came up from the sea, the third beast was *"like a leopard, which had upon the back of it four wings of a fowl; the beast had also four heads"* (Daniel 7:6). This beast that is like a leopard also symbolizes the Grecian Empire. Alexander's army did speed across the continents conquering kingdom after kingdom with the quickness and cunning of a leopard. So, again, a *beast* symbolizes an *empire*.

A new symbol is introduced with the vision of the leopard: *"The beast had also four heads"* (Daniel 7:6). The vision of the leopard with four heads parallels the vision of the goat with four horns. But, as the four horns coming up in place of the one great horn represented *the division of the rule* of the Grecian Empire, the four heads of the leopard represent *the division of the territory* of the empire. With the four horns on the goat and the four heads on the leopard, we have the division of both parts of an empire: the ruler and those who are ruled.

The four heads of the leopard symbolize the four kingdoms of the divided Grecian Empire. A *head*, therefore, symbolizes *a division of the territory of a beast.* The period of Grecian rule did not end with the death of Alexander but continued until the rise of Rome. Thus, the four divisions of the empire, represented by the four heads of the leopard, are still considered in Scripture to be the Grecian Empire.

This historic view of the Grecian Empire gives us a better understanding of the definition of a "head." A beast symbolizes an empire, in this case a leopard. This empire consists of four separate territories, each ruled by its own king. These four sovereign kingdoms are symbolized by the four heads of the leopard. Each head, therefore, is a division of the territory of the beast. More accurately, *a head is a kingdom that is part of an empire.*

Conclusion Report 7

- A *king* can represent a *kingdom.*
- Depicts the absolute authority of the ruler over the ruled.
- A *beast* represents a *king.*
- A *beast* represents a *kingdom.*
- A *king* and his *kingdom* can be seen as one.
- A *beast,* therefore, can represent both the *king* and his *kingdom,* either separately or as one depending on the context of the text.
- All the *kingdoms* of these visions are *empires.* Therefore, a beast can symbolize an *empire.*
- A *horn* represents a *king.*
- The *four horns* coming up in place of the great horn represents *a division of rule* within the empire.
- A *head* is a *kingdom* that is *a division of the land* within the empire. With the four notable horns replacing the great horn on the goat and the four heads seen on the leopard, we have the division of both parts of the empire: the ruler and those ruled. Multiple horns and heads of a beast signify that the empire consists of multiple kingdoms.

The Wild Beast

> *"After this I saw in the night visions, and behold a fourth beast, dreadful and terrible, and strong exceedingly; and it had great iron teeth: it devoured and brake in pieces, and stamped the residue with the feet of it: and it was diverse from all the beasts that were before it; and it had ten horns".*

(Daniel 7:7)

The fourth beast that Daniel saw rising from the sea is, in part, the Roman Empire.

This beast is not identified as an animal in the likeness of a lion or a bear, as were the preceding beasts. There is a purpose for this deviation from the pattern, which we will shortly see. But God did use the descriptive word wild to identify this beast in Hosea. There, God said of Israel, because my people have forgotten me, *"I will be unto them as a lion: as a leopard by the way will I observe them: ⁸I will meet them as a bear that is bereaved of her whelps, and will rend the caul of their heart, and there will I devour them like a lion: the wild beast shall tear them"* (Hosea 13:7– 8). In these two verses, we see four of our series of Gentile nations being used by God for His purpose to turn the rebellious nation to repentance.

This wild *beast* that represents the Roman Empire is an *empire*, just as were the first three beasts of Daniel's dream.

We need here to note Daniel's reaction at the sight of this beast— *"¹⁹Then I would know the truth of the fourth beast, which was diverse from all the others...²⁰and of the ten horns that were in his head"* (Daniel 7:19–20). Daniel recognized that this beast was different than the others, but it was the truth of the *ten horns* that he wanted to know.

When Daniel introduced his vision of the four beasts, he said that all four were *diverse one from another.* Scripture, however, seems to stress this diversity much more with the fourth beast when it states this beast shall be diverse from *"all kingdoms"* (Daniel 7:23). God stresses here that not only was this beast a separate kingdom as were the others, but that this kingdom was to be significantly different from all kingdoms that had preceded it—so different that it could not even be identified with any known animal. *"It was diverse from all the beasts that were before it [because] it had ten horns"* (Daniel 7:7). Further, Daniel was told *"the ten horns out of this kingdom are ten kings that shall arise"* (Daniel 7:24). We shall see that what makes the fourth beast so diverse is that these ten horns represent ten kings of a separable fifth kingdom.

The Kingdom of Iron

The fourth kingdom that was to follow Nebuchadnezzar is represented by the *"legs of iron" (Daniel 2:33)* of the great image. The interpretation given to Daniel is that *"the fourth kingdom shall be strong as iron: forasmuch as iron breaks in pieces and subdues all things: and as iron that breaks all these, shall it break in pieces and bruise" (Daniel 2:40)*.

The words used to describe this kingdom are much like those used to describe Daniel's fourth beast *whose teeth were of iron, and his nails of brass.* Just as the wild beast *devoured, broke in pieces, and stamped the residue with its feet* as it conquered all around it, this kingdom of iron *breaks all these* kingdoms that preceded it. We know from history that Rome conquered all of the territory of the previous empires of Greece, Medo-Persia, and Babylon. This kingdom of iron is therefore the Roman Empire.

I find it somewhat strange, however, that this fourth empire alone is described as one that "breaks in pieces" and "stamps the residue with its feet." All the preceding empires from Assyria to Greece built their empires by brute military force no different than did Rome. Since Daniel's prophecies are for his people and his holy city Jerusalem, as is expressed in Daniel 9:24, I believe there is a message to Israel in this description that applies specifically to what we will see as the fifth empire that engulfs the nation of today's Israel. Rome did destroy the Temple of the Jews to the point where no stone of the Temple was left upon another, decimated the city of Jerusalem, and slaughtered tens of thousands of its people, then scattered the remnant of the Jews throughout the lands and forbid their return upon pain of death. In short, Rome *devoured, broke in pieces,* and *stamped the residue with its feet* in their annihilation of Israel. The fifth empire represented by the ten horns on the head of the fourth beast, however, will bring *"great tribulation"* upon Jerusalem and upon Israel *"such as was not since the beginning of the world to this time, no, nor ever shall be" (Matthew 24:21)*.

A side note on the legs of iron. Some interpret the two legs of iron as the division of the Roman Empire into the eastern and western divisions of the empire that occurred toward the end of Roman rule. This dividing of the empire of iron into two divisions erroneously prompts the dividing of the empire represented by the feet and toes into the same two divisions. The problem with this theory is that this division of the image seen by Nebuchadnezzar begins with the split of the thighs of the kingdom of brass and not with the kingdom of iron. That the two legs of iron are pictured as divided in the vision of this great image has no relevance to this prophecy. There is, however, a division of the fourth kingdom of Nebuchadnezzar's image into two empires, but that corresponds to the division of the legs of iron from the feet of iron and clay, which portrays the division of the fourth and fifth empires of the great image.

The Kingdom of Iron and Clay

> *"⁴¹And whereas you saw the feet and toes, part of potter's clay, and part of iron, the kingdom shall be divided: but there shall be in it of the strength of iron, forasmuch as you saw the iron mixed with miry clay. ⁴²And as the toes of the feet were part of iron, and part of clay, so the kingdom shall be partly strong, and partly broken. ⁴³And whereas you saw iron mixed with miry clay, they shall mingle themselves with the seed of men: but they shall not cleave one to another, even as iron is not mixed with clay".*

> *(Daniel 2:41–43)*

The feet and the toes of Nebuchadnezzar's great image are both *part of potter's clay and part of iron.* Together, they are a fifth empire indicated by the change of material representing this empire. The feet as a unit represents the empire itself, while the ten toes represent the division of the empire into ten kingdoms.

The Kingdom of Ten Horns

Going back to Daniel's vision of the fourth empire, Daniel adds to his description of the wild beast that *"it had ten horns"* (Daniel 7:7) and was told of this, *"the ten horns out of this kingdom are ten kings that shall arise"* (Daniel 7:24).

There is a parallel between Daniel's dream of the wild beast with its ten horns and Nebuchadnezzar's dream of the great image with its legs of iron and its feet of iron and clay.

The feet of iron and clay is a fifth kingdom, in this case a confederacy rather than an empire, separate from the Roman Empire, its ten toes being the division of the territory into ten kingdoms. The ten horns of the wild beast, as kings, show the division of the rule of this fifth nation, with each king ruling one of the ten nations. The feet and toes of iron and clay, and the wild beast with ten horns on its head, also follow the pattern of the leopard with four heads being the division of the territory of the Grecian Empire into four kingdoms, while the four horns of the goat being the division of the rule of the four kingdoms of the Grecian Empire. However, there is one difference with the division of the elements of this kingdom. The feet of iron and clay, with its ten toes of iron and clay as a division of territory, and the head of the wild beast, with its ten horns on its head as a division of rule, describe this fifth kingdom as a confederacy.

We can now see how these beasts of Daniel's dream were not only *diverse one from another* in being separate empires, but that they are *diverse one from another* in their form.

The progression in the degree of diversity of each succeeding empire supports the concept of the wild beast representing both the fourth empire and a separable fifth kingdom in this series of Gentile empires:

The first empire comprises 1 king ruling 1 kingdom.

The second empire comprises 2 kings jointly ruling 1 kingdom.

The third empire began comprised of 1 king ruling 1 kingdom, which transitioned into 4 kings ruling 4 kingdoms.

The fourth and the fifth empires that were seen as one are comprised of 1 king ruling 1 empire in the distant past, and 10 kings ruling 10 kingdoms in the near future.

But why would Daniel have seen the fourth and fifth empires only as one? Part of the answer is that Daniel's message is to his people, especially to his people of today. Since his visions are for the nation of Israel, he did not see the period of the church. Thus, Daniel did not see the parenthesis in time when the nation of Israel would not exist. Israel was *"wounded to death" (Revelation 13:3)* by the Roman sword and disappeared from the face of the earth during the days of the fourth beast. It was to be during the days of the fifth beast that Israel was to be resurrected, and her *"deadly wound…healed."* From Daniel's view of Israel, these two beasts appeared together as one.

Another part of the answer is in the purpose of the vision of the four beasts that he saw arise from the sea. The vision of the fourth beast is to give us today who are living in *the time of the end* an understanding of that empire that is about to come into our world. This fifth empire will be much like the fourth in that the territory it rules will come from the territory of the fourth empire.It will also have the characteristics of the fourth empire, such as its great strength and brutality. And, it will destroy Jerusalem and the Temple as did the fourth empire.

The last part of the answer as to why Daniel saw this wild beast only as one beast is seen in the phrase *"the words are closed up and sealed till the time of the end" (Daniel 12:9).* The complete understanding of the vision and of the fourth beast is for those of the time of the end of this age. Daniel's vision could not be understood by earlier generations,
for if they would have understood what Daniel had seen, they would have known that the return of Jesus was long in coming.

"Blindness in part is happened to Israel, until the fullness of the Gentiles be come in" (Romans 11:25). This was said of the nation of Israel when they rejected Jesus as the Messiah, the Christ. The nation is still in this blindness. Thus, Israel's "eyesight" today is much like that of Daniel's—they do not yet see the church as part of God's plan. It is, therefore, the church who must understand Daniel's vision and take that message to Israel.

Conclusion Report 8

- A *king* can represent a *kingdom.*
- Depicts the absolute authority of the ruler over the ruled.
- A *beast* represents a *king.*
- A *beast* represents a *kingdom.*
- A *king* and his *kingdom* can be seen as one.
- A *beast* therefore can represent both the *king* and his *kingdom,* either separately or as one depending on the context of the text.
- All the *kingdoms* of these visions are *empires.* Therefore, a *beast* can symbolize an *empire.*
- A horn represents a *king.*
- The *four horns* coming up in place of the great horn represents *a division of rule* within the empire.
- A *head* is a *kingdom* that is a *division* of *land* within the empire.

With the four notable horns replacing the great horn on the goat and the four heads seen on the leopard, we have the division of both parts of the empire: the ruler and those ruled. Multiple horns and heads of a beast signify that the empire consists of multiple kingdoms.

- The *ten horns* of Daniel's wild beast represent *a division of the rule* of a fifth empire just as the toes of Nebuchadnezzar's image represent a division of the territory of the empire represented by the feet.

Postscript

I use the term empire generically in this portion of text as these ten kingdoms of the fifth empire will first unite as a confederacy prior to their morphing into an empire.

What may seem here as a minor point will be of considerable importance in understanding the rise of the Antichrist. Because this entity of ten nations forms as a confederacy I call it the League of Ten.

The League of Ten

The ten horns on the head of the wild beast represent the rulers of the fifth empire, the League of Ten. The horns positioned on the head of the fourth beast tell us that the kingdoms of these ten kings of the League are to come out of the territory that was once the Roman Empire.

The feet and toes of iron and clay of Nebuchadnezzar's image also represent the League of Ten. This empire is separate from and independent of the Roman Empire. We are told of this separation by the material types of Nebuchadnezzar's image: the Roman Empire being represented by iron; the League of Ten represented by iron and clay. The iron in the feet, and in the toes, does not say that the League is in some manner the empire that was Rome because this fifth empire is also of clay. Nor does the iron of this confederacy imply that some nation or nations have a special relationship or connection to Rome, as both the nations of iron and of clay will come from the territory of the old Roman Empire.

The iron mixed with clay describes the nature of the union between members of the League: *"And whereas you saw the feet and toes, part of potter's clay, and part of iron, the kingdom shall be divided"* (Daniel 2:41). Being part of iron and part of clay, two materials that do not bond one with another, speaks to the cause of why this *kingdom shall be divided*, that of lineage. Nine nations will be of the lineage of Ishmael, one will be of the lineage of Isaac; nine will be Muslim, one will be Jewish.

"And whereas you saw iron mixed with miry clay, they shall mingle themselves with the seed of men: but they shall not cleave one to another, even as iron is not mixed with clay" (Daniel 2:43). *They* have mingled *themselves with the seed of men* [purposely changed tense]: they are neighboring countries in the same land, and often they are literally neighbors on the same land. Israel and its neighbors are active trading partners, and many workers in Israel are from neighboring countries. Yet, they remain in conflict with each other *even as iron is not mixed with clay*. They at times form treaties one with another and will eventually form a confederacy joining themselves together as one.

Even though they come together in this confederacy, *they shall not cleave one to another* as one nation will lead others of the League in the conquest of three other nations of the League.

Another Little Horn

As Daniel *"considered the horns"* of the wild beast, *"there came up among them another little horn, before whom there were three of the first horns plucked up by the roots: and, behold, in this horn were eyes like the eyes of man, and a mouth speaking great things"* (Daniel 7:8). He was told of this that *"the ten horns out of this kingdom are ten kings that shall arise: and another shall rise after them: and he shall be diverse from the first, and he shall subdue three kings"* (Daniel 7:24). Horns in this vision of the four beasts are kings. A "little" horn must then be a "little" king, a prince who has not yet come to power as a king. This *little horn* is the *"prince that shall come"* of Daniel 9 that *"shall confirm the covenant with many."* This second little horn is the Antichrist.

The Antichrist will therefore come on the prophetic scene as a prince within one of the ten nations that will form the League of Ten. While yet a prince, he will represent his nation at the signing of the agreement that forms the League. Shortly thereafter, this prince must rise to the position of king of his nation, for it is as a king that he will attack and conquer three of the other nations of the League, one of which is Israel.

"And he shall speak great words against the most High, and shall wear out the saints of the most High, and think to change times and laws: and they

shall be given into his hand until a time and times and the dividing of time" (Daniel 7:25). A *time* is a year; *times* is two years. The period of *a time and times and the dividing of time* when Israel *shall be given into his hand* is three and a half years, specifically the 42-month period of the Antichrist's rule *(Revelation 11:2; 13:5). The saints of the most High* are those who not only accept Jesus as the Messiah during the 1,260 days of the Two Witnesses *(Revelation 11:3)* but also take him as their Lord and Savior.

"I beheld then because of the voice of the great words which the horn spake: I beheld even till the beast was slain, and his body destroyed, and given to the burning flame" (Daniel 7:11). The *burning flame* is the *"lake of fire"* of *Revelation 19:20* into which the Antichrist is cast at his defeat at the battle of Armageddon. Thus, the *beast* that *was slain* is here the ruler of the empire. Note then that *horn* and *beast* are used interchangeably as the ruler of the empire.

The Kingdom of Stone

Nebuchadnezzar saw the birth of a sixth empire in his dream of the great image. This empire was depicted by a stone *[that] was cut out without hands, which smote the image upon his feet that were of iron and clay, and broke them to pieces.* Daniel did not see this *stone* that *was cut out without hands* in his dream of the four beasts, but he describes the kingdom of this *stone* nevertheless, adding considerably to our knowledge of just who will rule this last empire.

Nebuchadnezzar's dream:

> *"34You watched until a stone was cut out without hands, which smote the image upon his feet that were of iron and clay, and broke them to pieces. 35Then was the iron, the clay, the brass, the silver, and the gold, broken to pieces together, and became like the chaff of the summer threshing floors; and the wind carried them away, that no place was found for them; and the stone that smote the image became a great mountain, and filled the whole earth"*

> *(Daniel 2:34-35)*

Nebuchadnezzar's dream interpreted:

> *"And in the days of these kings shall the God of heaven set up a kingdom, which shall never be destroyed; and the kingdom shall not be left to other people, but it shall break in pieces and consume all these kingdoms, and it shall stand for ever"*

(Daniel 2:44)

Daniel's dream of the four beasts:

> *"[11]I beheld then because of the voice of the great words which the horn spoke:
> I beheld till the beast was slain, and his body destroyed, and given to the
> burning flame. [12]As concerning the rest of the beasts, they had their dominion
> taken away: yet their lives were prolonged for a season and time. [13]I saw in
> the night visions, and behold, one like the Son of man came like the clouds
> of heaven, and came to the Ancient of days, and they brought him near before
> him. [14]And there was given him dominion, and glory, and a kingdom, that
> all people, nations, and languages, should serve him: his dominion is an
> everlasting dominion, which shall not be destroyed"*

(Daniel 7:11–14)

Daniel's dream interpreted:

> *"[21]I beheld, and the same horn made war with the saints, and prevailed
> against them; [22]until the Ancient of days came, and judgment was given to
> the saints of the most High: and the time came that the saints possessed the
> kingdom….[26]But the judgment shall sit, and they shall take away his
> dominion, to consume and to destroy it unto the end. [27]And the kingdom
> and dominion, and the greatness of the kingdom under the whole heaven,
> shall be given to the people of the saints of the most High, whose kingdom is
> an everlasting kingdom, and all dominions shall serve and obey him"*

(Daniel 7:21–22, 26–27)

The apostle John saw the coming of this kingdom and wrote,

> *"[11]I saw heaven opened, and behold a white horse; and he that sat upon him
> was called Faithful and True, and in righteousness he does judge and make
> war. [12]His eyes were as a flame of fire, and on his head were many crowns;
> and he had a name written, that no man knew, but he himself. [13]And he
> was clothed with a vesture dipped in blood: and his name is called The Word
> of God. [14]And the armies which were in heaven followed him upon white
> horses, clothed in fine linen, white and clean. [15]And out of his mouth goes a
> sharp sword, that with it he should smite the nations: and he shall rule them
> with a rod of iron"*

(Revelation 19:11–15)

The stone that Nebuchadnezzar saw *cut out without hands* is this rider on the white horse whose name is called *the Word of God.* John had earlier said of Jesus that *"in the beginning was the Word, and the Word was with God, and the Word was God" (John 1:1).* Jesus had spoken of himself as this stone when he said, *"The stone which the builders rejected, the same is become the head of the corner" (Matthew 21:42).* The cornerstone is that stone that guides the construction of the entire building. With this, Jesus was saying that he will be the one who will rule this kingdom of the *stone.*

This second coming of Jesus to the earth itself will thus be to establish his kingdom on earth. He will strike the image *upon his feet that were of iron and clay,* giving the time of his coming as *in the days of these kings* of the League of Ten. *Out of his mouth goes a sharp sword, that with it he should smite the nations;* so with the power of his word shall the *iron, the clay, the brass, the silver, and the gold,* [be] *broken to pieces together.* This is saying that all of the governments of this earth that man has created shall be *like the chaff of the summer threshing floors; and the wind carried them away, that no place was found for them* because he shall rule them *with a rod of iron. "The stone that smote the image became a great mountain, and filled the whole earth" (Daniel 2:43).* The *mountain* speaks of his *government.* The view of the *stone* becoming a *great mountain* is saying that *"the government shall be upon his shoulder...and of the increase of his government...there shall be no end" (Isaiah 9:6–7).* Isaiah also said of this *great mountain* that, *"²It shall come to pass in the last days, that the mountain of the Lord's house shall be established in the top of the mountains, and shall be exalted above the hills; and all nations shall flow unto it... ³for out of Zion shall go forth the law, and the word of the Lord from Jerusalem. ⁴And he shall judge among the nations" (Isaiah 2:2–4).* The *mountain of the Lord's* house is here speaking of two aspects of his government: that it *shall be established in the top of the mountains,* reigning supreme, *exalted above the hills,* the lower levels of government, and that *out of Zion shall go forth the law,* the physical location of his government being located in Jerusalem.

Note that Daniel also states of the rule of this sixth kingdom that *"the kingdom and dominion...shall be given to the people of the saints of the most High" (Daniel 7:27).* The *people* who will be given rule with Jesus over this last empire will be those who are *"redeemed...by the blood [of Jesus] out of every kindred, and tongue, and people, and nation"* who will be made *"unto our God kings and priests: and [they] shall reign on the earth"* *(Revelation 5:9–10).*

This empire will not be an ethereal empire, an intangible spiritual realm existing within a secular world. This last empire the world will see will be a theocracy, yes, but it will be as real to the touch, sight, and sound as any that preceded it.

The Crown, the Last of the Symbols

There are no crowns seen in these dreams of Nebuchadnezzar or Daniel. Yet there are crowns used in the portrayal of the Red Dragon and the Beast. Therefore, the use of the crown to define these three beasts must be discerned by other means. The crown has traditionally been used throughout history as a symbol of sovereignty. Thus, a crown placed upon the head of a man signifies that man to be a king. Using that concept, a crown on a horn of these beasts would in the same way make that horn sovereign in some manner. A crown placed on a head of a beast would in some manner make that head sovereign.

In the analysis of these three dreams, it has always been said that a *horn* is a king. However, in the portrayal of the Red Dragon, the Beast, and the False Prophet, some horns are shown with crowns and some are shown without crowns. How then are we to apply the symbols as defined in these three dreams to the interpretation of the three beasts of Revelation when there are such anomalies? The answer is simple; we must wait upon the Holy Spirit for guidance.

He had power to give life unto the image of the beast, that the image of the beast should both speak, and cause that as many as would not worship the image of the beast should be killed.

—Revelation 13:14 2

[2]This little horn could not have come out of the *four winds of heaven* as at times is taught. The four winds are an idiom for the four directions of the earth, meaning from all directions. It would have been pointless to state where the little horn came from if he came from "everywhere." It is the four notable horns that came *toward the four winds of heaven,* as Alexander's empire was split in every direction. It is also taught that this little horn is Rome. But Rome did not come out of either the kings or the kingdoms of Greece.

CHAPTER FOUR
The Image of the Beast

There is another entity yet not fully revealed, the Image of the Beast. This entity plays a significant role in the events of the coming days by deceiving many into worshipping it and the one it portrays, and will kill all in the empire ruled by the Antichrist who will not. Just what is this image that will become so powerful?

The Vision

[11]And I beheld another beast coming up out of the earth; and he had two horns like a lamb, and he spoke as a dragon. [12]And he exercises all the power of the first beast before him, and causes the earth and them which dwell therein to worship the first beast, whose deadly wound was healed.

[13]And he does great wonders, so that he makes fire come down from heaven on the earth in the sight of men. [14]And deceives them that dwell on the earth by those miracles which he had power to do in the sight of the beast; saying to them that dwell on the earth, that they should make an image to the beast, which had the wound by a sword, and did live.

[15]And he had power to give life unto the image of the beast, that the image of the beast should both speak, and cause that as many as would not worship the image of the beast should be killed.

[16]And he causes all, both small and great, rich and poor, free and bond, to receive a mark in their right hand, or in their foreheads: [17]And that no man might buy or sell, save he that had the mark, or the name of the beast, or the number of his name.

[18]Here is wisdom. Let him that has understanding count the number of the beast: for it is the number of a man; and his number is Six hundred threescore and six.

(Revelation 13:11-18)

An Image Defined

The understanding of the Image of the Beast starts with the word *image* itself. The Greek word that is here translated as *image is eikon,* which means *likeness.* This *likeness* may be a similarity in physical appearance, a similarity in character or manner, or even a similarity in spirituality.

One understanding of its use is seen in Paul's letter to the Colossians where he speaks of Jesus as the one *"who is the image [eikon] of the invisible God" (Colossians 1:15).* Paul is not saying that the physical appearance of Jesus is like that of God, but that the character of Jesus is like that of God. Another is in Romans 8:28 and 29 where eikon is used to portray a spiritual likeness: *"28And we know that all things work together for good to them that love God, to them who are the called according to his purpose. 29For whom he did foreknow, he also did predestinate to be conformed to the image [eikon] of his Son, that he might be the firstborn among many brethren."* Paul is saying that those who love God will become like, or be a likeness of, Christ. The use of *eikon* as a similarity in physical appearance is seen in the account of the chief priest's attempt to trap Jesus in a question of law by asking him if it was lawful for them to give tribute to Caesar. Jesus responded by saying, *"Show me a penny. Whose image [eikon] and superscription has it? They answered and said Caesar's" (Luke 20:24).* The image on the coin was that of Caesar that identified the coin as the currency of Rome.

In each of these examples, *eikon* is used to mean a *likeness* in the sense of duplication or copy.

Thus *eikon* does mean *image.* However, *eikon* is never used to mean a graven image. When the New Testament text speaks of a graven image or an idol, meaning a created object typically of stone, wood, or metal, the Greek word *eidolon* (idol) is used.

Today, *eidolon* could also apply to any constructed device, mechanical or electrical, such as a robot, a computer, or even a hologram.

Therefore, the *image of the beast* cannot be an idol or a graven image since the word *eikon* and the context of the text in which *eikon* is used does not allow it. In the given examples, and in other verses where *eikon* is used, the *image* is the *likeness* of some aspect of a man, the Son of Man, or of God. The *image of the beast is, therefore, a likeness of or is patterned after, a personage.*

The Image Identified

Now that we know the *image* of the beast is not an idol, we need to go back to the vision and identify the players in this prophecy:

> *¹¹And I beheld another beast* [the empire of the False Prophet] *coming up out of the earth; and he* [the empire of the False Prophet] *had two horns like a lamb, and he spoke as a dragon. ¹²And he* [the empire of the False Prophet] *exercises all the power of the first beast* [the empire of the Antichrist] *before him, and causes the earth and them which dwell therein to worship the first beast* [the empire of the Antichrist], *whose deadly wound was healed.*
>
> *¹³And he* [the first of the two rulers of the empire of the False Prophet] *does great wonders, so that he* [the first of the two rulers] *makes fire come down from heaven on the earth in the sight of men. ¹⁴And deceives them that dwell on the earth by those miracles which he* [the first of the two rulers] *had power to do in the sight of the beast* [the Antichrist]; *saying to them that dwell on the earth, that they should make an image to the beast* [the empire of the Antichrist], *which had the wound by a sword, and did live. ¹⁵And he* [the first of the two rulers] *had power to give life unto the image of the beast* [identity to be determined], *that the image of the beast* [identity to be determined] *should both speak, and cause that as many as would not worship the image of the beast* [identity to be determined] *should be killed.*
>
> *¹⁶And he* [the second of the two rulers] *causes all, both small and great, rich and poor, free and bond, to receive a mark in their right hand, or in their foreheads: ¹⁷And that no man might buy or sell, save he* [the people] *that had the mark, or the name of the beast, or the number of his name.*

The first part of the vision, verses 11 and 12, speaks of empires, identified by how they are described. It is the empire of the False Prophet that has the *two horns*. It is the empire of the Antichrist that is *the first beast, whose deadly wound was healed.* The second and third parts of the vision, verses 13 through 17, speak of the rulers of these empires. That these verses speak of the rulers rather than the empires is more difficult to discern, but there are clues in the text that affirm this.

Verse 12 states that it is the empire of the False Prophet that *causes* [makes (YLT)*] the earth and them which dwell therein to worship* [bow before (YLT)] the first beast, whose deadly wound was healed. Note that here both rulers (the two horns) of the empire of the False Prophet *make* the people *bow before* the first beast. Young's Literal Translation (YLT) is used in part here because it portrays a more accurate sense of the strong control of the False Prophet over the people than what is implied by the King James Version.

These two men will go beyond "leading and instructing" to outright control of the people. One will use religion, the other money. Since the two together are called the False Prophet, this implies that both men in their own way will be prophets (messengers) of their god, Satan. Both will use practices and methods in their "messages" that we might ascribe to a prophet of God. Both are false prophets because they bring a false message of salvation, a saving of man from the chaos in the world around him. Since both rulers of this empire are false prophets in their own manner, the message of the empire itself becomes a false message. It makes sense, therefore, that the empire itself would be called a "False Prophet."

Each ruler of the empire of the False Prophet thus uses a different means to enforce this "worship." What is arbitrarily labeled "the first" of the two rulers *does great wonders so that he makes, fire come down from heaven on the earth in the sight of men. And deceives them that dwell on the earth by those miracles.* Because this man of authority *does great wonders* that we typically associate with religious practices, he is deemed to be the head of the Ministry of Religion in the empire. The other ruler in the empire labeled as "the second" of the two rulers *causes all, both small and great, rich and poor, free and bond, to receive a mark in their right hand, or in their foreheads* in order to *buy or sell.* This man of authority within the empire of the False Prophet is, therefore, deemed to be the head of the Ministry of Finance.

Both have the same purpose—to *cause the earth and them which dwell therein to worship the first beast.* One will do so by deception, the other by force.

It is the head of the Ministry of Religion who deceives *them that dwell on the earth* so that *they should make an image to the beast, which had the wound by a sword, and did live.* Note that it is *them that dwell on the earth,* those who are deceived *by those miracles* of the religious ruler, who are to make this image. To make is *poieō,* meaning *to do.* In this context, to do expresses the concept of to *bring about* or *to make possible* the ability of a person to act rather than to *construct* a physical object. Note also that here it is said that this image is to be made *to* the beast, not *of* the beast. This image is therefore to be made so as to be of benefit to the beast, to draw people to worship the beast. The *beast* here is the Antichrist.

The Ministry of Religion *deceives them that dwell on the earth* and tells them *that they should make an image to the beast.* The way this workforce is described, it appears as if this project involves a considerable number of *them* that dwell on the earth, certainly more than just a handful of people. It is the great number of this "workforce" that is the impetus to the making of the image.

It is also the minister of religion who will have the *power to give life unto the image of the beast, that the image of the beast should both speak, and cause that as many as would not worship the image of the beast should be killed.* The *image* that is to be made is now spoken of as an image of the beast, an image of the Antichrist. Here is the key to the mystery of its identity. The *image of the beast* is a man who will be an *eikon, a likeness,* of the first beast. This man will be a clone, so to speak, of the Antichrist—the same in authority, in character, and in spirit, and likely, in ethnicity and culture as well. This man will be the "prophet" who gives the empire of the False Prophet its name.

How can the masses *make* this image if the *image of the beast* is a man? As previously stated, *to make* here is the Greek *poieō,* meaning to do. Poieō as used in other verses of Scripture gives us guidance to its use in this verse. By example, *poieō* means *to do* an action that will bring about a reaction. Jesus said of those who believe in him that he *"has made (poieō) us kings and priests unto God" (Revelation 1:6).* Through the shedding of his blood on the cross, Jesus has appointed us *kings and priests* and at the appointed time will rule with him. We see here an action resulting in a reaction; in this case, the reaction is an appointment to a position of supreme authority. This example of *to do* is most applicable to the situation of the masses of people who will *make* the Image of the Beast, for their acts will also result in an appointment.

The masses who have heard the teachings of this man and who have witnessed his miracles will validate him in the sight of the Antichrist as the supreme religious authority under his rule by their worship of him. Essentially, with their focus of worship on him and their belief in his miracles, this man fulfills their desire for a prophet (or a messiah, or maybe their long-awaited imam) and by public proclaim make him so. Just as God chooses a man as His prophet and gives him credence, the world will choose a man as their (false) prophet and give him credence. It is man who decides to reject God, and by doing so accepts Satan by default. (Here we have Babylon the Great, the Mother of Harlots and Abominations of the Earth in all her glory.) It is man who creates this *image,* the same as if it were a man who carved a wooden image or cast a golden idol.

And he [the head of the Ministry of Religion] *had power to give life unto the image of the beast, that the image of the beast should both speak and cause that as many as would not worship the image of the beast should be killed.* This is saying that this man who will be the likeness of the Antichrist in authority will have the power to fulfill the role as this new prophet.

Therefore, it is this religious leader, the *image of the beast, who causes the earth and them that dwell therein to worship the first beast* by first drawing their worship to him as their religious authority. He thus becomes a valuable tool of the Antichrist, drawing people by deception to also worship the Antichrist.

We can see how this process works by the following verses that tell the tangled tale of the False Prophet, the Beast, and the Red Dragon. There are two reoccurring themes of worship and power that define the relationship between the rulers of these three empires. Through the downward transfer of power and the upward transfer of worship, we can see how the Image of the Beast fits in. First, we see Satan's power and authority transferred down to the Antichrist: *"I stood upon the sand of the sea, and saw a beast rise up out of the sea, having seven heads and ten horns, and upon his horns ten crowns… 2and the dragon gave him his power, and his seat, and great authority"* (Revelation 13:1–2).

What we see with Satan and the Antichrist we also see with the Antichrist and the Image of the Beast of the empire of the False Prophet: *"11And I beheld another beast coming up out of the earth; and he had two horns like a lamb, and he spake as a dragon. 12And he exercises all the power of the first beast"* (Revelation 13:11–12). The power and authority of Satan has transferred downward through the first beast to the False Prophet.

Thus, both rulers of the empire of the False Prophet will have the power of the Antichrist and will speak as Satan.

Worship, on the other hand, begins with the people, *"them that dwell on the earth"* (Revelation 13:14). Using the power received from Satan through the Antichrist, the Image of the Beast will deceive the people who will, in turn, worship him. And he will *"cause that as many as would not worship the image of the beast should be killed"* (Revelation 13:15).

Further, the Image of the Beast *"causes the earth and them which dwell therein to worship the first beast" (Revelation 13:12)*. Thus, we see the flow of worship upward from the Image of the Beast to the Antichrist. Next, we see the worship of the Antichrist flow upward to Satan for *"they worshipped the dragon which gave power unto the beast" (Revelation 13:4)*.

Power will be given to the Antichrist by Satan to make war with those who profess Jesus as the Christ. As the Antichrist defeats these who are hated by the world, the world will give him glory and honor. But again, the people are worshipping Satan, for these acts are truly those of Satan; the Antichrist is only the visible face. It is still Satan who will be worshipped, even if by proxy.

Satan's goal is to be worshipped. Is not that the heart of the spiritual battle that has raged from Adam to Armageddon? Satan said, *"[13]I will ascend into heaven, I will exalt my throne above the stars of God…[14]I will be like the most High" (Isaiah 14:13–14)*. He tempted Jesus, saying, All the kingdoms of the world will I give you, if you will fall down and worship me *(Matthew 4:8–9)*. He is still trying to set his thrown above God's. Paul, speaking of an event in our near future, said that he is the one *"who opposes and exalts himself above all that is called God, or that is worshipped; so that he as God sits in the temple of God, showing himself that he is God" (2 Thessalonians 2:4)*.

But, you say, Paul is not speaking about Satan but about *"that man of sin…the son of perdition"* who is the Antichrist. He is. But Satan has come very literally to this earth.

He will soon possess the body of the man who is the Antichrist. The two will be as one. No matter how you look at it, Satan will be the one who will be worshipped. That is the mission of the Image to the Beast.

Revelation 17:2 states of *"Babylon the great,"* the world that man has created, that, *"is fallen, is fallen, and is become the habitation of devils, and the hold of every foul spirit, and a cage of every unclean and hateful bird."* From this statement describing the depravity of the spirit within *all that dwell on the earth* in the last days of this age, and the statement that all the world *worshipped the dragon*, it appears that people may literally and openly worship Satan.

I will tell you the mystery of the woman, and of the beast that carries her.

—Revelation 17:9

CHAPTER FIVE
Babylon the Great, a Mystery No Longer

The seventeenth chapter of Revelation describes a woman, identified as Babylon the Great, the Mother of Harlots and Abominations of the Earth, and the beast that carries her, having seven heads and ten horns. When John was shown this vision of the woman, an angel said to him, *"I will tell you the mystery of the woman, and of the beast that carries her" (Revelation 17:6).* The angel told John of the mystery, but the mystery itself was not revealed to him. The woman and the beast that carries her are yet a mystery, at least for the moment. That both the woman and the beast that carries her are a mystery yet today is evidenced by the myriad of theories of their identity that have brought considerable confusion to the understanding of the events of the end of the age.

This subject is introduced at this point because we have fresh in our minds the understanding of the symbols that describe the three beasts of Revelation and of their application in defining the empires they represent. This lays the foundation for the revealing of the mystery of the beast that carries the woman, and thus, the revealing of the mystery of the woman herself.

Space does not permit a detailed explanation here of all the Scripture pertinent to the mystery of the woman. Thus, my focus is only on revealing the identity of the woman and the beast that carries her with the intent of laying a foundation for the understanding of the kingdom of the Antichrist.

The Description of the Woman and the Beast That Carries Her

17: [3]*So he carried me away in the spirit into the wilderness: and I saw a woman sit upon a scarlet colored beast, full of names of blasphemy, having seven heads and ten horns. [4]And the woman was arrayed in purple and scarlet color, and decked with gold and precious stones and pearls, having a golden cup in her hand full of abominations and filthiness of her fornication: [5]And upon her forehead was a name written, [a] mystery, BABTLON THE GREAT, THE MOTHER OF HARLOTS AND ABOMINATIONS OF THE EARTH.*

[6]*And I saw the woman drunken with the blood of the saints, and with the blood of the martyrs of Jesus: and when I saw her, I wondered with great admiration. [7]And the angel said unto me, Wherefore did you marvel? I will tell you the mystery of the woman, and of the beast that carries her, which has the seven heads and ten horns. [8]The beast you saw was, and is not; and shall ascend out of the bottomless pit, and go into perdition: and they that dwell on the earth shall wonder, whose names were not written in the book of life from the foundation of the world, when they behold the beast that was, and is not, and yet is.*

[9]*And here is the mind which has wisdom. The seven heads are seven mountains, on which the woman sits. [10]And there are seven kings: five are fallen, and one is, and the other is not yet come; and when he comes, he must continue a short space. [11]And the beast that was, and is not, even he is the eighth, and is of the seven, and goes into perdition. [12]And the ten horns which you saw are ten kings, which have received no kingdom as yet; but receive power as kings one hour with the beast. [13]These have one mind, and shall give their power and strength unto the beast. [14]These shall make war with the Lamb, and the Lamb shall overcome them: for he is Lord of lords, and King of kings: and they that are with him are called, and chosen, and faithful.*

[15]*And he said unto me, The waters which you saw, where the whore sits, are peoples, and multitudes, and nations, and tongues. [16]And the ten horns which you saw upon the beast, these shall hate the whore, and shall make her desolate and naked, and shall eat her flesh, and burn her with fire. [17]For God has put in their hearts to fulfill his will, and to agree, and give their kingdom unto the beast, until the words of God shall be fulfilled. 18And the woman which you saw is that great city, which reigns over the kings of the earth.*

18: [1]*And after these things I saw another angel come down from heaven, having great power; and the earth was lightened with his glory. And he cried mightily with a strong voice, saying, Babylon the great is fallen, is fallen, and is become the habitation of devils, and the hold of every foul spirit, and a cage of every unclean and hateful bird. For all nations have drunk of the wine of the wrath of her fornication, and the kings of the earth have committed fornication with her, and the merchants of the earth are waxed rich through the abundance of her delicacies.*

(Revelation 17:3–18; 18:1–3)

The Judgment of the Great Whore

17: ¹And there came one of the seven angels which had the seven vials, and talked with me, saying unto me, Come here; I will show unto you the judgment of the great whore that sits upon many waters: ²With whom the kings of the earth have committed fornication, and the inhabitants of the earth have been made drunk with the wine of her fornication.

18:⁴And I heard another voice from heaven, saying, Come out of her, my people, that you be not partakers of her sins, and that you receive not of her plagues. ⁵For her sins have reached unto heaven, and God has remembered her iniquities. ⁶Reward her even as she rewarded you, and double unto her double according to her works: in the cup which she has filled fill to her double. ⁷How much she has glorified herself, and lived deliciously, so much torment and sorrow give her: for she says in her heart, I sit a queen, and am no widow, and shall see no sorrow. ⁸Therefore shall her plagues come in one day, death, and mourning, and famine; and she shall be utterly burned with fire: for strong is the Lord God who judges her.

⁹And the kings of the earth, who have committed fornication and lived deliciously with her, shall bewail her, and lament for her, when they shall see the smoke of her burning, ¹⁰Standing afar off for the fear of her torment, saying, Alas, alas that great city Babylon, that mighty city! for in one hour is your judgment come. ¹¹And the merchants of the earth shall weep and mourn over her; for no man buys their merchandise any more: ¹²The merchandise of gold, and silver, and precious stones, and of pearls, and fine linen, and purple, and silk, and scarlet, and all thyine wood, and all manner vessels of ivory, and all manner vessels of most precious wood, and of brass, and iron, and marble, ¹³And cinnamon, and odors, and ointments, and frankincense, and wine, and oil, and fine flour, and wheat, and beasts, and sheep, and horses, and chariots, and slaves, and souls of men.

¹⁴And the fruits that your soul lusted after are departed from you, and all things which were dainty and goodly are departed from you, and you shall find them no more at all. ¹⁵The merchants of these things, which were made rich by her, shall stand afar off for the fear of her torment, weeping and wailing, [16]And saying, Alas, alas that great city, that was clothed in fine linen, and purple, and scarlet, and decked with gold, and precious stones, and pearls! [17]For in one hour so great riches is come to nought. And every shipmaster, and all the company in ships, and sailors, and as many as trade by sea, stood afar off, [18]And cried when they saw the smoke of her burning, saying, What city is like unto this great city! [19]And they cast dust on their heads, and cried, weeping and wailing, saying, Alas, alas that great city, wherein were made rich all that had ships in the sea by reason of her costliness! for in one hour is she made desolate. [20]Rejoice over her, your heaven, and you holy apostles and prophets; for God has avenged you on her.

[21]And a mighty angel took up a stone like a great millstone, and cast it into the sea, saying, Thus with violence shall that great city Babylon be thrown down, and shall be found no more at all. [22]And the voice of harpers, and musicians, and of pipers, and trumpeters, shall be heard no more at all in you; and no craftsman, of whatsoever craft he be, shall be found any more in you; and the sound of a millstone shall be heard no more at all in you; [23]And the light of a candle shall shine no more at all in you; and the voice of the bridegroom and of the bride shall be heard no more at all in you: for your merchants were the great men of the earth; for by your sorceries were all nations deceived. [24]And in her was found the blood of prophets, and of saints, and of all that were slain upon the earth.

19: [1]And after these things I heard a great voice of much people in heaven, saying, Alleluia; Salvation, and glory, and honor, and power, unto the Lord our God: [2]for true and righteous are his judgments: for he has judged the great whore, which did corrupt the earth with her fornication, and has avenged the blood of his servants at her hand. [3]And again they said, Alleluia. And her smoke rose up for ever and ever. [4]And the four and twenty elders and the four beasts fell down and worshipped God that sat on the throne, saying, Amen; Alleluia.

(Revelation 17:1, 2; 18:4–24; 19:1–4)

The Mystery of the Beast

The angel, speaking to John concerning the understanding of this mystery, states, *"Here is the mind which has wisdom"* (17:9). Thus, we are told, "Start here." The woman is carried by a beast *having seven heads and ten horns.* But we have seen two beasts that could fit this description of having seven heads and ten horns: the Red Dragon and the Beast. The mind that has wisdom is to determine from the information now given to John as to which of these beasts is the one on which the woman sits. Wisdom is the proper application of knowledge. We now have the knowledge (the understanding) of the symbols used to define the empires of the Red Dragon and the Beast. To begin the revealing of the mystery of Babylon the Great, we must now properly apply that knowledge.

The Seven Heads

"The seven heads are seven mountains, on which the woman sits" (17:9). Historically, kings built their fortresses on the tops of mountains (or hills, as the case may be), as the high places of the land were the easiest from which to defend against an invading force. The kings ruled from these fortresses; thus, the seat of government, the heart of the kingdom was situated on a mountaintop.

It was a natural association for the people of the day to identify mountains with governments. Yet today, this is the proper allegoric use in the east for the word *mountain*. Scripture speaks of the place of rule, the seat of government, of Jesus in this same manner:

> *¹But in the last days it shall come to pass, that the mountain of the house of the lord shall be established in the top of the mountains, and it shall be exalted above the hills; and people shall flow unto it. ²And many nations shall come, and say, Come, and let us go up to the mountain of the lord, and to the house of the God of Jacob; and he will teach us of his ways, and we will walk in his paths: for the law shall go forth of Zion, and the word of the lord from Jerusalem.*

> *(Micah 4:1–2)*

The seven heads of the scarlet-colored beast are here said to be seven mountains, which represent seven governments. This does not change our definition of a *head* of a beast as a *kingdom* but rather complements the definition with the use of the symbol of a *mountain* to represent the *government* of the kingdom. The purpose in this vision of a head representing the government, the human component of the kingdom, rather than the whole of the kingdom, has more to do with the relationship between the woman and the heads of this beast than on identifying the beast itself; but it still helps to identify the beast.

"And there are seven kings" (17:10). "And the beast that was, and is not, even he is the eighth" (17:11). "And the ten horns which you saw are ten kings" (17:12). This scarlet-colored beast upon which the woman sits thus has eighteen kings who must now be accounted for.

The Set of Seven Kings

Of this set of seven kings of verse 10 that are the rulers of the seven governments of verse 9, *five are fallen, and one is, and the other is not yet come.* From John's perspective the five of the set of seven kings that had fallen, passed out of existence, would have been of the Assyrian, Egyptian, Babylonian, Medo-Persian, and Grecian empires. The one that is would be of the Roman Empire that was in existence at the time this vision was given to John. The king who had *not yet come* that would *continue a short space* will be of the empire of the Antichrist that will come out of the League of Ten.

These seven kings are the representative kings of the kingdoms depicted by the seven heads with seven crowns in the description of the Red Dragon in Revelation 12:3.

The Set of Ten Kings

The government that has *not yet come* is the government of the *ten horns,* which John saw that *are ten kings, which have received no kingdom as yet but receive power as kings one hour with the beast.* This describes the government of the confederacy of the League of Ten that is the seventh head of the Red Dragon.

This set of ten kings is depicted by the ten horns of the Red Dragon described in Revelation 12:3 and as the ten horns with crowns in the description of the Beast in Revelation 13:1.

Identification of the Beast That Carries the Woman

The *scarlet-colored beast* of Revelation 17:3 that is depicted as carrying the woman has eighteen kings who were numbered in verses 10 through 12. Only ten kings can be found within the empire of the Beast that arises from the sea. But eighteen kings are found within the empire of the Red Dragon.3 Therefore, the beast *having seven heads and ten* horns that is depicted as carrying the woman—*BABYLON THE GREAT, THE MOTHER OF HARLOTS AND ABOMINATIONS OF THE EARTH*—is the Red Dragon. But the Red Dragon is itself only representative of the true source of that which supports the woman.

The Eighth King

Scripture has identified the scarlet-colored beast as the empire of the Red Dragon and now brings our attention to the ruler of that empire. John was told, *"the beast that was, and is not, even he is the eighth, and is of the seven, and goes into perdition" (17:11)*. The seven are these seven kings of the seven governments of the kingdoms that are the seven crowned heads of the Red Dragon. Satan is king over these seven as the ruler of that empire. As the ruler of the empire he is *of the seven*, meaning he is a part of the empire of these seven kings, but as ruler, Satan is *the eighth* king of this scarlet-colored beast. (As stated earlier, Satan is not represented by a horn as are the other kings, as a horn only represents a man, not a spirit.)

When John was told of the mystery of the woman, and of the beast that carries her, he was told that *"the beast you saw was, and is not; and shall ascend out of the bottomless pit, and go into perdition: and they that dwell on the earth shall wonder, whose names were not written in the book of life from the foundation of the world, when they behold the beast that was, and is not, and yet is"* (17:8).4 Now we see that *"the beast that was, and is not, even he is the eighth, and is of the seven, and goes into perdition" (17:11)*. (A beast can represent either an empire or the ruler of the empire depending upon the context in which the word is used.) And here we see that Satan, as the eighth king, is the beast *that was, and is not, and yet is, and is the one who will ascend out of the bottomless pit, and go into perdition.*

Therefore, the *scarlet colored beast* represents Satan in this vision, the real power that supports the woman.

The angel explaining the mystery of this beast does so from the viewpoint of the time of final judgment of the beast (for all *whose names were not written in the book of life* from every age shall, at that time, *behold the beast that was, and is not, and yet is*). From this time perspective, the beast *was, and is not, and yet is*. Prior to this time of judgment, Satan had access to the people of the earth. To them, he was an adversary, a lion walking about the earth, seeking whom he may devour (1 Peter 5:8). Through deception, he had done to all people as he had done to Eve, tempting them to sin. But at the time of the judgment of the harlot, *"I an angel [will] come down from heaven, having the key of the bottomless pit and a great chain in his hand. 2And he [will lay] hold on the dragon, that old serpent, which is the Devil, and Satan, and bound him a thousand years. 3And [will] cast him into the bottomless pit, and shut him up, and set a seal upon him, that he should deceive the nations no more, till a thousand years should be fulfilled"* (Revelation 20:1–3). However, *"7when the thousand years are expired, Satan shall be loosed out of his prison, 8and shall go out to deceive the nations which are in the four quarters of the earth"* (Revelation 20:7–8). Therefore, Satan was on the earth, able to deceive people. But, being bound a thousand years, he is not on the earth to be able to deceive. After the thousand years, he will be *loosed out of his prison and will again be on the earth to deceive people; thus, he yet is. Furthermore, "the devil that deceived them was cast into the lake of fire and brimstone, where the beast and the false prophet are, and shall be tormented day and night for ever and ever"* (Revelation 20:10). Therefore, it is also Satan that is the beast that John saw that *shall ascend out of the bottomless pit and go into perdition.*

A Critical Clarification

The set of ten kings *which have received no kingdom as yet* are said to *give their power and strength unto the beast.* This *beast* is identified in verse 11 as *the beast that was, and is not,* the one that *goes into perdition.* Therefore, this *beast* to which these ten kings will *give their power and strength* is Satan, not the Antichrist. (After all, the Antichrist himself will be one of those ten kings, so it seems illogical to say that he is to give this *power and strength* unto himself.)

These ten kings *receive power as kings one hour with the beast,* indicating that they rule in the confederacy for a very short period of time. Note that it is the kings who are to *receive power* for a short time; the nations they rule, however, may be in existence for some time prior to the time of their rule. Note also that it is the kings who are to *receive* power, but it does not say Satan gives them this power; it is God who will give them their rule, for He is the author of the wrath that they will bring upon Israel.

Verse 13 states that these ten kings, in turn, *shall give their power and strength unto the beast,* unto Satan, meaning they work on behalf of Satan. Again, the Antichrist is one of those ten kings. Verse 14 states, *"These shall make war with the Lamb, and the Lamb shall overcome them: for he is Lord of lords, and King of kings: and they that are with him are called, and chosen, and faithful."* This verse that speaks of the battle of Armageddon confirms the time of rule of these ten kings.

The Age of the Woman

In verse 7 of chapter 17, it is said that the beast *which has the seven heads and ten horns is the beast that carries her,* indicating a relationship between the woman and the beast. The fact that the woman is shown sitting on the beast tells us that the woman and the beast must both exist at the same time in history.

It could be said that the empire of the Red Dragon began with the union of Satan and the kingdom of Assyria. The woman must therefore be at least as old as the Assyrian Empire. This fact alone eliminates all the theories taught today of the identity of the woman and of the city she is said to represent.

Who Controls Who?

"I will tell you the mystery of the woman, and of the beast that carries her, which has the seven heads and ten horns" (Revelation 17:7). This description of the *woman* clearly states that the scarlet-colored beast *carries her,* showing us that the beast supports the woman. We are told by this that the beast is in some manner not only in control of the woman but also aids her in her fornication. The *beast that carries* the woman is Satan. It is thus Satan that is the foundation on which the city of Babylon is built.

The Mystery of the Woman

"And there came one of the seven angels which had the seven vials, and talked with me, saying unto me, Come here; I will show unto you the judgment of the great whore" *(Revelation 17:1).* Thus, we are introduced to the mystery of *BABYLON THE GREAT, THE MOTHER OF HARLOTS AND ABOMINATION OF THE EARTH.* But note that John was told that he would be shown the judgment of the *great whore* as if this great whore was not new to him. How, then, did he know of this woman?

John had seen this woman previously, tucked between an account of the righteous and an account of the unrighteous as if this woman was the cause of this separation:

> *¹And I looked, and, lo, a Lamb stood on the mount Sion, and with him an hundred forty and four thousand, having his Father's name written in their foreheads. ²And I heard a voice from heaven, as the voice of many waters, and as the voice of a great thunder: and I heard the voice of harpers harping*

with their harps: ³And they sung as it were a new song before the throne, and before the four beasts, and the elders: and no man could learn that song but the hundred and forty and four thousand, which were redeemed from the earth.

⁴These are they which were not defiled with [the] women; for they are virgins. These are they which follow the Lamb wheresoever he goes. These were redeemed from among men, being the first fruits unto God and to the Lamb. ⁵And in their mouth was found no guile: for they are without fault before the throne of God... ⁸And there followed another angel, saying, Babylon is fallen, is fallen, that great city, because she made all nations drink of the wine of the wrath of her fornication.... ⁹If any man worship the beast and his image, and receive his mark in his forehead, or in his hand, the same shall drink of the wine of the wrath of God.

(Revelation 14:1–5, 8–9)

This Scripture shows us the two spiritual states of man, the redeemed and the unredeemed, and the cause that requires the need for redemption. I present here *the hundred and forty and four thousand* as an example of the redeemed. There is another story to be told of these hundred and forty and four thousand, but for my purpose here in identifying the woman, they are used as the example of the redeemed in the larger story that is told here. These who are *redeemed from among men* are thus an example of one spiritual state of all of mankind. Juxtaposed to the *hundred and forty and four thousand* are those who are given a warning; *If any man worships the beast and his image and receive his mark in his forehead, or in his hand, the same shall drink of the wine of the wrath of God.* These are the example in the larger story of those who are unredeemed, the other spiritual state of mankind. The *hundred and forty and four thousand* are (metaphorically) marked in their foreheads as belonging to God. Those who are given warning are (most likely to be) literally marked in their forehead as belonging to Satan.

Between the text that introduced those who are redeemed and the text that introduced those who are unredeemed, we are introduced to a woman and a city, as if to say, "Here is why these two are separated one from another." Of the woman it is said, *she made all nations drink of the wine of the wrath of her fornication. Fornication* is an illicit relationship—sin in the eyes of God. Thus, again, our text relates to the spiritual condition of man. The phrase *the wine of the wrath of her fornication* is a poetic way of saying that there was a steep price to pay for this illicit relationship in which the woman is involved. Of the city it is said, *Babylon is fallen, is fallen, that great city.* Babylon is fallen *because* it has drunk of *the wine of the wrath of her fornication.* Yet, again, this speaks to the spiritual. This fall of Babylon is therefore not the destruction of the physical structures of this *great city* or of the demise of its government but, rather, its fall from spiritual righteousness. The woman of Revelation 14:4 is the *great whore* of Revelation 17:1 that John now sees.

The woman named Babylon the Great is herself a *"great whore"* *(Revelation 17:1).* Therefore, the woman is symbolic of an illicit relationship. But in verse 18, we are told that *"the woman which you saw is that great city, which reigns over the kings of the earth."* This *great city* by which she is identified is in turn symbolic of that with which the woman has of this woman. With that statement, man proclaimed, *"Let us set ourselves as supreme."* One might even say that *let us make us a name* is another way of saying *"The way of man is better than the way of God."*

God speaks in Isaiah 47 to a Babylon that has set herself as supreme. This may be the great city of Babylon of Nebuchadnezzar's time or Babylon the Great of our time, but the message is the same as to the world man has created:

> [1]*Come down, and sit in the dust, O virgin daughter of Babylon, sit on the ground: there is no throne, O daughter of the Chaldeans: for you shall no more be called tender and delicate....[3]Your nakedness shall be uncovered, yea, your shame shall be seen: I will take vengeance, and I will not meet you as a man....[8]you that are given to pleasures, that dwell carelessly, that say in your heart, I am, and none else beside me....[10]For you have trusted in your wickedness: you have said, None see me. Your wisdom and your knowledge, it has perverted you; and you have said in your heart, I am, and none else beside me.*

> *(Isaiah 47:1, 3, 8, 10)*[2]

Another way of putting this today: "The way of the world is better than the way of God." In a word, worldly.

That great city Babylon, that mighty city is the world that man has created in defiance of God. But God has said, *"You adulterers and adulteresses, know you not that the friendship of the world is enmity with God? Whosoever therefore will be a friend of the world is the enemy of God"* (James 4:4). This is why God has said, *"Come out of her, my people, that you be not partakers of her sins, and that you receive not of her plagues"* (Revelation 18:4). By saying *come out of her,* God is not telling people to leave a literal sinful city but, rather, to not take part in this world's sinful ways. Thus, the woman is seen as *"having a golden cup in her hand full of abomination and filthiness of her fornication"* (Revelation 17:4). The outward appearance of this illicit relationship with the world is thus depicted by this shiny gold cup, that which is appealing to man. But God looks on the inside, and what fills this cup is enmity with God.

The revealing of this mystery shows us *BABYLON THE GREAT, THE MOTHER OF HARLOTS, AND ABOMINATIONS OF THE EARTH* is man's illicit relationship with the world, *that great city* which he has built. We are again building the tower of Babel, not with bricks of clay but with bricks of the haughtiness of man so as to lift ourselves to heaven as gods. And how far has this construction project progressed? Dr. Richard Seed, in his desire to create man in the image of his choosing by producing genetically engineered "super babies" proclaims, "We are going to become gods, period. If you don't like it, get off. You don't have to contribute, you don't have to participate, but if you are going to interfere with me becoming a god, you're going to have trouble. There'll be warfare."[6]

But the psalmist asks, *"¹Why do the heathen rage, and the people imagine a vain thing? ²The kings of the earth set themselves, and the rulers take counsel together, against the Lord, and against his anointed, saying, ³Let us break their bands asunder, and cast away their cords from us"* (Psalms 2:1–3). When the Lord saw the city and the tower that man had built, He said, *"Behold, the people is one, and they have all one language; and this they begin to do: and now nothing will be restrained from them, which they have imagined to do"* (Genesis 11:6). Again, we have *all one language* in that the world has become a globalized society. And, it appears that *nothing [has been] restrained from [us], which [we] have imagined to do.*

Chapter 18 describes God's reaction to this construction project. In short, *"the lofty looks of man shall be humbled, and the haughtiness of men shall be bowed down, and the Lord alone shall be exalted in that day"* (Isaiah 2:11). *"Thus with violence shall that great city Babylon be thrown down, and shall be found no more at all"* (Revelation 18:21), for *"out of his mouth goes a sharp sword, that with it he should smite the nations: and he shall rule them with a rod of iron: and he treads the winepress of the fierceness and wrath of Almighty God. And he has on his vesture and on his thigh a name written, KING OF KINGS, AND LORDS OF LORD"* (Revelation 19:15).

And if you will not for all this hearken unto me, but walk contrary unto me; Then I will walk contrary unto you also in fury; and I, even I, will chastise you seven times for your sins.

—Leviticus 26:27–28

[3]The Antichrist, who is the representative king of the League of Ten of the first part of verse 10, will become one of the ten kings of the government of the league of the last part of verse 10. His participation as king within the League of Ten will occur sometime after his coming on the scene as a prince at the confederacy of the League and, prior to his position as king of an empire of only seven nations, the remnant of the League. Technically, then, the Antichrist could be counted twice for a short period of time in that number of eighteen.

[4]The statement, *they that dwell on the earth shall wonder, whose names were not written in the book of life from the foundation of the world, when they behold the beast that was, and is not, and yet is* has no application to the Antichrist. *They that dwell on the earth* refer to people, in contrast to angels, because both will *behold the beast.* These that *dwell on the earth* include all people from every age *whose names were not written in the book of life.* Those who lived prior to the age of the Antichrist would not *wonder* about this man as he has no relevance to them. They will, however, *wonder* about Satan because he indeed has a relevance to them.

[5]*"You have said in your heart, **I am**, and none else beside me."* With this statement, man proclaimed himself as God, for God had said unto Moses, *"Thus shalt thou say unto the children of Israel, I Am hath sent me unto you" (Exodus 3:14).*

[6]Cris Putnam and Thomas Horn, Exo-Vaticana (Missouri: Defender, 2013), 117.

CHAPTER SIX
A Bit of History

The Red Dragon, the Beast, and the False Prophet hold a prominent place in Scripture. Much has been said, and much written, of what these three beasts of Revelation are and who they are. But there has been essentially nothing on why they are. We will search out the *why* in this chapter. In doing so, we will put the nation of Israel into the context of the first six of the seven Gentile empires of the Red Dragon, both physically and spiritually. This will be done by looking at a bit of the history of Israel. This history will help us to understand the why of these three beasts. It will also help us to understand Israel's part in the coming of the League of Ten and the seventh Gentile empire.

God Takes a People
God told the people of Israel, *"I will take you to me for a people, and I will be to you a God: and you shall know that I am the Lord your God"* (Exodus 6:7).

When this was told the people they were not yet a nation—they were still in the iron furnace of Egypt. Moses was to take these people of Abraham, Isaac, and Jacob out of this land of bondage and into Canaan, the land God had earlier promised to Abraham and to his seed as a possession forever. During this exodus from Egypt, the Israelites would pause for nearly a year before Mount Sinai to receive the revelation of God's law. They were not only introduced to the principle by which they were to obey Him; they were instructed on the principle by which they were to occupy the land God had given them. These two principles were wholly entwined.

The heart of these entwined principles was this: *"2I am the Lord your God, which have brought you out of the land of Egypt, out of the house of bondage. [3]You shall have no other gods before me. [4]You shall not make unto you any graven image, or any likeness of any thing that is in heaven above, or that is in the earth beneath, or that is in the water under the earth"* (Exodus 20:2–4). God had chosen Israel; now Israel was to choose their god. *"[26]Behold, I set before you this day a blessing and a curse; [27]A blessing, if you obey the commandments of the Lord your God, which I command you this day: [28]And a curse, if you will not obey the commandments of the Lord your God, but turn aside out of the way which I command you this day"* (Deuteronomy 11:26–28). Briefly, the blessing was thus; *"if you shall hearken diligently unto the voice of the Lord your God, to observe and to do all his commandments which I command you this day, that the Lord your God will set you on high above all nations of the earth"* (Deuteronomy 28:1). And the curse: *"[25]When you shall beget children, and children's children, and you shall have remained long in the land, and shall corrupt yourselves, and make a graven image, or the likeness of anything, and shall do evil in the sight of the Lord your God, to provoke him to anger: [26]I call heaven and earth to witness against you this day, that you shall soon utterly perish from off the land whereunto you go over Jordan to possess it; you shall not prolong your days upon it, but shall utterly be destroyed. [27]And the Lord shall scatter you among the nations, and you shall be left few in number among the heathen, whither the Lord shall lead you"* (Deuteronomy 4:25–27).

Possessing the Land

> *"Now therefore hearken, O Israel, unto the statutes and unto the judgments, which I teach you, for to do them, that you may live, and go in and possess the land which the Lord God of your fathers gives you".*
> *(Deuteronomy 4:1)*

Israel's well-being and longevity in the land they were to possess were thus conditional on their obedience to God.

To possess the land of Canaan, God instructed the Israelites to drive the occupying nations out from before them (Deuteronomy 4:38), to make no covenant with them nor show them mercy but to utterly destroy them (Deuteronomy 7:2). They were to destroy their altars and cut down the groves of their altars, and they were to burn the graven images of their gods with fire (Deuteronomy 7:5). Israel was to destroy these nations and their graven images so that these nations would not be a snare unto the people and turn them from following God (Deuteronomy 7:40).

When the Israelites entered the land of Canaan, God was faithful in delivering the indigenous peoples into their hand, and *"the children of Israel went every man unto his inheritance to possess the land. [7] And the people served the Lord all the days of Joshua, and all the days of the elders that outlived Joshua, who had seen all the great works of the Lord, that he did for Israel"* (Judges 2:6–7). However, in time, the Israelites became unfaithful to God in not following through with the complete destruction of all those nations about them. *"[10] And there arose another generation after them, which knew not the Lord, nor yet the works which he had done for Israel. [11] And the children of Israel did evil in the sight of the Lord, and served Baalim: [12] And they forsook the Lord God of their fathers, which brought them out of the land of Egypt, and followed other gods, of the gods of the people that were round about them, and bowed themselves unto them, and provoked the Lord to anger"* (Judges 2:10-12).

So, the nations the Israelites were to destroy, but failed in doing so, became a snare unto the people. God's response? He said, *"You [were to] make no league with the inhabitants of this land; you [were to] throw down their altars: but you have not obeyed my voice: why have you done this? [3] Wherefore I also said, I will not drive them out from before you; but they shall be as thorns in your sides"* (Judges 2:2–3). And, these nations were as thorns in the sides of the Israelites.

The people sorely felt the consequences of their disobedience as, *"[14] the anger of the Lord was hot against Israel, and he delivered them into the hands of spoilers that spoiled them, and he sold them into the hands of their enemies round about, so that they could not any longer stand before their enemies. [15] Whithersoever they went out, the hand of the Lord was against them for evil, as the Lord had said, and as the Lord had sworn unto them: and they were greatly distressed"* (Judges 2:14–15).

For a period of nearly two hundred years, the Israelites found themselves first under one and then another master—the Philistines, the Canaanites, the Sidonians, the Amorites, the Hittites, the Moabites, the Ammonites, the Midianites, to name a few. *"[16] Nevertheless the Lord raised up judges, which delivered them out of the hand of those that spoiled them. [17] And yet they would not hearken unto their judges, but they went a whoring after other gods.... [18] And when the Lord raised them up judges, then the Lord was with the judge, and delivered them out of the hand of their enemies all the days of the judge: for it repented the Lord because of their groanings by reason of them that oppressed them and vexed them. [19] And it came to pass, when the judge was dead, that they returned, and corrupted themselves more than their fathers, in following other gods to serve them, and to bow down unto them; they ceased not from their own doings, nor from their stubborn way"* (Judges 2:16–19).

Israel Takes a King

In those days there was no king in Israel; God was to be their king. The people had received the Mosaic Law, which had instructed them in governance, and they were to look to Him for guidance.

During the period of the judges, the Israelites rarely, if ever, organized into a single unit. The people remained divided rather into separate tribes that administered themselves. What cooperative effort there appeared to be among the tribes was at the leadership of the judges, who arose only in times of greatest oppression. These judges appeared for the most part to be military commanders who organized intertribal armies and led them into battle against invading or occupying forces. These judges were raised up by the hand of God; they were not chosen by men. Samuel was to be the last of these judges.

"⁴Then all the elders of Israel gathered themselves together, and came to Samuel unto Ramah, ⁵And said unto him, Behold, you are old, and your sons walk not in your ways: now make us a king to judge us like all the nations" (1 Samuel 8:4–5). Whether the Israelites had all but abandoned God or had perceived some advantage to having an earthly king as did the surrounding nations the Scripture does not say, but they requested from Samuel that he give them a king. Samuel put this request before the Lord: *"And the Lord said unto Samuel, Hearken unto the voice of the people in all that they say unto you: for they have not rejected you, but they have rejected me, that I should not reign over them"* (1 Samuel 8:7). The account in 1 Samuel of this request makes it quite clear that God considered this desire for an earthly king to be an act of disobedience. However, God relented to the desire of the people and told Samuel to give them a king. But God also forewarned the elders that *"if you shall still do wickedly, you shall be consumed, both you and your king"* (1 Samuel 12:25).

According to Hebrew history, Saul thus was chosen by popular acclaim of the people, and Samuel anointed him with oil to symbolize his election as king.

Saul united the twelve tribes of Jacob into the nation of Israel. It appears as if he established his native town of Gibeah as its capital and gathered a small standing army. Saul seems to have been largely a military leader and was initially successful in his efforts in delivering this new nation out of the hands of those that had spoiled her.

Although Israel now had its earthly king in Saul, this king was still to obey *"the voice of the words of the Lord"* (1 Samuel 15:1). Saul, however, repeatedly failed to carry out God's instructions. Because Saul rejected the words of the Lord, God also rejected Saul as king and rent the kingdom from his hand, delivering Israel, and the king himself, into the hands of the Philistines *(1 Samuel 28:17–19).*

While Saul was yet king, God chose another to rule over Israel, a man after the heart of the Lord *(1 Samuel 13:14).* This man was David. After the death of Saul, David was initially anointed king only by the house of Judah *(2 Samuel 2:4);* it was another seven years before the elders of the remaining tribes of Israel accepted David as king *(2 Samuel 5:3),* thereby uniting all the tribes of Israel again into a unified nation.

David also became the king of the city-state of Jerusalem, which had never been a part of the territory occupied by Israel. He conquered this Jebusite city with his mercenary troops *(2 Samuel 5:6–9),* built a fort within the city, which was called the city of David, and made it his residence. He ruled Jerusalem as legal successor to the previous Jebusite ruler, with the city remaining a city-state separate from both the kingdoms of Judah and Israel for several centuries.

Under the leadership of David, what had been a loose federation of tribes became an empire, expanding the territory ruled by Israel to all of the land of Canaan from the Euphrates River in the north to the river of Egypt in the south. The multitude of nations that once had taken spoil of Israel now paid tribute to her. This complete reversal of fortune was due to one thing: David was obedient to the word of the Lord.

Upon the death of David, Solomon became the third, and the last, king of a united Israel. As a young man when he ascended to the throne, Solomon was concerned about his ability to rule what was now a mighty nation. He thus asked God to be given an understanding heart that he might judge the people committed to him. His request was granted, and riches and honor were added thereto, with a promise of length of days if he kept God's commandments. Solomon loved the Lord and walked in the statutes of David his father, his crowning achievement being the building of the Temple in Jerusalem.

The Scriptural account of Solomon's reign portrays a wise and shrewd king, at least for most of his reign. Solomon's downfall came in his old age, for he had taken many foreign wives *"of the nations concerning which the Lord said unto the children of Israel, You shall not go in to them, neither shall they come in unto you: for surely they will turn away your heart after their gods"* (1 Kings 11:2). And, his heart was turned away after the gods of his wives, even to the building of shrines to burn incense and sacrifice unto their gods.

"⁹And the Lord was angry with Solomon, because his heart was turned from the Lord God of Israel....¹¹Wherefore the Lord said unto Solomon, Forasmuch as this is done of you, and you have not kept my covenant and my statutes, which I have commanded you, I will surely rend the kingdom from you, and will give it to your servant...¹³Howbeit I will not rend away all the kingdom; but will give one tribe to your son for David my servant's sake, and for Jerusalem's sake which I have chosen" (1 Kings 11: 9, 11, 14).

Rehoboam, a son of Solomon, was to be anointed king over all Israel in the stead of Solomon while Solomon yet lived. Thus, all the congregation of Israel was to come to Shechem to make him king, and with them came Jeroboam, the servant of Solomon to whom the Lord was to give ten tribes of Israel to rule *(1 King 11:35)*. Then the people came and spoke to Rehoboam saying, *"Your father made our yoke grievous: now therefore make you the grievous service of your father, and his heavy yoke which he put upon us, lighter, and we will serve you"* (1 Kings 12:4). King Rehoboam took this matter under consideration, requesting advice from the old men who had stood before Solomon. Their reply was that if he would be a servant unto his people and serve them, then they would be his servants forever.

But Rehoboam forsook the counsel of the old men and took the counsel of the young men who now stood before him, who had told him to make the yoke upon the people even heaver. Thus, Rehoboam answered the congregation of Israel with these words: *"Now whereas my father did lade you with a heavy yoke, I will add to your yoke: my father has chastised you with whips, but I will chastise you with scorpions"* (1 Kings 12:11). Rehoboam's answer was actually that of the Lord's (1 Kings 11:11–13) to bring about that which He had said unto Solomon, that He would surely rend the kingdom from him, and would give it to his servant Jeroboam.

"So when all Israel saw that the king hearkened not unto them, the people answered the king, saying, What portion have we in David? neither have we inheritance in the son of Jesse: to your tents, O Israel: now see to your own house,

David. So Israel departed unto their tents" (1 Kings 12:16). Israel had rebelled against the house of David. *"²⁰And it came to pass, when all Israel heard that Jeroboam was come again, that they sent and called him unto the congregation, and made him king over all Israel: there was none that followed the house of David, but the tribe of Judah only. ²¹And when Rehoboam was come to Jerusalem, he assembled all the house of Judah, with the tribe of Benjamin" (1 Kings 12:20–21).* Thus, the mighty kingdom of David was divided.

Judah, Israel, and Jerusalem

The time is around 925 BC; the great nation of King David has been divided into the southern state of Judah and the northern state of Israel, and Jerusalem, still a city-state, added to the territory of the Hebrews. We are now at that point in history where, for the first time, the necessary pieces were in place for the fulfillment of Zachariah's vision of the four horns, although his vision was still some years distant.

Zachariah said of his vision, *"¹⁸Then lifted I up mine eyes, and saw, and behold four horns. ¹⁹And I said unto the angel that talked with me, What be these? And he answered me, These are the horns which have scattered Judah, Israel, and Jerusalem" (Zachariah 1:18–19).* Judah, Israel, and Jerusalem were the pieces that had to be in place to fulfill Zachariah's vision. Zachariah lived during the time of the Medo-Persian Empire, about four hundred years after the division of the nation of Israel. From this perspective, he was looking back in time at four Gentile empires, represented by these four horns, which had come against Judah, Israel, and Jerusalem. These were the Gentile empires of Assyria, Egypt, Babylon, and Medo-Persia. We know from Scripture that three more Gentile empires were yet to follow, those of Greece, Rome, and the League of Ten. The *phrase Judah, Israel, and Jerusalem* of Zachariah's vision is, therefore, of singular importance in his vision as that phrase identifies the time of the birth of the empire of the Red Dragon.

Israel and the Assyrian Empire

There was enmity between Judah and Israel, and Jeroboam feared that if the people of Israel were to go to Jerusalem to sacrifice in the house of the Lord, then the heart of his people would turn again unto Rehoboam king of Judah, and thus, they would rise up and kill him. *"Whereupon the king [Jeroboam] took counsel, and made two calves of gold, and said unto them, It is too much for you to go up to Jerusalem: behold your gods, O Israel, which brought you up out of the land of Egypt"* (1 Kings 12:28). Jeroboam built altars and offered sacrifices unto these golden calves, which he had devised of his own heart, and the people worshiped before them. Because of this disobedience of Jeroboam, *"who did sin, and who made Israel to sin"* (1 Kings 14:16), God was to root up Israel out of the land that he had given to their fathers and would scatter them *"beyond the river"* (1 Kings 14:15).

Israel was now to come face-to-face with the rising power of the Assyrian Empire to its north. One could say that it was the natural course of events for the expanding Assyrian Empire to eventually engulf the territory of Israel. But the Scriptures tell us that it was the God of Israel who stirred up the spirit of Tiglath-pileser, king of Assyria, and he carried the people of Israel away *(1 Chronicles 5:26)*.

Tiglath-pileser III (Pul in the Scriptures) came to the throne of Assyria in the year 745 BC. He was the first of an uninterrupted series of great soldiers on the throne who quickly brought the Assyrian Empire to the zenith of its power, establishing Assyrian sovereignty over the whole of Syria and Israel.

Tiglath-pileser's initial invasion of the northern state of Israel only brought about the demand of payment of tribute to Assyria *(2 Kings 15:19)*. This tribute was paid only for a short period of time before Israel, together with Damascus, agreed on a course of mutual resistance of payment. The result was a second invasion by Tiglath-pileser. This time, Israeli citizens were taken into exile, and most of the territory of Israel was lost. King Pekah of Israel was left only Mount Ephraim with the royal city of Samaria; the rest of the state of Israel was incorporated into the Assyrian system of provinces.7 The Israelite peasant population in these new provinces were left generally where they were as a subject people. The urban upper class was deported to Assyria as stated in 2 Kings 15:29, and in their place, Assyrian governors and officials and a new upper class from other parts of the empire, were sent to the new provinces. What remained of the state of Israel remained as a dependent vassal state.

In time, Israel again resisted the payment of tribute, this time turning to Egypt for assistance. Consequently, Shalmaneser V, then ruler of Assyria, besieged Samaria in 724 BC. Samaria withstood the siege for three years but finally fell in 721 BC at the beginning of the reign of Sargon. Sargon took another 27,290 Israelites into captivity, this time to Mesopotamia and Media, and the remnant of the state of Israel turned into the Assyrian province of "Samaria." To better manage its control over the territory, the Assyrians imported a new upper class from Babylon and Syria into the region to dwell among the remnant of Israelites who remained in the land. Thus, the northern state of Israel ceased to exist; only the southern state of Judah and the city-state of Jerusalem remained.

But Israel was not alone in her sins, for *"²²Judah did evil in the sight of the Lord, and they provoked him to jealousy with their sins which they had committed, above all that their fathers had done. ²³For they also built them high places, and images, and groves, on every high hill, and under every green tree"* (1 Kings 14:22–23). Thus, Judah did not escape the long reach of the Assyrian Empire.

Neither was the city-state of Jerusalem to escape the wrath of God by the hand of Assyria. God said of Jerusalem: *"²⁵You have built your high place at every head of the way, and have made your beauty to be abhorred, and have opened your feet to everyone that passed by, and multiplied your whoredoms…²⁸You have played the whore also with the Assyrians, because you were unsatiable; yea, you have played the harlot with them, and yet could not be satisfied…³⁹And I will also give you into their hand"* (Ezekiel 25, 28, 39).

In 733 BC, Jerusalem was attacked by the combined forces of Damascus and the state of Israel for the refusal of King Ahaz to join them in their rebellion against Tiglath-pileser. In an attempt to enlist help against his attackers, King Ahaz sent a gift from the Temple to Tiglath-pileser with an offer of surrender and a request for aid. Tiglath-pileser intervened in this local squabble, but the consequence was that Judah became a vassal state, paying tribute to the Assyrian Empire till the death of Sargon in 705 BC.

When anti-Assyrian uprisings in other parts of the empire preoccupied Sargon's successor, King Hezekiah of Judah used it as an opportunity to throw off Assyrian rule, at least for a time. When Sennacherib ascended to the Assyrian throne, he reasserted authority over Judah in 701 BC, taking forty-six of its fortified walled cities and small towns.[8] Hezekiah was able only to hold Jerusalem, which was encircled by Assyrian troops; he had no choice but to submit to Sennacherib. Hezekiah was allowed to stay on the throne of the city-state of Jerusalem, but only as a tributary vassal. The state of Judah was taken from him. Thus, *Judah, Israel, and Jerusalem* had become a part of the Assyrian Empire.

The greatest extent of the Assyrian Empire is shown in map 6.1. The territory of the ancient empire is overlaid the borders of today's nation

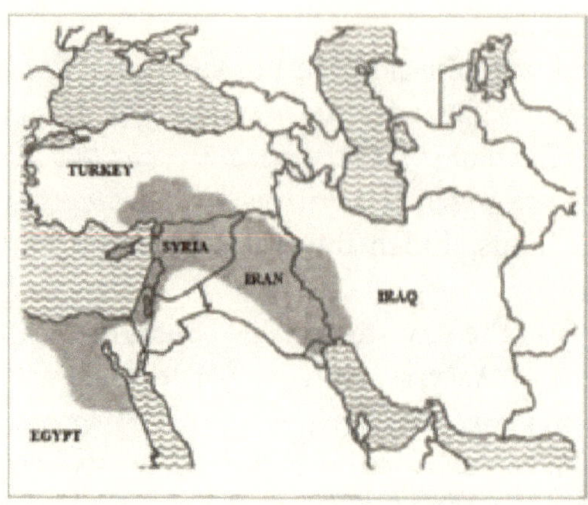

Map 6.1. The Assyrian Empire, circa 700 BC.

Israel and the Egyptian Empire

The Assyrian Empire reached its zenith in 663 BC when king Ashurbanipal of Assyria gained control over all of Egypt with the taking of Thebes, the capital city of Upper Egypt. But Ashurbanipal was not the warlord of the caliber of his forefathers, so the empire started to unravel as various conquered lands began to throw off Assyrian rule.

To the northeast of Nineveh, Assyria's capital city, the Medes consolidated its peoples when Cyaxares come to power in 633 BC and became a force to be reckoned with. To the southeast of Nineveh, new vigor came to the old kingdom of Babylon with the settlement of a new people into the region who called themselves "Chaldeans". In 625 BC, Nabopolassar united the Chaldean tribes and became king of this neo-Babylonian empire. In 612 BC, the alliance of the Medes and Babylonians marched against Nineveh and destroyed the city, bringing the Assyrian Empire near to its end.

To the south, Josiah, king of Judah, had been succeeding by degrees in breaking the dominance of Assyria. The Bible states of Josiah, *"Like unto him was there no king before him, that turned to the Lord with all his heart, and with all his soul, and with all his might, according to all the law of Moses; neither after him arose there any like him"* (2 Kings 23:25). At the death of Assyria's king Ashurbanipal, Josiah purified the Temple in Jerusalem by removing the symbols of the Assyrian cults, which had marked that of foreign domination and national humiliation since the reigns of Manasseh and Ahaz, and brought to the people the most radical religious reforms in Judah's history. He also stopped paying tribute, which meant complete independence from Assyria. He perused the restoration of the rule of the house of David in the former state of Israel. The laws of Deuteronomy, which made idolatry punishable by death, were enforced as former Israelite territory was regained.

> *"[26]Notwithstanding the Lord turned not from the fierceness of his great wrath, wherewith his anger was kindled against Judah, because of all the provocations that Manasseh had provoked him withal. [27]And the Lord said, I will remove Judah also out of my sight, as I have removed Israel, and will cast off this city Jerusalem which I have chosen, and the house of which I said, My name shall be there"* (2 Kings 23:26–27).[2]

This brings us to Egypt. Further south, Pharaoh Necho II was on his way north to assist Assyria in repelling Babylon, hopping to save a residue of Assyrian power as a buffer against the rising threats in the north and at the same time to regain possession of that part of Canaan that had once been controlled by Egypt. Josiah was opposed to Necho's support of Assyria, as he had aligned Judah with those who were fighting for Assyria's downfall and had no intent of trading Assyrian domination for Egyptian. In 609 BC, Josiah's forces, in an attempt to slow the advance of the Egyptians, intercepted those of Necho near Megiddo. Josiah was mortally wounded in the battle and his army defeated.

Pharaoh Necho continued on toward Northern Mesopotamia and the city of Harran, situated between the Euphrates and Tigris Rivers, where what remained of the Assyrian forces had retreated. Necho joined Ashur-uballit II, Assyria's last king, and engaged the forces of king Nabopolassar of Babylon, but to no avail. The Assyrian Empire was conquered by the Babylonians. Failing to achieve his purpose, Necho turned back across the Euphrates and established a headquarters in Syria. There he assumed the role of overlord of the territories of Syria, Judah, Israel, and Jerusalem.

In the interim, Jehoahaz had ascended to the throne of Judah at the death of Josiah and had continued Josiah's policies. Now Pharaoh Necho imprisoned Jehoahaz and placed Eliakim on the throne of Judah, changing his name to Jehoiakim to show that this new king was subject to Egypt. Pharaoh Necho reduced the dominions of Jehoiakim to the pre-Josiah period, limiting them to the city-state of Jerusalem and the old state of Judah. The provinces of the territory of the former state of Israel were administered as Egyptian provinces. Judah, Israel, and Jerusalem had become a part of the Egyptian Empire. The territory of the Egyptian Empire after the fall of the Assyrian Empire is shown in map 6.2.

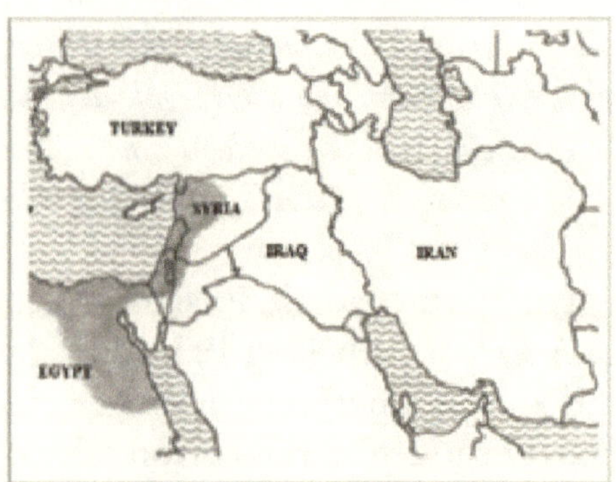

Map 6.2. The Egyptian Empire after the fall
of the Assyrian Empire.

Israel and the Babylonian Empire

After their joint victory over the Assyrians in 609 BC, the Medes and the Babylonians divided the empire of Assyria between them.

The Medes annexed the north and northeast; Babylon the south and southwest. Nebuchadnezzar, then crown prince, was sent to take possession of Babylon's new territories. Israelite and Syrian territories had fallen to king Nabopolassar, but Egypt had taken control of these Babylonian territories. Thus, in early 605 BC, Pharaoh Necho made an attempt to repulse the Babylonians. An allied army of Egyptians and Assyrians attacked the Babylonians near Carchemish in the same region where four years previous, Necho had been defeated in his attempt to assist the last king of Assyria.

Nebuchadnezzar beat them into nonexistence. The Battle of Carchemish was the end of the Assyrian Empire, and Egypt was reduced to a second-rate power. With this victory, Babylon became master of the Middle East.

To take control of Israelite territory, Nebuchadnezzar besieged Jerusalem in the third year of the reign of Jehoiakim, *"and the Lord gave Jehoiakim king of Judah into his hand" (Daniel 1:2)*. The year was 606 BC.[10] Jehoiakim was taken captive to Babylon along with *"[3]certain of the children of Israel, and of the king's seed, and of the princes; [4]Children in whom was no blemish, but well favored, and skillful in all wisdom, and cunning in knowledge" (Daniel 1:3–4)*. The prophet Daniel was among those taken. A portion of the vessels of the Lord's house was also taken to Babylon, and Judah put under heavy tribute.

In time, Nebuchadnezzar reinstated Jehoiakim to the throne of Judah, but as a vassal king. After three years of subjection to Babylon, Jehoiakim ceased paying the tribute to Babylon and gave his allegiance to Egypt, hoping to make himself independent. But God had told Jehoiakim that Judah was to serve Nebuchadnezzar, so now God sent Nebuchadnezzar against him for his disobedience. Nebuchadnezzar invaded Judah in 598 BC and laid siege to Jerusalem. The city fell in 597 BC.

> *"[13]And [Nebuchadnezzar] carried out thence all the treasures of the house of the Lord, and the treasures of the king's house…. [14]And he carried away all Jerusalem, and all the princes, and all the mighty men of valor, even ten thousand captives, and all the craftsmen and smiths: none remained, save the poorest sort of the people of the land. [15]And he carried away Jehoiachin to Babylon…. [16]And all the men of might, even seven thousand, and craftsmen and smiths a thousand, all that were strong and apt for war, even them the king of Babylon brought captive to Babylon" (2 Kings 24:13–16)*.

Jehoiakim had died during this siege of Jerusalem and been succeeded by Jehoiachin. Upon the fall of the city, Nebuchadnezzar deposed Jehoiachin and installed Zedekiah on the throne. *"[18]Zedekiah was twenty and one years old when he began to reign, and he reigned eleven years in Jerusalem…[19]And he did that which was evil in the sight of the Lord, according to all that Jehoiakim had done. [20]For through the anger of the Lord it came to pass in Jerusalem and Judah….that Zedekiah rebelled against the king of Babylon" (2 Kings 24:18–20)*.[11] From the wording of verse 20, it appears that God put the thought of this civil rebellion into Zedekiah's mind to use it as the impetus to bring judgment against Judah and Jerusalem for their spiritual rebellion, for God had said:

> *"I will utter my judgments against them touching all their wickedness, who have forsaken me, and have burned incense unto other gods, and worshipped the works of their own hands" (Jeremiah 1:16).*
>
> *"²⁸Therefore thus says the Lord; Behold, I will give this city into the hand of the Chaldeans, and into the hand of Nebuchadnezzar king of Babylon, and he shall take it: ²⁹And the Chaldeans, that fight against this city, shall come and set fire on this city, and burn it with the houses, upon whose roofs they have offered incense unto Baal, and poured out drink offerings unto other gods, to provoke me to anger...³¹that I should remove it from before my face, ³²because of all the evil of the children of Israel and of the children of Judah, which they have done to provoke me to anger, they, their kings, their princes, their priests, and their prophets, and the men of Judah, and the inhabitants of Jerusalem. ³³And they have turned unto me the back, and not the face: though I taught them, rising up early and teaching them, yet they have not hearkened to receive instruction. ³⁴But they set their abominations in the house, which is called by my name, to defile it. ³⁵And they built the high places of Baal....to cause their sons and their daughters to pass through the fire unto Molech; which I commanded them not, neither came it into my mind, that they should do this abomination, to cause Judah to sin. ³⁶And now therefore thus says the Lord, the God of Israel, concerning this city....It shall be delivered into the hand of the king of Babylon by the sword, and by the famine, and by the pestilence" (Jeremiah 32:28–36).*
>
> *"⁴Thus says the Lord God of Israel; Behold, I will turn back the weapons of war that are in your hands, wherewith you fight against the king of Babylon, and against the Chaldeans, which besiege you without the walls, and I will assemble them into the midst of this city. ⁵And I myself will fight against you with an outstretched hand and with a strong arm, even in anger, and in fury, and in great wrath. ⁶And I will smite the inhabitants of this city, both man and beast: they shall die of a great pestilence. ⁷And afterward, says the Lord, I will deliver Zedekiah king of Judah, and his servants, and the people, and such as are left in this city from the pestilence, from the sword, and from the famine, into the hand of Nebuchadnezzar king of Babylon, and into the hand of their enemies, and into the hand of those that seek their life: and he shall smite them with the edge of the sword; he shall not spare them, neither have pity, nor have mercy" (Jeremiah 21:4–7).*

In 586 BC, after an eighteen-month siege, the walls of Jerusalem were breached, the Temple burned, and the city destroyed. A great many of its people lay dead by famine, pestilence, and the sword. All who survived the siege were taken captive to Babylon, except for the very poorest of the land. Judah and Jerusalem were made a Babylonian province, and the Davidic monarchy that had ruled in Jerusalem for four centuries ended. *Judah, Israel, and Jerusalem* had become a part of the Babylonian Empire.

The greatest extent of the Babylonian Empire is shown in map 6.3.

Map 6.3. The Babylonian Empire of
Nebuchadnezzar, circa 600 BC.

Postscript

As we look at these events in history, we need to occasionally pause and consider the hand of God in these events. Again, one could say that the history written here is the natural rise and fall of kingdoms; it's just a coincidence that the Israelites were caught in the middle. But God had foretold the fate of the house of Israel:

> [1]*Hear you this word which I take up against you, even a lamentation, O house of Israel. [2]The virgin of Israel is fallen; she shall no more rise: she is forsaken upon her land; there is none to raise her up.*

> *(Amos 5:1–2)*

God also had foretold of who was to bring this about:

> *O Assyrian, the rod of my anger, and the staff in their hand is my indignation.*
>
> (Isaiah 10:5)

Concerning the fall of Egypt and the rise of Babylon:

> *¹ The word of the Lord which came to Jeremiah the prophet against the Gentiles; ²Against Egypt, against the army of Pharaohnecho king of Egypt, which was by the river Euphrates in Carchemish, which Nebuchadnezzar king of Babylon smote....⁸Egypt rises up like a flood, and his waters are moved like the rivers; and he said, I will go up, and will cover the earth; I will destroy the city and the inhabitants thereof.*
>
> (Jeremiah 46:1–2, 8)

But God said otherwise:

> *⁹Come up, you horses; and rage, you chariots; and let the mighty men come forth...¹⁰For this is the day of the Lord God of hosts, a day of vengeance, that he may avenge him of his adversaries: and the sword shall devour, and it shall be satiate and made drunk with their blood: for the Lord God of hosts has a sacrifice in the north country by the river Euphrates...²⁴The daughter of Egypt shall be confounded; she shall be delivered into the hand of the people of the north....²⁶into the hand of Nebuchadnezzar king of Babylon.*
>
> (Jeremiah 46:9–10, 24, 26)

And concerning the house of Israel:

> *⁶And now have I given all these lands into the hand of Nebuchadnezzar the king of Babylon, my servant...⁸And it shall come to pass, that the nation and kingdom which will not serve the same Nebuchadnezzar the king of Babylon, and that will not put their neck under the yoke of the king of Babylon, that nation will I punish, says the Lord, with the sword, and with the famine, and with the pestilence, until I have consumed them by his hand.*
>
> (Jeremiah 27:6, 8)

There was, and yet is, a purpose for God's hand in these events.

Israel and the Medo-Persian Empire

The Medes had acquired the northern part of Assyrian territory as the spoils of war for their joint effort with the Babylonians in the collapse of the Assyrian Empire. By the time Nabonidus came to the throne of the Babylonian Empire in 555 BC, the Medes had extended their empire from the region of the Black Sea along the northern border of the Babylonian Empire to the Persian Gulf along its southern border and nearly to the Indus River to the west. Nabonidus, in fear of the rising power of the Medes, joined forces with Cyrus, king of the Persian kingdom, to overthrow Astyages, king of the Median Empire. Cyrus was the grandson of Astyages. The Persians were thus Iranians, as were the Medes but to this point were still subjugated by the Medes. With the overthrow of the Median Empire, Cyrus amalgamated the Medes and Persians to become the ruler of the Medo-Persian Empire. Now Babylon faced an even greater threat in the rising power of the Medo-Persian Empire.

Cyrus turned against Nabonidus in 539 BC. Median forces led by Gobryas, considered to Babylonian Empire to the Persian Gulf along its southern border and nearly to the Indus River to the west. Nabonidus, in fear of the rising power of the Medes, joined forces with Cyrus, king of the Persian kingdom, to overthrow Astyages, king of the Median Empire. Cyrus was the grandson of Astyages. The Persians were thus Iranians, as were the Medes but to this point were still subjugated by the Medes. With the overthrow of the Median Empire, Cyrus amalgamated the Medes and Persians to become the ruler of the Medo-Persian Empire. Now Babylon faced an even greater threat in the rising power of the Medo-Persian Empire. Cyrus turned against Nabonidus in 539 BC. Median forces led by Gobryas, considered to Israelites. *Judah, Israel, and Jerusalem* had become a part of the Medo-Persian Empire.

The greatest extent of the Medo-Persian Empire is shown in map 6.4.

Map 6.4. The Medo-Persian
Empire, circa 500 BC.

Israel and the Grecian Empire

The expanding Medo-Persian Empire reached the Mediterranean seaboard when, in 546 BC, Cyrus the Great conquered the Lydian Empire in western Asia Minor. Lydia was then primarily Greek colonial cities. The Greeks called a halt to any further Persian advance when in 491 BC they defeated the Persian armies of Darius I who had attacked the Greek mainland, and eleven years later destroyed the Persian fleet of Xerxes. For the next two centuries, the Greeks and the Persians eyed each other warily across the Aegean Sea.

"And it happened, after that Alexander son of Philip, the Macedonian, who came out of the land of Chittim, had smitten Darius king of the Persians and Medes, that he reigned in his stead, the first over Greece, and made many wars, and won many strong holds....and ruled over countries, and nations, and kings, who became tributaries unto him" (1 Maccabees 1:1–4, KJV).

Macedonia was an ancient kingdom of Greek heritage situated at the northern periphery of the classical Greek city-states which prominently dotted the Greek peninsula. The rise of Macedonia from this small kingdom to one which came to dominate a great part of the known world began with the ascendancy of Philip II to the throne in 359 BC. In response to multiple attacks upon his homeland, Philip II reconstructed the Macedonian army with new tactics and equipment and initiated a political campaign that came to dominate the Greek mainland.

He was instrumental in the formation of a federation of Greek states that would guarantee peace in Greece and would provide him with military forces for his war against the Medo-Persian Empire which had taken the Greek colonial cities of Asia. Philip II was assassinated in 336 BC, early in the campaign against Persia. Philip's son Alexander III (the Great) succeeded his father to the throne and continued the campaign against the Medo-Persian Empire.

Alexander crossed the Hellespont separating Europe from Asia in 334 BC, invading Persian-ruled Asia Minor. In a series of decisive battles, Alexander broke the power of the Medo-Persian Empire, overthrowing King Darius III in 330 BC and eventually conquering the entirety of the empire. Judah, Israel, and Jerusalem had become a part of the Grecian Empire.

The greatest extent of Alexander's Empire is shown in map 6.5.

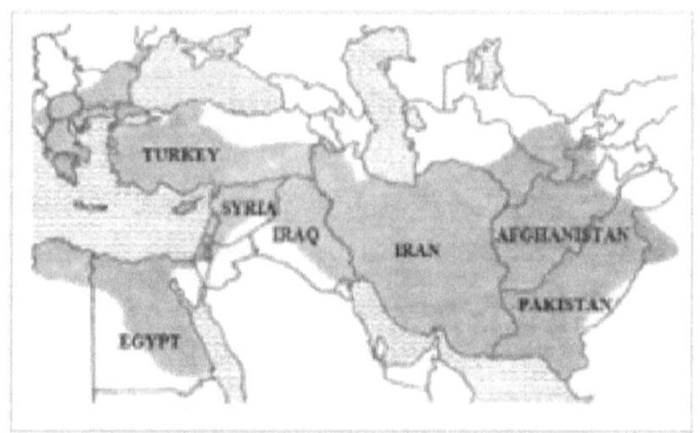

Map 6.5. The Grecian Empire of
Alexander, circa 323 BC.

Israel and the Division of Alexander's Empire

Upon Alexander's death in 323 BC his great empire was divided, eventually settling the territory into four kingdoms as a result of the War of the Kings in 301 BC. To the north of Jerusalem was the Seleucid Empire[12], to the south the Ptolemaic Empire[13], both led by kings who had been commanders in Alexander's army.[14] The territory of Judah, Israel, and Jerusalem was initially a part of the Ptolemaic Empire. However, Jerusalem came under Seleucid rule when in 200 BC Antiochus III defeated Ptolemaic forces at the Battle of Panium. The Jews had joined Antiochus with the intent to throw off the yoke of the Gentiles, but rather than throwing off the rule of Egypt now ended up under Syrian rule.

After defeating Ptolemaic forces in Egypt, Antiochus III moved to secure the Ptolemaic coastal towns of Greece and independent Greek cities in Asia Minor. He then invaded the European mainland in 196 BC and again in 192 BC. The Seleucid Empire was now to feel the power of Rome. Seeing a threat on its eastern frontier, the Romans routed Antiochus from Greece, forcing him to withdraw to Asia. In 190 BC, Antiochus III was defeated in Asia Minor and was forced to agree to the humiliating Peace of Apamea. Seleucid territories were taken from him, and a heavy tribute levied on the Seleucid Empire. This was the beginning of the decline of the Seleucid Empire.

Judah had become essentially autonomous since the time of Nehemiah's governorship of Jerusalem under Medo-Persian rule, and neither Alexander the Great nor the Ptolemaic kings had made any serious effort to interfere in its affairs. This was to change when in 175 BC Antiochus IV Epiphanes seized power in the Seleucid Empire. By this time, Jerusalem society had absorbed much of the culture of the Greeks, except in its general adherence to monotheism. This Greek influence had a devastating effect on the Jew's relationship with God and with Mosaic Law. The office of High Priest was now gained by whoever paid the highest tribute to Antiochus IV, usually by taxes on their own people. There was, thus, considerable hostility, even murder, between those vying for High Priest.

When it was rumored that Antiochus had died, believing that there was a lapse of authority in the kingdom, one who had been disposed as High Priest by the current high bidder attacked Jerusalem with his private army in an attempt to regain his position. Antiochus IV, believing that Judah had rebelled against royal authority, sought to mollify this religious culture. To do so, he attempted to convert the God of the troublesome Jews to Greek gods in order to Hellenize their religion. Antiochus had a statue of the Greek god Zeus placed in the Temple in Jerusalem and placed other Greek gods in temples throughout Judah (now named Judea) and Samaria. He then "sent letters by messengers unto Jerusalem and the cities of Judah that they should follow the strange laws of the land, and forbid burnt offerings, and sacrifice, and drink offerings, in the temple....to the end that they might forget the law….and whosoever would not do according to the commandment of the king, he said, he should die" (1 Maccabees 1:44–50). This edict was enforced by a garrison of Syrian soldiers that now had been posted in Jerusalem. This act of Antiochus IV provoked a rebellion in 167 BC by faithful believers led by Judas, called Maccabaeus.

Israel's Freedom from Gentile Rule

The Maccabean leaders recognized the power and influence of Rome early in their war against the Syrians. In 161 BC, Judas sent envoys to the Roman Senate to make a league of amity and confederacy with them in the hope that the Romans would help them to be liberated from the yoke of the Syrians (1 Maccabees 8:17). Their proposal of alliance was accepted, as the uprising of Judea against the Seleucid king Antiochus IV Epiphanes suited Roman political ambitions in the region. The terms of the treaty as presented in 1 Maccabees 8 committed the Jews to come to the defense of Rome, and Rome to the defense of the Jews. Thus, while Judea was still rebelling against Syrian domination, Rome was treating Judea as an independent nation.

When in 140 BC, Rome heard that Jonathan, the second Maccabean to rule Judea, was dead, and Simon was ruler and High Priest, Rome wrote to Simon "to renew the friendship and league which they had made with Judas and Jonathan his brother" (1 Maccabees 14:18), confirming the status of Judea as an independent state. At this time, the Syrian king, Demetrius, also confirmed Simon as High Priest "and made him one of his friends, and honored him with great honor. For he had heard say, that the Romans had called the Jews friends and confederates and brethren….that Simon should be their governor and high priest" (1 Maccabees 14:38–41). This last statement indicates the strength of Roman influence in the Seleucid world at this time. In 142 BC, the Hasmonean Dynasty15 began under the leadership of Simon Maccabaeus who served as ruler and High Priest. In time, Judea occupied the territory that had once been the kingdoms of Judah and Israel.

Israel and the Roman Empire

In 67 BC, the Roman Senate ordered Gnaeus Pompeius Magnus, a military and political leader known as Pompey, to put an end to the menace of pirates in the eastern Mediterranean. After quelling the pirate problem, he decided to intervene in the affairs of the kingdoms of the eastern sphere of Roman influence that were slowly coming under the thumb of the Roman Empire.

During this time, the two sons of the Judean queen Alexandra-Salome had started a bloody civil war. In 63 BC, Pompey intervened in this civil war at the request of one of the sons, the outcome being that Judea became a protectorate of Rome. The installation of Herod the Great as king of Israel in 37 BC ended the Hasmonean dynasty. In AD 6, Judæa became an autonomous part of the Roman province of Syria, ruled by a Roman official appointed by the emperor. *Judah, Israel, and Jerusalem* had become a part of the Roman Empire.

A map of the greatest extent of the Roman Empire is shown in Map 6.6.

Map 6.6. The Roman Empire at its
greatest extent, circa AD 116.

Israel and the League of Ten

We have been reviewing a bit of the history of the kingdoms that are represented by the heads of the beast that is the Red Dragon. There is yet one more head of this beast, the seventh, which is the League of Ten. This kingdom is yet to come. So, what can we discern of this coming kingdom from history?

- First and foremost, *Judah, Israel, and Jerusalem* must be a part of the confederation that will form the League of Ten. This die was cast by God—just as *Judah, Israel, and Jerusalem* were a part of the first six kingdoms of the Red Dragon, so must *Judah, Israel, and Jerusalem* be a part of the seventh.
- This seventh kingdom must encompass all of Israel.
  Within the phrase *Judah, Israel, and Jerusalem* are the twelve tribes of Jacob and all the land that was greater Israel. As we have seen in this bit of history, the twelve tribes of Jacob may have been scattered to the four winds, and their land divided by the empires that conquered them, yet both the people and the land were still contained within the borders of the conquering kingdoms.
- The other nine nations of the League of Ten that comprise the seventh kingdom will be Israel's neighbors, contiguous with the land that is Israel. From history, we see that the first six Gentile kingdoms represented as heads of the Red Dragon were comprised of nations contiguous in some manner with *Judah, Israel, and Jerusalem.* Set by this pattern, the seventh kingdom must also be comprised of Israel's neighbors.

That the League of Ten will be comprised of nations neighboring Israel is confirmed in Scripture, for God had said of the Israel that had gone into captivity, *"2they sin more and more, and have made them molten images of their silver, and idols according to their own understanding, all of it the work of the craftsmen…7Therefore I will be unto them as a lion: as a leopard by the way will I observe them: 8 I will meet them as a bear that is bereaved of her whelps, and will rend the caul of their heart, and there will I devour them like a lion: the wild beast shall tear them"* (Hosea 13:2, 7–8).

As we have seen, it was by God's hand that the *lion* (the Babylonian Empire), the *bear* (the Medo-Persian Empire), the *leopard* (the Grecian Empire), and the *wild beast* (the Roman Empire) consumed the nation of Israel for her sin. Note that these *"beasts"* came upon Israel in the singular, meaning that it was first just the lion, then just the bear, then the leopard, and in turn the wild beast that was Rome.

Now we need to consider another beast: *"1And I stood upon the sand of the sea, and saw a beast rise up out of the sea, having seven heads and ten horns, and upon his horns ten crowns, and upon his heads the name of blasphemy. ²And the beast which I saw was like unto a leopard, and his feet were as the feet of a bear, and his mouth as the mouth of a lion: and the dragon gave him his power, and his seat, and great authority" (Revelation 13:1–2).*

What God is saying here is that this time, He will be unto them as a composite of parts of the previous beasts.

This seventh kingdom of which *Judah, Israel, and Jerusalem* will become a part will not only be of modern nations out of the territory of the Roman Empire *(Daniel 7:7)* but also will be of modern nations in whole or in part out of the territories of the Grecian Empire (*like unto a leopard*), the Medo-Persian Empire (*the feet of a bear*), and the Babylonian Empire (*the mouth of a lion*). That the other nine nations of the League of Ten are today Israel's neighbors will be confirmed in detail in a later chapter, "The Roadmap for Peace."

- The nation of Israel will become a conquered territory and a subjugated people, ruled by a Gentile king as the confederation of the League of Ten morphs into the empire of the Antichrist. Again, we follow the pattern set by the preceding six kingdoms of the empire that is the Red Dragon. We really don't need to justify this conclusion by the pattern set by history since the Scripture itself is replete with descriptions of Antichrist's coming rule over Israel. Yet, that a pattern has been established by God to guide our understanding of this seventh Gentile kingdom that is to come must be recognized.

The Why of the Red Dragon

The seven Gentile kingdoms of the Red Dragon exist for the purpose of God's wrath upon the nation of Israel for their disobedience.

When God took the Israelites out of their bondage in Egypt, He told them they were to be His people, a people *"above all people"* (Deuteronomy 10:15). But this was not to be as simple as it sounds, for He was also to be their God, and they were to know He was the Lord their God (Exodus 6:7). With that came an expectation of obedience:

¹²And now, Israel, what does the Lord your God require of you, but to fear the Lord your God, to walk in all his ways, and to love him, and to serve the Lord your God with all your heart and with all your soul, ¹³To keep the commandments of the Lord, and his statutes, which I command you this day for your good?

(Deuteronomy 10:12–13)

With this expectation came a choice:

²⁶ Behold, I set before you this day a blessing and a curse; ²⁷A blessing, if you obey the commandments of the Lord your God, which I command you this day: ²⁸And a curse, if you will not obey the commandments of the Lord your God, but turn aside out of the way which I command you this day. (Deuteronomy 11:26–28) Therefore: ¹⁶Take heed to yourselves, that your heart be not deceived, and you turn aside, and serve other gods, and worship them; And then the Lord's wrath be kindled against you.

(Deuteronomy 11:16)

Therefore:

¹⁶Take heed to yourselves, that your heart be not deceived, and you turn aside, and serve other gods, and worship them; And then the Lord's wrath be kindled against you.

(Deuteronomy 11:16)

But they did turn aside time and time again out of the way that Yahweh had commanded. And, they were chastised time and time again for their disobedience. They had been warned that if they yet *"will not for all this hearken unto me, but walk contrary unto me; Then I will walk contrary unto you also in fury; and I, even I, will chastise you seven times for your sins"* (Leviticus 26:27–28). The seven heads of the Red Dragon are the Lord's wrath of this sevenfold curse.

Postscript

One may wonder why God would raise up such great empires to conquer the small kingdoms of Judah, Israel, and Jerusalem. God chose these Gentile kingdoms as a tool to carry out His wrath on a disobedient people. He thus gave the leaders of these Gentile kingdoms the means and the mind to conquer the lands around them that would include Judah, Israel, and Jerusalem. But God did not micromanage their ambitions; they would, by human nature, conquer all they possibly could. And some conquered much.

I saw in the right hand of him that sat on the throne a book written within and on the backside, sealed with seven seals.

—Revelation 5:1

[7] Martin North, *The History of Israel* (New York: Harper & Brothers, 1958), 260.

[8] The History of Israel, 268.

[9] By this time in history, the northern state of Israel had essentially melded into the territories of the conquering nations with little reference in Scripture of its existence; God had indeed removed the northern state of Israel from His sight.

[10] Jehoiakim reigned in Jerusalem and Judah over a period of eleven years. Historians differ as to the time of his reign, commonly giving 609 or 608 BC as the starting date under the vassalage of Pharaoh Nechoh, and an ending date of 599 or 598 under the vassalage of King Nebuchadnezzar.

[11] Note that Scripture is still separating the city-state of Jerusalem from the state of Judah with the phrase "it came to pass in Jerusalem and Judah."

[12] Often referred to as the Syrian Empire.

[13] Often referred to as the Egyptian Empire.

[14] These empires were an extension of the Grecian Empire of Alexander the Great since the territories of the divided empire and their kings were still Greek/Macedonian.

[15] The name Hasmonean comes from Asamoneus ("War of the Jews", 1, 1.3), the father of Mattathias who initiated the rebellion by slaying one of his countrymen who was offering a sacrifice to a Greek god and the king's officer who compelled the Jews to do so.

CHAPTER SEVEN
Hoofbeats of the Four Horsemen

The breaking of the seven seals of the scroll held in the hand of God of Revelation 5:1 and the reading of its contents put the preceding chapters into context for a full view of these days of the end of the age.

John's Vision

4:¹And after this I looked, and behold, a door was opened in heaven: and the first voice which I heard was as it were of a trumpet talking with me; which said, Come up here, and I will show you things which must be hereafter.

²And immediately I was in the spirit: and, behold, a throne was set in heaven, and one sat on the throne. ³And he that sat was to look upon like a jasper and a sardine stone: and there was a rainbow round about the throne, in sight like unto an emerald. ⁴And round about the throne were four and twenty seats: and upon the seats I saw four and twenty elders sitting, clothed with white raiment; and they had on their heads crows of gold.

⁵And out of the throne proceeded lightnings and thunderings and voices; and there were seven lamps of fire burning before the throne, which are the seven Spirits of God. ⁶And before the throne there was a sea of glass like unto crystal: and in the midst of the throne, and round about the throne, were four beasts full of eyes before and behind. ⁷And the first beast was like a lion, and the second best like a calf, and the third beast had a face as a man, and the fourth beast was like a flying eagle. ⁸And the four beasts had each of them six wings about him; and they were full of eyes within: and they rest not day and night, saying Holy, holy, holy, Lord God Almighty, which was, and is, and is to come.

[9]And when those beasts give glory and honor and thanks to him that sat on the throne, who lives for ever and ever, [10]The four and twenty elders fall down before him that sat on the throne, and worship him that lives for ever and ever, and cast their crowns before the throne, saying, :[11]You are worthy, O Lord, to receive glory and honor and power: for you have created all things, and for your pleasure they are and were created.

5:[1]And I saw in the right hand of him that sat on the throne a book written within and on the backside, sealed with seven seals. [2]And I saw a strong angel proclaiming with a loud voice, Who is worthy to open the book, and to loose the seals thereof? [3]And no man in heaven, nor in earth, neither under the earth, was able to open the book, neither to look thereon.

[4]And I wept much, because no man was found worthy to open and to read the book, neither to look thereon. [5]And one of the elders said unto me, Weep not: behold, the Lion of the tribe of Judah, the Root of David, has prevailed to open the book, and to loose the seven seals thereof. [6]And I beheld, and, lo, in the midst of the throne and of the four beasts, and in the midst of the elders, stood a Lamb as it had been slain, having seven horns and seven eyes, which are the seven Spirits of God sent fourth into all the earth. [7]And he came and took the book out of the right hand of him that sat upon the throne. [8]And when he had taken the book, the four beasts and four and twenty elders fell down before the Lamb, having every one of them harps, and golden vials full of odors, which are the prayers of saints.

[9]And they sung a new song, saying You are worthy to take the book, and to open the seals thereof: for you were slain, and have redeemed us to God by your blood out of every kindred, and tongue, and people, and nation; [10]And have made unto our God kings and priests: and we shall reign on the earth.

[11]And I beheld, and I heard the voice of many angels round about the throne and the beasts and the elders: and the number of them as ten thousand times ten thousand and thousands of thousands: [12]Saying with a loud voice, Worthy is the Lamb that was slain to receive power, and riches, and wisdom, and strength, and honor, and glory, and blessing.

[13]And every creature which is in heaven, and on the earth, and is under the earth, and such as are in the sea, and all that are in them, heard I saying, Blessing, and honor, and glory, and power, be unto him that sits upon the thrown, and unto the Lamb for ever and ever. [14]And the four beasts said, Amen. And the four and twenty elders fell down and worshipped him that lives for ever and ever.

(Revelation 4:1–5:14)

The Scroll Sealed with Seven Seals

To comprehend what is revealed when the seals of the scroll are broken, we must first know what the scroll itself represents and then identify those who are witness to the breaking of the seals. Thus, we start with the meaning of the scroll.

Why?

There does not appear to have been any explanation of this scene viewed by John, yet he *wept much* when he heard that *no man in heaven, nor in the earth, neither under the earth, was able to open the book, neither to look thereon* (5:4). Why then did John react with such sorrow when he saw this scene in heaven? Why did John weep? It is said that he wept because there was no man able to break the seals and to read the scroll. But that is not the complete answer. The complete answer is found only when the question is complete: what was so important about this scroll that John wept much when it could not be read?

The answer is found in the traditions of the Israelites. John needed no introduction to what he was witness to, for it was a scene right out of the customs of his people, and he knew it well. John knew that he was now witnessing a real estate transaction—specifically, a redemption of land.

Possession of the Land

Possession of the land given to them by God was a very important part of the life of the people of Israel. So much so that it was their custom, instituted by God, which a man should forever own his land. A man could rent or sell his land, or otherwise be alienated from his land, but only temporarily. At some point, the land must be returned to him as its rightful owner. One manner in which land was returned was that required by the year of Jubilee, a Hebrew festival celebrated every fiftieth year. In the year of Jubilee, it was simply required that all land be returned to its rightful owner. Knowing this, land contracts or debts incurred were made with the remaining years till the Jubilee in mind. The other manner in which land could be returned was by payment of the debt against the land. This could be done by a kinsman redeemer, one who had the legal authority to receive the land because of his relationship to the owner. The actual act of the redeeming of land in either case was performed in full view of the people. The redeeming of land was thus a common sight among the Israelites.

The Custom of a Deed

It was the custom to record a deed when a parcel of land was transferred from the owner to a temporary overseer. The deed was a description of the land and its contents written in a scroll. The deed was made secure by a wax seal that closed up the scroll. The deed (scroll) may have been sealed with more than one seal if the land to be transferred was sizable, as the task of describing a land having many vineyards, fields, buildings, and other items of importance, would take some time to record. If the scribe ceased his writing for any reason, a seal would have been placed in the scroll at that point to secure the written portion of the document. When the scribe resumed his writing, he would continue in the unsealed portion of the scroll, which, in turn, would be sealed. A scroll containing the description of a sizable piece of property could therefore have several seals.

An example of creating such a real estate deed is given in Jeremiah 32:7–12:

> *7 Behold, Hanameel the son of Shallum your uncle shall come unto you saying, Buy you my field that is in Anathoth: for the right of redemption is yours to buy it. 8 So Hanameel my uncle's son came to me in the court of the prison according to the word of the Lord, and said unto me, Buy my field, I pray thee, that is in Anathoth, which is in the country of Benjamin: for the right of inheritance is yours, and the redemption is yours; buy it for thyself. Then I knew that this was the word of the Lord. 9 And I bought the field of Hanameel my uncle's son, that was in Anathoth, and weighed him the money, even seventeen shekels of silver. 10 And I subscribed the evidence, and sealed it, and took witnesses, and weighed him the money in the balances. 11 So I took the evidence of the purchase, both that which was sealed according to the law and custom, and that which was open: 12 And I gave the evidence of the purchase unto Baruch the son of Neriah, the son of Maaseiah, in the sight of Hanameel mine uncle's son, and in the presence of the witnesses that subscribed the book of the purchase, before all the Jews that sat in the court of the prison.*

There is quite a revealing statement made in verse 11 of Jeramiah's account. The custom was to *subscribe* (write) two copies of the *evidence of the transaction,* one *which was sealed according to the law and custom and one which was open* to read. We see that God did likewise. The scroll *sealed according to the law and custom* is that which was *written within and on the backside, sealed with seven seals* which John sees in the right hand of God. This copy is sealed so that its content is secured from fraudulent changes. That copy *which was open* for us to read was written in the book of Revelation, the one we are now reading.

Redeeming the Land

When the land was to be redeemed, the scroll was taken to a public place to be read aloud.

Only the rightful owner of the land had the authority to break the seals of the scroll and to read what was written therein. Israelite custom, however, did allow another to redeem the land in the owner's stead as shown in the example above. This surrogate had to be a kinsman of the owner in order to have authority as a redeemer; thus, a kinsman redeemer. The redeemer also had to have the ability to pay the redemption price; the kinsman redeemer would have to pay the fair price of the debt on the land. Lastly, the kinsman redeemer had to come forward willingly and to accept the responsibility for the land. There was no requirement that forced a kinsman to redeem the land.

In the village square, local residents who knew the land to be redeemed and who knew the rightful owner of the land and of his kinsman would be witness to the reading of the deed. As the scroll was read, the witnesses would compare that which was described in the deed with the land to be redeemed and, thus, validate the transfer. Thereby, only the one with proper authority could take possession of the land.

The Deed in the Hand of God

The scene that John was familiar with on earth he now sees in heaven. He needed no explanation of the scene because he knew the significance of the event taking place before the throne of God. John knew that he was witnessing the redeeming of land.

The scroll in the hand of God is the deed to that land. Our text states that John *wept much* when he heard that no man was able to take this scroll from the hand of God, break its seals, and read its contents. The scroll itself is, therefore as important to this scene as is the one who is able to take the scroll and break its seals.

John knew that when there was no man who could take the scroll and break the seals, there was no man who could redeem the land. This meant the loss of the land to its owner. Since the deed to this real estate was held in the hand of God, he must have known that the land to be redeemed here was this earth. When the angel proclaimed that no man had the authority to redeem this land it must have seemed to John that the ownership of this earth was lost, and thus, he wept.

The Land to be Redeemed

The scroll held in the hand of God is *written within and on the backside* (5:1), telling us that this deed is indeed to a very sizable land, requiring not only the front of the scroll to record all that is on the land but the backside of the scroll as well. The scroll was also *sealed with seven seals.* The number seven, signifying completeness, tells us that this deed contains all of this earth and that it will be redeemed completely.

The Land Owner

If this scroll is indeed the deed to this earth, and it is the earth that is to be returned to its rightful owner, who owns it, and who now has dominion over it?

God created the earth, so it is His. In *Genesis 1:26*, we are told that God gave Adam dominion *"over all the earth."* Adam, in turn, gave dominion over to Satan through his disobedience to God.

Evidence of Satan's dominion over this earth is shown in the account of Satan's temptation of Jesus in the wilderness. Satan took Jesus *"⁸up into an exceeding high mountain, and showed him all the kingdoms of the world, and the glory of them; ⁹and said unto him, All these things will I give you, if you will fall down and worship me"* (Matthew 4:8–9). Satan must have had dominion over this earth, for when he offered all the kingdoms of this world to Jesus, Jesus did not dispute the validity of his offer.

Satan still has dominion over this earth today. This does not mean that Satan is in control, or that God is limited in His authority. God is in control—it is by His protocol that Satan has authority to act. In that manner, Satan has dominion over this earth.

The Kinsman Redeemer

When John saw the scroll in the hand of God, he heard an angel ask, *Who is worthy to open the book, and to loose the seals thereof? (5:2).* But the answer was *No man in heaven, nor in earth, neither under the earth, was* able to open the book *(5:3).* There is no man who can claim rightful ownership of this earth. Neither can any man pay the price to redeem it.

Yet, John is told that there is one who *has prevailed to open the book, and to loose the seven seals thereof (5:5).*

His credentials are identified as the *Lion of the Tribe of Judah, the Root of David* in verse 5, and as *a Lamb as it had been slain* in verse 6. This is Jesus. It is Jesus who steps forward as the redeemer of this earth. Since Jesus is the only begotten Son of the Father *(John 1:14)* he is the kinsman of the owner. Since the world was lost by sin, Jesus paid the fair price of the debt by which the land was lost by shedding his blood for the sins of the world. Lastly, Jesus gave his life willingly to pay the price, that the will of the Father might be done *(Luke 22:42).* Thus, Jesus is the kinsman redeemer and is worthy and willing to open the seals and to read the scroll.

The Description of the Land

When Jesus breaks the seals, we see a description of the land that is being returned to its owner. Rather than describing the contents of the land by numerating the orchards, fields, buildings, and such, the scroll sealed with seven seals identifies the land by the events that are occurring on that land. As each seal is broken, John is thus shown some aspect of what is occurring on the earth.

The Witnesses

Just as there were witnesses to the reading of the scroll on earth, there are witnesses to this same proceeding in heaven. These witnesses are just as critical to the process now seen by John as it was to the process on earth, for without the presence of the proper witnesses, even the first seal of the scroll could not be broken, and the redemption of the earth could not be validated.

When John saw the throne that was set in heaven, he also saw in a position of considerable prominence that *round about the throne were four and twenty seats: and upon the seats I saw four and twenty elders sitting, clothed with white raiment; and they had on their heads crowns of gold (4:4).* This is the first time these twenty-four elders have been seen in any vision of heaven. The identification of these twenty-four elders is of utmost importance, for they represent the presence of the proper witnesses to this process of redemption.

The word translated as *seats* is *thronos*, meaning *thrones.* The *throne* represents authority and judgment, for Revelation 20:4 states that those who sit on these thrones will sit in judgment of those who reject the gift of eternal life offered freely by Jesus. The twenty-four seated on these thrones have the societal position of elder. Elders in Scripture are those worthy of speaking on behalf of others because of their knowledge and wisdom acquired through longevity of life.

An example of the elders of Israel acting with authority on behalf of the people is seen in the choosing of their king: *"So all the elders of Israel came to the king [for David was king of Judah] to Hebron; and king David made a league with them in Hebron before the Lord: and they anointed David king over Israel" (2 Samuel 5:3).* This institution of eldership as a part of Israelite societal custom was also a part of the church: *"Let the elders that rule well be counted worthy of double honor, especially they who labor in the word and doctrine" (1 Timothy 5:17).*

Eldership was a separate institution from the priesthood as evidenced from the many Scriptural references that speak of the two as separate entities. An example of this is a statement made by Matthew concerning the "trial" of Jesus: *"When the morning was come, all the chief priests and elders of the people took counsel against Jesus to put him to death" (Matthew 27:1).* Since elders as a whole are separate from the priesthood, these twenty-four elders before the throne do not represent the twenty-four courses of priests established by King David, although there is no evidence given in Scripture that a priest could not also be an elder. Neither are these twenty-four elders a class of angels for *they had on their heads crowns of gold;* angels are never given crowns.

As we have seen, an elder represents a group of people and acts on their behalf or in their stead. Thus, the elders in a society would collectively represent the whole of the people of that society. This institution of eldership has existed in most every society throughout history and is still prevalent in many societies today.

These elders seated before the throne in heaven are clothed with white raiment, a sign of one whose name is written in the book of life *(Revelation 3:5)*. They wear crowns, *stephanos,* which are victor's crowns. There are four victor's crowns given to the saints: a crown of rejoicing *(1 Thessalonians 2:19);* a crown of righteousness *(2 Timothy 4:8);* a crown of life *(James 1:12);* and a crown of glory *(1 Peter 5:4)*. They will cast their crowns before the throne in worship of God *(Revelation 4:10)*. The descriptions given of the elders thus far tell us that they themselves are redeemed from the earth.

When Jesus takes the scroll from the hand of God *the four beasts and four and twenty elders [will fall] down before the Lamb, having every one of them harps, and golden vials full of odors, which are the prayers of saints. And they [will sing] a new song, saying, You are worthy to take the book, and to open the seals thereof: for you were slain, and have redeemed us to God by your blood out of every kindred, and tongue, and people, and nation; And have made us unto our God kings and priests: and we shall reign on the earth (5:9–10).* Only the twenty-four elders are in view in these two verses, for the four beasts have no need of redemption, nor will they be made kings or priests or reign on the earth.

In this song, the twenty-four elders proclaim that Jesus has *redeemed **us** to God by your blood out of every kindred, and tongue, and people, and nation: And have made **us** unto our God kings and priests: and **we** shall reign on the earth.* The words "us" and "we" as they are used in these verses are not a direct reference back to the twenty-four elders but are a reference to another distinct and separate group. The word translated as "us" in the King James Version in these two verses is *hemas.*

Hemas is not literally "us" in the Greek but has a more neutral connotation such as "men" or "them". *Young's Analytical Concordance* states that there are "various readings of the Greek New Testament" concerning its application here. However, *Young's* does not say what other variations of this word there could be. Other translations of the Bible, such as the New International Version, use "men" in place of "us" in verse 9 and "they" in verse 10. These two verses therefore point to those whom these elders represent who have been (note past tense) *redeemed…to God out of every kindred, and tongue, and people, and nation.*

Later, John will see those represented by these elders: *"9After this I beheld, and, lo, a great multitude, which no man could number, of all nations, and kindreds, and people, and tongues, stood before the throne, and before the Lamb, clothed with white robes, and palms in their hands; 10And cried with a loud voice, saying, Salvation to our God which sits upon the throne, and unto the Lamb"* (Revelation 7:9–10). Just as the twenty-four elders had proclaimed of Jesus, *you were slain, and have redeemed [us/them] to God by your blood out of every kindred, and tongue, and people, and nation, the great multitude is now said to be of all nations, and kindreds, and people, and tongues.*

This great multitude of saints are therefore standing before the throne as Jesus takes the scroll from the hand of God. These saints must be in place before the throne prior to Jesus taking the scroll, as they are the witnesses required in order for the kinsman redeemer to break the seals and to read what was written therein. These saints are the only ones who can meet the requirements of a proper witness, as it is these saints who lived in the "village", it is these saints who had intimate knowledge of the land, and it is these saints who had personal knowledge of the owner of the land and of the kinsman redeemer.

Now, why the number twenty-four? The twenty-four elders represent the entirety of the saints from the time of Adam till the instant of the Rapture; basically, witnesses that can validate events throughout the ages. Adam witnessed the loss of the land to Satan and knew personally the cause of the loss, and those living at the time of the Rapture can give account of current events. John himself helps us with the number. *He "saw the holy city, new Jerusalem, coming down from God out of heaven, prepared as a bride adorned for her husband"* (Revelation 21:2). Although Jerusalem is not the bride of Christ, it does in many ways represent his bride. The city *"had a wall great and high, and had twelve gates, and at the gates twelve angels, and names written thereon, which are the names of the twelve tribes of the children of Israel"* (Revelation 21:12). *"And the wall of the city had twelve foundations, and in them the names of the twelve apostles of the Lamb"* (Revelation 21:14). The twelve tribes of Israel pictured as the twelve gates of the city depict the gateway by which the world was to come to the knowledge of God. The twelve apostles pictured as the foundation of the city depict the foundation that supports the gates. Even though the word of God came through Israel, the foundation on which the word of God has been sustained has been the New Testament church. Therefore, throughout the ages, God employed both Israel and the church for mankind to come to the knowledge of God. These twenty-four elders not only represent believers from every age, but they also represent the whole of believers who are now seen before the throne.[16]

Breaking the First Seal

6:¹And I saw when the Lamb opened one of the seals, and I heard, as it were the noise of thunder, one of the four beasts saying, Come and see. ²And I saw, and behold a white horse: and he that sat on him had a bow; and a crown was given unto him: and he went forth conquering, and to conquer.

(Revelation 6:1-2)

Breaking the Second Seal

³And when he had opened the second seal, I heard the second beast say, Come and see. ⁴And there went out another horse that was red: and power was given to him that sat thereon to take peace from the earth, and that they should kill one another: and there was given unto him a great sword.

(Revelation 6:3-4)

Breaking the Third Seal

⁵And when he had opened the third seal, I heard the third beast say, Come and see. And I beheld, and lo a black horse; and he that sat on him had a pair of balances in his hand. ⁶And I heard a voice in the midst of the four beasts say, A measure of wheat for a [denarius], and three measures of barley for a [denarius]; and see thou hurt not the oil and the wine.

(Revelation 6:5)

Breaking the Fourth Seal

6:⁷And when he had opened the fourth seal, I heard the voice of the fourth beast say, Come and see. ⁸And I looked, and behold a pale horse: and his name that sat on him was Death, and Hell followed with him.

> *And power was given unto them over the fourth part of the earth, to kill with sword, and with hunger, and with death, and with the beasts of the earth.*
>
> *(Revelation 6:7-8)*

The Four Beasts Before the Throne

Before we address what is depicted by these four seals, we need to identify the four beasts that present these seals, for their identity guides our understanding of the scenes depicted when these four seals are broken. Of most importance to their identity is that these four beasts are *in the midst of the throne, and round about the throne.* Thus, they are very special in the sight of God. The *first beast was like a lion, and the second beast like a calf, and the third beast had a face as a man, and the fourth beast was like a flying eagle.* Each of these four is spoken of as a *beast* in this text. *Beast* here is translated from the Greek *zōon*, literally, a *living creature.* They are spoken of elsewhere in Scripture as cherubim, literally, *held fast* in Hebrew. John saw each beast as having six wings, and each was *full of eyes within (Revelation 4:8)* as if they see all things. We thus picture them as angels who are all-seeing. These four beasts represent God's creation and the life He has placed on the earth; man and the creatures we were to watch over.

These four beasts are seen elsewhere in the Bible, which helps us to understand why they are chosen to introduce these four seals and to decipher the earthly scenes depicted by the breaking of the seals. In the following verses, they are described as watching over events occurring on the earth, or not occurring, as the case may be:

> *[8]I saw by night, and behold a man riding upon a red horse, and he stood among the myrtle trees that were in the bottom; and behind him were there red horses, speckled, and white. [9]Then said I, O my lord, what are these? And the angel that talked with me said unto me, I will show you what these be. [10]And the man that stood among the myrtle trees answered and said, These are they whom the Lord has sent to walk to and fro through the earth. [11]And they answered the angel of the Lord that stood among the myrtle trees, and said, We have walked to and fro through the earth, and, behold, all the earth sits still, and is at rest.*
>
> *(Zachariah 1:8–11)*

¹And I turned, and lifted up mine eyes, and looked, and, behold, there came four chariots out from between two mountains; and the mountains were mountains of brass.

²In the first chariot were red horses; and in the second chariot black horses; ³And in the third chariot white horses; and in the fourth chariot grisled and bay horses. ⁴Then I answered and said unto the angel that talked with me, What are these, my lord? ⁵And the angel answered and said unto me, These are the four spirits of the heavens, which go forth from standing before the Lord of all the earth. ⁶The black horses which are therein go forth into the north country; and the white go forth after them; and the grisled go forth toward the south country. ⁷And the bay went forth, and sought to go that they might walk to and fro through the earth: and he said, Get you hence, walk to and fro through the earth. So they walked to and fro through the earth. ⁸Then cried he upon me, and spake unto me, saying, Behold, these that go toward the north country have quieted my spirit in the north country.

(Zachariah 6:1–8)

These verses from the beginning chapters of Zachariah are put into perspective with God's warning: *"Turn you now from your evil ways, and from your evil doings" (Zachariah 1:6).* These four beasts that John now sees standing before the Lord of all the earth had walked to and from through the earth throughout the ages and had witnessed, to put it bluntly, a world of sin. The words of Zachariah 1:11 *"all the earth sits still, and is at rest"* and *6:8 "have quieted my spirit"* attest to the scarcity of the spirit of God working within the inhabitants of the earth. This state of affairs is now reflected in the scenes we see as the first four seals are broken.

This Set of Four Seals

These four seals are presented to us as a set. We see this in that each of the four scenes revealed by the breaking of a seal is introduced by one of the four living creatures that are before the throne, and that each reveals a rider on a horse. Only the first four seals are presented in this manner. Because they are presented to us as a set, we will analyze them as a set.

As the first seal is broken, one of the four beasts tells John to *Come and see.* John said, *I saw, and behold a white horse; and he that sat on him had a bow; and a crown was given unto him: and he went forth conquering, and to conquer (6:2).* We will come back to identify this rider.

As the second seal is broken, John again is told to, *come and see,* by the second beast. John said, *There went out another horse that was red: and power was given to him that sat thereon to take peace from the earth, and that they should kill one another: and there was given unto him a great sword (6:4).* The rider of this horse is often called War, but this rider may represent more than military conflict. It may be conflict of all sorts that *take peace* from mankind. As the third seal is broken, John is told by the third beast to *Come and see.* John then *beheld, and lo a black horse; and he that sat on him had a pair of balances in his hand. And [he] heard a voice in the midst of the four beasts say, A measure of wheat for a [denarius], and three measures of barely for a [denarius]; and see you hurt not the oil and the wine (6:6).* A denarius was the wage for a day's labor. The rider of this horse is called Famine, as the scarcity of the basic foods of barley and wheat would imply. But the command to *hurt not the oil and the wine tells* us that there is more to this scene than simply famine. That oil and wine, more costly items, apparently will yet be easily acquired by others suggests the broader concept of inequity found in a fallen world. As the fourth seal is broken, John hears the fourth beast say, *Come and see.* When John looked, he *beheld a pale horse: and his name that sat on him was Death, and Hell followed with him (6:8).* The rider of this horse is Death. This *death* is the physical death brought to man by the sin of Adam. Note that *hell (hades, the unseen world* in the original Greek text) follows the death of all men.

Our objective now is to identify the rider on the white horse. In the visions of the second, third, and forth seals, the riders on the horses are, in short, War, Famine, and Death. Each of these is a simile, a very real event, but not something that could literally ride a horse. Following the pattern established by these three riders, the rider on the white horse must therefore also be a simile, something very real but something that cannot literally ride a horse. This rider is Spiritual Deception.

The conclusion that the rider on the white horse is Spiritual Deception is based on three facts. The first we have already seen by the established pattern of the three following seals.

If the rider is a simile such as is War, Famine, or Death, the rider on the white horse cannot be a man, as a man can very literally ride a horse. This fact eliminates the Antichrist as the rider. It also eliminates Jesus as the rider.

The second is a matter of chronology as the breaking of the first seal is considered to occur concurrent with the beginning of the Tribulation Period. The rider on the white horse is thus seen already successful in conquering as the Tribulation begins while the Antichrist is not given power to conquer until the 42-month period of the last half of the Tribulation.[17] The Scripture does not indicate in any manner his conquering anything prior to his invasion of Israel at the midpoint of the Tribulation Period. He therefore can not be the one who *went forth conquering, and to conquer* at the start of the "Tribulation Period." This fact also eliminates the Antichrist as the rider.

The third fact is that which is stated by Jesus in Matthew 24. As Jesus departed the Temple during the days preceding his crucifixion, his disciples came to him speaking of the magnificence of the buildings of the Temple. Jesus answered them, saying, *"See you not all these things? Verily I say unto you, There shall not be left here one stone upon another, that shall not be thrown down"* (Matthew 24:2). Some of the disciples came to him later and said, *"Tell us, when shall these things be? and what shall be the sign of your coming, and of the end of the [age]?"* (v. 3). Jesus answered them, saying, *"Take heed that no man deceive you. 5 For many shall come in my name, saying, I am the Christ; and shall deceive many. 6And you shall hear of wars and rumors of wars:* see that you be not troubled; for these things must come to pass, but the end is not yet. *7For nation shall rise against nation, and kingdom against kingdom: and there shall be famine, and pestilences, and earthquakes, in diverse places. 8All these are the beginning of sorrows"* (vv:4–8).

This order of events described by Jesus that were to foreshadow his return parallels the order of events depicted by the breaking of the seals of the scroll. The first sign given is of spiritual deceptions—*Take heed that no man deceive you. For many shall come in my name, saying, I am the Christ; and shall deceive many.* The second sign given by Jesus is of war, the third famine, and the fourth things that bring death. From a comparison of the signs given by Jesus of his coming and of the end of the age and the events occurring on the earth as the seals are broken comes the third fact; by the pattern established by these prophecies, the spiritual deception spoken of by Jesus is the rider on the white horse seen by John.

The picture we are given when the first seal is broken is one similar to that seen in Revelation 19:11–16 that depicts the coming of Jesus. The rider of the first seal comes on a white horse, as will Jesus. This rider wears a crown, whereas Jesus will wear many crowns. He has a bow; Jesus will have a sharp sword. This rider goes out to conquer. Jesus has already conquered; his coming will be to rule. In the vision revealed by the breaking of the first seal, God has thus given us an image of spiritual deception by the appearance of one similar to Jesus. Similar, but not the same. The Antichrist will be a part of this Spiritual Deception, but Jesus tells us that *"many shall come in my name, saying, I am Christ: and shall deceive many" (Matthew 24:5).* Just as there will be many wars, many famines, and many deaths, there will also be many spiritual deceptions.

It was said of these riders that *"power was given unto them over the fourth part of the earth to kill with the sword and with hunger, and with death, and with the beasts of the earth" (Revelation 6:8).* The fourth part of the earth is the portion of the earth's territory over which these riders have significant power at any given time; it is not the amount of people killed by these riders, as is often claimed. The fact that these riders of Deception, War, Famine, and Death are riding on horses indicates mobility or variability of location that mimics other prophetic visions, such as Zechariah's where the riders *are they whom the Lord hath sent to walk to and fro through the earth.* Jesus also said of the events depicted in the first seals that they will occur *"in diverse places" (Matthew 24:7)* leaving us with a sense of occurrences in divergent and distant places. The territory over which they have power over at any one time has been spread quite globally.

The breaking of the first four seals therefore depict the sad state of affairs on the earth as the Tribulation begins. It must be noted that the events depicted are brought about by man-they are not judgments of God. Note also that all these things began with a spiritual deception (the first on the list) that caused the fall of man. Thus, as John looks down on the land that is to be redeemed, he sees what man has wrought on the earth throughout the ages. Jesus said of these things, *"these are the beginning of sorrows" (Matthew 24:8).* There is nothing new in these events; there have been spiritual deceptions, wars, famines, disasters, and pestilences of every sort throughout history.

Thus, these events do not start at the breaking of a seal but are events already occurring on the land to be redeemed as the seals are broken. The Tribulation Period, therefore, starts off with things on earth pretty much as normal, although "normal" is getting worse by the day.

Essentially, the first four seals are broken together as a group with the intent to show that not only are these events occurring as the seals are broken but that they are occurring concurrently throughout the earth in random order or in any combination thereof as they have throughout history. It is reasonable to believe these events will occur repeatedly throughout the entire Tribulation Period and that they will increase in intensity and number as the world approaches Armageddon.

Postscript

The terms Tribulation Period, and its abbreviated form, Tribulation, are used often when speaking of prophetic events concerning the last days of this age. These terms pre se are not found in the Bible, but the time period they refer to is spoken of often and in many ways in the Bible. The term Tribulation Period is a creation of man; it refers to the time of the last seven years of this age, after which Jesus will return to rule this earth. This seven-year period comes out of the ninth chapter of Daniel where a messenger from God tells him that *"Seventy weeks are determined upon thy people and upon thy holy city, to finish the transgression, and to make an end of sins, and to make reconciliation for iniquity, and to bring in everlasting righteousness, and to seal up the vision and prophecy, and to anoint the most Holy"* (Daniel 9:24). These weeks, meaning a group of seven in old English terms of the King James Bible, are periods of seven years each. From history we understand that the last week of these seventy weeks, or a remaining period of seven years of this prophecy, is yet to be fulfilled.

Breaking the Fifth Seal

[9]And when he had opened the fifth seal, I saw under the altar the souls of them that were slain for the word of God, and for the testimony which they held: [10]And they cried with a loud voice, saying, How long, O Lord, holy and true, do you not judge and avenge our blood on them that dwell on the

earth? [11] *And white robes were given unto every one of them; and it was said unto them, that they should rest yet for a little season, until their fellow servants also and their brethren, that should be killed as they were, should be fulfilled.*

(Revelation 6:9-11)

Note first that *the souls of them that were slain* will be gathering *under the altar.* This is a very unique group of saints, for they are shown here set apart at their death from the other saints that John will see before the throne of the Father. Note also that even though this scene is of a gathering taking place in heaven, it still depicts what is occurring on the land being redeemed as that is where these saints are being slain.

Verse 9 does not specify which of the two altars of the Temple this *altar* would be where they are gathering, but later in verse 3 of the eighth chapter, both *the altar* and *the golden altar* are spoken of, implying *the altar* here would be the Altar of Burnt Offering. This reference also tells us these two altars are the two altars in the Temple which is in heaven. The Altar of Burnt Offering, also called the Brazen Altar, stood in the Temple court in front of the Holy Place and was that upon which animal sacrifices were offered in the earthly Temple. The gathering under the Altar of Burnt Offering in heaven of *the souls of them that were slain* depicts the death of those on the earth who will be *"beheaded for the witness of Jesus, and for the word of God, and which had not worshipped the beast, neither his image, neither had received his mark upon their foreheads, or in their hands"* *(Revelation 20:4).* That they will be gathering *under* the altar is telling us that *the souls of them that were slain* will be *covered* by the blood sacrifice of Jesus.

Note next that the scene depicted at the breaking of the fifth seal also follows the pattern of events established in Matthew 24. Verses 9 through 14 of Matthew 24 set the stage as verses 15 through 21 declare, *"When you therefore shall see the abomination of desolation, spoken of by Daniel the prophet, stand in the holy place…then shall be great tribulation, such as was not since the beginning of the world to this time, no, nor ever shall be."* The time of the abomination of desolation is defined by *Daniel 9:27* as the midpoint of the seven-year Tribulation Period. The world as a whole may well be in tribulation at this point, but this scene applies strictly to the nation of Israel:

³For, lo, the days come, says the Lord, that I will bring again the captivity of my people Israel and Judah, says the Lord: and I will cause them to return to the land that I gave to their fathers, ⁴and they shall possess it. And these are the words that the Lord spoke concerning Israel and concerning Judah. ⁵For thus says the Lord; We have heard a voice of trembling and fear, and not of peace. ⁶Ask you now, and see whether a man does travail with child? Wherefore do I see every man with his hands on his loins, as a woman in travail, and all faces are turned into paleness? ⁷Alas! For that day is great, so that none is like it: it is even the time of Jacobs's trouble; but he shall be saved out of it.

(Jeremiah 30:3–7)

Luke's account of these events follows the same pattern set in Matthew's account. *The time of Jacobs's trouble begins when, as Luke puts it, "you shall see Jerusalem compassed with armies, then know that the desolation thereof is nigh" (Luke 21:20).* The time of *Jacob's trouble* thus begins with the Antichrist's invasion of Jerusalem. The mark of the beast, at least as it concerns the inhabitants of Israel, will not be required of the Jews until that day or soon thereafter. Therefore, the slaying of those who will not worship the beast nor take his mark will only occur during the 42 months of the last half of the Tribulation Period.

Those who will be gathering under the altar in heaven who *were slain for the word of God, and for the testimony which they held,* are the first distinct group of saints to be identified at the breaking of the seals. We will see these martyrs later as their number is fulfilled.

Breaking the Sixth Seal, Scene One

¹²And I beheld when he had opened the sixth seal, and, lo, there was a great earthquake; and the sun became black as sackcloth of hair, and the moon became as blood; ¹³And the stars of heaven fell unto the earth, even as a fig tree casts her untimely figs, when she is shaken of a mighty wind. ¹⁴And the heaven departed as a scroll when it is rolled together; and every mountain and island were moved out of their places. ¹⁵And the kings of the earth, and the great men, and the rich men, and the chief captains, and the mighty men, and every bondman, and every free man, hid themselves in the dens and in the rocks of the mountains; ¹⁶And said to the mountains and rocks, Fall on us, and hide us from the face of him that sits on the throne, and from the wrath of the Lamb: ¹⁷For the great day of his wrath is come; and who shall be able to stand?

(Revelation 6:12-17)

This first scene of the sixth seal is God's answer to those gathering under the altar who are crying out to God to *judge and avenge our blood on them that dwell on the earth*. God's answer here is a glimpse of what was yet to come upon *them that dwell on the earth*. What John sees as he breaks the sixth seal mimics the words of Matthew; *"²⁹Immediately after the tribulation of those days shall the sun be darkened, and the moon shall not give her light, and the stars shall fall from heaven, and the powers of the heavens shall be shaken: ³⁰And then shall appear the sign of the Son of man in heaven: and then shall all the tribes of the earth mourn, and they shall see the Son of man coming in the clouds of heaven with power and great glory"* (Matthew 24:29–30).

This first scene of the sixth seal thus looks ahead very briefly to the final days of the Tribulation Period to give those crying out for God to avenge their blood a view of the wrath of Jesus avenging an unrepentant world. Still unrepentant, those still remaining yet acknowledge the supreme authority of God and their accountability to Him, for they cry out, *"Hide us from the face of him that sits on the throne, and from the wrath of the Lamb"* (Revelation 6:10).

The Kinsman Avenger

When Jesus takes the scroll sealed with seven seals from the right hand of God and begins to break the seals and to read what was written therein, he will be fulfilling the role of a Kinsman Redeemer. As the Kinsman Redeemer, Jesus is taking back land that had been lost. But we see in the opening scene of the sixth seal that there is another redeeming which must also take place if the earth is to be returned to God, and that is the redeeming of the blood of His servants.

We are shown in Numbers 35 verses 33 and 34 this need for the redeeming, or the cleansing, of the earth itself; *"³³So you shall not pollute the land wherein you are: for it defiles the land: and the land cannot be cleansed of the blood that is shed therein, but by the blood of him that shed it. ³⁴Defile not the land which you shall inhabit, wherein I dwell; for I the Lord dwell among the children of Israel."*

What Scripture is saying here is that when the land in which the Lord dwells is defiled by shed blood, that land can only be cleansed by the shedding of the blood of the one who shed that blood. Jesus will dwell on the land that he will redeem, for he will rule that land for the 1,000 years of the Millennium. Just as the land could not remain defiled when God dwelt amongst the Israelites, the earth can not remain defiled when Jesus again comes to live among men. To cleanse the earth that has been defiled by the shed blood of the righteous, those who shed that righteous blood must have their blood shed in return. The shedding of the blood of those remaining on the earth that will be seen in the breaking of the seventh seal is the redeeming of the blood of the servants of God and thus the cleansing of the land by the hand of Jesus. This cleansing of the land of the blood shed by the righteous is, therefore, also a part of the redemption of the earth.

In Numbers, and again in Deuteronomy, we see God instructing Moses to establish cities of refuge from the *"avenger of blood" (Deuteronomy 19:12)*. If a man was killed, either by accident or by purpose, the slayer of the man could find refuge from the avenger, that is if he could get to the safety of a city of refuge before he is caught, and he himself killed by the avenger of blood. Once in the city of refuge, the manslayer would be brought before the congregation in judgment for the death of another. If found guilty of slaying a man in malice, the manslayer was delivered *"into the hand of the avenger of blood, that he may die" (Deuteronomy 19:12)*. From these texts, we find that there was a kinsman who had the responsibility of avenging the death of another, one who is here called the avenger of blood.

When the seventh seal is broken, John will see an angel that will come and stand at the brazen altar in heaven, *"³having a golden censer; and there will be given to him much incense, that he should offer it with the prayers of all saints upon the golden altar which was before the throne. 4And the smoke of the incense, which will come with the prayers of the saints, will ascend up before God out of the angel's hand" (Revelation 8:3–4)*. The prayers of the saints that are here offered up to God are not only the cries of those who will be gathered under the brazen altar but are the prayers of all the saints.

After the prayers of the saints are offered up to God, the angel will then take the censor and fill it with fire from the brazen altar and cast that fire unto the earth (Revelation 8:5).

In the casting of the fire from the altar of sacrifice is found God's answer to the prayers of these martyred saints, for Jesus is about to avenge the blood of his servants.

Because those who are gathering under the altar are heirs of God and joint-heirs with Christ (Romans 8:17), they are kinsman of Jesus. Thus, I call this avenger of blood the Kinsman Avenger.

The Sixth Seal, Scene Two

> *7:¹And after these things I saw four angels standing on the four corners of the earth, holding the four winds of the earth, that the wind should not blow on the earth, nor on the sea, nor on any tree.*
>
> *(Revelation 7:1)*

The four winds that should not blow at this time is a restraining of the avenging wrath of the Lamb during the first three and a half years of the Tribulation Period. Later, in the breaking of the seventh seal, we will see these same four winds begin to blow in the opening salvos of his wrath: *"⁷The first angel sounded, and there followed hail and fire mingled with blood, and they were cast upon the earth: and the third part of trees was burnt up, and all green grass was burnt up. ⁸And the second angel sounded, and as it were a great mountain burning with fire was cast into the sea: ⁹and the third part of the sea became blood; And the third part of the creatures which were in the sea, and had life, died; and the third part of the ships were destroyed"* (Revelation 8:7–9).

> *²And I saw another angel ascending from the east, having the seal of the living God: and he cried with a loud voice to the four angels, to whom it was given to hurt the earth and the sea, ³Saying, Hurt not the earth, neither the sea, nor the trees, till we have sealed the servants of our God in their foreheads.*
>
> *(Revelation 7:2-3)*

The *seal of the living God* is a mark of ownership. His seal *in their foreheads* is metaphoric; it is stated here to tell us that those who are about to be sealed belong to God. This angel is coming *from the east*, indicating that the source is God Himself. This angel is also *ascending*, implying that those who are being sealed are on the earth below.

> *⁴And I heard the number of them which were sealed: and there were sealed an hundred and forty and four thousand of all the tribes of the children of Israel. ⁵Of the tribe of Juda were sealed twelve thousand. Of the tribe of Reuben were sealed twelve thousand. Of the tribe of Gad were sealed twelve thousand. ⁶Of the tribe of Aser were sealed twelve thousand. Of the tribe of Nephthalim were sealed twelve thousand. Of the tribe of Manasses were sealed twelve thousand. ⁷Of the tribe of Simeon were sealed twelve thousand. Of the tribe of Levi were sealed twelve thousand. Of the tribe of Issachar were sealed twelve thousand. ⁸Of the tribe of Zabulon were sealed twelve thousand. Of the tribe of Joseph were sealed twelve thousand. Of the tribe of Benjamin were sealed twelve thousand.*

> *(Revelation 7:4-8)*

Many wonder why this list of the tribes of Israel is not given in order of the birth of the sons of Jacob or why the tribe of Dan is missing. The selection of names and the order in which they are listed is to tell the message of the *hundred and forty and four thousand* through the meaning of their names.[18] Dan, meaning "judgment", is not needed for the message, but Manasseh, meaning "causing to forget", is. Here is their message:

We will praise the Lord for He has seen our afflictions. We are many and are blessed for in our wrestling against our adversaries He has made us forget all our toil. The Lord has heard us and is joined with us. The Lord has given us our wages for He has given us a great gift; He has added to us the Son of His right hand.

The Son of His right hand is defined in *Acts 2:32–33:* "*³²This Jesus has God raised up, whereof we all are witnesses. ³³ Therefore being by the right hand of God exalted, and having received of the Father the promise of the Holy Ghost, he has shed forth this, which you now see and hear.*"

The time of their sealing is during the period of tranquility when *the four winds of the earth…should not blow.* In Israel, it is the time of the 1,260 days of the protection from *"the face of the serpent"* (Revelation 12:14). It is *"In that day [that] there shall be a fountain opened to the house of David and to the inhabitants of Jerusalem for sin and for uncleanness"* (Zechariah 13:1). Therefore, the time of their sealing is the time of the first half of the Tribulation Period.

We will see these *hundred and forty and four thousand of all the tribes of the children of Israel* again when the seventh seal is broken. For now, it is sufficient to note that these *"which were redeemed from the earth"* (Revelation 14:3) are the second distinct group of saints to be identified at the breaking of the seals.

The Sixth Seal, Scene Three

> 7:*9After this I beheld, and, lo, a great multitude, which no man could number, of all nations, and kindreds, and people, and tongues, stood before the throne, and before the Lamb, clothed with white robes, and palms in their hands; *10*And cried with a loud voice, saying, Salvation to our God which sits upon the throne, and unto the Lamb. *11*And all the angels stood round about the throne, and about the elders and the four beasts, and fell before the throne on their faces, and worshipped God, *12*Saying, Amen: Blessing, and glory, and wisdom, and thanksgiving, and honor, and power, and might, be unto our God for ever and ever. Amen.*

> *(Revelation 7:9-12)*

John now actually sees the saints that have been standing before the throne, those whom the twenty-four elders represent, those who are the witnesses required to be before the throne in heaven in order for the kinsman redeemer to break the first seal and to begin to read the scroll.

> *13And one of the elders answered, saying unto me, What are these which are arrayed in white robes? and whence came they? *14*And I said unto him, Sir, you know. And he said to me, These are they which came out of great tribulation, and have washed their robes, and made them white in the blood of the Lamb. *15*Therefore are they before the throne of God, and serve him day and night in his temple: and he that sits on the throne shall dwell among them. *16*They shall hunger no more, neither thirst anymore; neither shall the sun light on them, nor any heat. *17*For the Lamb which is in the midst of the*

throne shall feed them, and shall lead them unto living fountains of waters: and God shall wipe away all tears from their eyes.

(Revelation 7:13-17)

These *which came out of great tribulation* are the third distinct group of saints seen by John at the breaking of the seals. *This great tribulation* from which they are to come is universally spoken of as The Great Tribulation (note capitalization). The Great Tribulation is a technical term created by man simply by how it is used. A "technical term" is defined as a word or phrase that has a specific (singular) meaning. This particular term is derived from the words of Matthew 24:21: *"For then shall be great tribulation, such as was not since the beginning of the world to this time, no, nor ever shall be."* The Great Tribulation is often used in reference to the last half of the Tribulation Period, which is a suitable use of the term—to a point. That point is that this technical term is used erroneously when applying it to the breadth of the world, as in *all nations, and kindreds, and people, and tongues* as spoken of in *Revelation 7:9.* But Matthew's *great tribulation* is the time of *Jacob's trouble,* not Henry's, and Pierre's, and Zhang Jie's, but Jacob's alone. Matthew's message of *great tribulation* is tribulation that will come specifically upon Israel. That it is meant to be Israel's alone is confirmed by the following passages:

And when you shall see Jerusalem compassed with armies, then know that the desolation thereof is nigh.

(Luke 21:20)

[1]Behold, the day of the Lord comes, and your spoil shall be divided in the midst of you. [2]For I will gather all nations against Jerusalem to battle; and the city shall be taken, and houses rifled, and the women ravished; and half the city shall go forth into captivity, and the residue of the people shall not be cut off from the city.

(Zechariah 14:1–2)

[22] For these be the days of vengeance, that all things which are written may be fulfilled. [23] But woe unto them that are with child, and to them that give suck, in those days! for there shall be great distress in the land, and wrath upon this people. [24] And they shall fall by the edge of the sword, and shall

be led away captive into all nations: and Jerusalem shall be trodden down of the Gentiles, until the times of the Gentiles be fulfilled.

(Luke 21:22–24)

And at that time shall Michael stand up, the great prince which stands for the children of your people: and there shall be a time of trouble, such as never was since there was a nation even to that same time.

(Daniel 12:1)

⁴And these are the words that the Lord spoke concerning Israel and concerning Judah. ⁵For thus says the Lord; We have heard a voice of trembling, of fear, and not of peace. ⁶Ask you now, and see whether a man does travail with child? wherefore do I see every man with his hands on his loins, as a woman in travail, and all faces are turned into paleness? ⁷Alas! for that day is great, so that none is like it: it is even the time of Jacob's trouble, but he shall be saved out of it.

(Jeremiah 30:4–7)

These verses speak of Matthew's *great tribulation* only in terms of Israel as Matthew was speaking to his Jewish disciples. This tells us that Matthew's *great tribulation* was not meant to apply to the world as a whole. Therefore, the *great multitude, which no man could number* standing before the throne that is to come out of the *great tribulation* of Revelation 7:14 are not those who will come out of The Great Tribulation that is Israel's alone. This is not to say that the Gentile world will not also have *great tribulation* during the last half of the Tribulation Period. The point here is that the time of great tribulation of Revelation 7:14 does not apply to the Tribulation Period, much less to the time of The Great Tribulation.

What then is the *great tribulation* of Revelation 7:14? It is life—life in a fallen world. Those who have remained faithful to God through millennia have seen tribulations because of their faith in a righteous God, a "tribulation" not often considered by the Western world, which has seen little of this in past centuries. (But it's coming folks!) Jesus said to his disciples that this fallen world will *"deliver you up to be afflicted, and shall kill you: and you shall be hated of all nations for my name's sake" (Matthew 24:9).* Many have walked in the footsteps of the disciples. We need not spend time enumerating the atrocities afflicted upon those faithful to God throughout the centuries as the Bible, the history books, and the nightly news are replete with accounts of the millions of lives slaughtered, of churches and homes, and even of entire villages, torched, and of the countless thousands driven from their homelands because they loved the Lord.

This is the *great tribulation* witnessed by those now standing before the throne of God.

We will see, as the seals are continued to be broken, that there will be few who will receive Jesus as Lord and Savior during the seven years of the Tribulation. Paul, speaking to those Gentile nations, kindreds, peoples, and tongues, said, *"I would not, brethren, that you should be ignorant of this mystery, lest you should be wise in your own conceits; that blindness in part is happened to Israel, until the fullness of the Gentiles be come in"* (Romans 11:25). I speak in various chapters of this spiritual blindness of Israel and of the time this blindness will be lifted. But before this blindness is removed from the Jews, the fullness of the Gentiles must occur. God here is thus speaking of two spiritual events, a closing of the door to the Gentiles and an opening of another to the Jews.

The line is slowly being drawn between those Gentiles who believe in Jesus and those who continue to reject him. When there are no Gentiles willing to cross that line to Christ, the harvest, *the fullness of the Gentiles,* will be complete. God will then turn from the Gentiles and turn again to Israel and *"there shall be a fountain opened to the house of David and to the inhabitants of Jerusalem for sin and for uncleanness"* (Zechariah 13:1). We will see in the coming pages that the Gentiles of *all nations, and kindreds, and people, and tongues* will have set their faces against God and hardened their hearts to His message of repentance. There will be few who will come out of The Great Tribulation to stand in righteousness before the throne of God for John to see.

Postscript

What is shown with the breaking of the first six seals is that John's text does not necessarily present the events of his visions in the order in which they will actually occur on earth. We will see, as John's account continues to unfold, that the visions portrayed are presented more by subject matter than by chronological order, although there is still a general progression of events through time in his visions. That the first four seals were presented to us as a set with the single subject, that of the mess man has made of this world, was a clue to how John was to present the story of the breaking of the seals of the scroll. We have seen in the fifth and sixth seals another subject, the distinct sets of saints that will appear in heaven during the period, of the Tribulation.

From the context of the verses that speak of these saints, and by other pertinent Scriptures found elsewhere throughout the Bible, we are able to discern the time frame of these appearances, which are not addressed in the text of the scroll in the chronological order of their actual arrival in heaven. This "disorder" is evident again at the breaking of the sixth seal where what is described as the wrath of the lamb will not actually occur until late in the breaking of the seventh seal. But because this "out of place" description of a future event is important to the understanding of the subject that was at hand, it is given in disorder. This is to remind us not to get hung up trying to put John's text in neat chronological order.

Breaking the Seventh Seal

> 8:[1]*And when he had opened the seventh seal, there was silence in heaven about the space of half an hour.*
>
> *(Revelation 8:1)*

The subject is now the wrath of the Lamb. All heaven is silent in awe and expectation of the horrific events that are about to come upon the earth and its inhabitants. The time is the midpoint of the Tribulation Period. Up to this point in time, there has been no wrath or judgment from God upon the earth.[12] The role of Jesus in these coming events is as the Kinsman Avenger.

> [2]*And I saw the seven angels which stood before God; and to them were given seven trumpets. [3]And another angel came and stood at the altar, having a golden censer; and there was given unto him much incense, that he should offer (it) with the prayers of all saints upon the golden altar which was before the throne. [4]And the smoke of the incense, which came with the prayers of the saints, ascended up before God out of the angel's hand. [5]And the angel took the censer, and filled it with fire of the altar, and cast it into the earth: and there were voices, and thunderings, and lightnings, and an earthquake.*

⁶And the seven angels which had the seven trumpets prepared themselves to sound.

(Revelation 8:2-6)

The sound of a trumpet was historically a call to action. Here, the sounding of the trumpets is as the voice of God commanding the wrath that is to come.

This wrath begins with the casting of fire from the altar of sacrifice, which is in heaven, onto those who remain on the earth, *"for they have shed the blood of saints and prophets, and [God will give] them blood to drink; for they are worthy"* (Revelation 16:6). This begins God's response to the prayers for vengeance of those gathering under the altar.

The First Angel Sounds

⁷The first angel sounded, and there followed hail and fire mingled with blood, and they were cast upon the earth: and the third part of trees was burnt up, and all green grass was burnt up.

(Revelation 8:7)

The Second Angel Sounds

⁸And the second angel sounded, and as it were a great mountain burning with fire was cast into the sea: and the third part of the sea became blood; ⁹And the third part of the creatures which were in the sea, and had life, died; and the third part of the ships were destroyed.

(Revelation 8:8-9)

The Third Angel Sounds

¹⁰And the third angel sounded, and there fell a great star from heaven, burning as it were a lamp, and it fell upon the third part of the rivers, and upon the fountains of waters; ¹¹And the name of the star is called Wormwood: and the third part of the waters became wormwood; and many men died of the waters, because they were made bitter.

(Revelation 8:10-11)

The Fourth Angel Sounds

[12] And the fourth angel sounded, and the third part of the sun was smitten, and the third part of the moon, and the third part of the stars; so as the third part of them was darkened, and the day shone not for a third part of it, and the night likewise.

(Revelation 8:12)

With the sounding of these four trumpets, we see the wrath of Jesus directed upon all aspects of the ecological world, which will have a significant effect on man. We can try to put the cause of these events as some natural event of nature, but God is not limited to waiting for some "act of nature" to occur so that He can act in coordination with it; God is capable of creating any act of nature He so desires, whenever He so desires. This wrath is poured out worldwide.

[13] And I beheld, and heard an angel flying through the midst of heaven, saying with a loud voice, Woe, woe, woe, to the inhabiters of the earth by reason of the other voices of the trumpet of the three angels, which are yet to sound!

(Revelation 8:13)

The woes to come, however, are a totally different story. The coming woes of the sounding of the next three trumpets will come directly and very purposefully upon men themselves.

The Fifth Angel Sounds; The First Woe Comes

9:[1] And the fifth angel sounded, and I saw a star fall from heaven unto the earth: and to him was given the key of the bottomless pit. [2] And he opened the bottomless pit; and there arose a smoke out of the pit, as the smoke of a great furnace; and the sun and the air were darkened by reason of the smoke of the pit. [3] And there came out of the smoke locusts upon the earth: and unto them was given power, as the scorpions of the earth have power. [4] And it was commanded them that they should not hurt the grass of the earth, neither any green thing, neither any tree; but only those men which have not the seal of God in their foreheads. [5] And to them it was given that they should not kill them, but that they should be tormented five months: and their torment was as the torment of a scorpion, when he strikes a man. [6] And in those days shall men seek death, and shall not find it; and shall desire to die, and death shall flee from them.

(Revelation 9:1-6)

It's obvious that these locusts are not the small insects that we are familiar with, for they are told not to hurt the grass of the earth nor any green thing, which would be their natural food. Rather, what comes out of the bottomless pit are spiritual beings, fallen angels, often called demons. These are the angels who followed Satan in his rebellion against God. There appears to be at least two general classes of fallen angels: those who are free to roam the earth, seeking to indwell the bodies of men (Matthew 12:43–45) and those who are in a place of continual confinement bound by chains of darkness who are reserved for use in judgment (2 Peter 2:4). The *bottomless pit* from which these demons come is best described from the original Greek as a very deep dungeon. It is from this place of confinement that these *locusts* are loosed to bring torment upon mankind *as the torment of a scorpion, when he strikes a man.* This torment is extreme, for *in those days shall men seek death because of their pain but they shall not find it.*

This torment will come to *only those men which **have not** the seal of God in their foreheads.* Those with *the seal of God are,* at the least, the *hundred and forty and four thousand of all the tribes of the children of Israel* who are now taking the gospel of Jesus to the ends of the earth. There may be others with the seal of God who have responded to their message of the saving grace of Jesus who will also be protected, as *the seal of God* is a metaphoric sign of having salvation in Jesus. (The Bible does not specifically state this protection is offered only to the hundred and forty and four thousand.) These only will not suffer this wrath of the Lamb. Since the Israelite evangelists will be scattered worldwide, reason would tell us that the extent of this torment will also be worldwide.

[7]And the shapes of the locusts were like unto horses prepared unto battle; and on their heads were as it were crowns like gold, and their faces were as the faces of men. [8]And they had hair as the hair of women, and their teeth were as the teeth of lions. [9]And they had breastplates, as it were breastplates of iron; and the sound of their wings was as the sound of chariots of many horses running to battle. [10]And they had tails like unto scorpions, and there were stings in their tails: and their power was to hurt men five months. [11]And

they had a king over them, which is the angel of the bottomless pit, whose name in the Hebrew tongue is Abaddon, but in the Greek tongue has his name Apollyon. (Revelation 9:7-11)

The physical description of these locusts is nothing like any known insect, giving reason to also believe that they are spiritual beings. Their leader is a fallen angel as he also is *of the bottomless pit* as are those he commands. His name is *Destroyer.*

One may wonder why God would bring such terrible pain upon people for so long a time. But He has now brought all of mankind to the final point of decision—choose eternal life in the presence of God or eternal death absent from God. With these *locusts,* God brings about a real-time contrast between the only two given choices man has: eternal protection or eternal torment

[12]One woe is past; and, behold, there come two woes more hereafter.

(Revelation 9:12)

The Sixth Angel Sounds; The Second Woe Begins

[13]And the sixth angel sounded, and I heard a voice from the four horns of the golden altar which is before God, [14]Saying to the sixth angel which had the trumpet, Loose the four angels which are bound [at][20] the great river Euphrates. [15]And the four angels were loosed, which were prepared for an hour, and a day, and a month, and a year, for to slay the third part of men. [16]And the number of the army of the horsemen were two hundred thousand: and I heard the number of them. [17]And thus I saw the horses in the vision, and them that sat on them, having breastplates of fire, and of jacinth, and brimstone: and the heads of the horses were as the heads of lions; and out of their mouths issued fire and smoke and brimstone. [18]By these three was the third part of men killed, by the fire, and by the smoke, and by the brimstone, which issued out of their mouths. [19]For their power is in their mouth, and in their tails: for their tails were like unto serpents, and had heads, and with them they do hurt.

(Revelation 9:13-19)

Loose the four angels which are bound…for to slay the third part of men. This *army of the horsemen* that are to be *two hundred thousand* strong that are commanded by four angels having been loosed from their bonds are typically said to be a two-hundred-million-man army of men from Asia. But this army now described by John is visioned to be quite similar in kind to the army that he saw coming out of the bottomless pit, which was commanded by an angel that had also been bound in that same bottomless pit. Just as the angel of the bottomless pit and the army of "locusts" he led were fallen angels (demons), the four angels now loosed from their bonds and their army of two hundred million are also demons. That the angel of the bottomless pit and the four angels at the river Euphrates are bound by God is one sure indication that these armies are demons, for angels in allegiance with God would have no need to be bound.

A force of two hundred million men may potentially be raised out of the area of the Far East, but it would be more logical that any army of men raised out of the east would be the armies of *"the ten kings of the east"* of *Revelation 16:12* that will come on the scene later at the time of Armageddon. Scripture does not speak of the necessity of the army of *two hundred thousand* to have the waters of the *great river Euphrates* dried up so they can move against those who they are to kill. But Scripture does say that when the sixth angel later pours out his vial upon the river Euphrates, *the water thereof was dried up, that the way of the kings of the east might be prepared.* A great army of men with their war machines would need the Euphrates to be dried up in order to cross in mass—demon armies are not so encumbered. This is another indication that these two armies of the first and second woes are demons.

Note that thus far, God is not using man to inflict His wrath.

20And the rest of the men which were not killed by these plagues yet repented not of the works of their hands, that they should not worship devils, and idols of gold, and silver, and brass, and stone, and of wood: which neither can see, nor hear, nor walk: 21Neither repented they of their murders, nor of their sorceries, nor of their fornication, nor of their thefts.

(Revelation 9:20-21)

And the rest of the men which were not killed…yet repented not. From this statement, it is evident that repentance from sin is still an option offered by Jesus. Yet, we see that man has at this point in time hardened their hearts and set their faces against God. Even though the salvation message of the gospel of Jesus is still being presented to the Gentiles by the hundred and forty and four thousand Israelite evangelists, we see here evidence that there will be few of The Great Tribulation who will repent of their works and stand in righteousness before the throne of God for John to see. The second woe is complete.

Postscript

I'm not picking on the Gentiles here, but the vast majority of the nations, and kindreds, and peoples, and tongues are Gentiles. The spiritual situation of the nation of Israel will be addressed shortly as there will be those of the house of Jacob who will turn to Jesus during the Tribulation Period. However, they still will not be the *great multitude, which no man could number* of Revelation 7:9.

A Break in the Pattern of the Text of the Scroll

We have been witnessing the wrath that is to come upon the earth and its inhabitants as the trumpets of the seven angels of the seventh seal are sounded. But at this point, there is a break in this pattern of the sounding of trumpets.

There are still angels with a message to present, but there is no accompanying sound of a trumpet. Thus, we depart from a view of worldwide events from our perspective to a view of Israel's world from God's perspective. The subject is still the wrath of the Lamb, but that wrath is, for the moment, shown to be wholly upon and unique to the nation of Israel.

The Message to John

> 10:¹ *And I saw another mighty angel come down from heaven, clothed with a cloud: and a rainbow was upon his head, and his face was as it were the sun, and his feet as pillars of fire.*
>
> *(Revelation 10:1)*

Note first that this angel does not sound a trumpet, and second, this angel is of royal stature (if such a term could be used for an angel).

One may think that this *mighty angel* is Jesus himself because of the majestic description given of this messenger. However, later in verses

5 and 6, this messenger *"lifted up his hand to heaven, And swear by him that lives for ever and ever, who created heaven, and the things that therein are, and the earth, and the things that therein are, and the sea, and the things which are therein."*

The one who created heaven and earth is Jesus. Thus, this *mighty angel* is telling us that his message is true by the Word of God (John 1:1–3). The majestic description given of this mighty angel may be a message in itself to us that the message he brings is of special importance to God.

> *²And he had in his hand a little book open: and he set his right foot upon the sea, and his left foot on the earth...*
>
> *(Revelation 10:2)*

This *little book* is open in the hand of the messenger inferring that the information written within is to be revealed to John. That this book is little implies that it contains only a portion of a larger text. But because it is brought by such a mighty messenger, its message is still of unusual importance.

> *³And [the mighty angel] cried with a loud voice, as when a lion roars: and when he had cried, seven thunders uttered their voices. ⁴And when the seven thunders had uttered their voices, I was about to write: and I heard a voice from heaven saying unto me, Seal up those things which the seven thunders uttered, and write them not.*
>
> *(Revelation 10:3-4)*

The *seven thunders* are the voice of God. Since seven is the number of completion or completeness, it appears that the message of the seven thunders may concern *"the mystery of God"* that will *"be finished"* (v. 7). John was told not to reveal what he heard, implying that there were just some things the world was not yet ready to receive.

Verses 1–4 above are interesting in that they show John's viewpoint of events is no longer from heaven but now is from earth. Verse 1 tells us that John saw this angel with the little book *come down from heaven.* In verse 4, he hears *a voice from heaven.* These are stated from an earthly perspective. This is the first time we see such wording since the seals began to be broken. When John heard the words of the seven thunders, he was told to *write them not.* This is also the first we see of John recording his visions at the breaking of the seals. If we think about it, it would have seemed strange if John would have grabbed an inkhorn and a sheaf of parchment when he heard a voice from heaven telling him to *"come up here" (Revelation 4:1).*

> *⁵And the angel which I saw stand upon the sea and upon the earth lifted up his hand to heaven, ⁶And swear by him that lives for ever and ever, who created heaven, and the things that therein are, and the earth, and the things that therein are, and the sea, and the things which are therein, that there should be time no longer: ⁷But in the days of the voice of the seventh angel, when he shall begin to sound, the mystery of God should be finished, as he has declared to his servants the prophets.*
>
> *(Revelation 10:5-7)*

This is simply saying that we are coming to the end of the story. God has shown His prophets the mystery of God through prophecy, and now it is time to fulfill what has been told.

> *⁸And the voice which I heard from heaven spoke unto me again, and said, Go and take the little book which is open in the hand of the angel which stands upon the sea and upon the earth. ⁹And I went unto the angel, and said unto him, Give me the little book. And he said unto me, Take it, and eat it up; and it shall make your belly bitter, but it shall be in your mouth sweet as honey. ¹⁰And I took the little book out of the angel's hand, and ate it up; and it was in my mouth sweet as honey: and as soon as I had eaten it, my belly was bitter. ¹¹And he said unto me, You must prophesy again [about] many peoples, and nations, and tongues, and kings.*
>
> *(Revelation 10:8-11)*

As John took this *little book* from the mighty angel and began to eat it (take to himself the information contained therein), it was to be *sweet as honey* in his mouth as he spoke the words of God's message. But as he began to digest (to understand) what this little book was saying, it made his *belly bitter* because of the bitter message he now was to tell. We are about to see why this message is brought to John by such a mighty angel and why its message turns John's belly bitter. The *peoples, and nations, and tongues, and kings* he is to prophecy about form a world unique to Israel. Ezekiel had a like experience:

> *2:⁸But you, son of man, hear what I say unto you; Be not you rebellious like that rebellious house: open your mouth, and eat that I give you. ⁹And when I looked, behold, an hand was sent unto me; and, lo, a roll of a book was*

therein; [10] *And he spread it before me; and it was written within and without: and there was written therein lamentations, and mourning, and woe.*

3: [1] *Moreover he said unto me, Son of man, eat that you find; eat this roll, and go speak unto the house of Israel. 2 So I opened my mouth, and he caused me to eat that roll. 3 And he said unto me, Son of man, cause your belly to eat, and fill your bowels with this roll that I give you. Then did I eat it; and it was in my mouth as honey for sweetness. 4 And he said unto me, Son of man, go, get you unto the house of Israel, and speak with my words unto them.*

(Ezekiel 2:8–10, 3:1–4)

Just as Ezekiel was told to take a bitter message to a rebellious Israel, John was to *prophesy again [about] many peoples, and nations, and tongues, and kings* who manifest the wrath of the Lamb which is yet to be poured upon the rebellious house of Israel. John's message is told in the following text.

Postscript

Since John was to give this message to those of his day, it seems out of place for this message to be in a text that was to describe what was to occur in the last days of this age. But its inclusion here does make sense if we remember that there were two copies of this title deed written, and one of those copies was to remain open for all to read throughout the ages. It would have been reasonable then to include these instructions to John in this deed, for what he was to prophecy was not only of events to occur on earth in the days the sealed scroll was to be opened but were to be a warning for the people of his day as to what was to come upon them if they continued on the rebellious path they were traveling.

Verse 11 in the KJV above reads, *You must prophesy again before many peoples, and nations, and tongues, and kings.* The word *before* presents a picture of John as standing in front of many people, telling them his message. This picture is not quite right as the Greek word translated as *before* in verse 11 is *epi*, meaning *on, upon, over*. Thus, I used the word *about* in place of *before* to give a more accurate picture of John's task. John was to prophecy *about* many peoples, and nations, and tongues, and kings. Thus, like Ezekiel's message, John's message of the *little book* is also about those people, their nations, and their kings who have, and will yet, come against *Judah, Israel, and Jerusalem*, as we are about to see in Revelation's chapters 11, 12 and 13.

The Wrath of Jesus Upon Israel

We are still in the time of the wrath of the seventh seal. And, we are still looking at events occurring on the land that is being redeemed. The subject is still the wrath of the Lamb, but the focus of John's vision is now singularly on the nation of Israel.

> *11:¹And there was given me a reed like unto a rod: and the angel stood, saying, Rise, and measure the temple of God, and the altar, and them that worship therein. ²But the court which is without the temple leave out, and measure it not; for it is given unto the Gentiles: and the holy city shall they tread under foot forty and two months. ³And I will give power unto my two witnesses, and they shall prophesy a thousand two hundred and threescore days, clothed in sackcloth... ⁷And when they shall have finished their testimony, the beast that ascends out of the bottomless pit shall make war against them, and shall overcome them, and kill them.*

> *(Revelation 11:1-3, 7)*

These verses are a concise synopsis of events that depict the very essence of the seven years of the Tribulation Period for the nation of Israel. They sum up the whole of God's redemption of His chosen people and complete His wrath upon a rebellious nation.

In this vision now before John, God has gathered the whole house of Jacob *"unto their own land"* and has *"left none of them any more there"* in the countries into which they had been scattered because of their iniquity (Ezekiel 39:23–29). Thus, all whom God considers to be His chosen people will now reside in Israel. This is critical for us to understand, for God will deal with His chosen people essentially as a corporate body. In this respect, all will be given the same opportunities and will receive the same consequences. During these seven years, every individual of the house of Jacob will be brought personally to a final point of decision concerning Jesus as their Messiah, and also their acceptance or rejection of him as their righteousness; there will be no escape from this decision this time!

After "digesting" the little book, John was told to measure the temple, the altar, and them who worship therein. John's viewpoint of events is now from earth rather than heaven. Therefore, this Temple and the worshipers he is to *measure* are to be those found in Jerusalem. To *measure* is God's manner of telling John to take stock of the situation, to consider what His chosen people are doing.

We are now in the time period when the third Temple has been built, and the Jews again are sacrificing according to the ancient Hebrew practices of the Law whereby they are seeking forgiveness for their sins by the shedding of the blood of animals.[21] The Bible does not tell us when these animal sacrifices began again, but they must have begun at the latest sometime very early in the first half of the Tribulation Period. Juxtaposed to those in the Temple covering over their sins with the blood of animals are those outside the Temple hearing the words of the Two Witnesses telling of the sacrifice of Jesus their Messiah, which takes away their sins by his shed blood on the cross of Calvary.[22] All will have to decide shortly which sacrifice they will take as theirs.

Both scenarios described in these few short verses above allude to two distinctively different time periods of the Tribulation: the first a period of tranquility conducive to contemplation and decision, the second a period of the wrath of the Lamb and the consequences of those decisions.

First, a Time of Tranquility

The stage is typically set in our thinking of the Tribulation Period by Daniel's prophecy of the time of the *"seventy weeks" (Daniel 9:24–27)* that are determined upon Daniel's people and upon Jerusalem. This prophecy states in verse 27 that *"he shall confirm the covenant with many for one week"* (actually, one period of seven years), which we take as the event starting the seven years of the Tribulation. The one here who is said to *confirm the covenant is "the prince that shall come"* of verse 26. (This prophecy is examined in detail in a later chapter, "The Seventy Sevens of Daniel.")

This *covenant with many* that will be ratified at the start of the *week* is considered to be, at least in part, a peace treaty between Israel and her neighbors. Thus, Israel will have a reprieve from the militant advances of the surrounding nations during the first half of the Tribulation Period. This time of tranquility is confirmed by the vision John is about to see that is given in the twelfth chapter of Revelation.

In symbolic language, John describes the age-old conflict between Israel, depicted as a woman crowned with twelve stars, and those surrounding nations, depicted as a red dragon with seven heads, which scatter the Israelites to the four winds. In this vision, John sees the Jews fleeing from their captive nations back into Israel where they will be protected from those nations, still intent on the annihilation of Israel despite the treaty.

This period of protection of 1,260 days is the first half of the Tribulation Period, which is concurrent with the time of this peace treaty (Revelation 12:6, 14). (This prophecy of the 1,260 days of Israel's protection from the surrounding nations is examined in detail in a later chapter "The (non)Flight of the Woman".)

Israel's focus during this time of tranquility turns to the theological conflict now developing within Jerusalem between the old covenant between God and man represented by the sacrifice of animals ongoing in the Temple, and the new covenant represented by the sacrifice of Jesus, which is being told by the Two Witnesses on the streets of the city.

Spiritual blindness had come upon Israel (Romans 11:25) on that fateful day Jesus rode into Jerusalem to present himself to the people for their inspection of the "sacrificial lamb."[23] The people had believed Jesus was their anticipated king, but they did not believe Jesus was their righteousness. For this *"God [gave] them the spirit of slumber, eyes that they should not see, and ears that they should not hear"* (Romans 11:8, quoting Isaiah 29:10) *"for the wisdom of their wise men shall perish, and the understanding of their prudent men shall be hid"* (Isaiah 29:14). Now, as the *two witnesses* come on the scene, this spiritual blindness is lifted that their eyes may see and their ears may hear, for *"in [this] day there shall be a fountain opened to the house of David and to the inhabitants of Jerusalem for sin and for uncleanness"* (Zachariah 13:1), for the Lord had said, *"I will pour upon the house of David, and upon the inhabitants of Jerusalem, the spirit of grace and of supplications: and they shall look upon me whom they have pierced"* (Zachariah 12:10).24 These Two Witnesses now presenting Jesus to the people may be Enoch and Elijah, two great men of God who were taken up to heaven without seeing death. It would be reasonable for God to send two from the Old Testament time of the Law and the Prophets to tell of Jesus as their Messiah, and as their sacrifice, since that is where the spiritual mind of the Jew is still to this day.

During this three-and-a-half-year period of somewhat peaceful tranquility in Israel, *the four winds* of the wrath of the Lamb are also quiet (Revelation 7:1–4). It is during this time of tranquility that *"the remnant of her seed,"* referring to the woman crowned with twelve stars, will choose *"the commandments of God, and have the testimony of Jesus Christ" (Revelation 12:17).* This includes the 144,000 of the tribes of the children of Israel that will be sealed with their Father's name written in their foreheads during this period of tranquility.

Then the Wrath of the Lamb

John had been told not to measure the outer court[25] of the Temple, *for it is given unto the Gentiles: and the holy city shall they tread under foot forty and two months.* He was also told that when the Two Witnesses *have finished their testimony, the beast that ascends out of the bottomless pit shall make war against them, and shall overcome them, and kill them.*[26] Both of these acts, Jerusalem being taken captive by the multitude of armies under the leadership of the Antichrist and the Two Witnesses being killed by Satan, are both expressions of the wrath of the Lamb upon the nation of Israel during the last half of the Tribulation Period.

Zachariah had written of this day: *"Awake, O sword, against my shepherd, and against the man that is my fellow, says the Lord of hosts: smite the shepherd, and the sheep shall be scattered…" (Zachariah 13:7a).* The *sword* is the *Antichrist,* and the shepherd is the king of Israel. *"7bAnd I will turn my hand upon the little ones. 8And it shall come to pass, that in all the land, says the Lord, two parts therein shall be cut off and die; but the third shall be left therein. 9And I will bring the third part through the fire, and will refine them as silver is refined, and will try them as gold is tried: they shall call on my name, and I will hear them: I will say, It is my people: and they shall say, The Lord is my God" (Zachariah 13:7b–9).* Zachariah is speaking in this passage of the consequences of those choices made between the two competing sacrifices. In both scenarios, the consequences involve the wrath of the Lamb, but the wrath upon each group is different one from the other. It is important for us to understand that it was God who had said, *I will turn my hand upon the little ones,* speaking specifically of His chosen people. I will come back to this thought shortly.

Again, Daniel's prophecy of the time of the *seventy weeks* comes into view as the one who *"shall confirm the covenant with many for one week"* will *"in the midst of the week…cause the sacrifice and the oblation to cease, and for the overspreading of abominations he shall make it [the Temple] desolate" (Daniel 9:27)*. The Temple sacrifices will be stopped, and the Temple will shortly thereafter be destroyed: *"There shall not be left here one stone upon another, that shall not be thrown down" (Matthew 24:2)*. (This is actually Jesus taking away the people's ability to sacrifice the blood of animals.)

Those who will choose the sacrifice of animals and reject the sacrifice made by Jesus will be the *two parts* of the whole house of Jacob that *shall be cut off and die*. The *third part* who will choose the sacrifice of Jesus and receive him as their Lord and Savior will be brought *through the fire* and refined as silver is refined and tried as gold is tried. This trial by fire is the demand to take the mark of the Beast that will now be required by all in the empire the Antichrist is forming. Those who will not take the mark nor worship the image of the Beast will be beheaded for their witness of Jesus (Revelation 13:15, 20:4). It would appear, then, that the consequences of both groups are the same in that all of the house of Jacob are killed in some manner. But those who choose the sacrifice of animals will die the death of the transgressor (to be *cut off*); their destination is the eternal lake of fire (Revelation 20:15). Those who choose the sacrifice of Jesus are those seen gathering under the altar in heaven; they shall be kings and priests and will reign on earth with Jesus (Revelation 5:10). This wrath is Jacob's trouble.

The Wrath of the Antichrist vs. the Wrath of the Lamb

This wrath of Jacob's trouble is quite often claimed to be the wrath of the Antichrist or the wrath of Satan and not the wrath of God. Both the Antichrist and Satan do bring wrath upon Israel out of their hatred of God's chosen people. But it is God who said, *I will turn my hand upon the little ones*. Even though Satan, the Antichrist, and others in authority are the ones swinging the sword, so to speak, it is God who is in control, it is God's program, and it is God's wrath; the others are just the tools by which God delivers His wrath.

Continuing the Account of the Two Witnesses

11:⁴These are the two olive trees, and the two candlesticks standing before the God of the earth. ⁵And if any man will hurt them, fire proceeds out of their mouth, and devours their enemies: and if any man will hurt them, he must in this manner be killed.

⁶These have power to shut heaven, that it rain not in the days of their prophecy: and have power over waters to turn them to blood, and to smite the earth with all plagues, as often as they will.

⁷And when they shall have finished their testimony, the beast that ascends out of the bottomless pit shall make war against them, and shall overcome them, and kill them.

⁸And their dead bodies shall lie in the street of the great city, which spiritually is called Sodom and Egypt, where also our Lord was crucified. ⁹And they of the people and kindreds and tongues and nations shall see their dead bodies three days and an half, and shall not suffer their dead bodies to be put in graves. 10And they that dwell upon the earth shall rejoice over them, and make merry, and shall send gifts one to another; because these two prophets tormented them that dwelt on the earth.

¹¹And after three days and an half the spirit of life from God entered into them, and they stood upon their feet; and great fear fell upon them which saw them. ¹²And they heard a great voice from heaven saying unto them, Come up here. And they ascended up to heaven in a cloud; and their enemies beheld them.

¹³And the same hour was there a great earthquake, and the tenth part of the city fell, and in the earthquake were slain of men seven thousand: and the remnant were affrighted, and gave glory to the God of heaven.

(Revelation 11:4-13)

Even with this devastating event wrought by the wrath of the Lamb upon Jerusalem, the Jews still *gave glory to the God of heaven,* so they still had some positive relationship with God. This is in contrast to a later outpouring of the wrath of God where man *"blasphemed the name of God, which had power over these plagues: and they repented not to give him glory"*

(Revelation 16:8–9) —additional evidence of the absences of a great revival amongst mankind during the great *tribulation.*

A Vital Footnote to Chapter Eleven

[14] The second woe is past; and, behold, the third woe comes quickly.

(Revelation 11:14)

This is a curious verse, for it seems quite out of place here. The text describing the second woe was complete in 9:20, and the start of the third woe is still some distance in the text ahead. Its placement here may be a sort of bookmark, for the account of the wrath of the Lamb poured exclusively upon Israel skips over a significant, yet unrelated, event in the remainder of chapter 11 and continues the account of the wrath upon Israel in detail in chapters 12 and 13 as if these two chapters are a footnote to chapter 11. Thus, we temporally leave chapter 11 to look at that footnote.

The purpose for this footnote is, in part, for John, for the information contained in these two chapters is the prophetic message he is to deliver concerning the *many peoples, and nations, and tongues, and kings* who manifest the wrath of the Lamb that is poured upon the rebellious house of Jacob. Whether he was given more information, possibly from the messages of the *seven thunders,* which he was told not to write, we do not know. But it seems he would need more details about the many peoples and nations he is to tell of than what he could glean from these two chapters. But keep in mind that there is an open copy of the scroll that is in God's hand that is for the church to read. Therefore, this footnote is also for the church today, for we are now the prophets who are to tell of the *many peoples, and nations, and tongues, and kings* who will soon manifest that wrath again upon Israel. We now have the understanding of the words of Daniel to help us today to fill in the blanks of the story of these two chapters.

What we see in chapters 12 and 13 is the foundational outline of God's plan for dealing with the disobedience of the nation of Israel. The symbols used to tell the story, and the story itself, is interpreted in detail throughout *The Mystery of Prophecy* so only a minimum of verses of these two chapters will be addressed here in further detail.

¹And there appeared a great wonder in heaven; a woman clothed with the sun, and the moon under her feet, and upon her head a crown of twelve stars…³And there appeared another wonder in heaven; and behold a great red dragon, having seven heads and ten horns, and seven crowns upon his heads.

(Revelation 12:1, 3)

This vision is first and foremost about the *woman clothed with the sun*, the nation of Israel. We know of this *great red dragon*. It's the *many peoples, and nations, and tongues, and kings* that John is to present. The existence of the Red Dragon now exceeds 2,700 years.

²And she being with child cried, travailing in birth, and pained to be delivered…⁴And the dragon stood before the woman which was ready to be delivered, for to devour her child as soon as it was born. ⁵And she brought forth a man child, who was to rule all nations with a rod of iron: and her child was caught up unto God, and to his throne.

(Revelation 12:2, 4-5)

This speaks of Satan's adversarial relationship with God. In this vision seen by John, this adversarial relationship manifests itself through proxies. Satan and God do not battle face-to-face but act through man and, at times, angels. Here, God uses that adversarial nature of Satan who, in turn, uses the *many peoples, and nations, and tongues, and kings* of the empire of the Red Dragon to bring wrath upon the Woman; that is the underlying premise of the story that is told in the opening verses of the prophecy.

⁶And the woman fled into the wilderness, where she has a place prepared of God, that they should feed her there a thousand two hundred and threescore days.

(Revelation 12:6)

From the opening verses that presented the broad scope of God's plan for dealing with the disobedient Israelites, the text now begins to give some details of the means by which He will complete the plan. We see here God gathering the Jews back into the land of their forefathers from which they had been scattered. Once they are fully gathered, He will provide them protection *from the face of the serpent*, meaning Satan and his proxies, for a period of *a thousand two hundred and threescore days.*

During that time of Israel's tranquility, God will meet with them face-to-face and will bring His chosen people to a final point of decision.

> *⁷And there was war in heaven: Michael and his angels fought against the dragon; and the dragon fought and his angels, ⁸And prevailed not; neither was their place found any more in heaven. ⁹And the great dragon was cast out, that old serpent, called the Devil, and Satan, which deceives the whole world: he was cast out into the earth, and his angels were cast out with him.*
>
> *(Revelation 12:7-9)*

This is God putting Satan into a position where Satan will ramp up his persecution of the Jews from which *the woman [will flee] into the wilderness.* The Jews essentially began this flight back to their homeland in the late 1800s, which escalated during the 1940s. That flight is not yet complete. We see today the rise of anti-Semitism throughout the world, which may be the impetus for the remnant of the Jews to flee from where they have been scattered. Since the Woman's flight into the wilderness has begun, this war in heaven is a done deal.

> *¹⁰And I heard a loud voice saying in heaven, Now is come salvation, and strength, and the kingdom of our God, and the power of his Christ: for the accuser of our brethren is cast down, which accused them before our God day and night. ¹¹And they overcame him by the blood of the Lamb, and by the word of their testimony; and they loved not their lives unto the death. ¹² Therefore rejoice, you heavens, and you that dwell in them. Woe to the inhabiters of the earth and of the sea! for the devil is come down unto you, having great wrath, because he knows that he has but a short time.*
>
> *(Revelation 12:10-12)*

The *accuser* is Satan who had been before God continuously to this point telling of the sins of the people so as to tempt God into condemning them. Although this scene takes place in heaven, it depicts what is occurring on the land that is being redeemed for those who *overcame* Satan by the blood of the Lamb and by the word of their testimony and *loved not their lives unto the death* are the third part of Israel who will be refined by the fire of God's wrath. This message is, thus, for Israel. Because this voice John hears speaks of *our* brethren, this voice is likely the chorus of voices of the Raptured saints standing before God who are now proclaiming these Jews are their brothers in Christ.

> *[13] And when the dragon saw that he was cast unto the earth, he persecuted the woman which brought forth the man child. [14] And to the woman were given two wings of a great eagle, that she might fly into the wilderness, into her place, where she is nourished for a time, and times, and half a time, from the face of the serpent.*
>
> *(Revelation 12:13-14)*

This is essentially a repeat of the verses above where the Woman was to flee into the wilderness where she is to be protected for a period of a *thousand two hundred and threescore days*. But we learn several things from this repeated text:

- Because this story of the persecution of the Jews, their flight back to their homeland, and their protection there for a period of time is here told twice, these events are very important to God. Therefore, we need to pay special attention to them.
- Here we are actually told that the Jews flee back to their homeland due to the persecution of Satan. (That the wilderness they will flee into is the land of ancient Israel is proven in a later chapter, "The (non)Flight of the Woman".)
- The time of the protection of the Jews from *the face of the serpent* occurs for a period of time while they are in Israel.
- This time of protection of a *thousand two hundred and threescore days* is here defined as *a time, and times, and half a time*. This is three and a half years, a *time* being a year, and *times* being two years. This proves that the theory of "a day in prophecy always represents a year" is invalid;when a day is to represent a year, God will tell us, as He did in Numbers 14:34 and Ezekiel 4:6.

15And the serpent cast out of his mouth water as a flood after the woman, that he might cause her to be carried away of the flood. 16And the earth helped the woman, and the earth opened her mouth, and swallowed up the flood which the dragon cast out of his mouth. 17And the dragon was wroth with the woman, and went to make war with the remnant of her seed, which keep the commandments of God, and have the testimony of Jesus Christ.

(Revelation 12:15-17)

The *remnant* of Israel's seed is *the third* part of the Jewish population that will not be killed as transgressors. These *which keep the commandments of God* will be challenged by their new master to take the mark of the Beast. When they refuse, they will be beheaded (Revelation 20:4).

John is now given a look at the last set of events in this outline of God's plan for Israel:

1And I stood upon the sand of the sea, and saw a beast rise up out of the sea, having seven heads and ten horns, and upon his horns ten crowns, and upon his heads the name of blasphemy. 2And the beast which I saw was like unto a leopard, and his feet were as the feet of a bear, and his mouth as the mouth of a lion: and the dragon gave him his power, and his seat, and great authority.

3And I saw one of his heads as it were wounded to death; and his deadly wound was healed: and all the world wondered after the beast. 4And they worshipped the dragon which gave power unto the beast: and they worshipped the beast, saying, Who is like unto the beast? who is able to make war with him?

5And there was given unto him a mouth speaking great things and blasphemies; and power was given unto him to continue forty and two months. 6And he opened his mouthin blasphemy against God, to blaspheme his name, and his tabernacle, and them that dwell in heaven.

7aAnd it was given unto him to make war with the saints, and to overcome them…

(Revelation 13:1-7a)

John now sees the emergence of the Antichrist's empire, which is to complete the Lamb's wrath upon Israel as the last *forty and two months* of the Tribulation Period begin.

> *7b* *[A]nd power was given him over all kindreds, and tongues, and nations.*

> *(Revelation 13:7b)*

The *kindreds, and tongues, and nations* over which the Antichrist is now given power is *all* of the nations of the League of Ten; one of which he is king, three that he has conquered by force of arms, and six that willingly relinquished their nations to him. This is the full extent of the territory the Antichrist will rule. Going back to the beginning of verse 7—*And it was given unto him to make war with the saints, and to overcome them*—speaks then of just the believers in Christ within the lands of the empire he now controls.

> *8* *And all that dwell upon the earth shall worship him, whose names are not written in the book of life of the Lamb slain from the foundation of the world.*

> *(Revelation 13:8)*

It is difficult to say here as to just who *all that dwell upon the earth* really includes, as the Greek word used here is *gē*, which could be interpreted either as *earth* or as *land*. Because we are now dealing with two entities, Antichrist the man and Satan the spirit, which indwells within him, *the earth* could refer to either of two different realms of real estate. Because this portion of text is dealing with Israel, *the earth* could be limited to just *the land* of the empire in which Israel is a part. The worship of Satan may then be the religion of just the realm of the Antichrist. But *they* who *worshipped the dragon* could plausibly be *all the world*, "the earth" as we often call it, who has *wondered after the beast*. The Bible says of this time, *"Babylon the great"*, the world man has created with indifference toward God, *"is fallen, is fallen, and is become the habitation of devils, and the hold of every foul spirit"* (Revelation 18:2). Considering the spiritual state of man in the later days of the Tribulation, it is quite reasonable then to believe that *all that dwell upon [global] earth will worship Satan.*

⁹ If any man have an ear, let him hear. ¹⁰ He that leads into captivity shall go into captivity: he that kills with the sword must be killed with the sword. Here is the patience and the faith of the saints.

(Revelation 13:9-10)

God has taken His protective hand off the Jewish people during this time of wrath:

⁶ For I will no more pity the inhabitants of the land, says the Lord: but, lo, I will deliver the men every one into his neighbour's hand, and into the hand of his king: and they shall smite the land, and out of their hand I will not deliver them…⁹Then said I, I will not feed you: that that dies, let it die; and that that is to be cut off, let it be cut off… ¹¹ so the poor of the flock that waited upon me knew that it was the word of the Lord.

(Zachariah 10:6, 9, 11)

Here is the patience and the faith of those who will not worship the image of the beast.

¹¹ And I beheld another beast coming up out of the earth; and he had two horns like a lamb, and he spake as a dragon. ¹² And he exercises all the power of the first beast before him, and causes the earth and them which dwell therein to worship the first beast, whose deadly wound was healed. ¹³ And he does great wonders, so that he makes fire come down from heaven on the earth in the sight of men, ¹⁴ And deceives them that dwell on the earth by the means of those miracles which he had power to do in the sight of the beast; saying to them that dwell on the earth, that they should make an image to the beast, which had the wound by a sword, and did live. ¹⁵ And he had power to give life unto the image of the beast, that the image of the beast should both speak, and cause that as many as would not worship the image of the beast should be killed. ¹⁶ And he causes all, both small and great, rich and poor, free and bond, to receive a mark in their right hand, or in their foreheads: ¹⁷ And that no man might buy or sell, save he that had the mark, or the name of the beast, or the number of his name. ¹⁸ Here is wisdom. Let him that has understanding count the number of the beast: for it is the number of, a man; and his number is Six hundred threescore and six.

(Revelation 13:11-18)

This beast that John sees as *coming up out of the earth* could also be viewed as coming from *the land* that is the territory of the Antichrist's empire.

If this would be the correct viewpoint, it would confirm that this bureaucratic empire originates from within the territory ruled by the Antichrist.

> *15 And he had power to give life unto the image of the beast, that the image of the beast should both speak, and cause that as many as would not worship the image of the beast should be killed.*
>
> *(Revelation 13:15)*

It is one of the two leaders of this bureaucratic empire that *causes all, both small and great, rich and poor, free and bond, to receive a mark in their right hand, or in their foreheads.* The monetary system used by the Antichrist may be the same or similar monetary system used elsewhere in the world at the time, but the *all, both small and great,* applies only to those residing within the limited territory ruled by the Antichrist. It may be even limited to just the Jewish population of the empire as the yellow star of David was used in parts of Europe in the 1940s.

Returning to the Place of the Bookmark

We had been in chapter 11 looking at the angel's instructions to John to consider those in the Temple who were sacrificing the blood of animals while the Two Witnesses where outside the Temple gates telling of the sacrifice of the blood of Jesus when we were interrupted by the notice of the footnote of chapters 12 and 13.

That text focused narrowly upon Israel and the wrath of the lamb upon her people. As we now go back to complete chapter 11, our focus returns again to the broad view of the whole of the land that is being redeemed. We are still in the breaking of the seventh seal and the wrath of the Lamb, and are awaiting the coming of the third woe.

The Seventh Angel Sounds

We had been told earlier that in the days of the voice of the seventh angel, when he shall begin to sound, the mystery of God should be finished, as he has declared to his servants the prophets. We are now at that point where the text of the scroll begins to speak of events that complete the mystery of God.

The Saint's Proclamation

> *15And the seventh angel sounded; and there were great voices in heaven, saying, The kingdoms of this world are become the kingdoms of our Lord, and of his Christ; and he shall reign for ever and ever. 16And the four and twenty elders, which sat before God on their seats, fell upon their faces, and worshipped God, 17Saying, We give you thanks, O Lord God Almighty, which are, and were, and are to come; because you have taken to you your great power, and have reigned.*
>
> *(Revelation 11:15-17)*

Those *great voices,* now heard as the seventh angel sounds his trumpet, are of those standing before the throne of God who are represented here by the twenty-four elders. They are the ones proclaiming, *The kingdoms of this world are become the kingdoms of our Lord, and of his Christ.* They are the only ones in all of heaven to fall upon their faces and worship God as the title deed of this earth has now been redeemed by Jesus, as they alone validate this real estate transaction; this, in a way, is their victory also.

In the order of events, Jesus has not yet taken physical possession of the land being redeemed, but he now is the proprietor of that land. He now reigns, but the redemption story is not yet complete.

The Judgment Seat of Christ

> *18And the nations were angry, and your wrath is come, and the time of the dead, that they should be judged, and that you should give reward unto your servants the prophets, and to the saints, and them that fear your name, small and great; and should destroy them which destroy the earth.*
>
> *(Revelation 11:18)*

It is still those saints standing before the throne who are speaking here. The past tense tone used intimates that we now are well into the time of the wrath of the Lamb, which is here acknowledged by the nations.

The subject is the Judgment Seat of Christ, the time of rewards given to the saints.

The phrase *the time of the dead* is making a differentiation between those believers having been caught up to heaven (Raptured) before the start of the Tribulation Period and those who had ascended to heaven during the Tribulation Period. The Raptured saints include both the *"dead in Christ"* (a physical death) and those *"which are alive"* (who also are *in Christ*) who were caught up together with them (1 Thessalonians 4:16–17). The "Tribulation saints" on the other hand were all killed for their belief in Jesus; thus, they are differentiated as *the dead* spoken of here.

The Raptured saints appear to be petitioning Jesus for these Tribulation Saints to receive their reward just as they will. This petition would extend to all who will accept Jesus as Lord and Savior after the time of the Rapture. Other than the hundred forty and four thousand of the tribes of Israel and those who refuse to take the mark of the Beast who we know will die during the Tribulation Period, the Bible is silent concerning others who may come to Jesus during this time. It would be reasonable to believe that these unidentified believers would also now be dead, considering the circumstances of the time.

That *the time of the dead* is now at hand such *that [Jesus] should give reward unto [his] servants the prophets, and to the saints,* intimates that all those who would have received Jesus as Lord have now done so, and paid the price of death. There will be no others who will come to Jesus beyond this point in time.

> *19 And the temple of God was opened in heaven, and there was seen in his temple the ark of his testament: and there were lightnings, and voices, and thunderings, and an earthquake, and great hail.*
>
> *(Revelation 11:19)*

This is God's answer to their petition. Opening the Temple to show the *ark of his testament* is a sign to the saints that God's covenant is still in effect for those who believe in Him.

That these Tribulation Saints *should be judged,* as will the other saints, is a glorious event. The "Judgment Seat of Christ," often spoken of as the "Bēma Seat," is an English phrase that expresses the intent of Paul's use of the Greek word *bēma* in 2 Corinthians 5:9–10: *"⁹Wherefore we labor, that, whether present or absent, we may be accepted of him. ¹⁰For we must all appear before the judgment [bēma] seat of Christ; that every one may receive the things done in his body, according to that he has done, whether it be good or bad."* Paul uses many allusions to Greek athletic contests in the epistles so this *bēma* seat is in keeping with its original use among the Greeks as a place where rewards are given or lost depending on how one "runs the race" rather than a place where a ruler would sit to make decisions and pass sentence. While salvation is a gift given by grace, the Bible does speak of rewards given or lost on how one has used their life for the Lord. Paul said of this labor:

> *⁸ Now he that plants and he that waters are one: and every man shall receive his own reward according to his own labor. ⁹For we are laborers together with God: you are God's husbandry, you are God's building. ¹⁰According to the grace of God which is given unto me, as a wise masterbuilder, I have laid the foundation, and another builds thereon. But let every man take heed how he builds thereupon. ¹¹For other foundation can no man lay than that is laid, which is Jesus Christ. ¹²Now if any man build upon this foundation gold, silver, precious stones, wood, hay, stubble; ¹³Every man's work shall be made manifest: for the day shall declare it, because it shall be revealed by fire; and the fire shall try every man's work of what sort it is. ¹⁴If any man's work abide which he has built thereupon, he shall receive a reward. ¹⁵If any man's work shall be burned, he shall suffer loss: but he himself shall be saved; yet so as by fire.*
>
> *(1 Corinthians 3:8–15)*

The Hundred Forty and Four Thousand Redeemed

> *14: ¹And I looked, and, lo, a Lamb stood on the mount Sion, and with him an hundred forty and four thousand, having his Father's name written in their foreheads. ²And I heard a voice from heaven, as the voice of many waters, and as the voice of a great thunder: and I heard the voice of harpers harping with their harps: ³And they sung as it were a new song before the throne, and before the four beasts, and the elders: and no man could learn that song but the hundred and forty and four thousand, which were redeemed from the earth. ⁴These are they which were not defiled with [the] women; for they are virgins. These are they which follow the Lamb wheresoever he goes. These were redeemed from among men, being the first fruits unto God and*

to the Lamb. ⁵And in their mouth was found no guile: for they are without fault before the throne of God.

(Revelation 14:1-5)

This completes the account of the *hundred forty and four thousand* who were sealed early in the first half of the Tribulation Period with their Father's name. These were the first to respond to the message of the Two Witnesses; thus, they were *the firstfruits unto God and to the Lamb* as the spiritual blindness was lifted from the eyes of the Jews. They were *virgins,* meaning they were pure in spirit, *without fault before the throne of God,* for they were *not defiled with [the] women,* the world that is *Babylon the Great* of Revelation 17:5.

The time these hundred forty and four thousand will be seen in heaven with Jesus will be late in the last half of the Tribulation Period. Because they are seen together on Mount Zion, it can be presumed that every one of the hundred forty and four thousand have now been killed for the word of God. They will be killed during the same time period as those who will not take the mark of the Beast. The deaths of both of these groups of saints depict what has been occurring to those who are being redeemed who are on the land that also is being redeemed. But note that these hundred forty and four thousand will not be gathering under the altar in heaven at their death, as will those who will be beheaded for refusing to take the mark of the beast. Certainly, the hundred forty and four thousand would not take the mark if confronted, so there is something uniquely different between the two groups of martyrs. It appears that the hundred forty and four thousand will never be under the authority of the Antichrist and, thus, will not be confronted with the requirement to take the mark. This is to say that those martyrs gathering under the altar in heaven will be those living within the territory under the Antichrist's rule while the hundred forty and four thousand will be dispersed throughout the nations outside the rule of the Antichrist. (This is an indication that the Antichrist will not rule over all the earth.)

A Warning for Today's World

The verses we are about to read are not intended to be read by Jesus when he opens the sealed scroll in the hand of God. They are for those who now read this unsealed copy of that scroll. They are forewarning.

⁶And I saw another angel fly in the midst of heaven, having the everlasting gospel to preach unto them that dwell on the earth, and to every nation, and kindred, and tongue, and people, [7]Saying with a loud voice, Fear God, and give glory to him; for the hour of his judgment is come: and worship him that made heaven, and earth, and the sea, and the fountains of waters.

(Revelation 14:6-7)

It's as if these words were meant to be hidden from our understanding until this time, just as were the words of Daniel. If this world is not yet in this hour of judgment, we soon will be.

This angel does not preach the Gospel of Jesus; that is the responsibility of the believers. This is just God's way of saying that His word will be spread to *every nation, and kindred, and tongue, and people* before *the hour of his judgment* is complete; there will be no excuse for ignorance of God's Word when standing before Him in judgment.

[8]And there followed another angel, saying, Babylon is fallen, is fallen, that great city, because she made all nations drink of the wine of the wrath of her fornication.

(Revelation 14:8)

A simple statement of fact describing the spiritual state of affairs of today's world. Revelation 18:2 puts it this way: *"Babylon the great is fallen, is fallen, and is become the habitation of devils, and the hold of every foul spirit, and a cage of every unclean and hateful bird." Babylon* is this world man has created with his indifference toward the only true and living God. There is nothing new in this; man has been at enmity with God through all of history. But we are fast approaching the point where the society and institutions of man will be void of all vestiges of God and will become wholly *the habitation of devils and the hold of every foul spirit.*

That Babylon has *made all nations drink of the wine of the wrath of her fornication* is poetic language simply saying man's relationship with this spiritually defunct world is an illicit relationship that will exact a wrathful price for those who will not turn to Jesus.

[9]And the third angel followed them, saying with a loud voice, If any man worship the beast and his image, and receive his mark in his forehead, or in his hand, [10]The same shall drink of the wine of the wrath of God,

which is poured out without mixture into the cup of his indignation; and he shall be tormented with fire and brimstone in the presence of the holy angels, and in the presence of the Lamb: ¹¹And the smoke of their torment ascends up for ever and ever: and they have no rest day nor night, who worship the beast and his image, and whosoever receives the mark of his name.

(Revelation 14:9-11)

The scenario of the mark of the beast was extensively presented previously in the general outline of the message of the scroll in the hand of God. For this subject to appear again in the context of this portion of the scroll is a good illustration that this section of the text is indeed meant as a warning for the people today.

Not all will be forced by threat of death to take the mark of the Beast as the Antichrist will not rule the world. But there will be a considerable population within the nations of the Antichrist's empire that may be forced to take his mark, as the Jews will be. We have focused our attention on the Jews who will be threatened by pain of death to take the mark of the Beast and to worship his image, but God is also concerned for the souls of other ethnic groups within the empire. Thus, a warning to them also. And, there likely will be others outside the realm of the Antichrist's authority that may be inclined to worship him that would be wise to heed this warning.

¹²Here is the patience of the saints: here are they that keep the commandments of God, and the faith of Jesus. ¹³And I heard a voice from heaven saying unto me, Write, Blessed are the dead which die in the Lord from henceforth: Yea, says the Spirit, that they may rest from their labors; and their works do follow them.

(Revelation 14:12-13)

A simple statement of assurance: there is peace beyond the physical death of a believer in Jesus.

[14]And I looked, and behold a white cloud, and upon the cloud one sat like unto the Son of man, having on his head a golden crown, and in his hand a sharp sickle. [15]And another angel came out of the temple, crying with a loud voice to him that sat on the cloud, Thrust in your sickle, and reap: for the time is come for you to reap; for the harvest of the earth is ripe. [16]And he that sat on the cloud thrust in his sickle on the earth; and the earth was reaped.

(Revelation 14:14-16)

This is a depiction of the First Resurrection. In this context, to be resurrected is to be literally brought forth before the Father. The First Resurrection is one of type as well as one of time. As for type, the First Resurrection is a resurrection unto eternal life in the presence of God. It is the resurrection of those whose names are written in *"the book of life"* that John speaks of in Revelation 20:12.

Revelation 20:6 states of these believers, *"Blessed and holy is he that has part in the first resurrection: on such the second death has no power."* As for time, the First Resurrection is the first to occur, but includes a multitude of resurrections—the resurrection of Jesus and those of the Rapture are the most noted. Those who will be continuing to gather one by one under the sacrificial altar in heaven as they are beheaded for rejecting the mark of the Beast is an example of multiple resurrections through a period of time. The First Resurrection includes all those *in Christ* no matter when throughout time they are brought forth before God.

The one sitting on the cloud *like unto the Son of man* is Jesus. He is the one doing the harvesting of the righteous, just as we see in 1 Thessalonians 4:16–17: *"[16]For the Lord himself shall descend from heaven with a shout, with the voice of the archangel, and with the trump of God: and the dead in Christ shall rise first: [17]Then we which are alive and remain shall be caught up together with them in the clouds, to meet the Lord in the air."* The *crown* upon the reaper's head in John's vision is *stephanos* in Greek, a crown of victory rather that a crown of authority. The *sharp sickle* he holds is the symbol of harvest.

[17]And another angel came out of the temple which is in heaven, he also having a sharp sickle. [18]And another angel came out from the altar, which had power over fire; and cried with a loud cry to him that had the sharp

sickle, saying, Thrust in your sharp sickle, and gather the clusters of the vine of the earth; for her grapes are fully ripe. ¹⁹And the angel thrust in his sickle into the earth, and gathered the vine of the earth, and cast it into the great winepress of the wrath of God. ²⁰And the winepress was trodden without the city, and blood came out of the winepress, even unto the horse bridles, by the space of a thousand and six hundred furlongs.

(Revelation 14:17-20)

This is a depiction of the Second Resurrection. It's the second in type and the last to occur. This is a resurrection unto the second death, an eternal separation from God of all who reject Him.

The *great winepress of the wrath of God* is the Great White Throne Judgment of unbelievers described by John in Revelation 20:11–15:

¹¹ And I saw a great white throne, and him that sat on it, from whose face the earth and the heaven fled away; and there was found no place for them. ¹² And I saw the dead, small and great, stand before God; and the books were opened: and another book was opened, which is the book of life: and the dead were judged out of those things which were written in the books, according to their works. ¹³ And the sea gave up the dead which were in it; and death and hell delivered up the dead which were in them: and they were judged every man according to their works. ¹⁴ And death and hell were cast into the lake of fire. This is the second death. ¹⁵ And whosoever was not found written in the book of life was cast into the lake of fire.

The great mass of humanity that will appear before the *great white throne* and be judged in the *winepress of the wrath of God* is visualized by the extent of the blood that flows from that winepress.

Preparing for the Third Woe

15: ¹And I saw another sign in heaven, great and marvelous, seven angels having the seven last plagues; for in them is filled up the wrath of God.

(Revelation 15:1)

We return our focus again to the "description" of the real estate that is being redeemed with the breaking of the seven seals of the scroll held in the hand of God. The breaking of the seventh seal that announced the coming wrath of the Lamb upon this earth and its inhabitants now seems almost like ancient history in this running account of events in this redeeming process. The seventh trumpet of the seventh seal has now sounded, and we are about to see John's account of the third and last woe. This woe is the last of the wrath that will come upon this earth. This wrath is now spoken of as the wrath of God, not as the wrath of the Lamb.

The Victorious Martyred Redeemed

> *²And I saw as it were a sea of glass mingled with fire: and them that had gotten the victory over the beast, and over his image, and over his mark, and over the number of his name, stand on the sea of glass, having the harps of God. ³And they sing the song of Moses the servant of God, and the song of the Lamb, saying, Great and marvelous Lord, and glorify your name? for you only are holy: for all nations shall come and worship before you; for your judgments are made manifest.*
>
> *(Revelation 15:2-4)*

These who now sing the song of victory are those who had been gathering under the sacrificial altar in heaven as they were beheaded for the witness of Jesus. As they had cried out to God to avenge their blood, they were told to wait while the rest of their brethren were killed as they were should be fulfilled. The number of those who would not take the mark of the beast or worship him must now be complete, as they are now seen on what appears to be *a sea of glass mingled with fire*. This sea of glass may be the great laver of water that stood beside the altar of sacrifice that was at times spoken of *as the great sea*. This laver was used by those at the sacrificial altar to wash their hands before entering the Holy place. If this is so, it would indicate their presence before God.

The Third Woe

> *⁵And after that I looked, and, behold, the temple of the tabernacle of the testimony in heaven was opened: ⁶And the seven angels came out of the temple, having the seven plagues, clothed in pure and white linen, and having their breasts girded with golden girdles. ⁷And one of the four beasts gave unto the seven angels seven golden vials full of the wrath of God, who lives for ever*

and ever. [8]And the temple was filled with smoke from the glory of God, and from his power; and no man was able to enter into the temple, till the seven plagues of the seven angels were fulfilled. 16:[1]And I heard a great voice out of the temple saying to the seven angels, Go your ways, and pour out the vials of the wrath of God upon the earth.

(Revelation 15:5-8, 16:1)

These seven "angels" who will pour out the wrath of God upon the earth are not angelic beings but men redeemed from the earth. These angels, *messengers* in the original Greek, are *clothed in pure and white linen.* Only those redeemed by the blood of the Lamb are described with such apparel *"for the fine linen is the righteousness of saints" (Revelation 19:8).* And, *"the armies which were in heaven,"* those very same saints, will follow Jesus *"upon white horses, clothed in fine linen, white and clean" (Revelation 19:14)* into the battle of Armageddon. Further, it is *one of the four beasts,* one of the cherubim that represent the creation of the earth and all the creatures thereon, that give these seven "angels" the golden vials that are full of the wrath of God.

The First Vial is Poured Out

[2]And the first went, and poured out his vial upon the earth; and there fell a noisome and grievous sore upon the men which had the mark of the beast, and upon them which worshipped his image.

(Revelation 16:2)

Those who have the mark of the Beast are singled out for wrath. But why is such a qualifying statement as that given here even stated? All those who did not take the mark or did not worship his image have all been beheaded (Revelation 20:4)! If the Antichrist ruled the world, who else would there be but those who had the mark? Could it be that the Antichrist will not rule the world, leaving a third group of people unscathed by this wrath?

The Second Vial is Poured Out

[3]And the second angel poured out his vial upon the sea; and it became as the blood of a dead man: and every living soul died in the sea.

(Revelation 16:3)

The Third Vial is Poured Out

> *⁴And the third angel poured out his vial upon the rivers and fountains of waters; and they became blood. ⁵And I heard the angel of the waters say, You are righteous, O Lord, which are, and where, and shall be, because you have judged thus. ⁶For they have shed the blood of saints and prophets, and you have given them blood to drink; for they are worthy. ⁷And I heard another out of the altar say, Even so, Lord God Almighty, true and righteous are your judgments.*
>
> *(Revelation 16:4-7)*

The Fourth Vial is Poured Out

> *⁸And the fourth angel poured out his vial upon the sun; and power was given unto him to scorch men with fire. ⁹And men were scorched with great heat, and blasphemed the name of God, which had power over these plagues: and they repented not to give him glory.*
>
> *(Revelation 16:8-9)*

The Fifth Vial is Poured Out

> *¹⁰And the fifth angel poured out his vial upon the seat of the beast; and his kingdom was full of darkness; and they gnawed their tongues for pain, ¹¹And blasphemed the God of heaven because of their pains and their sores, and repented not of their deeds.*
>
> *(Revelation 16:10-11)*

Again, there is a qualifying statement as to who is to receive this wrath; it will be just the kingdom of the Beast that will *be full of darkness.* And, it will be only those in *his kingdom* that will *gnaw their tongues for pain.* If the Antichrist was ruling the world, the entire world would be in darkness, and people the world over would gnaw their tongues for pain. Why then would the text state that only that land that is the Antichrist's kingdom will be full of darkness?

The Sixth Vial is Poured Out

¹² And the sixth angel poured out his vial upon the great river Euphrates; and the water thereof was dried up, that the way of the kings of the east might be prepared.

(Revelation 16:12)

This is a preview of what is about to come, a mass movement of armies heading toward Israel.

¹³And I saw three unclean spirits like frogs come out of the mouth of the dragon, and out of the mouth of the beast, and out of the mouth of the false prophet. ¹⁴For they are the spirits of devils, working miracles, which go forth unto the kings of the earth and of the whole world, to gather them to the battle of that great day of God Almighty.

(Revelation 16:13-14)

And this is the driving force behind this mass movement of armies.

¹⁵Behold, I come as a thief. Blessed is he that watches, and keeps his garments, lest he walk naked, and they see his shame.

(Revelation 16:15)

This is Jesus speaking to those who read this unsealed copy of the seven-sealed scroll. His message is to many a warning, to others an encouragement.

He is speaking of the Rapture, the gathering of his bride (1 Thessalonians 4:15–17). Just as a thief does not nail a sign on your front door telling you when he will come to rob your house, neither does Jesus tell us when he will come to take those who believe in him. He is telling each and every one of us to be prepared *"for in such an hour as you think not the Son of man comes"* (Matthew 24:44). To those who had not received Jesus as Lord and Savior will on that day face the horrors described above; that is why *"now is the day of salvation"* (2 Corinthians 6:2). To those who have received Jesus, this is a message of encouragement to remain steadfast in the Lord and watch expectantly for his return.

¹⁶And he gathered them together into a place called in the Hebrew tongue Armageddon.

(Revelation 16:16)

This gathering of armies is in preparation for *the battle of that great day of God Almighty.* The location is considered to be the vast plain stretching out below the ancient city of Megiddo in northern Israel. This valley has been the site of many great battles throughout history.

The battle to be fought is not to take the city of Jerusalem or to conquer the Jews, as that is now history. This battle is to prevent Jesus from taking taking possession of that real estate that had been forfeited to Satan by sin.

The Seventh Vial is Poured Out

> *[17]And the seventh angel poured out his vial into the air; and there came a great voice out of the temple of heaven, from the throne, saying, It is done.*
>
> *[18]And there were voices, and thunders, and lightnings; and there was a great earthquake, such as was not since men were upon the earth, so mighty an earthquake, and so great. [19]And the great city was divided into three parts, and the cities of the nations fell: and great Babylon came in remembrance before God, to give unto her the cup of the wine of the fierceness of his wrath. [20]And every island fled away, and the mountains were not found. [21]And there fell upon men a great hail out of heaven, every stone about the weight of a talent: and men blasphemed God because of the plague of the hail; for the plague thereof was exceeding great.*
>
> *(Revelation 16:17-21)*

This is the scene of the sixth seal shown to those who were gathering under the altar in heaven that was God's answer to their cries to judge and avenge their blood on them who dwell on the earth.

Taking Possession of the Redeemed Land

> *[11]And I saw heaven opened, and behold a white horse; and he that sat upon him was called Faithful and True, and in righteousness he does judge and make war.*
>
> *[12]His eyes were as a flame of fire, and on his head were many crowns; and he had a name written, that no man knew, but he himself. [13]And he was clothed with a vesture dipped in blood: and his name is called The Word of God.*

¹⁴And the armies which were in heaven followed him upon white horses, clothed in fine linen, white and clean.

¹⁵And out of his mouth goes a sharp sword, that with it he should smite the nations: and he shall rule them with a rod of iron: and he treads the winepress of the fierceness and wrath of Almighty God. ¹⁶And he has on his vesture and on his thigh a name written, King Of Kings, And Lord Of Lords.

¹⁷And I saw an angel standing in the sun; and he cried with a loud voice, saying to all the fowls that fly in the midst of heaven, Come and gather yourselves together unto the supper of the great God; ¹⁸That you may eat the flesh of kings, and the flesh of captains, and the flesh of mighty men, and the flesh of horses, and of them that sit on them, and the flesh of all men, both free and bond, both small and great.

¹⁹And I saw the beast, and the kings of the earth, and their armies, gathered together to make war against him that sat on the horse, and against his army. ²⁰And the beast was taken, and with him the false prophet that wrought miracles before him, with which he deceived them that had received the mark of the beast, and them that worshipped his image. These both were cast alive into a lake of fire burning with brimstone.

²¹And the remnant were slain with the sword of him that sat upon the horse, which sword proceeded out of his mouth: and all the fowls were filled with their flesh.

In the later years you shall come into the land that is brought back from the sword.

—Ezekiel 38:8

16 Appendix: "The Old Testament Believers Join the Church."

17 Revelation 13:5 states that *"power was given unto him to continue forty and two months." Continue here means to maintain without interruption;* it does not mean *to carry on with some previous action.* Therefore, the 42-month period of uninterrupted rule is the last half of the Tribulation Period.

18 Meaning of the names: Juda - Now I will praise the Lord (Genesis 29:35) Reuben - yhvh has looked upon my affliction (Genesis 29:32) Gad - A troop comes (Genesis 30:11)
Aser - Happy, blessed (Genesis 30:13) Nephthalim - I have wrestled (Genesis 30:8) Manasseh - Made me forget all my toil (Genesis 41:51) Simeon - The Lord has heard (Genesis 29:33) Levi - Joined to me (Genesis 29:34) Issachar - Given my wages (Genesis 30:18) Zabulon - Endowed with a good gift (Genesis 30:20) Joseph - Add to me another son (Genesis 30:24) Benjamin - You shall have this son also. (Genesis 35:17–18)

19 We see no evidence of wrath or judgment from God upon the earth during the first half of the Tribulation Period. That does not mean there will be no "tribulation" during that time. There very well may be tribulation, even great tribulation, but it will be the acts conceived and wrought by man.

20 At in the original Greek, in in the KJV.

21 But *"it is not possible that the blood of bulls and of goats should take away sins" (Hebrews 10:4).*

22 For this reason, Jesus came as a man to take *"away the first [sacrifices under the Law], that he may establish the second…[by which]…we are sanctified through the offering of the body of Jesus Christ once for all" (Hebrews 10:9–10).*

23 Jesus entered Jerusalem on the day each household was to choose a lamb for their sacrifice on the evening of the Passover in remembrance of the lamb's blood that saved the Israelites in Egypt. Just as the people were to take the sacrificial lamb to themselves for four days to observe the lamb for its perfection, Jesus also presented

himself to the people for inspection as their sacrificial lamb. As the chosen Passover lambs were sacrificed in their proper time, so too did Jesus shed his blood for the salvation of believers five days after presenting

[24] Jerusalem, as spoken of in most of these passages, is representative of all the people of Israel.

[25] There always has been an outer court of the Gentiles outside the Temple gates. This court was not to be "measured" because the issue of Temple sacrifices will be strictly a Jewish issue having no relevance for the Gentiles.

[26] *[T]he beast that ascends out of the bottomless pit* is put in the future tense here so as to identify Satan as the one who will kill the Two Witnesses. This is in reference to Revelation 17:8: *"The beast that you saw was, and is not; and shall ascend out of the bottomless pit, and go into perdition."*

CHAPTER EIGHT
Back from the Sword

God has said:

[17]When the house of Israel dwelt in their own land, they defiled it by their own way and by their doings: their way was before me as the uncleanness of a removed woman. [18]Wherefore I poured my fury upon them for the blood that they had shed upon the land, and for their idols wherewith they had polluted it: [19]And I scattered them among the heathen, and they were dispersed through the countries: according to their way and according to their doings I judged them.

(Ezekiel 36:17–19)

[20]And the heathen shall know that the house of Israel went into captivity for their iniquity: because they trespassed against me, therefore hid I my face from them, and gave them into the hand of their enemies: so fell they all by the sword.

(Ezekiel 39:23)

[21]But I had pity for mine holy name, which the house of Israel had profaned among the heathen, wherever they went. [22]Therefore say unto the house of Israel, thus says the Lord God; I do not this for your sakes, O house of Israel, but for my holy name's sake, which you have profaned among the heathen, where you went. [23]And I will sanctify my great name, which was profaned among the heathen, which you have profaned in the midst of them; and the heathen shall know that I am the Lord, says the Lord God, when I shall be sanctified in you before their eyes. [24]For I will take you from among the heathen, and gather you out of all countries, and will bring you into your own land.

(Ezekiel 36:21–24)

A Wound by the Sword

Throughout the period of subjugation by this series of Gentile empires the nation of Israel still lived. However, in AD 135, Rome crushed a Jewish rebellion for independence that put a pause to the redemption of His chosen people. A Roman army of twelve legions destroyed Jerusalem, and 50 fortified towns and 985 villages were razed.[27] The majority of the Jewish population was killed, exiled, or sold into slavery. The names Judah and Israel where wiped off the map and replaced with Syria Palæstina after the Philistines, the ancient enemies of the Jews.[28] Jerusalem was reestablished as the pagan colony of Aelia Capitolina, and Jews were forbidden from entering the city on pain of death. Thus, the nation of Israel was "wounded to death" by the Roman sword—every part of *Judah, Israel, and Jerusalem* ceased to exist, and the remnant of Jacob was scattered throughout the world. What had been the territory of *Judah, Israel, and Jerusalem* became a part of other empires after Rome, such as the Ottoman and the British Empires. However, none of those after Rome appears as a head of the Red Dragon as there was no Israel; the formation of the League of Ten was therefore held in abeyance.

The Resurrection of the Land That Was Israel

And of the land that was defiled, God said:

> *[1]Son of man, prophesy unto the mountains of Israel, and say, You mountains of Israel, hear the word of the Lord: [2]Thus says the Lord God; Because the enemy has said against you, Aha, even the ancient high places are ours in possession: [3]Therefore prophesy and say, Thus says the Lord God; Because they have made you desolate, and swallowed you up on every side, that you might be a possession you are taken up in the lips of talkers, and are an infamy of the people: [4]Therefore, you mountains of Israel, hear the word of the Lord God; Thus says the Lord God to the mountains, and to the hills, to the rivers, and to the valleys, to the desolate wastes, and to the cities that are forsaken, which became a prey and derision to the residue of the heathen that are round about….[8]O mountains of Israel, you shall shoot forth your branches, and yield your fruit to my people of Israel; for they are at hand to come. [9]For, behold, I am for you, and I will turn unto you, and you shall be tilled and sown: [10]And I will multiply men upon you, all the house of Israel, even all of it: and the cities shall be*

inhabited, and the wastes shall be built…. ³⁴And the desolate land shall be tilled, whereas it lay desolate in the sight of all that passed by. ³⁵And they shall say, This land that was desolate is become like the garden of Eden; and the waste and desolate and ruined cities are become fenced, and are inhabited. ³⁶Then the heathen that are left round about you shall know that I the Lord build the ruined places, and plant that that was desolate: I the Lord have spoken it, and I will do it.

(Ezekiel 36:1–4, 8–10, 34–36)

The Resurrection of the People That Was Israel

God also said to the mountains of Israel:

I will cause men to walk upon you, even my people Israel; and they shall possess you, and you shall be their inheritance

(Ezekiel 36:12)

And He said of His people:

¹²I will open your graves, and cause you to come up out of your graves, and bring you into the land of Israel. 13And you shall know that I am the Lord, when I have opened your graves, O my people, and brought you up out of your graves, 14And shall put my spirit in you, and you shall live, and I shall place you in your own land: then shall you know that I the Lord have spoken it, and performed it….²¹Behold, I will take the children of Israel from among the heathen, where they be gone, and will gather them on every side, and bring them into their own land: ²²And I will make them one nation in the land upon the mountains of Israel; and one king shall be king to them all: and they shall be no more two nations, neither shall they be divided into two kingdoms any more at all….²⁵And they shall dwell in the land that I have given unto Jacob my servant, wherein your fathers have dwelt; and they shall dwell therein.

(Ezekiel 37:12–14, 21–22, 25)

The Deadly Wound Healed

On the 14th of May 1948, Israel's "deadly wound was healed" as the twelve tribes of Jacob together proclaimed the resurrection of the nation of Israel. God had said of this day, *"⁷Before she travailed, she brought forth; before her pain came, she was delivered of a man child. ⁸Who has heard such a thing? who has seen such things? Shall the earth be made to bring forth in one day? or shall a nation be born at once? for as soon as Zion travailed, she brought forth her children"* (Isaiah 66:7–8).

First to come under the rule of this nation that was *"brought back from the sword"* (Ezekiel 38:8) were the *"tents of Judah,"* the land outside the old city walls of Jerusalem so that *"the glory of the house of David and the glory of the inhabitants of Jerusalem [would] not magnify themselves against Judah"* (Zechariah 12:7). But on the 7th of June 1967, Israel retook the old city, *"and Jerusalem [was] inhabited again in her own place, even in Jerusalem"* (Zechariah 12:6). Thus, *Judah, Israel, and Jerusalem* was again complete. It is now possible for Israel to become a part of the League of Ten to begin the healing of the spirit of the people of Israel.

And the king shall do according to his will; and he shall exalt himself, and magnify himself above every god, and shall speak marvelous things against the God of gods, and shall prosper till the indignation be accomplished: for that that is determined shall be done.

—Daniel 11:36

27 http://en.wikipedia.org/wiki/Bar_Kokhba_revolt 11/6/2010.
28 Ibid.

CHAPTER NINE
The King of the North

The most definitive statements of the origin and the identification of the Antichrist are recorded in the eleventh chapter of Daniel. Here, Daniel records in great detail a running account of a conflict between two kings, the king of the north and the king of the south. The account of these two kings begins in 305 BC, but does not end until the return of Jesus. This vision given to Daniel is for Israel, for the Scripture speaks of *"what shall befall your people in the later days" (Daniel 10:14).* Yet, this vision is for the entire world for all nations will come to war at the command of this king of the north.

Pay Attention!

The account of the vision itself of the conflict between these two kings is given in the eleventh chapter of Daniel, but a prelude of considerable significance to this vision is given in the tenth chapter. There, an account unique in the Scriptures tells of the attempt of Satan to keep a message sent by God from being delivered to a mortal on earth who is seeking an answer from God.

This account gives us a wide-eyed view of very literal spiritual kingdoms well populated with fallen angels that exist between heaven and earth.

"In the third year of Cyrus king of Persia a thing was revealed unto Daniel" (Daniel 10:1). Daniel did not understand this revelation when he first received it, so he went before God seeking the understanding. *"In those days I Daniel was mourning three full weeks. ³I ate no pleasant bread, neither came flesh nor wine in my mouth, neither did I anoint myself at all, till three whole weeks were fulfilled" (vv. 2–3). After these twenty-one days of seeking an answer from God, "a certain man clothed in linen" (v. 5)* came to Daniel in a vision. This messenger spoke to Daniel, saying:

[11]O Daniel, a man greatly beloved, understand the words that I speak unto you, and stand upright: for unto you am I now sent…[12]Fear not, Daniel: for from the first day that you did set your heart to understand, and to chasten yourself before your God, your words were heard, and I am come for your words.

[13] But the prince of the kingdom of Persia withstood me one and twenty days: but, lo, Michael, one of the chief princes, came to help me; and I remained there with the kings of Persia. [14] Now I am come to make you understand what shall befall your people in the latter days: for yet the vision is for many days…[20] Then said he, Know you wherefore I come unto you? and now will I return to fight with the prince of Persia: and when I am gone forth, lo, the prince of Grecia shall come. [21] But I will show you that which is noted in the scripture of truth: and there is none that holds with me in these things, but Michael your prince.

(Daniel 10:11–15, 20–21)

Satan appears to be doing his best to keep the understanding of this revelation from Daniel. There is therefore something here of considerable concern to Satan that he does not want to be known. The reason for Satan's angst is that this revelation identifies the Antichrist as much as God will allow known before his revealing at the time of the Tribulation. For God to include this unique account, He is telling us to "pay attention to this," for He deems the understanding of this revelation to be of considerable importance.

The Three Kings of Persia

"And now will I show you the truth. Behold, there shall stand up yet three kings in Persia; and the fourth shall be far richer than all; and by his strength through his riches he shall stir up all against the realm of Grecia" (Daniel 11:2). There were to be three kings to follow Cyrus II (the Great) until a king *far richer than all* was to come to the throne of the Medo-Persian Empire. The three kings to follow Cyrus were Cambyses II, who ruled from 529 to 522 BC, Pseudo-Smerdis, who ruled in 522 BC, and Darius I, who ruled from 522 to 486 BC.

Cambyses II was the elder son of Cyrus the Great. He had his younger brother Bardiya (Smerdis) killed, apparently to protect his throne while he was invading Egypt.[22] However, an impostor who bore the likeness of Smerdis declared himself king while Cambyses was in Egypt. Cambyses died on his return home to deal with this "Pseudo-Smerdis." The impostor was murdered after a reign of eight months.[30] Darius I, later called the Great, one of the princes of the royal family and a leading general of Cambyses' army, was then proclaimed the rightful heir to the Medo-Persian throne.

The Fourth King of Persia

The fourth king from Cyrus the Great was Xerxes I, the eldest son of Darius I, who ruled the empire from 486 to 465 BC. Xerxes I was the richest and most powerful of Persian kings[31] and the one who was to *stir up all against the realm* of *Grecia*. He crossed the Hellespont (Dardanelles) and invaded Greece with a combined army and navy of 2,641,000 men.32 The invasion by land was reasonably successful at first with northern Greece falling to the invaders. But the Persian fleet was defeated at the battle of Salamis in 480 BC, and the tide of the invasion was turned. In time, the smaller but more disciplined Greek military forces prevailed.

From there, the vision skips over the remaining kings of Medo-Persia and introduces the king of the Grecian Empire.

A Mighty King, Alexander the Great

"And a mighty king shall stand up, that shall rule with great dominion, and do according to his will" (Daniel 11:3). This *mighty king* is Alexander III (the Great). Alexander the Great came to the throne of Macedonia when his father, Philip II, was murdered.

The small country of Macedonia had become a major power amongst the Greek city-states under Philip II who had a desire to destroy the great Persian Empire to the east that was the only significant threat to his rising power. Alexander inherited that plan and in 334 BC crossed the Hellespont leading forty thousand Greek troops and confronted the Persians head on. He conquered Asia Minor, then captured the great Phoenician city of Tyre in 332 BC, and by 331 BC occupied Egypt, a Medo-Persian province. He then turned east and took the Persian capital city of Babylon. Just three years later, he was in India, having conquered all in route.

His Kingdom Shall Be Broken

"And when he shall stand up, his kingdom shall be broken, and be divided toward the four winds of heaven; and not to his posterity, nor according to his dominion which he ruled: for his kingdom shall be plucked up, even for others beside those"

(Daniel 11:4). Alexander the Great died in 323 BC at the peak of his power, and his great kingdom was divided.

The monarchy was at first officially represented by two kings appointed in his place, Philip III Arrhidaeus, his mentally retarded half-brother, and Alexander IV, a son born after his death.[33] In 317 BC, Philip III Arrhidaeus was killed by Olympias, the mother of Alexander the Great, out of a desire to obtain the throne for her grandchild Alexander IV.[34] About 311 BC, King Alexander IV was put to death by Cassander, one of the many trying to grab a piece of Alexander's broken empire. Thus, Alexander's empire was being divided, but *not to his posterity*.

At the death of Alexander the Great, the central government was more in the control of three principal men other than the two young kings: Antipater, Alexander's viceroy in Europe, Perdiccas, Alexander's second-in-command, and Craterus, a military officer who now became the guardian of king Philip III Arrhidaeus.[35] Perdiccas was killed in a Macedonian mutiny, and Craterus was killed in battle. Antipater, who was then made sole guardian and viceroy of the two young kings, Philip III and Alexander IV, died in 319 BC. Therefore, neither was Alexander's kingdom divided *according to his dominion which he ruled*.

Four New Kingdoms Verse

Verse 4 states that Alexander's kingdom was to be *divided toward the four winds of heaven…for his kingdom shall be plucked up, even for others beside those* mentioned above. Many had set themselves up as local rulers resulting in the War of the Successors that raged on for many years seeing the passing of most of the original rulers. The War of the Kings at Ipsus in 301 BC eliminated the last potential re-unifier of Alexander's kingdom, and the old territory settled into four new kingdoms as shown in map 9.1.

Map 9.1. The kingdoms of Alexander's
successors after the War of the
Kings at Ipsus in 301 BC.

The Point of All This…

From this point on, Daniel's vision focuses on two of the four kings of these new kingdoms and on their successors. "The king of the north" refers to the ruler of the Seleucid Empire, Seleucus I and those who were to follow him to the throne of the Seleucid Empire. "The king of the south" refers to the ruler of the Ptolemaic Empire, Ptolemy I and those who were to follow him to the throne of the Ptolemaic Empire.

The terms north and south are used in regard to Israel, the Seleucid Empire being to the north and the Ptolemaic Empire to the south. The nation of Israel (more correctly, the remnant of the old kingdom of Judah) came under the control of one or the other of these two empires until 200 BC when Israel became a permanent part of the Seleucid Empire.

The fulfillment of the vision specific to the king of the north and the king of the south began in 305 BC at the beginning of the reign of these two kings and continues into our future. That part of the vision that has been fulfilled took place over a period of 141 years. Then, as if time did not exist, the narration continues into events not yet fulfilled as if speaking of the same king it was speaking of in 164 BC.

The King of the South

"And the king of the south shall be strong, and one of his princes; and he shall be strong above him, and have dominion; and his dominion shall be a great dominion" (*Daniel 11:5*). The first king of the south was Ptolemy I Soter *one of his,* Alexander's, generals.

The King of the North

Ptolemy I *shall be strong above him,* a reference to the first king of the north, Seleucus I Nicator, who had been a subordinate military officer under Ptolemy I.[36]

They Shall Join Themselves Together

> *"And at the end of years they shall join themselves together; for the king's daughter of the south shall come to the king of the north to make an agreement: but she shall not retain the power of the arm: neither shall he stand, nor his arm: but she shall be given up, and they that brought her, and he that begat her, and he that strengthened her in these times".*

> (*Daniel 11:6*)

The phrase *they shall join themselves together* refers back to verse 5 and reinforces the conclusion that verse 5 speaks of the king of the south and the king of the north, for it is these two kings who *shall join themselves together when the king's daughter of the south shall come to the king of the north to make an agreement.* This agreement was the marriage of Berenice, the daughter of Ptolemy II Philadelphus, the second king of Egypt, who married Antiochus II Theos, the third king of Syria, thereby joining the two kings together. Antiochus II divorced his wife Laodice to marry Berenice. Laodice stirred up her friends against Antiochus II and caused Berenice and her attendants to be put to death. Antiochus II reinstated Laodice, who then poisoned him and brought her son Seleucus II Callinicus to the throne of the Seleucid Empire.

The King of the South Attacks the King of the North…

"But out of the branch of her roots shall one stand up in his estate, which shall come with an army, and shall enter into the fortress of the king of the north, and shall deal against them, and shall prevail" (*Daniel 11:7*). Ptolemy III

Euergetes I, the brother of Berenice, *the branch of her roots*, next came to the throne of Egypt. (*His estate* refers back to Ptolemy II.) Ptolemy III invaded Syria and defeated Seleucus II Callinicus, the fourth king of the north.

"And he shall also carry captives into Egypt their gods, with their princes, and with their precious vessels of silver and gold; and he shall continue more years than the king of the north" (Daniel 11:8). This speaks of the spoils of Ptolemy's victory. He did *continue more years than the king of the north*, reigning four years longer than Seleucus II.

"So the king of the south shall come into his kingdom, and shall return into his own land" (Daniel 11:9). This affirms that Ptolemy III did invade Syria then return to Egypt.

So, the King of the North Attacks the King of the South…

"But his sons shall be stirred up, and shall assemble a multitude of great force: and one shall certainly come, and overflow, and pass through; then shall he return, and be stirred up, even to his fortress" (Daniel 11:10). His sons refers back to verse 9 and to the king into whose kingdom the king of the south shall enter, since these are the sons of Seleucus II. Seleucus III Ceraunus, and Antiochus III Magnus assembled an army to avenge themselves on Egypt, but Seleucus III died before an invasion was attempted. Antiochus III later led an army into Egypt, fulfilling the prophecy that only *one shall certainly come, and overflow, and pass through*.

The King of the South Triumphs

"And the king of the south shall be moved with choler, and shall come forth and fight with him, even with the king of the north: and he shall set forth a great multitude; but the multitude shall be given into his, hand" (Daniel 11:11). Ptolemy IV Philopater was *the king of the south that [came] forth [to] fight … the king of the north. He [that] shall set forth a great multitude* is in reference to Antiochus III who came with an army of seventy-five thousand men against Ptolemy IV. *But the multitude shall be given into his hand.* This *multitude* of soldiers was defeated by Ptolemy IV at Raphia near Egypt in 217 BC.[37]

"And when he has taken away the multitude, his heart shall be lifted up; and he shall cast down many ten thousands: but he shall not be strengthened by it" (Daniel 11:12). Ptolemy IV was unable to take advantage of his victory and signed an ignoble peace with Antiochus III.

The King of the North Attacks the King of the South, Again

"For the king of the north shall return, and shall set forth a multitude greater than the former, and shall certainly come after certain years with a great army and with much riches" (Daniel 11:13). Antiochus III was to again attack Egypt in 201 BC.

"And in those times there shall many stand up against the king of the south: also the robbers of your people shall exalt themselves to establish the vision; but they shall fall" (Daniel 11:14). The *many [that shall] stand up against the king of the south* speaks of the alliance Antiochus III formed with Philip III of Macedonia for this attack on Egypt. Apostate Jews, *the robbers of your people,* joined Antiochus to *establish the vision,* which speaks to the Jew's intent to throw off the yoke of the Gentiles. *But they shall fall*–Israel, rather than throwing off the Gentile rule of Egypt, ended up now under Syrian rule.[38]

"So the king of the north shall come, and cast up a mount, and take the most fenced cities: and the arms of the south shall not withstand, neither his chosen people, neither shall there be any strength to withstand" (Daniel 11:15). Antiochus III, *the king of the north,* utterly defeated Ptolemy V Epiphanes, the fifth king of the south.

"But he that comes against him shall do according to his own will, and none shall stand before him: and he shall stand in the glorious land, which by his hand shall be consumed" (Daniel 11:16). *He that comes against him* is the king of the north that came against the king of the south. *He [that] shall stand in the glorious land* speaks of Antiochus III, the king of the north, for control of the nation of Israel, *the glorious land,* transferred from Egypt to Syria after the Battle of Panium in 200 BC.

"He shall also set his face to enter with the strength of his whole kingdom, and upright ones with him; thus shall he do: and he shall give him the daughter of women, corrupting her; but she shall not stand on his side, neither for him" (Daniel 11:17).

Antiochus III gave his daughter, Cleopatra Syra, in marriage to Ptolemy V in a further effort to control Egypt. But she shall not stand on his side, supporting her husband rather than her father.

Then Invades Greece

"After this shall he turn his face unto the isles, and shall take many: but a prince for his own behalf shall cause the reproach offered by him to cease; without his own reproach he shall cause it to turn upon him" (Daniel 11:18). Antiochus III then turned toward Greece. He took the isles of the Aegean Sea and continued across the Hellespont. Greece was now allied with Rome, the rising power in the West. The Roman army utterly defeated Antiochus at the battle of Magnesia in late 190 BC.

"Then he shall turn his face toward the fort of his own land: but he shall stumble and fall, and not be found" (Daniel 11:19). Antiochus III, returning to Syria, was forced to levy taxes against the temple states in order to pay the tribute demanded by Rome as part of the price of peace. He was killed in 187 BC by an angry populace in an attempt to "collect" those taxes from the Temple of Bell in Elam.39

So Another King of the North

"Then shall stand up in his estate a raiser of taxes in the glory of the kingdom: but within a few days he shall be destroyed, neither in anger, nor in battle" (Daniel 11:20).

Seleucus IV Philopator succeeded his father Antiochus III as king of the north. Seleucus IV was a *raiser of taxes* in order to obtain tribute to pay Rome. In an effort to collect money, he sent his minister Heliodorus to Jerusalem to seize the Temple treasury. On his return, Seleucus IV was assassinated by Heliodorus.

A Pattern of Note

Daniel's prophecies are for the nation of Israel. Thus, when a Gentile nation appears in his prophecies it is always in connection with some interaction with Israel. We therefore should have seen some evidence of interaction between these two kings and the nation of Israel. However, this running conflict between the king of the north and the king of the south, as we have seen thus far, appears to have essentially nothing to do with Israel. Yet, therein lies the answer to one of the mysteries of prophecy.

The running conflict between the king of the north and the king of the south establishes a pattern that is most critical to the intent of the vision. What we were to learn from what has been presented thus far is that throughout the whole of this vision our focus is to be on the king of the north and the king of the south. Further, the message of the vision is to be understood by focusing on the one who is in *the position of* the king of the north. What we are about to see is that this has everything to do with today's Israel.

Yet Another King of the North

"And in his estate shall stand up a vile person, to whom they shall not give the honor of the kingdom: but he shall come in peaceably, and obtain the kingdom by flatteries" (Daniel 11:21). In his estate, that of Seleucus IV, stood up Antiochus IV Epiphanes. *They [that] shall not give the honor of the kingdom* were the rightful heirs to the Seleucid Empire. At the death of Seleucus IV, Antiochus, the heir to the throne of Syria was made king of the north. This Antiochus was the younger son of Seleucus IV and the nephew of Antiochus IV. Since Antiochus was about four or five years old, the throne was likely entrusted to the Queen Dowager.

He shall come in peaceably and obtain the kingdom by flatteries. Antiochus IV, who had been absent the country at the time of the death of Seleucus, now entered Syria with an army and a crown supplied by Eumenes II of Pergamum, a traditional enemy of Syria.[40] Before Antiochus IV and his foreign army came to open war with the government of Syria over the throne, an arrangement was found to which both sides could agree. Antiochus IV was accepted as king of the Seleucid Empire on the condition that he adopt the young Antiochus and share the throne with him.[41]

"And with the arms of a flood shall they be overflown from before him, and shall be broken; yea, also the prince of the covenant" (Daniel 11:22). This verse speaks of the destruction of the rightful government of the empire by Antiochus IV by threat of force. *The covenant* was the agreement made with Antiochus IV where he was to jointly rule with the young Antiochus, the prince of the covenant. Thus, Antiochus IV established himself on the throne.

"And after the league made with him he shall work deceitfully: for he shall come up, and become strong with a small people" (Daniel 11:23). Antiochus IV ruled jointly with the young Antiochus for nearly five years, then had Antiochus killed.[42] Therefore, *the honor of the kingdom,* the throne, was not given to Antiochus IV but was taken by him through threat of force and murder.

"He shall enter peaceably even upon the fattest places of the province; and he shall do that which his fathers have not done, nor his father's father; he shall scatter

among them the prey, and spoil, and riches: yea, and he shall forecast his devices against the strong holds, even for a time" (Daniel 11:23). This is a synopsis of the relationship of Antiochus IV Epiphanes with Israel. On his first entry into Jerusalem, Antiochus did *enter peaceably*. He was *"honorably received"* and *"was brought in with torchlight, and with great shoutings"* (2 Maccabees 4:22). Later, he *"took the city by force of arms…and there were destroyed within the space of three whole days fourscore thousand, whereof forty thousand sold than slain. Yet was he not content with this, but presumed to go into the most holy temple of all the world…and taking the holy vessels with polluted hands…he gave them away"* (2 Maccabees 5:11–16). Thus, he did *that which his fathers have not done, nor his father's father*—he sold the Jews as slaves and gave away the holy vessels of the temple, *scatter(ing) among them the prey, and spoil, and riches.*

Two years later, Antiochus, *"sent his chief collector of tribute unto the cities of Judah, who came unto Jerusalem with a great multitude, and spoke peaceable words unto them, but all was deceit: for when they had given him credence, he fell suddenly upon the city, and smote it very sore, and destroyed much people of Israel. And when he had taken the spoils of the city, he set it on fire, and pulled down the houses and walls thereof on every side…Then builded they the city of David with a great and strong wall, and with mighty towers, and made it a strong hold for them"* (1 Maccabees 1:29–33). Thus, Antiochus *forecast his devices against the strong holds of Israel.*

The King of the North Attacks the King of the South…

"And he shall stir up his power and his courage against the king of the south with a great army; and the king of the south shall be stirred up to battle with a very great and mighty army; but he shall not stand: for they shall forecast devices against him" (Daniel 11:25). Antiochus IV invaded Egypt in 170 BC. This was his first invasion of Egypt.

Initiated by the King of the South

Although the Scripture states in verse 25 that the king of the north *shall stir up his power and his courage against the king of the south*, it is important to note that this war was not started by Antiochus IV but by the king of the south. The Seleucid Empire had taken the area of Palestine from the Ptolemaic Empire after the battle of Panium in 200 BC, some thirty years earlier. Egypt had not forgotten this loss and now prepared the army to recover the lost territory.[43] Antiochus IV, however, was aware of Egypt's intentions and came against the king of the south before the southern army could even leave Egyptian soil.[44] The phrase *he shall not stand* refers to the king of the south, for the ensuing battle was a decisive victory for Antiochus IV.

"Yea, they that feed of the portion of his meat shall destroy him, and his army shall overflow: and many shall fall down slain" (Daniel 11:26). Early in his reign, Antiochus IV had sent Apollonius to Egypt to represent his interests there. Apollonius, residing in Egypt, was aware of Egypt's preparation for the invasion of Syria and forewarned Antiochus.[45]

This enabled Antiochus to prepare a preemptive strike, which was successful. *They that feed on a portion of his meat* that had a significant part in the defeat the king of the south is most likely referring to Apollonius. The phrase *his army shall overflow* is most likely speaking of Apollonius as representative of the king of the north.

The King of the North vs. the King of the South

"And both these kings' hearts shall be to do mischief, and they shall speak lies at one table; but it shall not prosper: for yet the end shall be at the time appointed" (Daniel 11:27). Immediately after his victory, Antiochus IV concluded an armistice with Ptolemy VI Philometor, the one now recognized as the king of the south. Ptolemy VI was yet a young man, just coming of age at this time. The real power of the throne appeared to be in the hands of two of his soldiers, Comanus and Cineas.[46] Immediately after the expiration of the truce, Antiochus gained possession of an important fortress at Pelusium, then advanced his army across the Delta toward Alexandria. Ptolemy was now forced to reconcile with Antiochus, and the two did meet to negotiate peace. Historians have differing opinions as to the details of the negotiations, but it is certain that Antiochus procrastinated in his deliberations, leaving the Egyptians completely in the dark as to his real intentions. All the while, he advanced his army steadily toward Alexandria. The result of all this was that Antiochus usurped the position as tutor of the young king Ptolemy. He therefore controlled Egypt without actually annexing it, thereby not risking a challenge to his authority in Egypt by Rome, the rising power in the region.[47]

But it shall not prosper is a reference to the agreement between Antiochus IV and Ptolemy VI. In time, the citizens of Egypt rebelled against this puppet rule, and a faction established a new government, appointing Cleopatra II, the sister of Ptolemy VI Philometor, and his brother, the younger Ptolemy, joint rulers.[48] The result was a war between the two Egyptian governments, the two younger rulers in Alexandria against Ptolemy VI and his ally Antiochus IV, who controlled most of the country outside of the city. Antiochus attacked Alexandria, but did not succeed in conquering it. He proclaimed victory, however, and then returned to Syria with his army. In the meantime, the two younger rulers in Alexandria had sent an embassy to Rome for help. The result of that call for help is given to us in verse 30.

"Then shall he return into his land with great riches; and his heart shall be against the holy covenant; and he shall do exploits, and return to his own land" (Daniel 11:28). In route back to Syria, Antiochus invaded Jerusalem *"and entered proudly into the sanctuary, and took away the golden altar, and the candlestick of light, and all the vessels thereof … He took also the silver and the gold, and the hidden treasures which he found. And when he had taken all away, he went into his own land, having made a great massacre, and spoken very proudly"* (1 Maccabees 1:21–24). (It should be noted that Israel was a part of Antiochus's empire at this time, even though the text implies that Israel and Syria were two different kingdoms, although at the time of this invasion of Jerusalem, Israel still retained considerable autonomy within the Seleucid Empire.)

The King of the North Attacks the King of the South, Again

"²⁹At the time appointed he shall return, and come toward the south; but it shall not be as the former, or as the later. ³⁰For the ships of Chittim shall come against him" (Daniel 11:29–30). With Antiochus IV back in Syria, the kings of the south, Ptolemy VI Philometor, Cleopatra II, and Euergetes II reconciled their differences and formed a single government in Egypt.

This meant the end of the alliance between Ptolemy VI and Antiochus IV, and, of course, the end of Antiochus's influence on Egypt. In response, Antiochus invaded Egypt the second time in the spring of 168 BC to reestablish his authority. *But it shall not be as the former*—Antiochus was now to face the power of Rome, *the ships of Chittim.* In response to Egypt's earlier call for help, Gaius Popillius Laenas, a Roman ambassador, appeared at the camp of Antiochus, which had advanced into Egypt as far as Alexandria. Laenas immediately delivered a written message from the Senate ordering Antiochus to leave Egypt with his army. When Antiochus expressed the desire to consult others about the Roman ultimatum, Laenas, disregarding all accepted standards of diplomacy, drew a circle in the earth around Antiochus with his walking stick and told him to answer the Roman command before crossing the line. Taken by surprise by this rude command, Antiochus accepted the Senate's decision and retreated from Egypt.

The Three Invasions of Verse 29

Antiochus IV *shall return, and come toward the south; but it* (this second invasion just described) *shall not be as the former* (the first invasion), or as the later (a third invasion). We will return to this critical verse since Antiochus IV did not invade Egypt a third time, nor has any past king of the north!

The King of the North and Israel

"For the ships of Chittim shall come against him: therefore he shall be grieved, and return, and have indignation against the holy covenant: so shall he do; he shall even return, and have intelligence with them that forsake the holy covenant" (Daniel 11:30). Forced out of Egypt by Rome, Antiochus now turned toward home. En route back to Syria, he attacked Jerusalem believing that the Jews had rebelled against his authority. The indignation against the holy covenant was the attempt a year later to Hellenize the Jews. Both of these acts were devastating to the Israelite community, but apostate Jews, *them that forsake the holy covenant,* were the root cause of both.

"And arms shall stand on his part, and they shall pollute the sanctuary of strength, and shall take away the daily sacrifice, and they shall place the abomination that makes desolate" (Daniel 11:31). As part of this attempt to Hellenize the Jews "the king sent an old man of Athens to compel the Jews to depart from the laws of their fathers, and not to live after the laws of God: And to pollute also the temple in Jerusalem, and to call it the temple of Jupiter[49] Olympius; and that in Garizim, of Jupiter the Defender of Strangers, as they did desire that dwelt in the place" (2 Maccabees 6:1–2). This edict was enforced by a garrison of Syrian soldiers that had been posted in Jerusalem after Antiochus's second invasion. These soldiers were the *arms [that] shall stand on his part* that would *pollute the sanctuary of strength.* A statue of Zeus was placed upon the altar in the Temple,[50] which was *the abomination that makes desolate.* Ten days later, a pig was sacrificed upon the idol altar, further desecrating the Temple.[51] With the desecration of the Temple, *the daily sacrifice* could no longer be conducted.

"And such as do wickedly against the covenant shall he corrupt by flatteries" (Daniel 11:32a). This speaks of the Jews who had turned from God and accepted the way of the Greeks. The writer of Maccabees said of them that, "in those days went there out of Israel

wicked men, who persuaded many, saying, Let us go and make a covenant with the heathen that are round about us: for since we departed from them we have had much sorrow. Then certain of the people were so forward herein that they went to the king, who gave them license to do after the ordinances of the heathen: Whereupon they built a place of exercise at Jerusalem according to the customs of the heathen: and made themselves uncircumcised, and forsook the holy covenant, and joined themselves to the heathen, and were sold to do mischief" (1 Maccabees 1:11–15).

"But the people that do know their God shall be strong, and do exploits And they that understand among the people shall instruct many: yet they shall fall by the sword, and by flame, by captivity, and by spoil, many days. Now when they shall fall, they shall be helped with a little help: but many shall cleave to them with flatteries. And some of them of understanding shall fall, to try them, and to purge, and to make them white, even to the time of the end: because it is yet for a time appointed" (Daniel 11:32b–35).

While many in Israel turned from God, others remained obedient to Him. Among those were Mattathias and his five sons, and a company of "mighty men of Israel, even all such as were voluntarily devoted unto the law" (1 Maccabees 2:42).

They rose up against the ungodly demands of Antiochus and "recovered the law out of the hand of the gentiles, and out of the hand of kings, neither suffered they the sinner to triumph" (1 Maccabees 2:47).

Even to the time of the end refers to the end of Gentile subjugation of Israel.[52] The Maccabeean revolt was eventually successful, yet *they [would] fall by the sword, and by flame, by captivity, and by spoil, many days.* In 142 BC, the Hasmonean Dynasty began under the leadership of Simon Maccabaeus who served as ruler and High Priest. In time, this remnant of Judea occupied the territory that had once been the kingdoms of Judah and Israel.

The Coming King of the North

[36]And the king shall do according to his will; and he shall exalt himself, and magnify himself above every god, and shall speak marvelous things against the God of gods, and shall prosper till the indignation be accomplished: for that that is determined shall be done. [36]Neither shall he

regard the God of his fathers, nor the desire of women, nor regard any god: for he shall magnify himself above all.

(Daniel 11:36–37)

There are four critical points to recognize in these two verses:

- This king is the king of the north. Verse 28 introduces the king of the north with the statement,

   "Then shall he return into his land with great riches; and his heart shall be against the holy covenant." The king of the north here is identified by historical events as Antiochus IV. Verse 29 continues with the statement that *"at the time appointed he shall return, and come toward the south."* This confirms that the subject introduced in verse 28 is the king of the north. From verse 28 to verse 35 *the king of the north* remains the subject of the text with no introduction of another king. Verse 36 begins with *"And the king shall do according to his will."* And is a conjunctive, attaching verse 36 to the previous verses. Therefore, this king that *shall do according to his will* is still the king of the north.

- This king of the north is not Antiochus IV Epiphanes.

   This king of the north *shall exalt himself, and magnify himself above every god…neither shall he regard the God of his fathers…nor regard any god.*

   Antiochus did take the title "Epiphanes," which today is said to be "God Manifest". But "Epiphanes" without "Theos" is "a title which [is] best translated as 'Illustrious,' i.e. as a rather vague honorific term without any specific claim to be a 'God in the Flesh.'"[53] Further, reports such as "He erected a statue of Zeus with his own face on it in the Holy Place, thereby proclaiming himself to be God"[54] can not be substantiated. In fact, the religion instituted in the Temple was not that of the worship of Antiochus, or even of Zeus, but of a cult of Ba'al Shamim, the old high-god of the Canaanites.[55]

   Antiochus IV though did take a special interest in Zeus, building one of the largest Greek temples in the world for Zeus Olympius in Athens.[56] But his worship of Zeus was not to the exclusion of the worship of other gods.[57] He built a temple to Jupiter Capitolinus at Antioch[58] and honored many other gods and mythological figures.[59]

The words of Daniel that this king of the north *shall exalt himself, and magnify himself above every god...neither shall he regard the God of his fathers...nor regard any god* certainly does not apply to Antiochus IV.

- This king of the north is the Antichrist.

Fourteen kings were to follow Antiochus IV to the Syrian throne before the Seleucid Empire fell to Rome. Thus, we see a gap in the lineage of kings in the Scriptural text. No Syrian king following Antiochus IV fulfilled the prophecy of verse 36, or any of the verses following. Further, no king of any age has yet fulfilled this prophecy. Therefore, Scripture is not only speaking here of a new king of the north but of a king of the north yet to come!

This future king of the north will magnify himself above every god. The apostle Paul spoke of this same man as *"³the son of perdition; ⁴who opposes and exalts himself above all that is called God, or that is worshipped; so that he as God sits in the temple of God, showing himself that he is God"* (2 Thessalonians 2:3–4). This king of the north will, however, repeat quite similarly the actions of Antiochus IV.

For example, this king of the north also shall speak marvelous things against the God of gods (Daniel 11:36), just as did Antiochus IV when he forbid the Jews to worship their God. But instead of having an idol placed in the Temple as did Antiochus, this new king will place himself in the Temple as God. The text thus transitions from the prototype of the antichrist to the Antichrist himself.

This king of the north that is yet to come *"shall prosper till the indignation be accomplished"* (Daniel 11:36). This indignation which is to be accomplished is defined by Daniel: *"At that time shall Michael stand up, the great prince which stands for the children of your people: and there shall be a time of trouble, such as never was since there was a nation even to that same time: and at that time your people shall be delivered, every one that shall be found written in the book"* (Daniel 12:1). This time of trouble that Daniel speaks of here is the *"time of Jacob's trouble"* spoken of in

Jeremiah 30:7, the time when God will take His people through a trial by fire to bring a disobedient nation back to Him. This is the 42 months that the Antichrist shall rule over Israel, Jerusalem, and the Jews as spoken of in Revelation 11:2 and 13:5.

This *indignation* of Daniel 11:36 that is to be *accomplished* is also the *"consummation"* of Daniel 9:27, showing again that *"the prince that shall come"* of Daniel 9:26 is now the king of the north.

- Position, Position, Position. A most critical point to recognize in this running account of the conflict between the king of the north and the king of the south is that the players are always identified as "king of…" Therefore, it is "position," not bloodline, that identifies the Antichrist.

King Him from the Land of Thin Air

"And at the time of the end shall the king of the south push at him: and the king of the north shall come against him like a whirlwind, with chariots, and with horsemen, and with many ships" (Daniel 11:40). A third king is universally interjected into this verse, having missed God's message of the running account of the conflict between the king of the south and the king of the north of the preceding verses. An example of the interjection of this third king:

Beginning in Daniel 11:36 we fast forward to the time of the end when modern versions of these two kings will go after the anti-Christ…. At the time when he moves to consolidate his grasp on the earth by going to Jerusalem, the King of the North and the King of the South will both try to stop him (Daniel 11:40).[60]

Here the writer is stating that *the king of the south* **and** *the king of the north* will **both** try to stop *him*. With this, a third king identified only as *him* is created out of whole cloth, appearing out of thin air!

Verse 40 begins with the statement that *at the time of the end shall the king of the south push at him.* By all rules grammar, the pronoun *him* refers back to the king of verse 36, the *king [that] shall do according to his will.* That king is *the king of the north.* Not only is that king *the king of the north* but that king is the Antichrist!

This point bears repeating—there is no third king interjected into verse 40 by Scripture. From verse 1 to verse 39, the battle has been between the king of the north and the king of the south. Through history, the men who were those kings came and went, but the battle remained between those who were the king of the north and the king of the south. That battle between these two kings continues into our future. This is the principal point that God is making with the use of such exacting historical detail.

Therefore, the King of the South Attacks the King of the North...

"And at the time of the end shall the king of the south push at him..." (Daniel 11:40a). This states that in the last days of this age, the king of the south will attack him, the king of the north of verse 36.

And the King of the North Retaliates

"And the king of the north shall come against him like a whirlwind, with chariots, and with horsemen, and with many ships" (Daniel 11:40b). When the king of the south comes against the king of the north, *the king of the north in turn shall come against him,* referring back to the king of the south. Simply, the king of the north retaliates against the advance of the king of the south.

The Third Invasion of Egypt

At this point, we go back to verse 29 and to the then king of the north, Antiochus IV. Verse 29 stated that *"at the time appointed he shall return, and come toward the south; but it shall not be as the former, or as the later."* This verse speaks of three invasions of Egypt by the king of the north. The invasion of Egypt that we are now seeing in verse 40 is that third invasion! Verse 29 implies that *the later,* or third invasion of Egypt, is to be *like the former,* the first invasion. A notable point of comparison here between the first and third invasions is that the king of the south precipitates both of these conflicts by an attack on the king of the north. This is just what we see in verse 40a.

When the king of the north does react to this threat, he advances south *"40clike a whirlwind, with chariots, and with horsemen, and with many ships; and he shall enter into the countries, and shall overflow and pass over...42He shall stretch forth his hand also upon the countries: and the land of Egypt shall not escape. 43But he shall have power over the treasures of gold and of silver, and over all the precious things of Egypt" (Daniel 11:40c–43).*

Just as in the *former* invasion, *the land of Egypt shall not escape* from this *later* invasion, and the king of the north again *shall have power over the treasures of gold and of silver, and over all the precious things of Egypt.*

The King of the North Conquers Israel

On his advance south toward Egypt, the king of the north *"shall enter also into the glorious land"* (Daniel 11:41). The glorious land is the land of Israel.

This is the invasion of Israel spoken of by Luke:

> *[20]When you shall see Jerusalem compassed with armies, then know that the desolation thereof is nigh. [21]Then let them which are in Judaea flee to the mountains; and let them which are in the midst of it depart out; and let not them that are in the countries enter thereinto. [22]For these be the days of vengeance, that all things which are written may be fulfilled. [23]But woe unto them that are with child, and to them that give suck, in those days! for there shall be great distress in the land, and wrath upon this people. [24]And they shall fall by the edge of the sword, and shall be led away captive into all nations: and Jerusalem shall be trodden down of the Gentiles, until the times of the Gentiles be fulfilled.*
>
> *(Luke 21:20–24)*

Zechariah described this invasion of Jerusalem this way:

> *"[1]Behold, the day of the Lord comes, and your spoil shall be divided in the midst of you. [2]For I will gather all nations against Jerusalem to battle; and the city shall be taken, and the houses rifled, and the women ravished; and half of the city shall go forth into captivity, and the residue of the people shall not be cut off from the city"* (Zechariah 14:1–2).

Daniel also spoke of this time of the fall of Jerusalem when he said that it would be *"the people of the prince that shall come [that] shall destroy the city and the sanctuary"* (Daniel 9:26).

God said, I will gather all nations against Jerusalem to battle. By *all nations* God means the nation of the Antichrist and the remaining nations of the League of Ten that form his empire. Those who shall go forth into captivity will be taken from Israel into the other nations of the Antichrist's empire just as was done by the previous Gentile conquerors.

The residue of the people that *shall not be cut off from the city* are in all probability the non-Jewish population of the city who are the *people of the prince that shall come who shall destroy the city and the sanctuary.*

The Time of the Later Invasion

The time of this *later* invasion within the schedule of events of the Tribulation Period is identified by Daniel 7:25: *"And he shall speak great words against the most High, and shall wear out the saints of the most High, and think to change times and laws: and they shall be given into his hand until a time and times and the dividing of time."* This is the last half of the Tribulation when *"the holy city shall they tread under foot forty and two months"* (Revelation 11:2).

Three Kings Plucked Up by the Roots

"Many countries shall be overthrown" (Daniel 11:41). The Scripture here does not say how many countries are overthrown as the king of the north advances south. However, from Daniel 7 verses 8 and 24, we know that three of the ten nations of the League of Ten are overthrown.

There may be other nations overthrown that are not members of the League, but a reference to them would not likely be given as they, would not be germane to the intent of the prophecy.

Daniel had seen this coming invasion of the south previously as he stated that he *"considered the horns [of the fourth beast], and, behold, there came up among them another little horn, before whom there were three of the first horns plucked up by the roots"* (Daniel 7:8). Two of these three *horns* that are to be *plucked up by the roots* are the kings of Israel and Egypt. I believe the third that is plucked up by the roots is also identified but not spoken of by name. (We will investigate that scenario in the chapter "The Roadmap for Peace".) The horn spoken of *as another little horn* is the king of the north, the Antichrist. Note that the first little horn seen by Daniel was Antiochus IV (Daniel 8:9).

The kings of Egypt and Israel, and that of the king of the north, are represented by horns of this fourth beast of Daniel 7. The kings of Egypt and Israel will be two of the *three of the first horns plucked up by the roots.* Thus, two nations of the League of Ten have been here identified.

"He shall enter into the countries, and shall overflow and pass over" *(Daniel 11:40).* This implies that the king of the north will travel through neighboring nations on his way south to Egypt. *"But these shall escape out of his hand, even Edom, and Moab, and the chief of the children of Ammon"* *(Daniel 11:41).* Edom, Moab, and Ammon were nations situated along the east bank of the Jordan River in the territory that is now the state of Jordan. Again, this implies that the king of the north will travel through neighboring nations on his way south. It well could be that the kings of those neighboring nations are some of the other kings of the League of Ten.

Something to contemplate is that *"the Libyans and the Ethiopians shall be at his steps" (Daniel 11:43).* I take this to mean at the steps of the king of the north. The *Gesenius' Hebrew-Chaldee Lexicon* defines that expression as "in his company." The *Soncino Commentary* states that *at his steps* is to be understood as either joining his army, or placing themselves at his beck and call. It would appear that this king of the north has the help of other nations overthrowing these three nations of the League. That scenario is also implied by Zachariah's words of chapter 14, verse 1. That does not necessarily mean that Libya and Ethiopia are other nations of the League of Ten.

The Origin of the Antichrist

The pattern set forth in the account of this running conflict between the past king of the north and the past king of the south identifies the origin of the coming king of the north. The historic portion of the vision of these two kings occurred over a period of 141 years. It's obvious, then, that those who filled the position of king of the north and of the south changed over time. Going from Antiochus IV to the Antichrist, we see a gap in time. Still, the words of the text speak as if there were but one king of the north and but one king of the south throughout the entirety of the prophecy, even when passing from historic events to future events. Therefore, it is the phrase *the king* of that is the key to our understanding of the origin of the Antichrist. The Antichrist is to come from **the position of** the king of the north!

The vision of the king of the north and the king of the south is in the context of the Seleucid and Ptolemaic Empires. Neither of these two empires exists today. However, following the pattern set forth in the vision, the future king of the north must come from the territory that was the Seleucid Empire, and the future king of the south must come from the territory that was the Ptolemaic Empire, just as did the past kings. That the future king of the south is the king of today's Egypt is quite straight forward as the territory of today's Egypt is essentially that of the old Ptolemaic Empire. It's a different story with the future king of the north since the territory of the Seleucid Empire has been divided amongst many of today's nations. However, it is still possible to narrow the field of potential candidate nations from which this future king of the north will come.

Narrowing the Field

When Seleucus I Nicator became king of the eastern provinces of Alexander the Great's empire, the territory included all or parts of modern Turkey, Armenia, Syria, Lebanon, Iraq, Iran, Kuwait, Afghanistan, Pakistan, Turkmenistan, Uzbekistan, and Tajikistan, as shown in map 9.2. The territories in the far eastern reaches of the empire were only tentatively held and were never a permanent part of the empire. Therefore, for the purpose of this analysis, they were considered lost to the Seleucids.

The nations that remain that could reasonably be considered to be the nation of the coming king of the north are Turkey, Syria, Lebanon, Jordan, Iraq, and Iran, shown in map 9.3.

Turkey and Iran are further eliminated as the military might of these two nations will be destroyed in the battle of Gog, of the land of Magog, as given in Ezekiel 38 and 39. Meshach, Tubal, and Togarmah, three of the nations named to be in league with Gog, were nations within the territory that is now Turkey. Persia is the ancient name of Iran. Thus, Turkey and Iran are two of the modern nations that attack Israel in the last days. God said of these nations that come against Israel that He would destroy their military might, leaving *"but the sixth part of you" (Ezekiel 39:2)*. This attack on Israel will occur sometime prior to the king of the north's invasion of Israel at the midpoint of the Tribulation. Following such destruction of their military forces, these nations would not have the capability to conquer either Israel or Egypt.

Map 9.2. The Seleucid Empire at
its greatest extent, circa 301 BC.

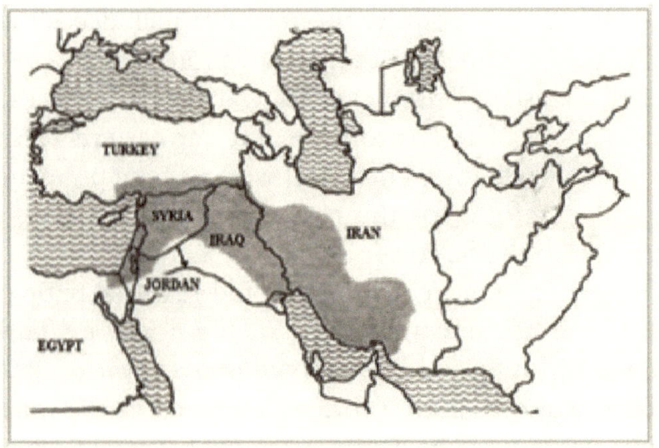

Map 9.3. The Seleucid Empire, circa 198 BC.

Jordan is also eliminated as a nation from which the king of the north could come. Verses 40 and 41 of Daniel 11 tell us that when the king of the north attacks Egypt, *"⁴⁰he shall enter into the countries, and shall overflow and pass over. ⁴¹He shall enter also into the glorious land, and many countries shall be overthrown: but these shall escape out of his hand, even Edom and Moab, and the chief of the children of Ammon."* As stated, Edom, Moab, and Ammon were nations situated along the east bank of the Jordan River in the territory that is now Jordan. Thus, Jordan will not fall to the king of the north as he advances south through Israel toward Egypt. Since Jordan is said to escape the advance of the king of the north, it can not be the country of which he is king.

Therefore, the conclusion on the origin of the Antichrist is that he will come from the position of king of one of the modern nations of Syria, Iraq, or Lebanon.

The Ethnic Identity of the Antichrist

The Antichrist will come from the position of king of modern Syria, Iraq, or Lebanon. These nations encompass a mix of ethnic groups which have settled in the region over several thousand years, although today most of the population is Arab. It is, therefore, most probable that the coming king of the north would be Arab. Further, as this king of the north invades and conquers three other nations of the League of Ten, the remaining six kings of the League will give their full allegiance to this king of the north. Since these six nations are neighboring Israel, they would likely also be Arab, and not likely to put their nations under the rule of one other than an Arab.

The Cultural Identity of the Antichrist

It was said of this king of the north that *"neither shall he regard...the desire of women" (Daniel 11:37)*. This statement identifies the religion of his culture. The statement that this king will not regard *the desire of women* is placed between the statement that he would not regard *the God of his fathers,* a statement of religious choice, and the statement that he would not regard *any god,* another statement of religious choice. The reference to *the desire of women* in this context must, therefore, be a statement of religious choice also.

In recent years, we have been awakened to the cultural world of Islam and to its fanatical subjugation of women that strips them of their humanity.

Riffat Hassan, professor of religious studies at the University of Louisville, sums up Islam's impact on women: "The way Islam has been practiced in most Muslim societies for centuries has left millions of Muslim women with battered bodies, minds and souls."61 It is not difficult to imagine *the desire of women* to be free from this bondage.

That this king shall not regard *the desire of women* as a matter of religious choice tells us that, at the least, the religious culture of this Arab king is Islam.

Putting this concept of "the desire of women" back into the context of Daniel 11:37, the text states *"neither shall he regard the God of his fathers, nor the desire of women, nor regard any god."* Since this king will not regard the *God of his fathers* nor regard *any god*, the phrase *the desire of woman* would, by following this pattern of not regarding gods, be saying that this king also will not regard Allah, the god of Islam.

One could argue from this that this king of the north will appear to have no religious affiliation, not even that of Islam. The last part of Daniel 11 verse 36 appears to agree with this, for there it is said that *"he shall exalt himself, and magnify himself above every god,"* thus showing no allegiance to any religion. Paul describes this king in the same manner, as one *"who opposes and exalts himself above all that is called God, or that is worshipped; so that he as God sits in the temple of God, showing himself that he is God" (2 Thessalonians 2:4).* The problem with this argument, however, however, is that the Scripture is not speaking of the man but rather of the one who indwells within the man. Daniel clarifies this: *"³⁸But in his estate shall he honor the God of forces: and a god whom his fathers knew not shall he honor with gold, and silver, and with precious stones, and pleasant things. ³⁹Thus shall he do in the most strong holds with a strange god, whom he shall acknowledge and increase with glory" (Daniel 11:38–39).* Therefore, when the Antichrist as *God sits in the temple of God* at the midpoint of the Tribulation, the world will see the man, but it will be Satan indwelling within the man that the world will hear *showing himself that he is God.* It is thus Satan that *exalts himself above all that is called God.*

With that said, could the Antichrist adhere to Islam prior to the time of his being possessed by Satan? We don't know the point in time when Satan enters the Antichrist, but Revelation 13:5 does tell us that *"there was given unto him a mouth speaking great things and blasphemies; and power was given unto him to continue forty and two months." The phrase to continue as used here is poieô, which means to do. It means to maintain without interruption a condition or a course of action.* It does not mean that this man is to "continue" in a condition that began prior to this 42-month period. This is saying that the man we call Antichrist will be given power to perform in that role for only the 42-month period of the last half of the Tribulation. And, it is *"the dragon" who will give him "his power, and his seat, and great authority" (Revelation 13:2).* That means this man will not have Satan's power during the first half of the Tribulation. It is reasonable then to consider that the Antichrist will not be possessed by Satan prior to his invasion of Jerusalem at the midpoint of the Tribulation. The fact then that he will be a prince, *"the prince that shall come" (Daniel 9:26),* in a position of authority within an Islamic nation with the responsibility to *"confirm the covenant" (Daniel 9:27)* would require him to be a Muslim at the beginning of the Tribulation. Further, his rise to the kingship of an Islamic nation would assuredly require him to be a Muslim.

The God of the Antichrist

"But in his estate shall he honor the God[62] of forces: and a god whom his father's knew not shall he honor with gold, and silver, and with precious stones, and pleasant things" (Daniel 11:38).

The word *forces* used in the phrase *the God of forces is maoz,* which means *stronghold or strength. Maoz* is used thirty-five times throughout the Bible and is most often translated as "fortress" or "stronghold" implying a place of refuge and protection or a source of strength. Jeremiah used this same word *maoz* when he proclaimed, *"O Lord, my strength, and my fortress [maoz], and my refuge in the day of affliction" (Jeremiah 16:19).* King David also used the word when he said of the deliverance from his enemies, *"The Lord is my rock, and my fortress [maoz], and my deliverer, my God, my rock, in whom I take refuge" (2 Samuel 22:2). David also said of God "In You, O Lord, do I put my trust…be you my strong [maoz] rock, for are my strength [maoz]" (Psalms 31:1–2, 4).* Jeremiah and David both spoke of God as the source of their strength [maoz] and of their protection [maoz].

The statement that this king shall *honor the God of forces* is saying that he shall honor the god of his strength, his support, and his protection. Revelation 13:2 says of the Antichrist that *"the dragon gave him his power, and his seat, and great authority."* This is whom he will honor; Satan is the *God of forces* of this king of the north!

A god whom his father's knew not shall he honor. It seems contradictory that this king of the north will *magnify himself above every god,* place himself in the Temple *showing himself that he is God,* and yet honor another as god. Again, we see in this two personages in one body. When Satan is thrown out of heaven and is *"cast out into the earth" (Revelation 12:9),* he comes very literally to this world and eventually takes up residence in this king.[63] Satan and the Antichrist will become one spiritually and will appear as one physically. Therefore, it is the man who shall honor the god of forces, but it is Satan in the form of the man whereby the king of the north shows himself that he is God.

The God of His Fathers

It was said of this king of the north that *"neither shall he regard the God of his fathers" (Daniel 11:37). God* here is the Hebrew *elohim,* the plural of *el. El* is *God, the Mighty One* used as a title of majesty and power. Although *el* is often used in reference to Yahweh, the God of the Jews, el is also used for any false god. We see this unmistakably in Daniel 11:36: *"And the king shall do according to his will; and he shall exalt himself, and magnify himself above every god [el], and shall speak marvelous things against the God [el] of gods [el]."* Thus, *el* can be translated as either *God* or *god* depending on the context of its use with the differentiation between the true and the false signified by the capitalization, as depicted in the phrase *the God [el] of gods [el].* Elohim as the plural of el as used in the *God of his fathers* could speak of *God,* meaning plural in form but singular in meaning as the Triune God, or as *gods,* the true grammatical plural.

God is capitalized in the phrase *the God of his fathers* in the King James Version, implying this god is the Triune God. Because it is capitalized, many view this as evidence that the Antichrist will be a Jew. However, an analytical look at the "gods" of verses 36 and 37 shows that *elohim* as used in the phrase the *God of his fathers* is correctly translated when it is the true grammatical plural *gods.* Verse 36 states that this king of the north *shall exalt himself, and magnify himself above every god, and shall speak marvelous things against the God of gods.* In this context, what the king of the north shall speak against the *God of gods* will be in the negative—in no regard of the *God of gods.* This covers the God of the Jews. Verse 37 begins with *neither shall he regard,* tying verse 37 to verse 36 by continuing the thought of verse 36. In putting these two verses together, there is the continuous thought that "He shall not regard the God of gods, neither shall he regard the god (or gods) of his fathers, nor the desire of women, nor regard any god." The list of the gods the Antichrist will not regard shows us that the God of gods is not the same as the god (or gods) of his fathers.

Other Clues to the Cultural Identity of the Antichrist

Another identifier of the culture of this king of the north is the method of choice for execution of its enemies. Just as crucifixions were the mark of Rome, so beheadings today are the mark of Islam. This cultural trait of Islam is also the mark of the Antichrist: *"I saw the souls of them that were beheaded for the witness of Jesus, and for the word of God, and which had not worshipped the beast, neither his image, neither had received his mark upon their foreheads, or in their hands"* (Revelation 20:4).

Another point that may have merit is Yasser Arafat's statement, "I do say that we must learn from (the prophet Muhammad's) steps and those of Salah a-Din."[64] What he was referring to was two infamous peace agreements made and then broken by these Muslim leaders. Muhammad made an agreement with the Arabian tribe of Koreish that was to last for ten years. Muhammad broke the agreement after only two years, using that time to consolidate his forces and grow stronger than his enemy. Salah al-Din al-Ayubbi became a legend when, during a cease-fire, he declared a jihad against the Crusaders and captured Jerusalem. Arafat said of his own peace agreements, "We respect agreements the way that the prophet Muhammad and Salah a-Din respected the agreement which they signed."[65] Does this sound familiar? *"He shall confirm the covenant with many for one week: and in the midst of the week he shall cause the sacrifice and the oblation to cease, and for the overspreading of abominations he shall make it desolate"* (Daniel 9:27).

Speaking of peace agreements, when Muhammad made the Khudaibiya agreement with the tribe of Koreish, he removed his title "messenger of Allah" from the agreement. This agreement was then referred to by others as the "inferior peace agreement." Did this absence of the title "high commander" somehow legitimize the breaking of that covenant? It is curious that it is only a prince of the nation, *the prince that shall come,* who puts his signature on this covenant that forms the League of Ten.

One would think that such an important document would be worthy of the signature of the "high commander." Is it the intent of having a *prince* confirm this covenant *with many* so as to qualify this covenant as an "inferior peace agreement"? After all, Surah 9:12 of the Qur'an does say, "If you fear treachery from any of your allies, you may fairly retaliate by breaking off your treaty with them." Remember, Israel will be an ally of this *prince that shall come* as a signatory to this *covenant.* As Daniel had said of this League, *"Whereas you saw iron mixed with miry clay, they shall mingle themselves with the seed of men: but they shall not cleave one to another, even as iron is not mixed with clay"* (Daniel 2:43).

And then there is this: He shall *"think to change times and laws"* (Daniel 7:25). *Times,* as in *"a time and times and the dividing of time,"* of the last half of verse 25 is in reference to the calendar used by the Antichrist. To *change times* is the replacement of the accepted world calendar by another of his choosing. Islam has its own calendar of twelve lunar months with its starting date based on the time of the migration of Mohammed from Mecca to Medina. It is considered a divine command to use the Islamic calendar.[66] To change…laws is to replace non-Islamic legal systems with Islamic Sharia law. Today there is a cry for Sharia law throughout the nations of the world wherever Muslims gather.

Destruction comes; and they shall seek peace, and there shall be none.

—Ezekiel 7:25

[29] *The Encyclopedia Americana*, 833.

[30] *International Bible Dictionary* (Plainfield, New Jersey: Logos International, 1977) 40.

[31] *Halley's Bible Handbook*, 351.

[32] Herodotus, *The Persian Wars III*, 62–79.

[33] From *Alexander to Cleopatra*, 5.

[34] Ibid.

[35] Ibid.

[36] http://en.wikipedia.org/wiki/Seleucus_I_Nicator, accessed 8/28/2011.

[37] Samuel K. Eddy, *The King is Dead : Stydies in the Near Eastern Resistance to Hellenism* 334 -31 B.C. (Lincoln: University of Nebraska Press, 1961), 200.

[38] Eddy, *The King is Dead,* 201.

[39] Ibid., 133.

[40] Otto Mørkholm, *Antiochus IV of Syria (Classica et mediaevalia, dissertationes VIII)* (Gyldendal, 1966), 41.

[41] Ibid., 49.

[42] Ibid., 42.

[43] Ibid., 67.

[44] Ibid., 73.

[45] Ibid., 68.

[46] ibid., 76.

[47] Ibid., 84.

[48] Ibid., 86.

[49] Jupiter is the Latin name for the Greek god Zeus.

[50] 1 Maccabees 1:54.

[51] 1 Maccabees 1:59.

[52] This was a reprieve in a lengthy period of Gentile rule, but it was not the end of the Time of the Gentiles.

[53] Samuel K. Eddy, *The King is Dead: Studies in the Near Eastern Resistance to Hellenism 334 -31 B.C.* (Lincoln: University of Nebraska Press, 1961), 133.

[54] http://www.raptureready.com/soap/seven2.html, *Seven Things You Have To Know To Understand End Times Prophecy ... Part 2,* Jack Kelley, accessed 9/20/2016.

[55] Samuel K. Eddy, *The King is Dead : Studies in the Near Eastern Resistance to Hellenism 334 -31 B.C.* (Lincoln: University of Nebraska Press, 1961), 212.

[56] Edwyn Robert Bevan, M.A., *The House of Seleucus, Vol. II* (New York: Barns & Nobel, Inc.), 148.

[57] Mørkholm, *Antiochus IV of Syria*, 131.

[58] Bevan, *The House of Seleucus*, 149.

[59] Mørkholm, *Antiochus IV of Syria*, 131.

[60] http://www.raptureready.com/featured/kelley/jack172.html accessed 9/5/11 *The Kings Of The North And The South.*

[61] Lisa Beyer, "The Women of Islam," November 25, 2001, *www.time.com/time/world/article/0,8599,185647,00.html.*

[62] "God" here is capitalized in the King James Version implying that the "god of forces" is Yahweh. The Hebrew word here is *eloah,* meaning *an object of worship,* which can mean any god.

[63] There are two men in the Bible who are called "the son of perdition", the one who *"as God sits in the temple of God, showing himself that he is God" (2 Thessalonians 2:3–4),* the man we call the Antichrist, and Judas Iscariot (John 17:12). What is translated as *perdition* is the Greek word *apoleia,* meaning *loss* or *destruction.* It is used in Revelation 17:8 as a place: *"The beast that you saw was, and is not; and shall ascend out of the bottomless pit, and go into perdition."* It is used again in verse 11: "And the beast that was, and is not, even he is the eighth, and is of the seven, and goes into perdition." The one who is spoken of here as going into perdition, or to destruction, is Satan. The two men who are called "the sons" of perdition are thus offspring of Satan in some manner. This connection to Satan is seen in Judas Iscariot, who was the disciple who betrayed Jesus by leading the chief priests to Jesus when they sought to kill him. When the time came that Jesus was to be crucified, *"Then entered Satan into Judas, surnamed Iscariot, being of the twelve. And he went his way, and communed with the chief priests and captains, how he might betray him unto them" (Luke 22:3–4). Then entered Satan into Judas,* this is the cause by which Judas could be called *the son of perdition.* But the purpose for him to be called by that name is to show us that as Satan entered Judas, he will in like manner enter the Antichrist.

[64] Egyptian Orbit TV, April 1998.

[65] Ibid.

[66] Endnote 49. Walid Shoebat and Joel Richardson, *God's War on Terror [Islam, Prophecy and the Bible]* (Top Executive Media, 2010), 86.

CHAPTER TEN
The Roadmap for Peace

"Land for Peace"—a cry we have heard for many years as the roadmap for peace in the Middle East. The concept of Israel forfeiting land to those intent on annihilating the very people of Israel for the hope of a peaceful existence is abhorrent to those who believe that God had given that land to Abraham as an everlasting possession. But we are about to see that land for peace may also be on God's roadmap for peace; it's just not the peace which the world is looking for.

Historical Events and Proposals

Following World War I, the Ottoman Empire, which had been the leading Islamic state in geopolitical, cultural, and ideological terms, was divided into several new nations creating the modern nations of the Middle East. The British and French partitioned the Middle Eastern part of the empire between them, with Iraq and Palestine becoming British-mandated territories under the League of Nations, and Syria and Lebanon becoming French-mandated territories. Palestine was later divided into two territories, Palestine on the west bank of the Jordan River, and Transjordan on the east bank, as shown in map 10.1. Palestine was placed under direct British administration, and the Jewish population allowed to increase, at least initially, while Transjordan was given to the Arabs.

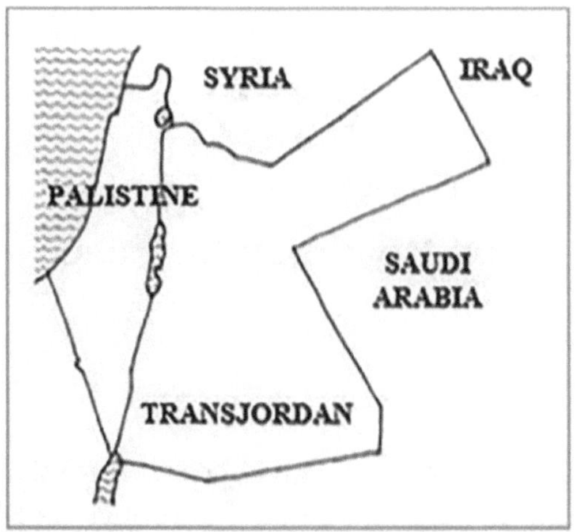

Map 10.1. The British Mandate of Palestine.

Most of these new territorial divisions achieved independence without unusual difficulty, but Palestine has remained a significant problem. Palestine was contentious from the beginning since the Palestine Mandate, reflecting the intent of the Balfour Declaration, required it as the site of a Jewish homeland. Palestine, the site of the ancient kingdom of Israel, had a significant Jewish population, yet the majority of the population was Arab-Muslim. Many different proposals have been made through the years to settle this issue of a Jewish homeland, including the creation of a Jewish state, with or without a significant Arab population, an Arab state, with or without a significant Jewish population, a single binational state, with or without some degree of division by ethnicity, or two states, one Jewish and one Arab. None were acceptable by both sides.

In November 1947, the United Nations General Assembly adopted Resolution 181 (II) recommending "to the United Kingdom, as the mandatory Power for Palestine, and to all other Members of the United Nations the adoption and implementation, with regard to the future government of Palestine, of the Plan of Partition with Economic Union." The plan was to partition Palestine into "Independent Arab and Jewish States," and the City of Jerusalem was to come under a "Special International Regime." This proposed division of the land is shown in map 10.2. Jewish leaders accepted the plan, but Arab leadership rejected it.

Almost immediately after the failure of the resolution, hostilities erupted between the Arab and Jewish communities. The conflicting forces of Arab nationalism and the Jew's quest for a homeland created a situation that the British, who had the obligation to maintain order, could neither resolve nor extricate themselves from. Britain thus withdrew from Palestine on May 14, 1948 at the termination of the British Mandate itself.

Map 10.2. Division of Palestine
in the 1947 UN resolution.

On that same day, the Jewish People's Council declared "the establishment of a Jewish state in Eretz Israel, to be known as the State of Israel." On May 15, 1948 Transjordan, Egypt, Syria, Iraq, and Palestinian Arab forces attacked Israel without success. As a result of the war, called the War of Independence, the state of Israel kept nearly all the area that had been recommended by the UN General Assembly Resolution 181 and took control of almost 60 percent of the area allocated to the proposed Arab state. Transjordan (Jordan) took the bulk of the West Bank land and the old city of Jerusalem. Egypt took Gaza. Israel after the 1948 War of Independence is demarcated by the shaded area in map 10.3.

Map 10.3. Land Occupied by Israel
after the 1948 War of Independence.

Israel was attacked again by Egypt, Syria, and Jordan in June 1967. In the Six Day War, Israel captured the rest of the area that had been part of the British Mandate of Palestine, taking the West Bank (including the old city of Jerusalem) from Jordan, the Gaza Strip from Egypt, and the Golan Heights from Syria. East Jerusalem was also annexed by Israel as part of its capital. The area controlled by Israel after the Six Day War of 1967 is shown in map 10.4.

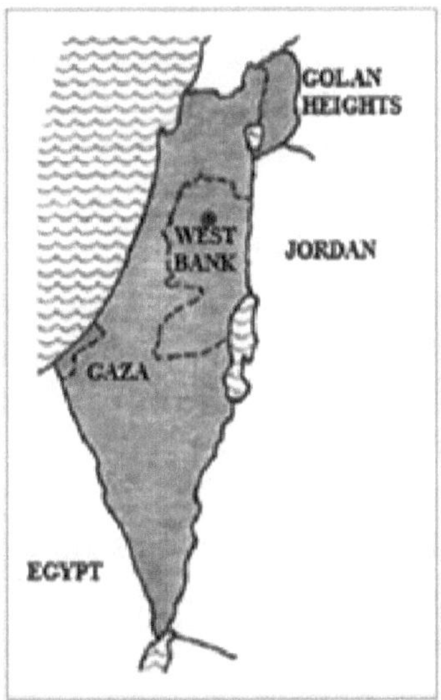

Map 10.4. Land occupied by Israel
after the 1967 Six Day War.

Israel withdrew from Gaza in 2005. The Gaza Strip forms part of the Palestinian territories, or occupied Palestinian territories, which include the West Bank and East Jerusalem, now claimed by the state of Palestine.

The state of Palestine is a state that was proclaimed in exile in 1988 when the Palestine Liberation Organization adopted the unilateral Palestinian Declaration of Independence. It claims the Palestinian territories, defined by the 1967 borders, and designates Jerusalem as its capital. In November 2012, two thirds of the member states of the United Nations recognized the state of Palestine, and the General Assembly passed a resolution giving Palestine status as a "non-member observer state," implicitly recognizing its sovereignty.

The Current Roadmap

The current "roadmap for peace" was drawn by President George W. Bush in a speech in 2002 by which peace was to come to Israel by the creation of an independent Palestinian state to exist side by side with the Israeli state. This new Arab state was to be formed on the West Bank of the Jordan River on land ceded by Israel in exchange for a cessation in Arab terrorism against Israel.

The first milestone on this "roadmap" was to be the appointment of a prime minister for the Palestinian government. The roadmap then had three following milestones, which were to lead to the ultimate goal of enduring peace. The first of these was to be an end to Palestinian violence and Israel's withdrawal from West Bank lands. The second was to be the creation of an independent Palestinian state. The third and last milestone was to be a permanent status agreement on final borders, clarification of the fate of Jerusalem, refugees and settlements, and an end of conflict with the Arab states agreeing to peace deals with Israel.

A leader was chosen for the Palestinian government, and there was initially some movement down this road for peace with Israel freeing about one hundred Palestinian political prisoners as a sign of goodwill, and a handful of Arab leaders announcing their support for the roadmap, promising to work on cutting off funding to "terrorist groups." But it wasn't long before a series of attacks by Palestinians and retaliatory actions by Israelis threatened to tear up the map. Peace talks and cease-fires followed, but neither side has complied with even the initial initial requirements of the roadmap; the Palestinian Authority hasn't succeeded in stopping Palestinian terrorism, and Israel has not withdrawn from West Bank lands. Thus, the roadmap was essentially folded up and put on the shelf.

Yet, the roadmap for peace is occasionally taken off the shelf, unfolded, and a detour erased.

The United Nations' implicit recognition of the sovereignty of the state of Palestine is a case in point. The position of the Palestinian Authority is still that the West Bank and the Gaza Strip should form the basis of a Palestinian state. World public opinion strongly supports this. What I find interesting is that it appears that Israel is becoming agreeable to this two-state solution.

The Requirement for a Palestinian State

To put all this into the context of God's roadmap for the peace that will come at the return and rule of Jesus, we go back to the eleventh chapter of Daniel, which states of the king of the north:

> *40 And at the time of the end shall the king of the south push at him: and the king of the north shall come against him like a whirlwind, with*

chariots, and with horsemen, and with many ships; and he shall enter into the countries, countries, and shall overflow and pass over. ⁴¹He shall enter also into the glorious land, and many (countries) shall be overthrown: but these shall escape out of his hand, even Edom, and Moab, and the chief of the children of Ammon. ⁴²He shall stretch forth his hand also upon the countries: and the land of Egypt shall not escape. ⁴³But he shall have power over the treasures of gold and of silver, and over all the precious things of Egypt: and the Libyans and the Ethiopians shall be at his steps.
(Daniel 11:40–43)

Here Daniel is describing the confrontation between the king of Egypt and the king of a country to the north of Israel. We know this king of the north to be the Antichrist and that he will come from either Syria, Iraq, or Lebanon to conquer Egypt. Daniel states that as this king of the north advances south toward Egypt, *he shall enter also into the glorious land.* The glorious land would be Israel. Daniel also states that *Edom and Moab, and the chief of the children of Ammon shall escape out of his hand.* When Daniel was given this vision, Edom, Moab, and Ammon were known by him to be kingdoms that had been primarily situated along the eastern bank of the Jordan River as shown in map 10.5.

Map 10.5. The ancient kingdoms
of Edom, Moab, and Ammon.

Thus, we are also told that the path of the king of the north is not likely through Jordan. With this, the path of the Antichrist from his position in the north moving southward toward Egypt is potentially defined; he will be pinched between the Mediterranean Sea and Jordan, as shown in map 10.6.

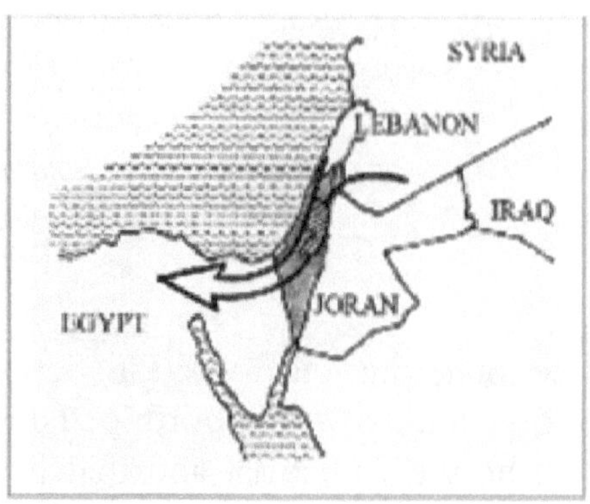

Map 10.6. The path of the king of the north.

It is clear from Daniel's words that the Antichrist will conquer Egypt, but it is critical at this point to keep in mind that when the Antichrist comes out of the north in his move against Egypt, there are three nations that will be overthrown: *"And the ten horns out of this kingdom are ten kings that shall arise: and another shall rise after them; and he shall be diverse from the first, and he shall subdue three kings" (Daniel 7:24)*. As the Antichrist advances toward Egypt, *he shall enter also into the glorious land. The glorious land* can only be the land of Abraham, Isaac, and Jacob, for that is the only land that God speaks of in such endearing terms.

The entering into *the glorious land* includes, but may not be limited to, the invasion of Israel spoken of by Jesus: *"[20]When you shall see Jerusalem compassed with armies, then know that the desolation thereof is nigh. [21]Then let them which are in Judaea flee to the mountains; and let them which are in the midst of it depart out; and let not them that are in the countries enter thereinto. [22]For these be the days of vengeance, that all things which are written may be fulfilled" (Luke 21: 20–22)*.

It is a curious thing that Israel is not identified by name in Daniel's prophecy, as are the other nations. Certainly, if other land areas could be identified by their ancient names, such as Edom, Moab and Egypt, *the glorious land* could have been identified as Israel, or Judah as the area was called at the time of Daniel's prophecy. It is also curious that the third nation that is to be overthrown is not identified.

(I can understand why the nation of the Antichrist is not specifically named here, even by an ancient place name, as his identity is not to be known until the time of the Tribulation.) The answer to that curiosity may be that the two unnamed nations that are to be overthrown along the Antichrist's path to Egypt is that both would be identified by the same place name—Judah. That may also be why such detail as that of *Edom, and Moab, and the chief of the children of Ammon* was given that narrowed the path of the advancing armies of the Antichrist, given to show us the location of the third king to be *subdued.* If an independent Arab state is created out of the lands of the West Bank, this state of Palestine and the state of Israel would both be in *the glorious land.*

As we watch the state of Palestine slowly come into being on the evening news, are we watching the tenth nation of the League of Ten being set into place? Would this be the last milestone marker on God's roadmap toward His peace?

I will gather all nations against Jerusalem to battle; and the city shall be taken.

—Zachariah 14:2

CHAPTER ELEVEN
The Fall of Jerusalem

"I will gather all nations against Jerusalem to battle; and the city shall be taken" *(Zechariah 14:2).* This line of Zechariah's prophecy describing the fall of Jerusalem to the Gentiles is most often quoted when attempting to identify the purpose for the gathering of the nations for the battle of Armageddon. But these words of Zachariah are speaking of the fall of Jerusalem that will occur several years prior to this infamous battle.

In this chapter, we will investigate this gathering of nations against the city of Jerusalem that Zachariah speaks of and the sequence of events concerning Jerusalem within which the city *shall be taken.*

Although this gathering of nations against Jerusalem to battle has no part in the battle of Armageddon, God still *will gather all nations* in Israel for a battle. In Revelation 16:13–16, the apostle John speaks of the final battle that is Armageddon, *"[13]I saw three unclean spirits like frogs come out of the mouth of the dragon, and out of the mouth of the beast, and out of the mouth of the false prophet.*

[14]For they are the spirits of devils, working miracles, which go forth unto the kings of the earth and of the whole world, to gather them to the battle of that great day of God Almighty…[16]And he gathered them together into a place called in the Hebrew tongue Armageddon." This gathering for the battle of Armageddon will not be for the purpose of taking the city of Jerusalem, nor will it be for the oft-stated intent of the annihilation of the nation of Israel. Thus, we will also investigate the purpose for the gathering of the nations for the battle of Armageddon.

Zachariah gives us a synoptic outline of events concerning the city of Jerusalem by describing five distinct periods of time:

- The prelude to the Tribulation Period; the gathering of the nations against Jerusalem in Zachariah 12:1–9.
- The first half of the Tribulation Period; the redemption of the Jews in Zachariah 12:10 through 13:6.
- The last half of the Tribulation Period; the fall of Jerusalem and the annihilation of Israel in Zachariah 13:7 through 14:2.
- The end of the Tribulation Period; the day of the battle of Armageddon in Zachariah 14:3–5.
- The Millennium in Zachariah 14:6–20.

The Prelude to the Fall

²Behold, I will make Jerusalem a cup of trembling unto all the people round about, when they shall be in the siege both against Judah and against Jerusalem. ³And in that day will I make Jerusalem a burdensome stone for all people: all that burden themselves with it shall be cut in pieces, though all the people of the earth be gathered together against it...

⁶In that day will I make the governors of Judah like an hearth of fire among the wood, and like a torch of fire in a sheaf; and they shall devour all the people round about, on the right hand and on the left: and Jerusalem shall be inhabited again in her own place, even in Jerusalem. ⁷The Lord also shall save the tents of Judah first, that the glory of the house of David and the glory of the inhabitants of Jerusalem do not magnify themselves against Judah.

⁸In that day shall the Lord defend the inhabitants of Jerusalem; and he that is feeble among them at that day shall be as David; and the house of David shall be as God, as the angel of the Lord before them. ⁹ And it shall come to pass in that day, that I will seek to destroy all the nations that come against Jerusalem.

(Zechariah 12:2–3, 6–9)

On May 14, 1948 the Jewish People's Council declared the establishment of the state of Israel as British forces withdrew from Palestine at the termination of the United Nations's British Mandate. Within hours of this declaration of independence, the Arabs launched an air attack on Tel Aviv, followed the next day by an invasion by surrounding Arab nations committed to the annihilation of Israel. Syria and Lebanon struck from the north; Iraq and Transjordan (renamed Jordan during the war) struck from the East; Egypt, assisted by contingents from Saudi Arabia and the Sudan, struck from the south; and the Arab Liberation Army composed of Palestinian Arabs, armed and officered by the British, along with volunteers from neighboring Arab countries struck from the interior.

The fledgling state of Israel had little that could be called an army—having not even a single cannon or tank. But against this coordinated assault by five well-trained Arab armies with overwhelming superiority in manpower, heavy armor, artillery, and air force, the Israelis won. Zachariah had foretold of this victory, for the prophecy states, *In that day shall the Lord defend the inhabitants of Jerusalem; and he that is feeble among them at that day shall be as David. And, as David had done, "they shall devour, and subdue with sling stones"* (Zachariah 9:15); an apt description of Israel's victory.

Prior to Israel's War of Independence, the United Nations had recommended the creation of independent Arab and Jewish states in its Partition Plan for Palestine, which was to follow the termination of the British Mandate. Israel had accepted the Partition Plan, but the Arab nations rejected the plan. The ensuing War of Independence resulted in this new state of Israel keeping nearly all the area that had been recommended by the Partition Plan and the taking of almost 60 percent of the area allocated to the proposed Arab state. But the old city of Jerusalem still remained under Arab control. However, the outcome of this war did fulfill Zachariah's words in that *The Lord also shall save the tents of Judah first, that the glory of the house of David and the glory of the inhabitants of Jerusalem do not magnify themselves against Judah.*

The phrase *tents of Judah* referred to the more rural areas outside the city of Jerusalem. Thus, Jerusalem's place in the new state of Israel would have to wait.

After the 1948 War of Independence, Arab nations maintained a state of hostility toward Israel. Terrorist incursions into Israel were commonplace, especially from Egypt. All land routes were blocked, restricting Israel's access to the rest of the world to air and sea only. Egypt then denied passage through the Suez Canal to Israeli-registered ships or to any ship carrying cargo to or from Israel. Further, Egypt closed the Straits of Tiran to Israeli shipping, blockading Israel's southern port of Eilat on the Red Sea that was crucial to her trade with Africa and Asia. Israel's army now was gaining strength. She struck back in 1956 with an operation lasting just one hundred hours. This Sinai Campaign put an end to Egypt's terrorist incursions into Israel and, with the taking of the entire Sinai Peninsula from Egypt, removed the Egyptian blockade of Eilat.

To encourage those of Zachariah's day who were still under the thumb of the Gentiles, God had said, *"[12]Turn you to the strong hold, you prisoners of hope: even today do I declare that I will render double unto you; [13]When I have bent Judah for me, filled the bow with Ephraim, and raised up your sons, O Zion, against your sons, O Greece, and made you as the sword of a mighty man"* (Zachariah 9:12–13). Now Judah had been bent, and the bow filled with Ephraim, a reference to this time of the united tribes of Israel when God would make the nation *as the sword of a mighty man. Your sons, O Greece,* is a generic reference to those Gentile nations who were to come against Israel;67 in this instance, it was Egypt that felt the sword of *Zion.*

In 1967, Israel was again alone against a powerful Arab coalition. This time it was Egypt, Syria, and Jordan in the Six Day War. But God had said, *In that day will I make the governors of Judah like an hearth of fire among the wood, and like a torch of fire in a sheaf; and they shall devour all the people round about, on the right hand and on the left.* Israel captured the rest of the area that had been part of the British Mandate of Palestine, taking the Gaza Strip from Egypt and the Golan Heights from Syria. Israel also took the West Bank from Jordan and with it the old city of Jerusalem. Zachariah had said *Jerusalem [would] be inhabited again in her own place, even in Jerusalem,* referring to Jerusalem's return to its place as the capital city of Israel.

Egypt and Syria, with support from Iraq, Jordan, Saudi Arabia, Kuwait, Libya, and other Arab nations, tried again in 1973, launching a sneak attack on Yom Kippur, the holiest of Jewish holidays. Again, the Israelis defeated the Arabs.

The Yom Kippur War was followed thereafter by an extended terrorist campaign from across its northern border from Lebanon where Palestinian terrorists had established their bases with the help of Syria. A long litany of such accounts as these could be told of this siege against Israel that began in 1947–48. Israel still is under this siege by the relentless attacks of its neighbors, whether it be by coordinated attacks by nations, by terrorist's rockets by the thousands that fly into Israel from Lebanon to its north or Gaza to its south, by terrorists who attack across Israel's border via tunnels, or by next-door neighbors blowing up buses and restaurants with bombs strapped to their bodies.

But there has been, and yet will be, a high price paid by those who come against Israel, for God had said, *I will make Jerusalem a cup of trembling unto all the people round about, when they shall be in the siege both against Judah and against Jerusalem.* And I believe that price has not yet been paid in full, for God had also said *it shall come to pass in that day, that I will seek to destroy all the nations that come against Jerusalem.* The destroying hand that has come with the "Arab Spring" and the rise of the Islamic Caliphate (as it is currently called) is only the beginning of the destruction coming on those who come against Israel. We know the attack by Gog of the land of Magog (Russia) and his allies (Turkey, Iran, Libya, and Sudan) is yet to come during this siege. Ezekiel describes their destruction:

> *2I will turn you back, and leave but the sixth part of you....4You shall fall upon the mountains of Israel, you, and all your bands, and the people that is with you: I will give you unto the ravenous birds of every sort, and to the beasts of the field to be devoured.... 6And I will send a fire on Magog, and among them that dwell carelessly in the isles: and they shall know that I am the Lord.*
>
> *(Ezekiel 39:2, 4, 6)*

The siege described in Zachariah 12 as we have witnessed this last seventy years or so is the persistent attack by *all the people round about* Israel intent on annihilating both the nation and the people. The period of this siege, in the simplest of terms, began at the time of the resurrection of the state of Israel. This siege will temporally end with the formation of the League of Ten at the start of the Tribulation Period.

The Tribulation Period Begins

> *I will pour upon the house of David, and upon the inhabitants of Jerusalem, the spirit of grace and of supplications: and they shall look upon me whom they have pierced, and they shall mourn for him, as one mourns for his only son, and shall be in bitterness for him, as one that is in bitterness for his firstborn.*

(Zechariah 12:10)

> *In that day there shall be a fountain opened to the house of David and to the inhabitants of Jerusalem for sin and for uncleanness.*

(Zachariah 13:1)

Scripture tells of three events that will occur on the first day of the Tribulation Period. The most visible to the world will be the gathering of representatives from ten Middle Eastern nations to sign the document ratifying the League of Ten. This is described in Daniel 9 where *"the prince that shall come"* of verse 26 *"shall confirm the covenant with many for one week"* of verse 27. Likely going unnoticed on that day will be the appearance of two strangers in Jerusalem who are identified in Scripture only as the *"two witnesses."* These two men *"shall prophesy a thousand two hundred and threescore days"* *(Revelation 11:3)*, the full time of the first half of the Tribulation Period. Unseen on that day, there also *"shall be a fountain opened to the house of David and to the inhabitants of Jerusalem for sin and for uncleanness"* *(Zachariah 13:1)*. This *fountain* is a spiritual outpouring from God who *"will pour upon the house of David, and upon the inhabitants of Jerusalem, the spirit of grace and of supplications"* *(Zachariah 13:1)*.

As Jesus rode into Jerusalem on that fateful Sunday morning five days before his crucifixion, *"⁴¹he beheld the city, and wept over it, ⁴²Saying, If you had known, even you, at least in this your day, the things which belong unto your peace! but now they are hid from your eyes"* *(Luke 19:41–42)*. The people believed Jesus was their king, but they did not believe Jesus was their righteousness.

Paul explained what Jesus meant as to *what belonged to [their] peace* that was to be *hid from [their] eyes*. He said in Romans 11:25 that *"blindness in part is happened to Israel, until the fullness of the Gentiles*[68] *be come in."* Paul said the people were spiritually ignorant of the truth that *"Christ is the end [the fulfillment] of the law for righteousness to everyone that believes"* *(Romans 10:1–4)*. As for this blindness, Paul was speaking of a spiritual blindness, for *"according as it is written, God has given them the spirit of slumber, eyes that they should not see, and ears that they should not hear"* (Romans 11:8, quoting Isaiah 29:10). Corporately, the Jews cannot finish their transgression, nor make and end of their sins, nor make reconciliation for their iniquity, nor bring in everlasting righteousness (Daniel 9:24) until this *blindness* is lifted.

As the Tribulation Period begins, *there shall be a fountain opened to the house of David and to the inhabitants of Jerusalem for sin and for uncleanness* as this *blindness* is lifted when the two witnesses tell of Jesus their Messiah. It is during this first half of the Tribulation that God *"will pour upon the house of David, and upon the inhabitants of Jerusalem, the spirit of grace and of supplications: and they shall look upon me whom they have pierced, and they shall mourn for him, as one mourns for his only son, and shall be in bitterness for him, as one that is in bitterness for his firstborn"* (Zechariah 12:10).

This is the time when the *"hundred and forty and four thousand of all the tribes of the children of Israel"* will be *"sealed"* (Revelation 7:4), *"having his [Jesus] Father's name written in their foreheads"* (Revelation 14:1). It is by these *hundred and forty and four thousand* that *"this gospel of the kingdom shall be preached in all the world for a witness unto all nations; and then shall the end come"* (Matthew 24:14).

This is the time when Israel *"is nourished for a time, and times, and half a time, from the face of the serpent"* (Revelation 12:14).

The Fall of Jerusalem

> *¹Behold, the day of the Lord comes, and your spoil shall be divided in the midst of you. ²For I will gather all nations against Jerusalem to battle; and the city shall be taken, and the houses rifled, and the women ravished; and half of the city shall go forth into captivity, and the residue of the people shall not be cut off from the city.*
>
> (Zechariah 14:1–2)

Here, Zachariah describes the event that begins the annihilation of the people of Israel and of the annihilation of the nation of Israel itself with the fall of Jerusalem. Luke also describes this opening salvo:

> *²⁰And when you shall see Jerusalem compassed with armies, then know that the desolation thereof is nigh. ²¹ Then let them which are in Judaea flee to the mountains; and let them which are in the midst of it depart out; and let not them that are in the countries enter thereinto. ²² For these be the days of vengeance, that all things which are written may be fulfilled. ²³ But woe unto them that are with child, and to them that give suck, in those days! for there shall be great distress in the land, and wrath upon*

this people. 24 And they shall fall by the edge of the sword, and shall be led away captive into all nations: and Jerusalem shall be trodden down of the Gentiles, until the times of the Gentiles be fulfilled.

(Luke 21:20–24)

As the result of this attack on Jerusalem:

- First, a clarification of the phrase all nations of Zachariah 14:2, the nations that are to be gathered against Jerusalem at this time. These are not the nations *"of the whole world"* of Revelation 16:14 that are gathered for the battle of Armageddon. *All nations* that are now gathered against Jerusalem to battle are nations of the League of Ten under the command of the coming king of the north. That the phrase *all nations* is used implies that all seven nations who will form the empire of the Antichrist are those who advance through the *glorious land* on their way to conquer Egypt (Daniel 11:41).

- Jerusalem will come under gentile occupation for three and a half years. *"But the court which is without the temple leave out, and measure it not; for it is given unto the Gentiles: and the holy city shall they tread under foot forty and two months"* (Revelation 11:1).

- The city of Jerusalem will be destroyed. *"The people of the prince that shall come shall destroy the city and the sanctuary"* (Daniel 9:26).

- The Temple will be destroyed. *"5And as some spoke of the temple, how it was adorned with goodly stones and gifts, he said, 6As for these things which you behold, the days will come, in the which there shall not be left one stone upon another, that shall not be thrown down"* (Luke 21:5, 6).

- Jerusalem will be made desolate. *"8And it shall come to pass, that in all the land, says the Lord, two parts therein shall be cut off and die; but the third shall be left therein. 9And I will bring the third part through the fire, and will refine them as silver is refined"* (Zechariah 13:8–9). As for *the third* part who will be refined by the fire— *"as many as would not worship the image of the beast should be killed"* (Revelation 13:15). Reason would tell us then that the *third part* of the Jews will die also. That pretty much covers the entire Jewish population of Jerusalem, and the entire Jewish population of all Israel as well, as this shall occur in *all the land.*

Jesus had said, *when you shall see Jerusalem compassed with armies, then know that the desolation thereof is nigh.* To be desolate is to be void of people. This is told from the perspective of God concerning the disposition of His chosen people; there will be other ethnic peoples remaining in Jerusalem who will be those who destroy *"the city and the sanctuary" (Daniel 9:26).*

- As Israel's capital city falls, the nation falls, and Israel will come under the direct rule of the Antichrist for three and a half years. *"I beheld, and the same horn made war with the saints, and prevailed against them" (Daniel 7:21). "And he [the leader of these armies] shall speak great words against the most High, and shall wear out the saints of the most High, and think to change times and laws: and they shall be given into his hand until a time and times and the dividing of time" (Daniel 7:25).*

- Israel's government will be eliminated. *"And the ten horns out of this kingdom are ten kings that shall arise: and another shall rise after them; and he shall be diverse from the first, and he shall subdue three kings" (Daniel 7:24).* Israel is one of the three that shall fall; *"7 Awake, O sword, against my shepherd, and against the man that is my fellow, says the Lord of hosts: smite the shepherd, and the sheep shall be scattered: and I will turn my hand upon the little ones. 8 And it shall come to pass, that in all the land, says the Lord, two parts therein shall be cut off and die" (Zachariah 13:7–8).*

- The nation of Israel will become part of the nation of the king of the North. *"He shall enter also into the glorious land, and many countries shall be overthrown" (Daniel 11:41). "And he shall plant the tabernacles of his palace between the seas [the Mediterranean Sea and the Dead Sea] in the glorious holy mountain [Zion]" (Daniel 11:45).* This annihilation of the nation of Israel is shown most clearly in the description of the empire of the Antichrist: *"And I stood upon the sand of the sea, and saw a beast rise up out of the sea, having seven heads and ten horns, and upon his horns ten crowns, and upon his heads the name of blasphemy" (Revelation 13:1).* There are ten kings depicted, but only seven nations. This shows that when the three kings will be *"uprooted" (Daniel 7:8),* their kingdoms will be absorbed into the kingdom of which the Antichrist is king.

"⁶How long shall it be to the end of these wonders? ...⁷it shall be for a time, times, and an half; and when he shall have accomplished to scatter the power of the holy people, all these things shall be finished" (Daniel 12:6–7).

The Time of the Fall

¹⁵When you therefore shall see the abomination of desolation, spoken of by Daniel the prophet, stand in the holy place, (whoso reads, let him understand:) ¹⁶ Then let them which be in Judaea flee into the mountains: ¹⁷ Let him which is on the housetop not come down to take anything out of his house: ¹⁸ Neither let him which is in the field return back to take his clothes. ¹⁹ And woe unto them that are with child, and to them that give suck in those days! ²⁰ But pray you that your flight be not in the winter, neither on the sabbath day: ²¹ For then shall be great tribulation, such as was not since the beginning of the world to this time, no, nor ever shall be.

(Matthew 24:15-21)

These words of Matthew tell of the same attack on the city of Jerusalem that Luke had described. Luke began his description of the fall of Jerusalem with the words, *"When you shall see Jerusalem compassed with armies" (Luke 21:20)*. Matthew begins his description of the fall of Jerusalem with the words, When you *therefore shall see the abomination of desolation*. With these words, Matthew identifies the time when the world *shall see Jerusalem compassed with armies*. (Note that in both Luke's account of this invasion of Jerusalem and in Matthew's account, a warning is given to all of today's Israel by the words *then let them which be in Judaea flee. Judaea* at the time of the prophecy was all that existed of greater Israel.)

Mathew was referring to Daniel's words of 9:27, which states, *"And he shall confirm the covenant with many for one week: and in the midst of the week he shall cause the sacrifice and the oblation to cease, and for the overspreading of abominations he shall make it desolate."* The one week is the seven-year period of the Tribulation; the midst of the week is the midpoint of those seven years. The ceasing of the sacrifice and the oblation at the midst of the week is the time of the *abomination of desolation*. When the Antichrist conquers Jerusalem, he enters the Temple of the Jews and *"exalts himself above all that is called God, or that is worshipped so that he as God sits in the temple of God, showing himself that he is God" (2 Thessalonians 2:4).* This brings about the *abomination of desolation* spoken of by both Matthew and Daniel.

Another measuring point given to us by which we can determine the time of the fall of Jerusalem comes from Jeremiah. As Matthew had said, *When you therefore shall see the abomination of desolation…then shall be great tribulation, such as was not since the beginning of the world to this time, no, nor ever shall be. Jeremiah had said of these same days: "5We have heard a voice of trembling, of fear, and not of peace. 6Ask you now, and see whether a man does travail with child? wherefore do I see every man with his hands on his loins, as a woman in travail, and all faces are turned into paleness? 7Alas! for that day is great, so that none is like it: it is even the time of Jacob's trouble" (Jeremiah 30:5–7).*

The time of Jacob's trouble is the last half of the Tribulation Period:

Therefore, the city of Jerusalem and the nation of Israel will fall to the Antichrist three and a half years prior to the battle of Armageddon. Israel, including Jerusalem, will become part of the nation in which the Antichrist is king and will remain there under his rule until Jesus returns to rule. Why then would the *three unclean spirits…go forth unto the kings of the earth and of the whole world, to gather them to the battle* to take the city of Jerusalem when the city, and all of Israel, is already theirs?

No Rescue for Israel

A claim often made concerning the battle of Armageddon is that Jesus returns at that time to rescue the Jews from the armies of the world that had gathered in Israel intent on taking the city of Jerusalem. This rescue they speak of is of the physical body. There is Scripture that speaks of Israel being saved, but this rescue will not be as they claim.

Jeremiah did say, *"Alas! for that day is great, so that none is like it: it is even the time of Jacob's trouble, but he shall be saved out of it" (Jeremiah 30:7).* But when Jeremiah said that Israel shall be saved, he was speaking of spiritual salvation, not physical safety. This is confirmed by Daniel who also spoke of this deliverance: *"And at that time shall Michael stand up, the great prince which stands for the children of the people: and there shall be a time of trouble, such as never was since there was a nation even to that same time: and at that time your people shall be delivered, everyone that shall be found written in the book" (Daniel 12:1).* The book Daniel refers to is *"the book of life" (Revelation 3:5).* Those names found written in the book thus include those who receive Jesus as Lord and Savior during this *time of trouble.* Their deliverance will be spiritual, not physical.

As we have seen, there will be *"a fountain opened to the house of David and to the inhabitants of Jerusalem for sin and for uncleanness" (Zachariah 13:1)* during the first half of the Tribulation Period. However, no provision is made for the "rescue" of the physical body beyond the midpoint of the Tribulation. God said of the days of the last half of the Tribulation:

> *⁷I will feed the flock of slaughter, even you, O poor of the flock. And I took unto me two staves; the one I called Beauty, and the other I called Bands; and I fed the flock. 8Three shepherds also I cut off in one month; and my soul lothed them, and their soul also that that is to be cut off, let it be cut off; and let the rest eat every one the flesh of another."*
>
> *(Zechariah 11:7–9)*

> *The three shepherds that will be cut off are the three kings that will be "plucked up by the roots".*
>
> *(Daniel 7:8, 24)*

A bit more information on the flock of slaughter is given us in Zachariah 13:7–9:

> *⁷Awake, O sword, against my shepherd [the king of Israel], and against the man that is my fellow, says the Lord of hosts: smite the shepherd, and the sheep shall be scattered: and I will turn my hand upon the little ones.⁸ And it shall come to pass, that in all the land, says the Lord, two parts therein shall be cut off and die; but the third shall be left therein. ⁹ And I will bring the third part through the fire, and will refine them as silver is refined, and will try them as gold is tried: they shall call on my name, and I will hear them: I will say, It is my people: and they shall say, The Lord is my God.*

The time of this *slaughter* is identified by the phrase *smite the shepherd, and the sheep shall be scattered* which is the fall of Jerusalem. The *poor of the flock* are the *"remnant"* of Israel *"which keep the commandments of God, and have the testimony of Jesus Christ" (Revelation 12:17).* They are *the third part* that God will take. They are those who will be *"beheaded for the witness of through the fire Jesus, and for the word of God, and which had not worshipped the beast, neither his image, neither had received his mark upon their foreheads, or in their hands" (Revelation 20:4).* Those who will be "rescued" will be those returning with Jesus on the day of Armageddon.

The Battle of Armageddon

> *Therefore wait you upon me, says the Lord, until the day that I rise up to the prey: for my determination is to gather the nations, that I may assemble the kingdoms, to pour upon them my indignation, even all my fierce anger: for all the earth shall be devoured with the fire of my jealousy.*
>
> *(Zephaniah 3:8)*

> *^{13} And I saw three unclean spirits like frogs come out of the mouth of the dragon, and out of the mouth of the beast, and out of the mouth of the false prophet. ^{14} For they are the spirits of devils, working miracles, which go forth unto the kings of the earth and of the whole world, to gather them to the battle of that great day of God Almighty....^{16} And he gathered them together into a place called in the Hebrew tongue Armageddon.*
>
> *(Revelation 16:13–14, 16)*

> *^{3} Then shall the Lord go forth, and fight against those nations, as when he fought in the day of battle. ^{4} And his feet shall stand in that day upon the mount of Olives, which is before Jerusalem on the east.*
>
> *(Zachariah 14:3–4)*

> *^{11} And I saw heaven opened, and behold a white horse; and he that sat upon him was called Faithful and True, and in righteousness he does judge and make war. ^{12} His eyes were as a flame of fire, and on his head were many crowns; and he had a name written, that no man knew, but he himself. ^{13} And he was clothed with a vesture dipped in blood: and his name is called The Word of God. ^{14} And the armies which were in heaven*

followed him upon white horses, clothed in fine linen, white and clean. 15 And out of his mouth goes a sharp sword, that with it he should smite the nations: and he shall rule them with a rod of iron: and he treads the winepress of the fierceness and wrath of Almighty God....19 And I saw the beast, and the kings of the earth, and their armies, gathered together to make war against him that sat on the horse, and against his army.

(Revelation 19:11–15, 19)

There is but one battle—*the battle of that great day of God Almighty.*
There is but one purpose for those gathered in the valley of Megiddo—*to make war against him that sat on the horse, and against his army.*
There is but one reason *to make war against him that sat on the horse,* to prevent the Kinsman Redeemer from taking possession of the redeemed land.

The people of the prince that shall come shall destroy the city and the sanctuary.

—Daniel 9:26

[67] The nations who attacked Israel came out of the territories of what was the Grecian Seleucid and Ptolemaic Empires.

[68] The fullness of the Gentiles is explained fully in The Seventy-Sevens of Daniel.

CHAPTER TWELVE
The People of the Prince That Shall Come

Within the prophecy of the Seventy Weeks that God has determined upon Daniel's people and upon his holy city is the statement, *"The people of the prince that shall come shall destroy the city and the sanctuary"* (Daniel 9:26), referring to the destruction of Jerusalem and the Temple. The interpretation of this phrase is of considerable importance to the understanding of the kingdom of the Antichrist and to the identification of the Antichrist himself. In this chapter, we will search out the mystery of *the people of the prince* and the time when they are to *destroy the city and the sanctuary.*

The Vision of the Seventy Weeks

[24]Seventy weeks are determined upon your people and upon your holy city, to finish the transgression, and to make an end of sins, and to make reconciliation for iniquity, and to bring in everlasting righteousness, and to seal up the vision and prophecy, and to anoint the most Holy.

[25]Know therefore and understand, that from the going forth of the commandment to restore and to build Jerusalem unto the Messiah the Prince shall be seven weeks, and threescore and two weeks: the street shall be built again, and the wall, even in troublous times.

[26]And after threescore and two weeks shall Messiah be cut off, but not for himself: and the people of the prince that shall come shall destroy the city and the sanctuary; and the end thereof shall be with a flood, and unto the end of the war desolations are determined.

[27]And he shall confirm the covenant with many for one week: and in the midst of the week he shall cause the sacrifice and the oblation to cease, and for the overspreading of abominations he shall make it desolate, even

*until the consummation, and that determined shall be poured upon the
desolate.*

(Daniel 9:24–27)

A Brief Explanation of the Vision

Daniel was told that God had set a time limit on the nation of Israel to complete seven requirements. These seven required something *of your people,* meaning the people of the linage of the twelve tribes of Jacob. Of these seven requirements, four were specific to the spiritual redemption of the people: *finish the transgression, make an end of sins, make reconciliation for iniquity, and bring in everlasting righteousness.* The remaining three required something also of *your holy city,* meaning the city of Jerusalem: *seal up the vision, [seal up] prophecy, and anoint the most Holy.* This is best explained as the events that would bring about the redemption of Israel itself, the restoration and sanctification of all that will comprise the nation that will be the inheritance of Jesus.

The time allotted was identified as *seventy weeks (seventy sevens of years),* a period of 490 years. The time allotted began at the commandment to rebuild the city of Jerusalem that was destroyed by Babylon's king Nebuchadnezzar in the sixth century BC. From the time the commandment was given until the coming *of the Messiah the Prince shall be seven weeks,* and threescore and two weeks, a period of sixty-nine weeks (v. 25). The city was rebuilt in the first forty-nine years of this period, thus the reference to the first *seven weeks.* The *Messiah the Prince* was Jesus, whose coming at that time was not as the *"King of Kings" (Revelation 19:16)* to rule over the people but as a servant unto the people; therefore as a prince.

After this period of sixty-nine weeks (483 years) *shall Messiah be cut off, but not for himself.* Jesus was to be crucified for payment of the sins of those who were to believe in him (v. 26). Thus, he was put on the cross five days after the end of the sixty-ninth week. Yet, his crucifixion did not occur during the time period of the seventieth week—the completion of the prophecy has been held in abeyance.

The next portion of verse 26 is the point of contention that we will address; *and the people of the prince that shall come shall destroy the city and the sanctuary.* The identification of *the prince* and *the people* of this prince, and the time that they *shall destroy the city and the sanctuary* is thus our focus.

Verse 27 describes events that are to be fulfilled during the last, the seventieth, week of the prophetic time period. *He [the prince that shall come] shall confirm the covenant with many for one week: and in the midst of the week he shall cause the sacrifice and the oblation to cease, and for the overspreading of abominations he shall make it desolate. The week that is spoken of twice in this verse is the time we identify as the seven years of the Tribulation Period.*

A Misleading Theory

It is commonly said that the Antichrist will be of the people who destroyed the city of Jerusalem and the Temple in AD 70. As the story typically goes:

> The greatest political leader in the history of Mankind will emerge from Europe…This conclusion is based upon a statement in Daniel 9:26.[69] The Antichrist will be of the people who destroyed the City of Jerusalem and the Jewish Temple in AD 70…The Roman army under general Titus Vespasian laid siege against Jerusalem destroying the city and the Jewish Temple not leaving one stone upon another as predicted by Jesus in Matthew 24:1–4. Many people conclude that because the Romans fulfilled this prophecy, the people of the prince (Antichrist) must be Europeans.[70]
>
> Since 'the prince that shall come' will come out of the Roman people, scholars conclude that the Antichrist will arise and take over the ten nations of the revived Roman Empire.[71] A reconstituted Roman Empire—that means Europe. It can only mean Rome and its environs: Italy, Germany, France, Holland, Belgium, and England; all of which and more were a part of the original Roman Empire.[72] With his European base consolidated and peace achieved in the Middle East, he will set forth to subdue the whole world.[73]

This theory brings grave error to the understanding of events of the last days.

Titus and the Temple

Jesus gave two prophecies that included the phrase *there shall not be left here one stone upon another,* a reference to a destruction of the Temple specifically and to Jerusalem in general. The unfolding of events of these two prophecies is distinctly different from one another. The first prophecy is that which Jesus spoke of as he wept over Jerusalem as he entered the city on an ass:

> *"⁴²If you had known, even you, at least in this day, the things which belong unto your peace! But now they are hid from your eyes. ⁴³For the days shall come upon you, that your enemies shall cast a trench about you, and compass you round, and keep you in on every side, ⁴⁴And shall lay you even with the ground, and your children within you; and they shall not leave in you one stone upon another; because you knew not the time of your visitation".*

(Luke 19:42–44)

The second prophecy is that recorded in Matthew 24, and again in Luke 21:

> *"⁵And as some spoke of the temple how it was adorned with goodly stones and gifts, [Jesus] said, ⁶As for these things which you behold, the days will come, in the which there shall not be left here one stone upon another, that shall not be thrown down".*

(Luke 21:5–6)

What brought Titus to Jerusalem was the sedition and tyranny in what was left of the Israelite nation, now only a Roman province called Judæa. By AD midsixties, several groups, too large to be called gangs and too small be called armies, were not only in rebellion against Roman authority but were roaming the land, robbing and killing their own countrymen, and invading neighboring territories. In response, Rome sent Vespasian, an experienced but aging Roman general, to restore order. Because of his age, his sons were sent with him, including Titus. Vespasian had sixty thousand fighting men under his command, including large war machines and a sizeable cadre of support personnel—it was not an army that moved with great speed. Over a period of four-plus years, this army moved through the land of Judæa, eventually taking all the cities surrounding Jerusalem.

Vespasian appeared to be in no hurry; he was known to set his camp up in the sight of a city and restrain "his soldiers, who were eager for war; he also shewed his army to the enemy in order to affright them, and to afford them a season for repentance, to see whether they would change their minds before it came to a battle, and at the same time he got things ready for besieging their strongholds."[74]

Often, there were emissaries sent out from the cities to negotiate surrender to the Roman army. Certainly, the people of Jerusalem knew the Roman legions were coming.

Many of the cities around Jerusalem were under siege for weeks before they fell; Jerusalem was under siege for months. And, the citizenry could not flee once a city was under siege. At the siege of Jerusalem under the command of Titus, those who tried to flee where nailed to crosses outside the city walls as a warning against such an attempt. Thus, Jesus had described this Roman invasion precisely when he said, *"Your enemies shall cast a trench about you, and compass you round, and keep you in on every side"* (Luke 19:43). These words describe siege warfare—the type of warfare waged by Titus. Does that make him *the prince that shall come* of Daniel 9:26?

When we look at the prophecy of Luke 21, we see a description of an invasion of Jerusalem that is in stark contrast to that described in Luke 19. Luke 21 states of this coming invasion, *"[20]When you shall see Jerusalem compassed with armies, then know that the desolation thereof is nigh. [21]Then let them which are in Judaea flee to the mountains; and let them which are in the midst of it depart out; and let not them that are in the countries enter thereinto"* (Luke 21:20–21). Matthew adds to the description of this invasion: *"[15]When you therefore shall see the abomination of desolation, spoken of by Daniel the prophet, stand in the holy place, (whoso reads, let him understand:) [16]Then let them which be in Judaea flee into the mountains: [17]Let him which is on the housetop not come down to take anything out of his house: [18]Neither let him which is in the field return back to take his clothes"* (Matthew 24:15–18). In these words of Jesus, we see another destruction of *the city* (in Luke) *and the sanctuary* (in Matthew). This invasion, rather than being a slow and methodological siege, is an invading force that comes with such speed through Judæa that the people are told to flee so fast they don't even have time to grab a coat on their way out the door.

The time of this destruction of the city and the sanctuary is found in Matthew 24:15: *"When you therefore shall see the abomination of desolation, spoken of by Daniel the prophet, stand in the holy place…"* There are only two abominations of desolation spoken of by Daniel: that of 8:11 and that of 9:27 (which is spoken of again in 12:11). The profaning of the Temple that stopped the daily sacrifices as described in chapter 8 was fulfilled in every respect by Antiochus IV Epiphanes two hundred years before the death of Jesus. He therefore could not have been speaking of that abomination of desolation. The second profaning of the Temple occurs at the midpoint of the last of Daniel's weeks when *"in the midst of the week he [the prince that shall come] shall cause the sacrifice and oblation to cease, and for the overspreading of abominations he shall make it [the temple] desolate" (Daniel 9:27)*. Jesus could have been speaking only of this second abomination of desolation, and he defines the time when it will occur.

When the disciples came to Jesus to show him the buildings of the Temple, *"Jesus said unto them, See you not all these things? Verily I say unto you, there shall not be left here one stone upon another that shall not be thrown down" (Matthew 24:2)*. Later, the disciples came to Jesus to ask about this destruction. It is very important here to understand what the disciples asked, and what Jesus answered. The disciples said, *"Tell us, when shall these things be? And what shall be the sign of your coming, and of the end of the world?" (Matthew 24:3)*. The disciples asked three questions: When will the Temple buildings be destroyed? What will be the sign of your return to the earth? What will be the sign of the end of the age? To these three questions, he gave only one answer.

There is no doubt by his answer, recorded in part by Matthew and in part by Luke, that the signs of his return to earth and the signs of the end of the age also apply to the time when the city and the sanctuary are to be destroyed. One of the signs Jesus gave to mark this time was that of the abomination of desolation spoken of by Daniel. Jesus, speaking of this abomination of desolation, said, *"For then shall be great tribulation, such as was not since the beginning of the world to this time, no, nor ever shall be (Matthew 24:21)*. Jesus also said of this time, *"For these be the days of vengeance, that all things which are written may be fulfilled" (Luke 21:22)*. These two statements are clearly references to the time of the end of this age and are bound by the text to the abomination of desolation spoken of by Daniel.

Certainly, Titus has no part in the prophecy of Luke 21:20 (*When you shall see Jerusalem compassed with armies, then know that the desolation thereof is nigh*) or of Mathew 24:15–16 (15When you therefore shall see the abomination of desolation… 16Then let them which be in Judaea flee). But Titus did have a part in the prophecy of Luke 19:43–44 (). But does that mean he is *the prince* of the people that *[43]your enemies shall cast a trench about you, and compass you round, and keep you in on every side, ⁴⁴And shall lay you even with the ground* shall come of Daniel 9:26?

Verse 27 of Daniel's prophecy identifies the *prince that shall come* of verse 26:

> ²⁶*The people of the prince that shall come shall destroy the city and the sanctuary; and the end thereof shall be with a flood, and unto the end of the war desolations are determined.*
>
> ²⁷*And he shall confirm the covenant with many for one week: and in the midst of the week he shall cause the sacrifice and the oblation to cease, and for the overspreading of abominations he shall make it desolate.*

He that *shall confirm the covenant of* verse 27 refers back to the *prince that shall come* of verse 26. He that *shall make it [the Temple] desolate* of verse 27 also refers back to *the prince that shall come* of verse 26. The one who *shall confirm the covenant* and then break it *in the midst of the week,* the one who *shall cause the sacrifice and the oblation to cease,* the one who *shall make* the Temple *desolate,* is the Antichrist. Conclusively, *the prince that shall come* of verse 26 is the Antichrist. Therefore, Titus is not *the prince that shall come* of Daniel 9:26.

The People of Titus

Does that mean that *the people* of the prince that shall come have no part in the events of AD 70? Even though *this prince that shall come* is not Titus, there is possibly some justification for the people of the prince that shall come to have a connection to the destruction of Jerusalem and the Temple in AD 70. I base this solely on one point— that part of verse 26 that says *the people of the prince that shall come [that] shall destroy the city and the sanctuary* appears to be out of sequence in the chronology of events of the prophecy. This is explained as follows.

The prophecy begins in verse 24 by giving a set time period, *seventy weeks,* for the completion of events. Verse 25 then identifies the event that begins the time count, and the event that ends the first period of sixty *the going forth of the commandment to restore and to build Jerusalem,* and the event that ends the first period of sixty-nine weeks, *unto the Messiah the Prince.* The event that restarts the count again for the remaining seventieth week is the *confirm[ing of] the covenant with many for one week* (v. 27). The event that marks the midpoint of this *one week* is the stopping of *the sacrifice and the oblation* (again in verse 27). From this point, the *week* extends to the event spoken of as *the consummation,* the end of the seventieth week, the end of the prophetic period.

What we have identified thus far is a number of events that denote important time markers of the prophecy, all recorded in chronological order. Now verse 26 states, *the people of the prince that shall come shall destroy the city and the sanctuary.* Logic would say that if the destruction of *the city and the sanctuary* applies to the time of the seventieth week, it would be recorded in verse 27 as the event that marks the midpoint of the seventieth week when *the prince that shall come* breaks *the covenant with many.* But it's not recorded in verse 27 but in verse 26, implying this destruction of *the city and the sanctuary* applies to a preceding time, that of AD 70. If this is correct, the intent of the placement of this phrase may be for the purpose of pointing us to the origin of *the prince that shall come* in our time by knowing who *the people of the prince* were who destroyed *the city and the sanctuary* in our past. Who then were *the people* who destroyed *the city and the sanctuary* in AD 70?

In the early years of the growth of the Roman Republic, the majority of the soldiers recruited to serve in the Roman armies (called legions) were from Rome and its environs. As the Republic expanded to include Europe, North Africa, and a large part of the Middle East, it became more and more difficult to man the entire Republic with soldiers only from Rome. With the transformation of the Roman Republic into the Roman Empire during the first century BC, Emperor Augustus made a series of reforms that led to significant changes where most of the soldiers recruited were from the provinces where their garrisons were located, changing the ethnic makeup of the Roman legions. With these reforms, the only Roman army that continued to consist mainly of men from Rome proper was the Praetorian Guard, an elite military unit whose mission was to guard the Emperor and Roman generals. The rest of the army was increasingly composed of citizens native to the provinces, the conquered territories of the empire distant from the capital city of Rome. Flavius Josephus, a first century Jewish historian, confirms this use of provincials when speaking of a disturbance between the Jews and Syrians who lived in Cesarea. He stated, "The Grecian part [a reference to the Syrians of the old Seleucid Empire] had the advantage of assistance from the soldiery; for the greatest part of the Roman garrison was raised out of Syria; and being thus related to the Syrian part, they were ready to assist it."75 According to both ancient historical records and modern scholarship, this change from Europeans to provincials in Roman legions was clearly the case in respect to the Eastern legions that destroyed Jerusalem and the Temple in AD 70.

Publius (or Gaius) Cornelius Tacitus (AD 56–117) was a senator and a historian of the Roman Empire who lived during the time of the destruction of Jerusalem. The surviving portions of his two major works, the *Annals* and the *Histories*, span the history of the Roman Empire from the death of Augustus in AD 14 to the death of emperor Domitian in AD 96. Tacitus details the specific legions and the peoples that composed the attacking army:

Early in this year Titus Caesar, who had been selected by his father to complete the subjugation of Judea…found in Judea three legions, the 5th, the 10th, and the 15th, all old troops of Vespasian's. To these he added the 12th from Syria, and some men belonging to the 18th and 3rd, whom had withdrawn from Alexandria. This force was accompanied by twenty cohorts of allied troops and eight squadrons of cavalry, by the two kings Agrippa and Sohemus, by the auxiliary forces of king Antiochus, by a strong contingent of Arabs, who hated the Jews with the usual hatred of neighbors, and lastly, by many persons brought from the capital and from Italy by private hopes of securing the yet unengaged affections of the Prince. With this force Titus entered the enemy's territory…At last encamped near Jerusalem.[76]

Below are listed the forces that were under Titus during the First Jewish-Roman War referenced by Tacitus and the location that history records for their garrisons:

Legions:[77]
- Legion V Macedonica: Garrisoned in Moesia, a Roman province situated in the Balkans.
- Legion X Fretensis: Garrisoned in Syria.
- Legion XII Fulminata: Garrisoned in Melitene, a city in southeastern *Turkey*.

- Legion XV Appolinaris: Garrisoned in Illyricum, a Roman province along the eastern shoreline of the Adriatic Sea. Legion XV was sent to Syria in AD 62 or 63.

These four legions [listed above] were all involved in the destruction of Jerusalem and the Temple. The legion, in particular, that went through the wall breach and set fire to the Temple was known as X Fretensis or the tenth legion. It was this particular legion that actually pulled down the entire Temple and made the Temple Mount its new base. It should be pointed out that each legion was composed of several smaller "cohorts." Below is a list of the actual cohorts that comprised the tenth legion and where they originally came from:

A. Thracum: Syria (Syrians)
B. IV Cohort Thracia: Bulgaria and Turkey (Turks)
C. Syria Ulpia Patraeorum: Petra in Edom (Nabatean Arabs)
D. IV Cohort Arabia (Arabs)[78]

Partial Legions:[79]

- Legion XVIII: Little is known of this legion, which was completely destroyed around AD 9. This eighteenth legion that was destroyed may have been European based. Since Tacitus references men of the eighteenth under Titus, the legion in AD 70 may have been a different legion as legion numbers were reused.
- Legion III Cyrenaica: A subunit of Legion III garrisoned in Egypt did take part in the siege of Jerusalem. This is likely those "whom had withdrawn from Alexandria."
- Legion III Gallica: This legion was garrisoned in Syria but may not be those referenced by Tacitus.

Allied Troops:

- Twenty cohorts of allied troops and eight squadrons of cavalry by the two kings Agrippa and Sohemus: Tacitus identifies these kings as the kings of Judea and Iturea, respectively.[80] Iturea (Ituraea in Luke 3:1) is the Greek name of one of the regional tribes near Galilee conquered by David. "The countries of Iturea and Judea were, upon the death of their kings Sohemus and Agrippa, annexed to the government of Syria."[81]

- The auxiliary forces of King Antiochus: Tacitus states in *The Annals*, "When tidings of these things were brought to Cestius it seemed good to him to march against the rebels. Wherefore he gathered together an army, taking the twelfth legion and auxiliaries, both horse and foot, and twelve thousand men from the three kings, to wit, Antiochus and Agrippa and Sohemus, of which twelve thousand the half were archers; and besides, many came of their own accord from the cities round about, who, though they knew but little of war, were full of zeal and hatred against the Jews."82

  (Gaius Cestius Gallus was legate of Syria during the early years of Rome's military campaign in the First Jewish-Roman War (AD 66–73). As legate, Cestius was a general of senatorial rank in the Roman army, and as such was the provincial governor of Syria. Cestius marched into Judea in AD 66 in an attempt to restore calm at the outset of the war. At his death in AD 67, General Vespasian was appointed to crush the rebellion.) What we see here is that the armies of Antiochus, as those of Agrippa and Sohemus, were Middle Eastern forces, not European. With the armies of these provincial kings came many "of their own accord from the cities round about."

  Flavius Josephus, a Jewish historian who actually fought the Roman legions within the city walls of Jerusalem in AD 70, confirms the report of Tacitus concerning regional forces. He states, "So Vespasian sent his son Titus, [who] came by land into Syria, where he gathered together the Roman forces, with a considerable number of auxiliaries from the kings in that neighborhood."[83]

- A strong contingent of Arabs, who hated the Jews with the usual hatred of neighbors: Josephus also confirms Tacitus's statement of there being a strong contingent of Arabs under

Titus by detailing the specific number of Arab soldiers who joined forces with the invading armies: "Malchus also, the king of Arabia, sent a thousand horsemen, besides five thousand footmen, the greatest part of which were archers; so that the whole army, including the auxiliaries sent by the kings, as well horsemen and footmen, when all were united together, amounted to sixty thousand."[84] This contingency of Arabs alone was greater in size than a full Roman legion.

- Many persons brought from the capital and from Italy by private hopes of securing the yet unengaged affections of the prince: There were some European forces, apparently citizens, with Titus.

Modern scholars of ancient Rome confirm the statements of the early historians and are in universal agreement that the overwhelming majority of the soldiers who destroyed Jerusalem in AD 70 were Eastern provincial recruits. Sara Elise Phang, PhD, author of *Roman Military Service, Ideologies of Discipline in the Late Republic and Early Principate,* writes, "Recruitment underwent major shifts from Italy in the early first century A.D. to the frontier provinces in the latter first and second centuries... That Italians were increasingly replaced in the legions during this period by provincials is in itself no longer a novelty among scholars... In the East, that is Asia Minor, Syria and Egypt, it seems clear that local recruitment was well under way under Augustus [d.14 A.D.], so that by his death only a very small number of legionaries derived from Italy or indeed any of the western provinces... Under Nero [d. 68A.D.], when the eastern legions required supplementation... it was to Cappadocia and Galatia that [Rome] looked for recruits. This was doubtless standard procedure. [The] legions of the East consisted largely of "orientals" (Middle Easterners) ... What had been an army of Italians was increasingly becoming an army of provincials owing no particular allegiance to, or common bond with the Senate or the urbs Roma... Increasingly they began to identify their interests with those of the provinces in which they were stationed.... By AD 69 Gallica III [one of the Legions that was involved in the destruction of Jerusalem], like other legions long stationed in the East, contained a very high proportion of men born in the eastern provinces."[85] Nigel Pollard, PhD, professor of Roman

History at Oxford University and author of *Soldiers, Cities, and Civilians in Roman Syria,* writes, "Legions based in Cappadocia [central Turkey], Syria, and Egypt were made up of recruits from Asia Minor, Syria, and Egypt."[86]

Tacitus had said, "With this force Titus entered the enemy's territory." Whether or not all these forces where directly involved in breaching the walls of Jerusalem and burning the Temple, the overriding majority of "the people" of Titus were from the Eastern part of the empire—from Eastern Europe, Asia Minor, the Middle East, and Egypt.

Certainly, *the people* that destroyed the city of Jerusalem and burned the Temple in AD 70 were not from Western Europe.

Just Who Were Roman?

There are those who argue that the ethnicity of the Roman legions is irrelevant. Under the heading of Strained Logic, Dr. David R. Reagan writes:

The plain sense meaning of this passage is that the Antichrist will come from the people who will destroy the Temple. Shoebat tries to dispel this meaning by arguing that the Roman legions that carried out the destruction of Jerusalem and the Temple in AD 70 were composed primarily of Syrians and Turks. He therefore concludes that the Antichrist will arise from the Syrians or Turks and will be a Muslim.[87] ...But Shoebat's argument here is really grasping at straws in the wind! For one thing, the ethnicity of the soldiers is irrelevant because the Romans never used mercenaries. All their soldiers were citizens of Rome. But it would not have made any difference if the legions had been composed of Australian Aborigines, for it was the Roman government that decided to destroy Jerusalem, it was the Roman government that gave the orders, and it was Roman generals who carried out the destruction. Rome was the rod of God's judgment and it is from the Roman people that the Antichrist will arise.[88]

Reagan states that it would not have made any difference who the legions had been composed of for it was the Roman government that gave the orders to destroy Jerusalem, and it was the Roman generals who carried out the destruction. That may have been the case for the Jerusalem of AD 70. But for the Jerusalem of tomorrow,

Scripture states that it will be *the people* who *shall destroy the city and the sanctuary;* it does not say that it will be *the prince* that *shall destroy the city and the sanctuary.*

If the destruction of the Temple of AD 70 is not what was in view in the prophecy of Daniel 9 then the ethnicity of the soldiers of first century Rome is irrelevant. And the fact that all the soldiers were citizens of Rome is also irrelevant. But if there is some foreshadowing by those who destroyed the Temple in AD 70 to *the people* who *shall destroy the city and the sanctuary* in the coming years then ethnicity of the soldiers of the past is relevant, for it points to the ethnicity of *the people of the prince that shall come,* and thus to the ethnicity of *the prince* himself. As for the ethnicity of the soldiers of first century Rome, have we become ignorant of geography? The people of Syria, Iraq, and Egypt were as "Roman" as were those of England, France, and Germany. And even Israel was "Roman." Was not Paul a Roman? (Acts 22:25–27)

Reagan states that "the ethnicity of the soldiers is irrelevant because the Romans never used mercenaries" and that "all their soldiers were citizens of Rome," thereby appearing to assert that the Roman legions were composed of soldiers recruited only from what is present-day Italy. But history tells us that Roman legions in the late first century AD were manned by those recruited primarily from the provinces where the legions were garrisoned. And, these provincial soldiers were no more mercenaries than an Italian recruited for a legion garrisoned in Italy.

A Side Note on Geography

Many have concluded that because the "Romans" fulfilled this prophecy, *the people of the prince* must be European, and thus, the Antichrist is of the European Union. What many appear to be ignorant of is that all prophecy concerning the coming days focuses on Israel. What does the European Union have to do with the nation of Israel?

The People of the Prince That Shall Come

There are four aspects to the phrase *the people of the prince that shall come shall destroy the city and the sanctuary.* They are identified below by the unmarked area of text.

• ~~The people of~~ *the prince that* ~~shall come shall destroy the city and the sanctuary.~~

- *The people ~~of the prince that shall come~~ shall destroy the city and the sanctuary.*
- *The people of the prince that ~~shall come shall destroy the city and the sanctuary.~~*
- *The people of the prince that shall come shall destroy the city and the sanctuary.*

The prince that shall come: This does not apply in any way to the Roman general Titus. The *prince* is the coming Antichrist who first comes on the scene when he confirms *the covenant* with *many* as a prince representing his country of origin.

The people shall destroy the city and the sanctuary: If *the people* of Daniel 9:26 does have application to those who destroyed the city of Jerusalem and the burning of the Temple in AD 70, then the people were people of Eastern Europe, Asia Minor, the Middle East, and Egypt.

The people of the prince that shall come: If *the people* in this phrase does apply to those who destroyed *the city and the sanctuary* in AD 70, then those of the past point to *the people of the prince that shall come* and to the origin of the Antichrist of the future. But how do we apply this concept? By etymology or by location? There was quite a mix of peoples within the Eastern nations of the Roman Empire in the first century AD, and there's still quite a mix today. Such a tangle could never be undone with what information we have at this point. However, we do have a good start by location.

If Daniel 9:26 does have application to the events of AD 70, then *the people* of Asia Minor, the Middle East, and Egypt point to *the people* of the nations that surround Israel today. Among those nations are the nine nations that will join with Israel to form the League of Ten.

The people of the prince that shall come shall destroy the city and the sanctuary: How are we to take this phrase if we take it in its entirety to interpret it as applying to a single event? The fact that *the prince that shall come* applies only to the Antichrist requires the destruction of *the city and the sanctuary* to be a future event and, therefore, *the people of the prince* to be those associated with the Antichrist at the time the city and the sanctuary are destroyed.

The phrase *the people of the prince that shall come that shall destroy the city and the sanctuary* has interesting phraseology in that it appears to distinguish *the people* as being somehow apart *from the prince*. What I am implying by this is that the people associated with the Antichrist who are those who participate in the actual destruction of Jerusalem and its Temple may not be the invading forces themselves but rather the local and regional citizenry favorable to the Antichrist. If a military force of a foreign nation was to invade Israel and destroy the city of Jerusalem, it would be said that (fill in the blank) nation destroyed Jerusalem, or that king (fill in the blank) destroyed the Temple. It appears out of the ordinary to say that such destruction was done by "the people" of the invading nation or by "the people" of the invading king.

Another phrase in this prophecy *is "seventy weeks are determined upon your people" (Daniel 9:24).* Here, another *people* are spoken of, those of Daniel. *Your people* of Daniel in a way were apart from Daniel in the same *way the people of the prince* are apart from the Antichrist. Daniel's people were not ruled by Daniel as a king, neither were Daniel's people led into battle by him as a military leader. *Your people* of verse 24 are simply of the same lineage as Daniel. Could it be then that *the people of the prince that shall come* are simply the people of the same lineage as the Antichrist?

The Arab population in Israel at the end of 2008 numbered nearly 1.5 million people. By 2030, it is expected to number nearly 2.5 million.[89] In the municipality of Jerusalem, with a population of 761,000 in 2009, Jews and other non-Arabs made up 65 percent of the population while Arabs made up 35 percent. According to data published by the Jerusalem Institute for Israel Studies, the growth rate of the Arab population in Jerusalem has been almost double the growth rate of the Jewish population.[90] If this trend continues, the Arab population will reach 40 percent by 2020 and 50 percent by 2035. And, almost all Arabs currently live in East Jerusalem, the site of the Temple.

Today they are called Palestinians, a contrived race created for political purposes by Arab nations. But most of the Palestinians living within the borders of Israel have come from those same Arab nations. Therefore, the Palestinians are of the same lineage of the Arab king of the North, just as the Jews are of the same lineage of Daniel. When the Antichrist invades Jerusalem as the king of an Arab nation,
there will be plenty of *the people* of this *prince* that shall come there to greet him upon his arrival.

As the city of Jerusalem falls under the authority of the Antichrist, there will be the opportunity for those who would destroy *the city and the sanctuary.* We have seen shadows of this in incidents such as the destruction of Joseph's tomb in Shechem in present-day Nablus when "Palestinians relentlessly hammered at the tomb with pick axes and hammers to pry the stones apart. Muslim mobs burned and destroyed Joseph's tomb and then danced in celebration. Over sixteen synagogues were desecrated in Judea, literally all the synagogues in Judea."91 Considering the hatred of the Arab population against the existence of a Jewish state, much less the existence of a Jewish temple, newly built in what they believe to be the capital city of their homeland, it is reasonable to believe that it could be the people and not the army of *the prince that shall come* that will *destroy the city and the sanctuary.*

***And the vision of the evening and the morning which was
told is true.***

—Daniel 8:26

.

69 Dr. David R. Reagan, "The Rise and Fall of the Antichrist, Is He Alive Today?—And Other Questions."
http://www.lamblion.com/articles/articles_tribulation7.php,2/298/12.

70 Rodrigo Silva, "The People of the Prince that Shall Come: Who Are They?" http://www.raptureready.com/soap/silva6.html, 7/25/08.

71 Grant R. Jeffrey, *Prince of Darkness* (Canada: Frontier Research Publications, 1994), 35.

72 David Breese, "Europe and the Prince That Shall Come," http://www.raptureme.com/terry/james4.html, 6/13/2003.

73 Reagan, "The Rise and Fall".

74 Josephus, *Wars of the Jews, Book III,* chapter 6.3.

75 Flavius Josephus, The Wars of the Jews, Book 2.13.7

76 Tacitus, The History, ed. Moses Hadas, trans. Alfred Church, William Brodribb (Modern Library: New York, 2003).

77 Jona Lendering, "The Roman Legions," http://www.livius.org/le-lh/legio/legions.htm, accessed 2/22/12.

78 Walid Shoebat and Joel Richardson, God' s War on Terror (2008 Top Executive Media) 352.

79 Jona Lendering, "The Roman Legions," http://www.livius.org/le-lh/legio/legions.htm, accessed 2/22/12.

80 Tacitus, The Annals, 205.

81 Ibid., 284–85.

82 Of the Doings of Cestius, The Baldwin Online Children's Literature Project,
http://www.mainlesson.com/display.php?author=church&book=jerusalem&story=cestius, 2/21/12.

83 Flavius Josephus, *The Complete Works of Josephus, The Wars of the Jews, Or the History of the Destruction of Jerusalem,* Book III, Chapter 1, Paragraph 3.

84 Ibid., Chapter 4, Paragraph 2.

85 Albert Kents, "Daniel 9:26: Who Are The People of the Prince to Come?" http://www.albertkents.org/%e2%80%9cdaniel-926-who-

are-the-people-of-the-prince-to-come%e2%80%9d/ accessed 3/1/12.

[86] Ibid. http://www.albertkents.org/%e2%80%9cdaniel-926-who-are-the-people-of-the-prince-to-come%e2%80%9d/ accessed 3/1/12.

[87] Shoebat, *God's War on Terror*, 349–53.

[88] David R. Reagan, "The Muslim Antichrist Theory: Walid Shoebat," http://www.lamblion.us/2011/02/muslim-antichrist-theory-walid-shoebat.html, accessed 3/12/12.

[89] "The Arab Population in Israel," http://www.gov.il/FirstGov/NewsEng/NewsEng_ArabPopulation.htm, 3/6/12.

[90] Lilach Shoval, "Arab Population in Jerusalem Growing, Study Says," http://www.ynetnews.com/articles/0,7340,L-3397174,00.html, 3/6/12.

[91] Walid Shoebat and Joel Richardson, *God's War on Terror [Islam, Prophecy and the Bible]*, 247.

CHAPTER THIRTEEN
2300 Evenings and Mornings

Verses from the eighth chapter of Daniel are far too often quoted as if they are the direct acts or defined character of the Antichrist. For example:

Daniel declared that "by peace [he] shall destroy many" (Daniel 8:25), indicating he will subtly use false peace treaties to conquer many nations.[22]

The Antichrist, energized by Satan (Daniel 8:24), will seem to have all the answers to the world's problems.[23]

He will take over the European Union through skillful intrigue (Daniel 8:23).[24]

Daniel 8:23–25 tells us … he "shall prosper, and practice" indicate that the Antichrist will bring about tremendous economic prosperity, at least initially.

His brilliant economic policies will transform and enhance world wealth as "through his policy also he shall cause craft [the economy] to prosper in his hand."[25]

He will be an intellectual genius (Daniel 8:23) … and quickly convince the ten leaders of the reunited Roman Empire (the G10) to give him complete control.[26]

The Antichrist will be a man totally possessed by Satan's power as Daniel 8:24 declares: "His power shall be mighty, but not by his own power."[27]

The problem with these quotes is that each one of these verses of Daniel 8 is of a man long dead, and the prophecies long fulfilled. Daniel 8 is an historical account of Antiochus IV Epiphanes who ruled the Seleucid Empire from 175 BC until his death in 164 BC. Antiochus IV is one of two men in the Bible identified as a "little horn"; the Antichrist is the other. That Antiochus IV and the Antichrist are both so identified instructs us to consider Antiochus as a prototype of the Antichrist; but **similar does not mean identical.** That means one can not arbitrarily quote a verse of Daniel 8 as applying verbatim to the Antichrist. Daniel 8 does have relevance to the last days of this age, but its application to any future event must be made with discernment, Scriptural context, and certainly with knowledge of the history of Antiochus IV. It is valuable then to our understanding of the Antichrist to know the history of Antiochus IV. It is also valuable to understand the spiritual condition of the people of Israel at the time of Antiochus and God's reaction to it since this tells us of God's reaction to the spiritual condition of the people of Israel today and to what He is about to do about that.

The Vision

> *³Then I lifted up mine eyes, and saw, and, behold, there stood before the river a ram which had two horns: and the two horns were high; but one was higher than the other, and the higher came up last. ⁴I saw the ram pushing westward, and northward, and southward; so that no beasts might stand before him, neither was there any that could deliver out of his hand; but he did according to his will, and became great.*
>
> *⁵And as I was considering, behold, an he goat came from the west on the face of the whole earth, and touched not the ground: and the goat had a notable horn between his eyes. ⁶And he came to the ram that had two horns, which I had seen standing before the river, and ran unto him in the fury of his power. ⁷And I saw him come close unto the ram, and he was moved with choler against him, and smote the ram, and brake his two horns: and there was no power in the ram to stand before him, but he cast him down to the ground, and stamped upon him: and there was none that could deliver the ram out of his hand.*
>
> *⁸Therefore the he goat waxed very great: and when he was strong, the great horn was broken; and for it came up four notable ones toward the four winds of heaven. ⁹And out of one of them came forth a little horn, which*

waxed exceeding great, toward the south, and toward the east, and toward the pleasant land.

[10]And it waxed great, even to the host of heaven; and it cast down some of the host and of the stars to the ground, and stamped upon them. [11]Yea, he magnified himself even to the prince of the host, and by him the daily sacrifice was taken away, and the place of his sanctuary was cast down. [12]And an host was given him against the daily sacrifice by reason of transgression, and it cast down the truth to the ground; and it practiced, and prospered.

[13]Then I heard one saint speaking, and another saint said unto that certain saint which spoke, How long shall be the vision concerning the daily sacrifice, and the transgression of desolation, to give both the sanctuary and the host to be trodden under foot? [14]And he said unto me, Unto two thousand and three hundred days; then shall the sanctuary be cleansed.

(Daniel 8:3–14)

The Interpretation

[15]And it came to pass, when I, even I Daniel, had seen the vision, and sought for the meaning, then, behold, there stood before me as the appearance of a man. [16]And I heard a man's voice between the banks of Ulai, which called, and said, Gabriel, make this man to understand the vision.

[17]So he came near where I stood: and when he came, I was afraid, and fell upon my face: but he said unto me, Understand, O son of man: for at the time of the end shall be the vision. [18]Now as he was speaking with me, I was in a deep sleep on my face toward the ground: but he touched me, and set me upright. [19]And he said, Behold, I will make you know what shall be in the last end of the indignation: for at the time appointed the end shall be.

[21]And the rough he goat is the king of Grecia: and the great horn that is between his eyes is the first king. [22]Now that being broken, whereas four stood up for it, four kingdoms shall stand up out of the nation, but not in his power.

[23]And in the later time of their kingdom, when the transgressors are come to the full, a king of fierce countenance, and understanding dark sentences, shall stand up. [24]And his power shall be mighty, but not by his own power: and he shall destroy wonderfully, and shall prosper, and practice, and shall destroy the mighty and the holy people. [25]And through his policy

*also he shall magnify himself in his heart, and by peace shall destroy many;
but he shall be broken without hand.*

*[26]And the vision of the evening and the morning which was told is
true: wherefore shut you up the vision; for it shall be for many days.*

(Daniel 8:21–26)

The Fulfillment

Alexander the Great and the division of his Grecian Empire were
foretold in verses 21 and 22: *The rough he goat is the king of Grecia: and the
great horn that is between his eyes is the first king. Now that being broken, whereas
four stood up for it, four kingdoms shall stand up out of the nation, but not in his
power.* After his death, Alexander's great empire was divided and
eventually consolidated into four smaller, less powerful empires. Only
two of those were important to Israel: the Seleucid Empire (often
referred to as the Syrian Empire), which lay to its north, and the
Ptolemaic Empire (often referred to as the Egyptian Empire), which was
to the south of Israel.

The Time of the End

Understand, O son of man: for at the time of the end shall be the vision (v. 17). This
verse needs to be put in perspective of the context of this prophecy, for
many are misled by the phrase *the time of the end*, applying this vision or
parts of it directly to the coming time of the end of this age and to the
Antichrist. There is an application of this vision to the coming events of
the Tribulation, but that application has also to be put in its proper
perspective.

Beside the statement in verse 17 that this vision is for *the time of
the end*, we are told that these events *shall be in the last end of the indignation*
(v. 18), and this *little horn* would appear *in the later time of their kingdom* (v.
23). The indignation was the period of Gentile rule over the Israelites
while the *last end of the indignation* was the time of tyrannical rule of
Jerusalem and Judah by Antiochus IV. His attempt to convert the
monotheistic Yahweh into a pantheon of Greek gods sparked the
rebellion of the Maccabees against Antiochus that brought an end to the
Seleucid rule of Judah and a temporary cessation of ruling Gentile
empires over Israel.

The rule of Antiochus IV was *in the later time of their kingdom.* The
kingdom, singular, speaks to Alexander's empire. *Their,* plural, speaks to
the kings of the kingdoms that formed by the division of Alexander's

empire. Thus, *their kingdom* defines a critical time distinction; it is not only the time of the Grecian Empire but is specifically the time of the divided Grecian Empire. *In the later time* of their kingdom further narrows the time of the coming of the king of fierce countenance as it points toward the end of the existence of the divided empire. By the time of Antiochus's reign, two of the four kingdoms no longer existed. The two remaining kingdoms, the Seleucid and Ptolemaic Empires, struggled on for a time after the reign of Antiochus IV before their demise. But it was in the period of Antiochus IV when Roman power subjugated the Greeks, which helped Israel achieve her independence from Gentile rule. *The time of the end* is therefore the time of the end of a long period of continuous rule by Gentile empires over the Israelites.

A Little Horn

And out of one of them came forth a little horn (v. 9). Out of one of these four lesser empires that formed from Alexander's empire was to come one identified as a *little horn*. This was Antiochus IV Epiphanes. Antiochus IV came on the scene when he was sent to Rome as a hostage demanded by the Romans after the battle of Magnesia where the Roman army defeated the Seleucid king Antiochus III.[20] Antiochus IV was the eldest son of Antiochus III and, thus, a prince of the Seleucid dynasty. As a prince, he was *a little horn.*

Antiochus IV spent twelve to thirteen years in Rome during which the second son of Antiochus III, Seleucus IV, ascended to the throne of Syria. Rome now demanded Demetrius, the eldest son of Seleucus IV, in exchange for Antiochus IV.[22] Leaving Rome, Antiochus IV went to Athens on his way back to Syria. While in Athens, he heard of the assassination of his brother. Seleucus IV had two sons: the eldest, Demetrius, was still a hostage in Rome, and the younger, Antiochus, was too young to assert his legitimate claim to the throne. The political power in Syria was thus usurped by the assassin, Heliodorus, the prime minister.

Antiochus IV, the only grown man of the Seleucid house, saw this as an opportunity to take the Syrian throne. Antiochus IV, however, lacked the material resources—money, soldiers, etc.—for asserting his claim. Assistance was now offered by Eumenes II, king of Pergamon (a kingdom in what is now western Turkey) to help the Syrian prince to take the Seleucid throne. Eumenes's forces escorted Antiochus to the Syrian border, provided him with money and an army, and gave him a crown and other royal insignia. Antiochus was now equipped to make his attempt to take the Syrian throne. Antiochus IV did eventually gain the Seleucid throne, *but not by his own power* (v. 24).

The Seleucid Empire had lost much of its territory in the years preceding the ascension of Antiochus IV to the throne. Rome had taken the Greek territories and much of Asia Minor while many of the far eastern kingdoms subjugated by Alexander the Great were in rebellion or had gained independence. The empire acquired by Antiochus IV, shown in map 13.1, now included only the south-central costal lands of modern Turkey, Syria, Israel, Lebanon, much of Iraq and Iran, and the west bank of Jordan.

Toward the South...

Antiochus waxed exceeding great, toward the south, and toward the east, and toward the pleasant land (v. 9).

To his south was Egypt. Antiochus attacked Egypt twice. The first invasion was successful, with Antiochus ruling the Ptolemaic Empire for a short period of time jointly with the young Egyptian king. Later, attempting to restore his lost authority, he invaded Egypt a second time. On this attempt, he was challenged by the rising power of Rome and retreated from Egypt.

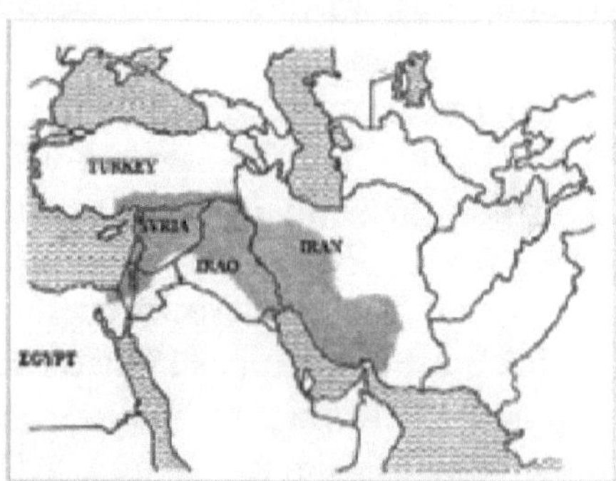

Map 13.1. The Seleucid Empire, circa 198 BC.

Toward the East...

To the east were Armenia, Media, Parthia, Persis, and other nations (today's northern and eastern Iran, Turkmenistan, Afghanistan, and Pakistan). The east had been "conquered," but Syria's control had been neither long-lived nor very firm in this part of the world. These nations had been generally subservient to Syria but never an integral part of the empire. They often rebelled, temporarily gained independence, and were subjugated again.

Antiochus had ascended to the Syrian throne in 175 BC, as the Roman Empire was coming to power in the west. Syria had been at war with Rome prior to Antiochus's ascension, and while Syria was preoccupied with the war in the west the eastern countries of Armenia[100], Media Atropatene[101], and Persis[102] ceased paying tribute and claimed independence.

Antiochus invaded Armenia and Media and reestablished Syrian authority. He also warred against Persis, but with little success.

To assure a greater dominance over the Oriental peoples in his empire, Antiochus also began a policy to Hellenize the eastern portions of the empire. Many old native towns of the east were made into Greek city-states that were to embody the social customs of the west. This involved change in their religious life and the Hellenization of the eastern gods.[103] The eastern gods were renamed or assimilated to Antiochus's Grecian gods. These renamed gods were also the religious symbols of the new imperial unity that Antiochus sought to create. This program of Hellenic urbanization generated widespread resistance in the east, which won him the name of Antiochus IV Epimanes or "Madman" by his contemporaries.[104]

Thus, Antiochus IV Epiphanes also *waxed exceeding great...toward the east.*

Toward the Pleasant Land

Israel had never gained independence from its Gentile neighbors after being conquered by Assyria. Rule over Israel transferred from the Assyrian Empire to the Egyptian, then to the Babylonian, Medo-Persian, and Grecian Empires. At the division of the empire of Alexander the Great, Israel's lot fell to the Ptolemaic Empire where it remained for over a century. Then in 200 BC, Egypt lost the province of Coele-Syria and Phoenicia, including Judah (what was left of the land that had been Israel) to the Seleucid Empire.

The Jew's transition from Egyptian to Syrian rule was accomplished without difficulties as the Jews readily accepted their new master. Antiochus III incorporated Judah into his empire without diminishing the Jew's political rights and guaranteed the right to live according to their ancestral laws and customs.[105] Judah was also recognized as a temple state with a wide measure of self-governance. The High Priest remained as Judah's political and spiritual leader, and at the same time became the head of the temple state and the representative of the Seleucid king.[106] By all accounts, "Peace and happiness reigned in Judea."[107]

However, *in the later time of their kingdom, when the transgressors are come to the full, a king of fierce countenance, and understanding dark sentences, shall stand up* (v. 23). In 175 BC, Antiochus IV, *the king of fierce countenance,* came to the throne of the Seleucid Empire. Judah was to feel the effects of his policy of Hellenization.

After his first invasion of Egypt, Antiochus "went up against Israel and Jerusalem with a great multitude, and entered proudly into the sanctuary, and took away the golden altar, and the candlestick of light, and all the vessels thereof…He took also the silver and the gold, and the precious vessels: also he took the hidden treasures which he found. And when he had taken all away, he went into his own land, having made a great massacre, and spoken very proudly" (1 Maccabees 1:20–25).

Two years later, Antiochus "sent his chief collector of tribute unto the cities of Judah, who came unto Jerusalem with a great multitude, and spoke peaceable words unto them, but all was deceit: for when they had given him credence, he fell suddenly upon the city, and smote it very sore, and destroyed much people of Israel. And when he had taken the spoils of the city, he set it on fire, and pulled down the houses and walls thereof on every side. But the women and children took they captive, and possessed the cattle" (1 Maccabees 1:29–32).

"Then builded they the city of David with a great and strong wall, and with mighty towers, and made it a strong hold for them. And they put therein a sinful nation, wicked men, and fortified themselves therein. They stored it also with armour and victuals, and when they had gathered together the spoils of Jerusalem, they laid them up there, and so they became a sore snare: for it was a place to lie in wait against the sanctuary, and an evil adversary to Israel. Thus they shed innocent blood on every side of the sanctuary, and defiled it: insomuch that the inhabitants of Jerusalem fled because of them: whereupon the city was made an habitation of strangers, and became strange to those that were born in her; and her own children left her" (1 Maccabees 1:33–38). Thus, Antiochus IV Epiphanes *waxed exceeding great…toward the pleasant land.*

The Transgressors…

And in the later time of their kingdom, when the transgressors are come to the full… (v. 23). These *transgressors* of the kingdom of the Seleucids were the Jews themselves for "in those days went there out of Israel wicked men, who persuaded many, saying, Let us go and make a covenant with the heathen that are round about us: for since we departed from them we have had much sorrow. So this device pleased them well. Then certain of the people were so forward herein, that they went to the king, who gave them license to do after the ordinances of the heathen: whereupon they built a place of exercise at Jerusalem according to the customs of the heathen: and made themselves uncircumcised, and forsook the holy covenant, and joined themselves to the heathen, and were sold to do mischief" (1 Maccabees 1:11–15).

Antiochus IV was to come to rule *when the transgressors were come to the full.* Antiochus was not solely responsible for the sad state of affairs of the Jews under his rule for the Jews where more than willing accomplices to their fate. It was the Jews who said, *let us go and make a covenant with the heathen.* It was the Jews who *went to the king, who gave them license to do after the ordinances of the heathen.* It was the Jews who *made themselves uncircumcised, and forsook the holy covenant.* From God's perspective, *the transgressors* here were the people of Israel. It was the very people that God had brought under Gentile rule generation after generation as chastisement for their disobedience to Him. Now, God was about to say, 'Enough!'

Led by the High Priest…

"But after the death of Seleucus, when Antiochus, called Epiphanes, took the kingdom, Jason[108] the brother of Onias labored underhand to be high priest, promising unto the king by intercession three hundred and threescore talents of silver, and of another revenue eighty talents: beside this, he promised to assign an hundred and fifty more, if he might have license to set him up a place for exercise, and for the training up of youth in the fashions of the heathen, and to write them of Jerusalem by the name of Antiochians. Which when the king had granted, and he had gotten into his hand the rule he forthwith brought his own nation to Greekish fashion…putting down the governments which were according to the law, he brought up new customs against the law. For he built gladly a place of exercise under the tower itself, and brought the chief young men under his subjection…that the priests had no courage to serve any more at the altar, but despising the temple, and neglecting the sacrifices, hastened to be partakers of the unlawful allowance in the place of exercise" (2 Maccabees 4:7–12, 14).

The writer of Maccabees states that "certain of the people were so forward herein, that they went to the king, who gave them license to do after the ordinances of the heathen" (1 Maccabees 1:13). It appears that the writer is here speaking of those who had acquired the position of High Priest by graft and deceit. God was about to use these very same men to bring about His chastisement of *the transgressors*.

Are Come to the Full

"By reason whereof sore calamity came upon them: for they had them to be their enemies and avengers, whose custom they followed so earnestly, and unto whom they desired to be like in all things" (2 Maccabees 4:16). In this brief statement, the writer describes the method of God's chastisement of those who "do wickedly against the laws of God" (2 Maccabees 4:17).

The very people whose customs the Jews so earnestly desired to follow were to become their enemies, and God was to use the apostate High Priests to bring it about.

"Three years afterward Jason sent Menelans [Menelaus, a Gentile]…to bear the money [tribute owed] unto the king…But he being brought to the presence of the king, when he had magnified him for the glorious appearance of his power, got the priesthood to himself, offering more than Jason by three hundred talents of silver. So he came with the king's mandate, bringing nothing worthy the high priesthood, but having the fury of a cruel tyrant, and the rage of a savage beast. Then Jason, who had undermined his own brother, being undermined by another, was compelled to flee into the country of the Ammonites" (2 Maccabees 4:23–26).

Later, during Antiochus's second invasion of Egypt, "when there was gone forth a false rumor, as though Antiochus had been dead, Jason [the disposed High Priest] took at the least a thousand men, and suddenly made an assault upon the city; and they that were upon the walls being put back, and the city at length taken, Menelans [the High Priest who had outbid Jason] fled into the castle: But Jason slew his own citizens without mercy" (2 Maccabees 5:5–6).

"Now when this that was done came to the king's ear, he thought that Judea had revolted: whereupon removing out of Egypt in a furious mind, he took the city by force of arms, and commanded his men of war not to spare such as they met, and to slay such as went up upon the houses. Thus there was killing of young and old, making away of men, women, and children, slaying of virgins and infants. And there were destroyed within the space of three whole days fourscore thousand, whereof forty thousand were slain in the conflict; and no fewer sold than slain. Yet was he not content with this, but presumed to go into the most holy temple of all the world; Menelans [the High Priest], that traitor to the laws, and to his own country, being his guide: And taking the holy vessels with polluted hands, and with profane hands pulling down the things that were dedicated by other kings to the augmentation and glory and honor of the place, he gave them away" (2 Maccabees 5:11–16).

"So when Antiochus had carried out of the temple a thousand and eight hundred talents, he departed in all haste unto Antiochia, weening in his pride to make the land navigable, and the sea passable by foot: such was the haughtiness of his mind. And he left governors to vex the nation …He sent also that detestable ringleader Apollonius with an army of two and twenty thousand, commanding him to slay all those that were in their best age, and to sell the women and the younger sort: Who coming to Jerusalem, and pretending peace, did forbear till the holy day of the sabbath, when taking the Jews keeping holy day, he commanded his men to arm themselves. And so he slew all them that were gone to the celebrating of the sabbath, and running through the city with weapons slew great multitudes" (2 Maccabees 5:21–26).

The stage had now been set. This conflict between two apostate Jews, neither worthy of the office of High Priest, was a reflection of the apostasy of all Israel; *the transgressors [had] come to the full.* Israel had turned their back to God, and God was about to turn His back to Israel.

The Hellenization of Yahweh

"Moreover king Antiochus wrote to his whole kingdom, that all should be one people, and everyone should leave his laws: so all the heathen agreed according to the commandment of the king. Yea, many also of the Israelites consented to his religion, and sacrificed unto idols, and profaned the sabbath. For the king had sent letters by messengers unto Jerusalem and the cities of Judea that they should follow the strange laws of the land, and forbid burnt offerings, and sacrifice, and drink offerings, in the temple; and that they should profane the sabbaths and festival days: and pollute the sanctuary and holy people: set up altars, and groves, and chapels of idols, and sacrifice swine's flesh, and unclean beasts: that they should also leave their children uncircumcised, and make their souls abominable with all manner of uncleanness and profanation: to the end they might forget the law, and change all the ordinances. And whosoever would not do according to the commandment of the king, he said, he should die" (1 Maccabees 1:39–50).

The cause of what Antiochus thought was a revolt against his authority was the existence of the authoritative position of the High Priest within the Jew's religious culture. It appears as if Antiochus came to realize that not only was this position of High Priest a threat to the empire but that the religion of the Jews as a whole was a threat, for now he *sent letters by messengers unto Jerusalem and the cities of Judah that they should follow the strange laws of the land.* In order that *all should be one people,* it appears Antiochus now attempted to Hellenize the culture of the Jews simply for ease of control, as he had the oriental peoples in the eastern kingdoms of his empire. To Antiochus, it was just a matter of the preservation of the empire. He was under siege by the Romans to the north, was struggling to regain lost territories in the east, and was heavily invested in his military exploitation of Egypt. Antiochus could ill afford the cost of military control of another rebellious segment of the empire, no matter what the cause.

The motive of Antiochus may have been one thing, but that of God was quite another. Antiochus was only the means by which God was to get the full attention of His wayward people.

God Turns His Back...

Daniel had been told of his vision that this *little horn* would come with great force against *the host of heaven* (Daniel 8:10), those whom God had chosen to be His people, and that *by him the daily sacrifice was [to be] taken away, and the place of his sanctuary was [to be] cast down* (v. 11).

The Israelites were commanded by the Law to sacrifice two lambs daily upon the altar, one lamb in the evening at the start of the Hebrew day, and one lamb in the morning (Exodus 29:38–43). The slain lamb represented a covenant of communion between God and the people of Israel. God said that at the place of the daily sacrifice is *"where I will meet you, to speak there unto you"* (Exodus 29:42).

The commandment of this sacrifice was given to the nation corporately; All were held to account. They were to first be obedient to God in their offer of the sacrifice, then would He commune with them. But now the Jews were sorely testing God's patience. The nation of Israel was already subjugated to Gentile rule because of their disobedience, but this generation had turned their back to God even more so than had their forefathers, and *the transgressors had now come to the full.* God was to get their attention—He was to turn his back to them by stopping the daily sacrifice. God was not to break the covenant of communion, but was about to bring about conditions due to the transgression of the people so that they could not fulfill the requirements to commune with Him. And, He would do that by using Antiochus.

"Not long after this [Jason's assault on Jerusalem] the king sent an old man of Athens to compel the Jews to depart from the laws of their fathers, and not to live after the laws of God: And to pollute also the temple in Jerusalem, and to call it the temple of Jupiter Olympius" (2 Maccabees 6:1–2). Thus, Antiochus began his program of Hellenization about a year after he had put down what he thought had been a revolt by the citizens of Jerusalem.

"Now the fifteenth day of the month Casleu, in the hundred forty and fifth year, they set up the abomination of desolation upon the altar, and builded idol altars throughout the cities of Judah on every side; and burnt incense at the doors of their houses, and in the streets. And when they had rent in pieces the books of the law which they found, they burnt them with fire. And whosoever was found with any the book of the testament, or if any committed to the law, the king's commandment was, that they should put him to death.... Now the five and twentieth day of the month they did sacrifice upon the idol altar, which was upon the altar of God" (1 Maccabees 1:54–59).

God's altar had been defiled, and the daily sacrifices ceased. Without this sacrifice, there could be no communion with God; He would not hear their voices.

And Gets the Attention of His People

In those days arose Mattathias, a priest, and his five sons who dwelt in the city of Modin. "The king's officers, such as compelled the people to revolt, came into the city Modin, to make them sacrifice. And when many of Israel came unto them, Mattathias also and his sons came together. Then answered the king's officers, and said to Mattathias on this wise, Thou art a ruler, and an honorable and great man in this city, and strengthened with sons and brethren: Now therefore come thou first, and fulfill the king's commandment, like as all the heathen have done, yea, and the men of Judah also, and such as remain at Jerusalem: so shalt thou and thy house be in the number of the king's friends, and thou and thy children shall be honored with silver and gold, and many rewards. Then Mattathias answered and spake with a loud voice, Though all the nations that are under the king's dominion obey him, and fall away every one from the religion of their fathers, and give consent to his commandments: Yet will I and my sons and my brethren walk in the covenant of our fathers. God forbid that we should forsake the law and the ordinances. We will not hearken to the king's words, to go from our religion, either on the right hand, or the left" (1 Maccabees 2:15–22).

"Now when he had left speaking these words, there came one of the Jews in the sight of all to sacrifice on the altar which was at Modin, according to the king's commandment.

Which thing when Mattathias saw, he was inflamed with zeal, and his reins trembled, neither could he forbear to show his anger according to judgment: wherefore he ran, and slew him upon the altar. Also the king's commissioner, who compelled men to sacrifice, he killed at that time, and the altar he pulled down. And Mattathias cried throughout the city with a loud voice, saying, Whosoever is zealous of the law, and maintaineth the covenant, let him follow me" (1 Maccabees 2:23–27). Thus began the revolt of those who observed the law of God, led by Judas, who was called Maccabeus, a son of Mattathias.

Within three years, Judas had driven the Syrians from the Temple at Jerusalem. "Then said Judas and his brethren, Behold, our enemies are discomfited: let us go up to cleanse and dedicate the sanctuary. Upon this all the host assembled themselves together, and went up into mount Sion. And when they saw the sanctuary desolate, desolate, and the altar profaned, and the gates burned up, and shrubs growing in the courts as in a forest…they rent their clothes, and made great lamentation…Then Judas appointed certain men to fight against those that were in the fortress [situated just outside the Temple walls], until he had cleansed the sanctuary…Now on the five and twentieth day of the ninth month, which is called the month Casleu, in the hundred forty and eighth year, they rose up betimes in the morning, and offered sacrifice according to the law upon the new altar of burnt offerings, which they had made. Look, at what time and what day the heathen had profaned it, even in that was it dedicated with songs, and citherns, and harps, and cymbals" (1 Maccabees 4:36–38, 41, 52–54). Thus, the altar was dedicated to the Lord on the very same day as it had been defiled.

2300 Evenings and Mornings

The events just described are referenced in the question: *"[13]How long shall be the vision concerning the daily sacrifice, and the transgression of desolation, to give both the sanctuary and the host to be trodden under foot? [14]And he said unto me, Unto two thousand and three hundred days; then shall the sanctuary be cleansed"* (Daniel 8:13–14).

The King James Version gives this time period as 2300 days. However, the phrase that is translated as *days* is in Hebrew *ereb boger,* which is *evening morning*. This phrase is used only this once in the Bible. The Scripture itself confirms the time period as 2300 evenings and mornings, as verse 26 of the same passage states *the vision of the evening and the morning which was told is true*. The time period of these events are thus 2300 evenings and mornings—1,150 days. Why would God use "evenings and mornings" instead of the simpler and more easily understood "days"?

The length of this period was measured in *evenings and mornings* because the focus of this vision is *concerning the daily sacrifice and the transgression of desolation;* in other words, God's response to the disobedience of the Jews. As stated earlier, the Israelites were commanded by the Law to sacrifice two lambs daily upon the altar, one lamb in the evening and one lamb in the morning—this was the *daily sacrifice*. The slain lamb represented a covenant of communion between God and the people of Israel. Without this sacrifice, there was no communion with God.

The time period between the heathen's sacrifice upon the idol's altar on Kislev 25 (Casleu in the Maccabees) in 167 BC and the Jew's offering of the sacrifice on the cleansed altar on Kislev 25 in 164 BC was a period of three years. The typical Jewish year was 354 days in length, depending on the monthly sighting of the new moon. This three-year period would have been around 1,063 days, including this second Kislev 25. If this period included an intercalated month,[109] there would have been about 1,093 days in this period. Because Daniel's 2300 evenings and mornings (1,150 days) does not fit into the period between the heathen's sacrifice, which defiled the Temple, and the Jew's sacrifice after the cleansing of the Temple, there have been many erroneous interpretations of this vision. But therein lies the problem—trying to fit the 2300 evenings and mornings into the time between the two sacrifices. Daniel 8:13 states that the time of this vision is the time *to give **both** the sanctuary **and** the host to be trodden under foot*, not just the sanctuary.

The point in time when the vision was to be completed is easy to identify, for Daniel was told *"Unto two thousand and three hundred [evenings and mornings]; then shall the sanctuary be cleansed" (Daniel 8: 14)*. The cleansing of the sanctuary indicates the absence of Syrian control over *both the sanctuary and the host*. We would expect the point in time the vision was to begin would also be identified by an event, one that would bring *both the sanctuary and the host* under Syrian control. But this starting event is not so easily identified considering that there were several Syrian incursions (for lack of a better description) into Jerusalem.

However, by following the chronology of events of the period, we can see what was happening in Jerusalem at the time the period of the 2300 evenings and mornings was to begin and see what event could mark the beginning of the period.

At the cleansing of the sanctuary, sacrifices were offered according to the Law upon the new altar of burnt offerings on the twenty-fifth day of Kislev (Casleu) "in the hundred forty and eighth year" (1 Maccabees 4:52).

At this point, I must digress momentarily to explain the dating system used by the writer of Maccabees. The "hundred forty and eighth year" was the 148th year of the Seleucid Era (SE). However, the writer used two different variants of the Seleucid Era concurrently.[110] The Macedonian system for dating of events was used concerning Seleucid history; the Babylonian[111] system was used concerning events of Jewish history. In Syria, the Seleucid Era began on the first of Dios (c. October) 312 BC. The Seleucid Era according to the Babylonian calendar was reckoned from the first of Nisan (c. April) 311 BC. (The relationship of the two Seleucid Era systems can be best visualized in figure 13.1 below.) This is a critical distinction as it clarifies some confusion in translating the dates of some of these events to the Gregorian calendar. (The Gregorian calendar did not exist at that early date, but extending this dating system back in time helps us to visualize the comparable dates.) The time of the cleansing of the sanctuary in 1 Maccabees 4:52 is thus by Babylonian reckoning, as the cleansing of the sanctuary was a Jewish event, with the year of 148 SE being 164 BC. This is shown graphically in figure 13.1. Kislev 25 according to the Babylonian calendar could occur at any time from late November to late December in the Gregorian calendar.

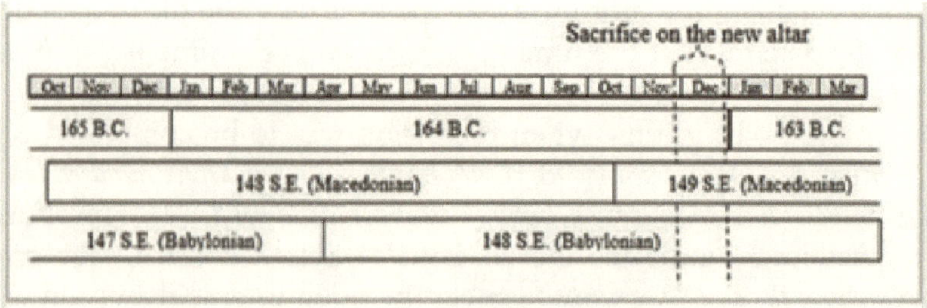

Figure 13.1. Variants of the Seleucid
Era (S.E.) calendar compared
to the Gregorian calendar.

Counting 2300 evenings and mornings (1,150 days) back in time from Kislev 25, sometime between late November and late December of 164 BC, the event we are looking for would have begun essentially three years and three months earlier, sometime between late August and late September of 167 BC when *both the sanctuary and the host [was] to be trodden under foot*. The time of the expected start of the 2300 evenings and mornings in relationship to other significant events of the period is shown in figure 13.2.

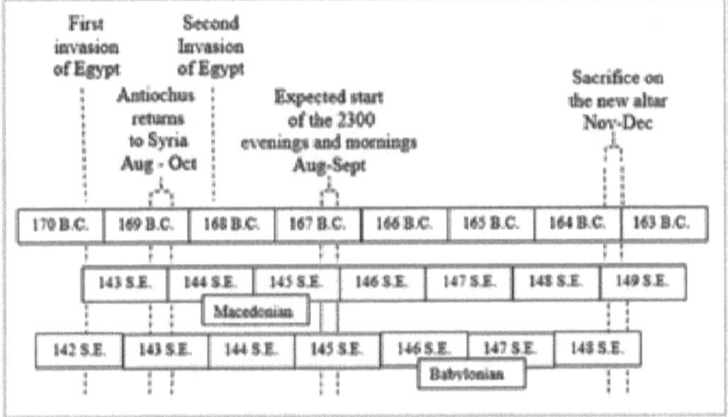

Figure 13.2. The time of the expected
start of the 2300 evening-mornings.

The First Invasion of Egypt

The first invasion of Egypt by Antiochus IV began in November of 170 BC. Victorious, he remained in Egypt into the following year. The writer of Maccabees tells us of his return that "after that Antiochus had smitten Egypt, he returned again in the hundred forty and third year, and went up against Israel and Jerusalem with a great multitude" (1 Maccabees 1:20). Again, we must consider the two different variants of the Seleucid Era. The date of 143 SE in 1 Maccabees 1:20 puts the return of Antiochus from this invasion of Egypt in the Macedonian period of 169 BC. Further, his return is sometime before the end of October 169 BC. This is shown graphically in figures 13.2 and 13.3.

The phrase *he returned again* puts this current incursion into Jerusalem in the perspective of a previous attempt to loot the Temple. There were several incursions by Antiochus into Jerusalem that we now have to keep track of in order to determine which may have been the starting event of the 2300 evenings and mornings.

It must be noted here that "an incursion by Antiochus" does not necessarily require Antiochus to be personally present at the time, but that, at the least, the incursion was at his command.

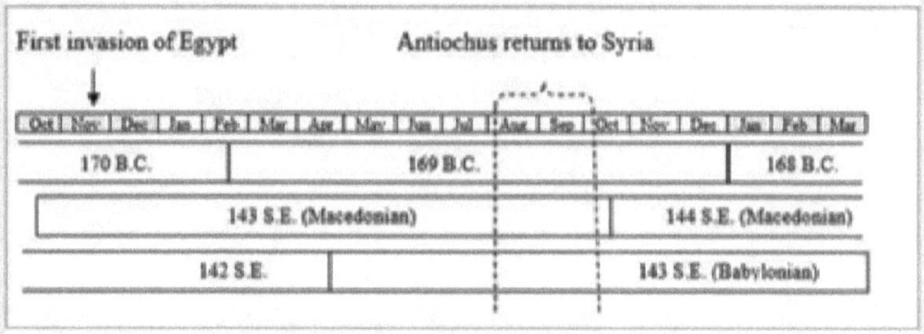

Figure 13.3. The first invasion
of Egypt by Antiochus.

The Second Invasion of Egypt

Antiochus IV began his second invasion of Egypt in the spring of 168 BC.[112] Upon his attack, Egypt hastily dispatched an embassy to Rome urging the Senate to send help. Rome, however, was preoccupied with its war with Macedonia to the north, which delayed any response. On June 22, 168 BC, Rome gained victory over Macedonia, ending the war and freeing Rome to intervene in this conflict between Syria and Egypt.113 Gaius Popillius Laenas was sent as an envoy to Antiochus, who was then just outside of Alexandria. Upon meeting Popillius,

Antiochus extended his hand in a friendly greeting. Popillius, however, placed in his hand the written decree of the Senate "to withdraw forthwith from Egypt"[114] and told him to read it. After reading the decree, Antiochus said he would take some time to consult with others to consider what he would do. But Popillius drew a circle around Antiochus with the stick he was carrying and told Antiochus that before he stepped out of that circle, he give him a reply to lay before the senate. Caught off guard with such a tact, Antiochus complied and accepted the Senate's ultimatum to leave. Thus, it was sometime after late June of 168 BC that Antiochus began his return to Syria. It is considered that Antiochus returned sometime in late summer or early fall of that year.

Antiochus was on his way north when he heard the news of Jason's attack on Jerusalem and marched against the city at that time. This attack was very devastating to both the city and the Temple, but Antiochus returned to Syria leaving the Jewish community essentially to its own administration. As such, this disposition of Jerusalem does not fit the requirement *to give both the sanctuary and the host to be trodden under foot.*

But a following incursion of Jerusalem a year later in 167 BC has all the earmarks of the event we are searching for.[115]

The Event That Began the 2300 Evenings and Mornings

"And after two years fully expired the king sent his chief collector of tribute unto the cities of Juda, who came unto Jerusalem with a great multitude, And spake peaceable words unto them, but all was deceit: for when they had given him credence, he fell suddenly upon the city, and smote it very sore, and destroyed much people of Israel" (1 Maccabees 1:29–30). "After two years fully" is a reference back to verse 20 of 1 Maccabees 1 and Antiochus's incursion into Jerusalem on his way back to Syria after his first invasion of Egypt in August or September of 169 BC. The time of this incursion is thus no earlier than August or September of 167 BC. (1 Maccabees 1 does not speak of Antiochus's incursion into Jerusalem on his return to Syria after his second invasion of Egypt a year earlier in 168 BC.)

"And when he had taken the spoils of the city, he set it on fire, and pulled down the houses and walls thereof on every side…. Then builded they the city of David with a great and strong wall, and with mighty towers, and made it a strong hold for them. And they put therein a sinful nation, wicked men, and fortified themselves therein. They stored it also with armour and victuals, and when they had gathered together the spoils of Jerusalem, they laid them up there, and so they became a sore snare: For it was a place to lie in wait against the sanctuary, and an evil adversary to Israel. Thus they shed innocent blood on every side of the sanctuary, and defiled it: Insomuch that the inhabitants of Jerusalem fled because of them: whereupon the city was made an habitation of strangers, and became strange to those that were born in her; and her own children left her" (1 Maccabees 1:31–38). Thus, *the host* was given *to be trodden under foot.*

"Her sanctuary was laid waste like a wilderness, her feasts were turned into mourning, her sabbaths into reproach her honor into contempt… Now the fifteenth day of the month Casleu, in the hundred forty and fifth year, they set up the abomination of desolation upon the altar, and builded idol altars throughout the cities of Juda on every side" (1 Maccabees 1:39, 54). Thus, *the sanctuary* was also given *to be trodden under foot.* (Verse 54 confirms the date of these events as 145 SE/167 BC)

In this we see a marked change in the manner of Syrian administration of the Jewish community. In the previous incursions of Jerusalem to plunder the Temple or to quell what was thought to be a revolt against Seleucid authority, Syrian troops had always left, leaving the city to its own customs and rule. Now the Jewish community came under the direct, and permanent, rule of Antiochus. Also, it was at this time that Antiochus began his attempt to Hellenize the God of the Jews, giving the sanctuary over to the Gentiles as well. This attack on Jerusalem in the August/September time frame of 167 BC fits well with the time period the 2300 evenings and mornings was to begin.

The Character of Antiochus IV Epiphanes

"23And in the later time of their kingdom, when the transgressors are come to the full, a king of fierce countenance, and understanding dark sentences, shall stand up. 24And his power shall be mighty, but not by his own power: and he shall destroy wonderfully, and shall prosper, and practice, and shall destroy the mighty and the holy people. 25And through his policy also he shall magnify himself in his heart, and by peace shall destroy many" (Daniel 8:23–25). In these verses we have a brief description of the character and ability of Antiochus IV. These verses give the impression that he was quite successful in his exploits, and to a degree, he was. But the exploits of Antiochus were for the most part only marginally successful and would not seem to satisfy the given description. However, the successes alluded to in these verses apply well to his exploits against Jerusalem. Thus, it is in this context that I attempt to explain these verses.

A King of Fierce Countenance

And in the latter time of their kingdom, when the transgressors are come to the full, a king of fierce countenance...shall stand up (v. 23). Antiochus dealt with Jerusalem with a strong, unrelenting hand. As one historian put it, "He had fundamentally the nature of the tyrant. He would suffer no conventional restraint upon his impulse."[116]

The two books of the Maccabees give us some explicit details of Antiochus's dealings with the citizens of Jerusalem, some of which is given above. There were three distinct objectives for his attacks on Jerusalem: the plundering of the Temple, the quelling of an apparent rebellion in Jerusalem, and the Hellenizing of Yahweh. Each will be briefly addressed to put the intent of Antiochus IV in historic perspective.

Antiochus's first successful invasion of Jerusalem was for the purpose of plundering the Temple (1 Maccabees 1:20–28). He went up against Jerusalem with considerable military force, the result of which was a great massacre of the citizenry. He entered the sanctuary and took the golden altar, the candlestick of light, and all the vessels of the Temple. He took also the riches of the Temple treasury. But Jerusalem was not the only victim of his plundering. "His spendthrift magnificence drove him to perpetual necessity, and before the end of his reign he had laid his hands on the riches of nearly all the temples in Syria."[117]

Antiochus's second invasion came about a year later when intelligence reached him during his second campaign in Egypt that Jerusalem had risen in support of the house of Ptolemy to his rear. What appeared to be a defection of the Jews came at a critical moment for Antiochus as he had just been ejected from Egypt by the power of Rome. Losing Egypt meant that he again would have a significant threat on his southern border, and Jerusalem, a city so near the Egyptian frontier, had to be made sure beyond question. "We can well believe that the passionate and willful nature of Antiochus took a direction of strong vindictiveness towards the treacherous city. On his return from Egypt he turned aside, and came to Jerusalem with a fierce countenance to wreak vengeance."118 Antiochus "took the city by force of arms, and commanded his men of war not to spare such as they met, and to slay such as went up upon the houses. Thus there was killing of young and old, making away of men, women, and children, slaying of virgins and infants. And there were destroyed within the space of three whole days fourscore thousand, whereof forty thousand were slain in the conflict; and no fewer sold than slain" (2 Maccabees 5:11–14). At this point in time, "Antiochus had not yet declared war on the Jewish religion. He had but chastised Jerusalem as another rebellious city might have been chastised."[119]

The weak spot in protecting Syria was now Jerusalem, but its people maintained an obstinate isolation by the religion of Yahweh. For the security of the empire, the Jews had to be brought into the fold. Thus, "Antiochus wrote to his whole kingdom, that all should be one people, and every one should leave his laws" (1 Maccabees 1:41–42). This was to be accomplished by force.

Now, for the third time, Syrian military forces invaded Jerusalem. Another massacre ensued as the city walls were razed, the city set on fire, and the women and children taken captive. The spoils of the city were taken and put in the city of David, which was now reconstructed as a military stronghold. A mixed force of mercenaries, including Jews, occupied the stronghold to enforce the royal decrees. There was now a need not merely to superficially identify the Jew's God with this or that Greek god but to transform thought and speech. "Imaginative and sentimental Hellenism was no doubt in part the motive which governed Antiochus, but there were considerations of policy as well. Some principle was needed to unite and fuse a realm whose weakness was that it had no national unity.
And Antiochus…sees such a principle in a uniform culture, resting upon a system of Greek cities, and obliterating or softening the old differences of race and tradition."[120] "Antiochus did not, from his point of view,

carry out a religious persecution - he took action that was political."[121] But to the Jews, he was fierce in every respect in doing so.

Understanding Dark Sentences

And in the latter time of their kingdom, when the transgressors are come to the full, a king … understanding dark sentences, shall stand up (v. 23). Dark here is *chidah*, meaning *a knot, acute hidden saying or thing*. This same word is used in Proverbs 1:5–6 which gives us the correct interpretation of *understanding dark sentences: "A wise man will hear, and will increase learning; and a man of understanding shall attain unto wise counsels: To understand a proverb, and the interpretation; the words of the wise, and their dark sayings."* Antiochus must have been intelligent and knowledgeable, capable of a depth of understanding that allowed him to decipher the complex or difficult. Certainly, he had an education like that of no other oriental king. Instead of growing up amongst eunuchs and courtiers, as was the custom of a prince, he had grown up in Rome amongst aristocracy and had become intimate with many of the men in whose hands the destiny of the world rested. It was said by one historian, "The effect of such surroundings can be traced in the character of Antiochus IV."[122]

His Power Shall Be Mighty

The Scripture states of Antiochus in verse 24 that *his power shall be mighty, but not by his own power: and he shall destroy wonderfully, and shall prosper, and practice, and shall destroy the mighty and the holy people.* Here it appears that the substantial power that Antiochus obtained was that which was to be used against Jerusalem. The focus of the vision of the 2300 evenings and mornings was God's move to correct the transgression of His *holy people*. From the pattern seen in A *Bit of History* where God used the power of Gentile empires to get the attention of His disobedient people, it could well be that God also was the power behind Antiochus and the events of the 2300 evenings and mornings.

He Shall Destroy Wonderfully

He shall destroy wonderfully, and shall prosper, and practice, and shall destroy the mighty and the holy people (v. 24b). *Destroy* is *schchath*, meaning *to mar or corrupt*. *Wonderful* is *pala*, meaning *singular*, not in a numerical sense but in type. To *destroy wonderfully* would imply a marring or corruption completed by a one-of-a-kind means or event. The Hellenization of Yahweh by

Antiochus was a *singular*, a one-of-a-kind, event in the history of Israel. To Antiochus, it was a method to strengthen his empire, but to the Israelites, this Hellenization of Yahweh did *destroy wonderfully*.

He Shall Prosper, and Practice

Prosper is *tsaleach*, meaning to *(cause to) go on*. *Practice is asah*, meaning *to do*. This simply states that Antiochus was successful in his actions to *destroy wonderfully…the mighty and the holy people of Israel*.

He Shall Destroy the Mighty and the Holy People

History records the tremendous destruction, spiritual as well as physical, which Antiochus wrought upon God's chosen people. Much of that destruction is recorded in these pages.

He Shall Cause Craft to Prosper

And through his policy also he shall cause craft to prosper in his hand (v. 25a). *Craft* is here *mirmah*, meaning *deceit*.

There are several examples of the deceit of Antiochus recorded in the annals of history. Three are given here:

- His first recorded act of deceit was in the means by which he came to the throne of the Seleucid Empire: *"And in his estate shall stand up a vile person, to whom they shall not give the honor of the kingdom: but he shall come in peaceably, and obtain the kingdom by flatteries"* (Daniel 11:21). *They [that] shall not give the honor of the kingdom* were the rightful heirs to the empire. At the death of Seleucus IV, Antiochus, the young son of Seleucus IV and heir to the throne of Syria, was made king. *He [that] shall come in peaceably, and obtain the kingdom by flatteries* was Antiochus IV. Antiochus IV, who had been absent the country at the time of the death of Seleucus, now entered Syria with an army and a crown supplied by Eumenes II of Pergamum, a traditional enemy of Syria.[123] Before Antiochus IV and his foreign army came to open war with the government of Syria over the throne, an arrangement was found to which both sides could agree. Antiochus IV was accepted as king of Syria on the condition that he adopt the young Antiochus and share the throne with him.[124] Antiochus IV ruled jointly with the young

Antiochus for nearly five years, then had Antiochus killed.[125] Therefore, *the honor of the kingdom*, the throne, was not given to Antiochus IV but was taken by him through threat of force, deceit, and murder.

- The empire was bankrupted under the administration of Antiochus, and in his want of funds, he looted the temples of the kingdom. In one such pillaging raid, he "sent his chief collector of tribute unto the cities of Judah, who came unto Jerusalem with a great multitude, and spoke peaceable words unto them, but all was deceit: for when they had given him credence, he fell suddenly upon the city, and smote it very sore, and destroyed much people of Israel" (1 Maccabees 1:29–30).

- After the initial victory of his first invasion of Egypt, Antiochus IV concluded an armistice with Ptolemy VI Philometor, the young king of Egypt. Immediately after the expiration of this truce, Antiochus gained possession of an important fortress at Pelusium, then advanced his army toward the capital city of Alexandria, forcing Ptolemy to reconcile with Antiochus. The two kings met to negotiate peace, but Antiochus procrastinated in his deliberations, leaving the Egyptians completely in the dark as to his real intentions. All the while, he advanced his army steadily toward Alexandria. The result was that Antiochus usurped the position as tutor of the young king Ptolemy. He therefore controlled Egypt without actually annexing it, thereby not risking a challenge to his authority in Egypt by Rome, the rising power in the region.

He Shall Magnify Himself in His Heart

And through his policy also…he shall magnify himself in his heart (v. 25b). We see evidence of this character trait in the accounts of the Maccabees of his raids on the Temple:

- "And after that Antiochus had smitten Egypt, he returned again in the hundred forty and third year, and went up against Israel and Jerusalem with a great multitude, And entered proudly into the sanctuary, and took away the golden altar, and the candlestick of light, and all the vessels thereof …And when he had taken all away, he went into his own land, having made a great massacre, and spoken very proudly" (1 Maccabees 1:20–24).

- "And so haughty was Antiochus in mind, that he considered not that the Lord was angry for a while for the sins of them that dwelt in the city, and therefore his eye was not upon the place" (2 Maccabees 5:17).

- "So when Antiochus had carried out of the temple a thousand and eight hundred talents, he departed in all haste unto Antiochia, weening in his pride to make the land navigable [row a boat across the land], and the sea passable by foot [walk on water]: such was the haughtiness of his mind" (2 Maccabees 5:21).

By Peace Shall Destroy Many

By peace shall [he] destroy many (v. 25c). *Peace* in this verse is *shalvah,* meaning *rest, ease, security.* Shalvah is translated as *peace* only this one time in Scripture. It is also translated once as *abundance,* three times as *prosperity,* and once as *quietness:*

> *Behold, this was the iniquity of your sister Sodom, pride, fullness of bread, and abundance [shalvah] of idleness was in her and in her daughters.*
>
> *(Ezekiel 16:49)*

> *For the turning away of the simple shall slay them, and the prosperity [shalvah] of fools shall destroy them.*
>
> *(Proverbs 1:32)*

> *I spoke unto you in your prosperity [shalvah]; but you said, I will not hear. This has been your manner from your youth, that you obeyed not my voice.*
>
> *(Jeremiah 22:21)*

The use of *shalvah* as *abundance* or *prosperity* in speaking of one as having an ample quantity or of being successful or thriving would normally be thought of in the sense of well-being. *Shalvah* as *peace* would then seem to fit well into this concept of well-being. However, in these verses, this *abundance* and *prosperity* is spoken of as a detriment, as having an abundance of harmful ways or of being successful in doing wrong. It's as if the Scripture is saying in these verses that those who possess this *shalvah* will not fare well for it. *Shalvah as peace* as used here in verse 25 is, therefore, something quite different from the typical concept of peace, that of a state of well-being or of an absence of conflict.

By peace (shalvah) Antiochus IV was to *destroy many*. But how did Antiochus destroy by rest, ease, or security?

From what historical information we have on the Seleucid administration of the Jewish community, there appears quite a paradigm change with the coming reign of Antiochus IV.

"Now when the holy city was inhabited with all peace, and the laws were kept very well, because of the godliness of Onias the high priest, and his hatred of wickedness, It came to pass that even the kings themselves did honor the place, and magnify the temple with their best gifts; Insomuch that Seleucus of Asia of his own revenues bare all the costs belonging to the service of the sacrifices" (2 Maccabees 3:1–3).

"But after the death of Seleucus, when Antiochus, called Epiphanes, took the kingdom, Jason the brother of Onias labored underhand to be high priest, promising unto the king by intercession three hundred and threescore talents of silver, and of another revenue eighty talents: beside this, he promised to assign an hundred and fifty more, if he might have license to set him up a place for exercise, and for the training up of youth in the fashions of the heathen, and to write them of Jerusalem by the name of Antiochians. Which when the king had granted, and he had gotten into his hand the rule he forthwith brought his own nation to Greekish fashion. And the royal privileges granted of special favor to the Jews... he took away; and putting down the governments which were according to the law, he brought up new customs against the law: for he built gladly a place of exercise under the tower itself, and brought the chief young men under his subjection....Now such was the height of Greek fashions, and increase of heathenish manners, through the exceeding profaneness of Jason, that ungodly wretch, and no high priest; that the priests had no courage to serve any more at the altar, but despising the temple, and neglecting the sacrifices, hastened to be partakers of the unlawful allowance in the place of exercise....Not setting by the honors of their fathers, but liking the glory of the Grecians best of all" (2 Maccabees 4:7–15).

That was the long way of saying that Antiochus "did not honor the place, or magnify the Temple." He gave the Jews ease *(shalvah)* from the Law of Moses. With the authorization of Antiochus, the Jews now acted as if they were no longer bound to the worship of Yahweh and were *secure (shalvah)* in doing as the heathen. Thus, *peace* is a suitable word to describe the mind-set of these apostate Jews; they were at peace in doing wrong. Further, Antiochus sold the high priesthood to the highest bidder, initiating a series of events that brought the destruction of Jerusalem and the death of tens of thousands of Jews. By these two acts alone, Antiochus was to *destroy many,* both in spirit and in body by this *peace.*

Bringing About the Abomination of Desolation

"And arms shall stand on his part, and they shall pollute the sanctuary of strength, and shall take away the daily sacrifice, and they shall place the abomination that makes desolate" (Daniel 11: 31). The details of how the Temple in Jerusalem was brought to complete desolation have been described elsewhere, so I will only address the root cause for its desolation here. At first glance, one would say that it was Antiochus IV with his troops that brought about the desolation of the Temple.

They did, but only in that they added the finishing touches to an already desolate building. The Jews in their desire to live like the rest of the world apart from the law of God did more in bringing about the abomination of desolation than did Antiochus. Antiochus was just the tool God used to get the attention of a disobedient people by stopping the sacrifices.

"And such as do wickedly against the covenant shall he corrupt by flatteries: but the people that do know their God shall be strong, and do exploits" (Daniel 11:32). But God always has a remnant that will stand strong for Him. In this case, Mattathias, his five sons, and a band of righteous believers stood strong against their apostate brethren and the demand of Antiochus for the Jews to depart from their faith to free Israel of Gentile rule.

Broken Without Hand

But he shall be broken without hand (v. 25c). Antiochus IV died at Tabae in Persis of a physical ailment shortly after a failed attempt to loot an Elymite temple. He died in the ninth month of the year 148 SE

(Babylonian), or shortly before November-December of 164 BC. His death was thus roughly contemporary with the restoration of the Temple in Jerusalem.[126]

And after you shall arise another kingdom inferior to you, and another third kingdom of brass, which shall bear rule over all the earth.

—Daniel 2:37–39

[22] Grant R. Jeffrey, *Final Warning* (Oregon: Harvest House Publishers, 1996), 164.

[23] Dr. David R. Reagan, "The Rise and Fall of the Antichrist, Is He Alive Today? And Other Questions." http://www.lamblion.com/articles/articles_tribulation7.php, accessed 2/298/12.

[24] Ibid.

[25] Grant R. Jeffrey, *Countdown to the Apocalypse* (Colorado: Water Brook Press, 2008), 61.

[26] Mark Hitchcock, *Who is the Antichrist?* (Oregon: Harvest House Publishers, 2011), 53.

[27] Grant R. Jeffrey, *Prince of Darkness* (Canada: Frontier Research Publications, 1994), 31.

[28] Mørkholm, *Antiochus IV of Syria*, 38.

[29] Ibid., 40.

[100] Ibid., 167.

[101] Samuel K. Eddy, *The King is Dead: Studies in the Near Eastern Resistance to Hellenism 334–31 B.C.* (Lincoln: University of Nebraska Press, 1961), 99.

[102] Ibid., 78.

[103] Ibid., 135.

[104] Ibid., 90.

[105] Ibid., 135.

[106] Ibid., 186.

[107] Mørkholm, *Antiochus IV of Syria*, 136.

[108] Jason was a Greek name. His Hebrew name was Jesus, which was discarded in his pursuit of Greek gods.

[109] An intercalary month of thirty days was added seven times during a nineteen-year cycle to correct their lunisolar calendar to the sun.

[110] Mørkholm, *Antiochus IV of Syria*, 160.

[111] Not to confuse this further, but the Hebrews used the Babylonian calendar.

[112] Mørkholm, *Antiochus IV of Syria*, 89–92.

[113] Ibid., 93.

[114] Eddy, *The King is Dead*, 211.

115 Ibid., 211–12.
116 Edwyn Robert Bevan, *The House of Seleucus, Vol. I* (New York: Barns & Nobel, Inc., 1966), 130.
117 Ibid., 157.
118 Ibid., 171.
119 Ibid., 172.
120 Ibid., 153.
121 Eddy, *The King is Dead,* 213.
122 Bevan, *The House of Seleucus,* 128.
123 Mørkholm, *Antiochus IV of Syria,* 41.
124 Ibid., 49.
125 Ibid., 42.
126 Ibid., 161.

CHAPTER FOURTEEN
Mistaken Identity

With a big bold print, Hal Lindsey announces the coming topic: **FOUR WOLRD EMPIRES.** Referring to Nebuchadnezzar's great image with its head of fine gold, its breast and arms of silver, its belly and thighs of brass, and its legs of iron, he begins to construct the empire of the Antichrist. He writes, "Daniel saw an image of four successive world empires. In order, he saw Babylon fall to the Medo-Persian Empire, who fell to the Greek Empire, which fell to the Roman Empire."[127] Thus, in an attempt to define the empire of the Antichrist, he begins with the concept of these historic empires as "world empires," and with this as his foundation ends with the Antichrist ruling the world.[128] He is not alone with this theory. It is universally proclaimed that the Antichrist will rule the world—and what is proclaimed is universally wrong. Satan will rule the world; the Antichrist will rule but ten nations.

If one would stop and think a bit of Lindsey's theory in view of history, one would realize there is something very wrong with his concept. He speaks of Nebuchadnezzar's image as four successive empires that ruled the world.

Then, he identifies the four world empires by saying that the Babylonian Empire fell to the Medo-Persian Empire, who fell to the Greek Empire, which fell to the Roman Empire. Where did these conquering empires come from? If we take, for example, the Babylonian Empire as ruling the world, did it not rule the Medes and the Persians? History tells us that the Medo-Persian Empire was not only an empire that existed for many years adjacent to the Babylonian Empire, but that its peoples and its lands never had been nor ever would be a part of the Babylonian Empire. How then could it be said that the Babylonians ruled the world when they did not even rule their own neighborhood? The Grecian Empire also existed separate from and totally independent of the Medo-Persian Empire before Alexander the Great conquered that "world empire." The rising Roman Empire also existed independently outside the rule of the Grecian Empire. And the story goes on.

How then can it be said that these four empires ruled the world? Reason should have told us somewhere along the line that something was not right with this theory that is the foundation on which a world empire ruled by the Antichrist is built.

A Foundation of Misconceptions

So then, how did it come about that the Antichrist is said to rule the world? In part, it's ignorance of world geography, and in part, a bit of Scripture that appears to support that ignorance.

When Daniel interpreted king Nebuchadnezzar's dream of a great image built of different metals, he told Nebuchadnezzar, *"[37]You, O king, are a king of kings: for the God of heaven has given you a kingdom, power, and strength, and glory. [38]And wheresoever the children of men dwell, the beasts of the field and the fowls of the heaven has he given into your hand, and has made you ruler over them all. You are this head of gold. [39]And after you shall arise another kingdom inferior to you, and another third kingdom of brass, which shall bear rule over all the earth"* (Daniel 2:37–39). The Bible does say here that the kingdoms of Babylon, Medo-Persia, and Greece shall bear rule over all the earth. Thus, Scripture itself does appear to say these three empires did rule what we have taken to be global earth—the operative words here are "does appear to say."

Then, when John *"stood upon the sand of the sea, and saw a beast rise up out of the sea, having seven heads and ten horns"* and said of this beast, *"[7] power was given him over all kindreds, and tongues, and nations"* (Revelation 13:1, 7), the theory of a world rule by the Antichrist became chiseled in stone. Again, the Scripture does appear to say by John's words that this last Gentile empire to rule over Israel will also have global rule. And, again, "does appear to say" are the operative words.

We take what the words of Nebuchadnezzar's dream portray at face value. Yet, the lands ruled by Nebuchadnezzar were only a small part of the inhabited world, even a small part of that corner of the world of which Nebuchadnezzar was a part. Map 14.1 shows the greatest extent of the rule of the Babylonian Empire, and it's obvious that Nebuchadnezzar did not rule the world. How then are we to take Daniel's interpretation of Nebuchadnezzar's dream or John's vision of the power that will be given to the beast that will rise up from the sea?

Map 14.1. The Babylonian Empire
at the time of Nebuchadezzar.

Putting Nebuchadnezzar's World into Context

The Bible may state things in particular ways that we at times do not notice, or that we choose to ignore. As for these empires bearing rule over all the earth, it's a matter of prophetic perspective, a matter of our understanding of how God tells the story of the rule of a select group of Gentile kingdoms over the nation of Israel.

In that respect, there are some things we must keep in mind that frame the prophetic prospective we are to see.

- The dreams of Nebuchadnezzar and Daniel apply uniquely to John's vision of the Red Dragon of Revelation 12 and the Beast of Revelation 13. Although each in their own way describes a series of Gentile kingdoms, the true subject of their visions is the nation of Israel.
- In the accounts of the Woman in conflict with the Red Dragon and the remnant of her seed in conflict with the Beast as seen in the breaking of the seventh seal, the wrath of Jesus is focused singularly on the nation of Israel. What we are to see is that the wrath of these two beasts is brought upon the Jews solely by those nations that make up these two beasts. The other nations of the world are never in view.
- The perspective we are given of the Beast in the text of Revelation 13 is not of the nations of the world but a view of a very select but limited set of Gentile nations that God brings against Israel in His wrath.

The four Gentile empires of Babylon, Medo-Persia, Greece, and Rome that were presented as world empires somehow set apart unto themselves from the other kingdoms of the world are, in reality, part of a set of seven Gentile kingdoms that are depicted by the seven heads of the Red Dragon. The remaining three kingdoms that have thus far been left out of this picture are the Assyrian and Egyptian Empires that begin the series of seven and the confederation of the League of Ten that ends the series. The Assyrian and Egyptian Empires and the confederation of the League of Ten are thus no different than the Babylonian Empire, or that of Medo-Persia, Greece, or Rome for that matter.

These seven, in and of themselves, complete the picture that we are to see concerning these kingdoms, meaning that from God's prophetic viewpoint of the Red Dragon, it's as if the other nations of the world do not exist.

When the vision of the Red Dragon confronting the Woman is put into proper context in the book of Revelation and interpreted within the context of the wrath of the Lamb of the seventh seal, we have a clear picture of these seven Gentile kingdoms as having been created by God specifically for the purpose of bringing that wrath upon Israel. The Red Dragon itself with its seven heads is the visual portrayal of the outline of the story of God's wrath upon a disobedient and rebellious people. The heads of the Dragon are thus seven chapters in Israel's story of disobedience. The Red Dragon is, therefore, a creation of God designed for His purpose; Satan, as ruler of this empire, is just the tool used to dispense that wrath.

Now, to put these four empires *which shall bear rule over all the earth* into God's perspective.

Continuing with the Babylonian Empire as our example, Daniel had told Nebuchadnezzar that it was the God of heaven who had given him a kingdom, and *wheresoever the children of men dwell…has he given into your hand, and has made you ruler over them all. But wheresoever* does have its limits. Now it's true that Nebuchadnezzar ruled over all the various peoples and nations that made up his empire; thus, he did rule *wheresoever* the children of men dwelt within the boundaries of his empire. But it's quite obvious that he did not rule over the people of the neighboring empires.

How then are we to take the words *all the earth?* Since God was the author of Nebuchadnezzar's dream, it is God's viewpoint from which we are to picture Israel within this empire. Israel was captive to the Babylonian Empire; thus, Nebuchadnezzar was the caretaker of her people. Further, the purpose for the existence of the Babylonian Empire, as with the other three of these empires, was to be the instrument of God's wrath upon the Jews. Then, from God's perspective, *all the earth* would be *all the land* of the Babylonian Empire within which Israel existed. (This is an acceptable transition in wording, since *earth, ara* in Hebrew, can be translated as *land,* just as well as *earth.*) Thus, *all the earth* in this context is *all the land* of the Babylonian Empire. Nebuchadnezzar then did bear rule over all the land that was the Babylonian Empire, including the land that was Israel. Therefore, *all the earth* in this passage does not mean all the planet Earth.

Now to that Scripture on which the theory of a one-world government ruled by the Antichrist so desperately hangs: *And I stood upon the sand of the sea, and saw a beast rise up out of the sea, having seven heads and ten horns, and upon his horns ten crowns… and power was given him over all kindreds, and tongues, and nations.*

John's vision of the opening verses of Revelation 13 depicts the rise of the empire of the Antichrist from the confederation of the League of Ten, the seventh head of the Red Dragon. All ten nations of the League are represented in the symbolization of the Beast, and all ten are now ruled by the Antichrist by one means or the other. These nations will come solely out of the territory of the ancient Roman Empire. But that part of the Roman Empire from which they will come is restricted to that part of Roman territory that was also occupied by the Grecian, Medo-Persian, and Babylonian Empires. That is why this beast which John saw *"was like unto a leopard [Greece], and his feet were as the feet of a bear [Medo-Persia], and his mouth as the mouth of a lion [Babylon]" (Revelation 13:2).*
These ten nations, which will be melded into seven by conquest in the formation of the empire of the Antichrist, are therefore *all* the *kindreds, and tongues, and nations* over which *power was given him.*

Chapter 13 is presented with only the view of the wrath of the Lamb being brought upon Israel solely by those *kindreds, and tongues, and nations* over which the Antichrist will rule. From God's prophetic viewpoint of the Beast, it's as if the other nations of the world do not exist.

A Bit of Reason, and a Dash of Logic

We have applied a bit of reason to the world that will be ruled by the Antichrist. Now we are going to add a dash of logic by looking at three accounts of that world of which he will rule. These come from the text of the scroll sealed with seven seals that is held in the right hand of God.

When the fifth seal of the scroll is broken, John sees under the altar in heaven the gathering of *"the souls of them that were slain for the word of God, and for the testimony which they held" (Revelation 6:9)*. When the seventh seal is broken, John sees the cause of their deaths: *"15I beheld another beast coming up out of the earth; and he had two horns like a lamb, and he spake as a dragon. 16And he causes all, both small and great, rich and poor, free and bond, to receive a mark in their right hand, or in their foreheads: 17And that no man might buy or sell, save he that had the mark, or the name of the beast, or the number of his name" (Revelation 13:15–17)*. But those who refuse to take this mark or refuse to worship this Beast become the *"souls of them that were beheaded for the witness of Jesus, and for the word of God, and which had not worshipped the beast, neither his image, neither had received his mark upon their foreheads, or in their hands" (Revelation 20:4)*. They are the ones gathering under the altar and crying out to God, asking, *"10How long, O Lord, holy and true, do you not judge and avenge our blood on them that dwell on the earth? 11And white robes were given unto every one of them; and it was said unto them, that they should rest yet for a little season, until their fellow servants also and their brethren, that should be killed as they were, should be fulfilled" (Revelation 6:10–11)*. The time of the deaths of these that will not take the mark of the Beast nor worship his name will be during the last half of the Tribulation Period, that period of time when the Antichrist ascends to power. At the last of the Tribulation, just as the last of the wrath of God is about to be poured out upon man, they will appear on *"a sea of glass mingled with fire" (Revelation 15:1)* indicating that their number will have been *fulfilled.*

The stage has now been set to apply a dash of that logic: *"And the first [angel] went, and poured out his vial upon the earth; and there fell a noisome and grievous sore upon the men which had the mark of the beast, and upon them which worshipped his image" (Revelation 16:2)*.

Those who will have the mark of the Beast will be singled out for this wrath. But singled out from amongst whom? Under a one-world rule of the Antichrist, only those *which had the mark of the beast or worshipped his image* would yet be alive on earth this late in the Tribulation Period. All those who will not take the mark or will not worship his image would have been killed as they are now seen in heaven. Then, who else is there but those who have taken the mark? If the only remaining souls left on earth will be those *which had the mark of the beast or them which worshipped his image,* why would God make such a vacuous statement as to who on the earth is to receive this wrath?

Logic therefore demands that there will yet be others remaining on the earth who are not to receive this wrath. These who are not to receive this wrath are of the nations that will not be under the authority of the Antichrist and thus will not be confronted with the Beast's requirement to take his mark. With this, the Antichrist simply can not rule the world.

When the sixth seal is broken, we see the hundred and forty and four thousand of all the tribes of Israel who will be the first fruits unto God as their spiritual blindness is lifted at the start of the Tribulation Period. It is believed that these become evangelists who will take the message of Jesus throughout the world late into the second half of the Tribulation Period. Later, at the breaking of the seventh seal, these hundred and forty and four thousand are seen standing with Jesus on heaven's Mount Zion. They were said to have been redeemed from among men, indicating a physical death. Considering the circumstances of the time of their ministry, it's most likely they too will be killed for their testimony of Jesus.

These hundred forty and four thousand will therefore be killed during the same time period as those who will be killed for refusing to take the mark of the Beast.

But these hundred forty and four thousand will not be gathering under the sacrificial altar in heaven at their death, as will those who will be confronted with the requirement to take the mark. Certainly, the hundred forty and four thousand would not take the mark if confronted, so there is something quite different between the two groups of martyrs. Logic tells us that the hundred forty and four thousand will never be under the authority of the Antichrist and thus will never be required to take the mark or worship his name. This is to say that those martyrs gathering under the altar in heaven will be those living within the territory under the Antichrist's rule, while the hundred forty and four thousand will be dispersed throughout the nations outside the rule of the Antichrist. This tells us that the Antichrist simply will not rule the world.

This last dash of logic also points to the existence of a boundary to the kingdom of the Beast: *"And the fifth angel poured out his vial upon the seat of the beast; and his kingdom was full of darkness; and they gnawed their tongues for pain" (Revelation 16:10).* Again, there is a qualifying statement specifying those who are to receive this wrath. It will be just the kingdom of the Beast that will be *full of darkness,* strongly implying that there are other kingdoms that will not be. And, it will be only those who are in *his kingdom* that will *gnaw their tongues for pain,* again implying that there will be others outside his kingdom that will not receive this wrath. If the Antichrist was ruling the world, would there be anyone outside of his kingdom? The Antichrist simply will not rule the world.

Beyond Misconceptions

There are many erroneous statements made about "world empires" that are intended to justify the concept of Babylon, Medo-Persia, Greece, and Rome, and only these four, as having ruled the world, thereby, by implication, requiring the empire of the Antichrist, as the revived Roman Empire, to also rule the world. At least some of this ignorance needs to be addressed to put these four empires into proper perspective of world history.

Tim LaHay claims, "These four animals, representing the four world kingdoms, are most interesting, for no world powers have existed other than the four described by Daniel."[129] But other "world powers" have existed beyond these four. Even if we were to limit the world powers to only those that contained the land that was Israel, the greatest of these would include the Umayyad Caliphate, which stretched from the western most part of Europe and North Africa all the way to India; the Ottoman Empire, which spanned three continents, controlling much of Western Asia, Eastern and Southeastern Europe, the Caucasus, and North Africa, and existed for seven centuries, the longest period of rule of any empire; and the British Empire, which was the largest empire in history, ruling approximately a quarter of the earth's total land area and, for over a century, was the foremost global power.

David Breese writes, "We must remember that only four great empires will rule the world in the entire history of man. These four great empires are: Babylon, Persia, Greece, and Rome."[130] But there have been many great empires throughout the history of man other than these four. Some of the other "great empires" (which did not rule over the land that was Israel) include the Mongol Empire, the largest contiguous empire in the history of the world, spanning from Eastern Europe across Asia, and the second largest empire in history after the British Empire, and the Russian Empire, which stretched from eastern Europe, across Asia, and into North America. It was the second largest contiguous empire the world has ever seen, surpassed only by the Mongol Empire, and was the third largest empire the world has ever seen.

Grant Jeffrey claims, "Two additional world empires, Greece and Rome, rose to prominence after Daniel. In those two thousand years since the days of Rome no one has been able to create a true fifth world empire."[131] Yet, it was said of the United Kingdom that it was "the empire on which the sun never sets" because of the global extent of its rule. That could not have been said even of Rome.

Then there were the great empires of the Incas and the Aztecs, and the great dynasties of China. The list could go on, but I think the point has been made that there were great empires throughout history that rivaled the four of Nebuchadnezzar's Nebuchadnezzar's and Daniel's visions. But the most important point in all of this is that the empires of Babylon, Medo-Persia, Greece, and Rome did not rule the world any more than did any of the other great empires.

What then of the rule of the Antichrist? We have seen the pattern in God's prophetic word of six Gentile empires that God has brought upon the nation of Israel. If the pattern of these six is to be followed in its application to the empire of the Antichrist, this would not be a world rule any more than were any of the others.

Further, any empire of global extent would contain the nation of Israel by default. But God's plan for Israel was not inclusion by default—it was designed to have Israel become a part of a specifically identified empire that rules only a part of this world, the part that includes the nation of Israel.

A Revived Roman Empire?

The most prevalent theory on the kingdom of the Antichrist is one of a one-world government founded upon the revival of the ancient Roman Empire via the European Union, which is to expand to include all nations of the world. This one-world government of the Antichrist is commonly called the Revived Roman Empire. I do not identify the kingdom of the Antichrist as the "Revived Roman Empire" as the concept portrayed by that title blinds us from what is happening right before our eyes. The kingdom of which the Antichrist will become a part will not be "revived," nor will it be "Roman," nor will it be an "empire."

The problem starts with "revived." It is the common belief that "Scripture foretold that the Roman Empire itself would be revived in a more powerful form to control all of earth."[132] The concept of the kingdom of the Antichrist as the Roman Empire coming back into existence comes primarily from Daniel 7 verses 23 through 27:

> *23Thus he said, The fourth beast shall be the fourth kingdom upon earth, which shall be diverse from all kingdoms, and shall devour the whole earth, and shall tread it down, and break it in pieces.*
>
> *24And the ten horns out of this kingdom are ten kings that shall arise: and another shall rise after them; and he shall be diverse from the first, and he shall subdue three kings.*
>
> *25And he shall speak great words against the most High, and shall wear out the saints of the most High, and think to change times and laws: and they shall be given into his hand until a time and times and the dividing of time. 26But the judgment shall sit, and they shall take away his dominion, to consume and to destroy it unto the end. 27And the kingdom and dominion, and the greatness of the kingdom under the whole heaven, shall be given to the people of the saints of the most High, whose kingdom is an everlasting kingdom, and all dominions shall serve and obey him.*

Daniel's telling of his vision of the *fourth beast* being *the fourth kingdom upon earth* is speaking in verse 23 of the ancient Roman Empire as the fourth in a series of Gentile empires God brings against the nation of Israel. This verse is Daniel's perspective from the days of Nebuchadnezzar, the Babylonian Empire being the first of the

Gentile empires. But verse 24 speaks of *ten kings that shall arise* from *out* of this kingdom that was *the fourth beast;* thus a fifth kingdom, another from *"out of the sea"* that becomes our Beast of Revelation 13:1. Verse 24 is from our perspective as evidenced from verses 25 through 27, which identify the time when these ten kings *shall arise* as the time of the return of *the saints* to rule all these kingdoms.

One of the mysteries of Daniel that apparently has not been previously revealed is that Daniel did not see the death and resurrection of the nation of Israel—the time period of the church. Israel was *"wounded to death" (Revelation 13:3)* during the time of the Roman Empire, and this *"deadly wound was healed"* at the time the *ten kings arise.* Daniel's prophecies were, and are, for the nation of Israel so it would not be strange if he was shown the kingdom of the Antichrist as an extension of the Roman Empire. However, there are in reality two separate and distinct kingdoms separated by two millennia spoken of in these verses. Therefore, all we can take from this is that the *ten kings* of the kingdom of the Antichrist *shall arise out* of the territory of the ancient Roman Empire.

It may be helpful in our understanding of Daniel's vision of this fourth beast and of the ten horns that are to arise from this beast if we take a look at a sample of some of these theories of the kingdom of the Antichrist as a revived Roman Empire and see why these theories fail Scripture.

Walid Shoebat states:

The Empire of the Antichrist will not be a new empire; it will be the revival of a previously great empire that will have suffered what the Bible calls a *"fatal head wound." (Revelation 13:3)* But the wound will be healed and the empire will be revived from the dead as it were.[133]

Shoebat has the correct concept in that a head of a beast is a kingdom. However, his choice of the Ottoman Empire as the "previously great empire" that is revived does not fit God's pattern, for *Judah, Israel, and Jerusalem* were never a part of the Ottoman Empire; Israel did not exist in any form at that time in history. The Ottoman Empire never was one of the heads of the Red Dragon, as was the Roman Empire, and thus could not be revived as the empire of the Antichrist.

Hal Lindsey, like several others, believes this "previously great empire" to be Rome. He states:

> Rome, as a political system received a mortal wound, lingers in mystery form, and then revives to the astonishment of the world.[134]

The problem with this theory is that the head that was *wounded to death* is one of the ten heads (represented by the ten crowned horns) of the *beast from the sea* (Revelation 13:1–3). The Roman Empire, on the other hand, is one of the seven heads of the Red Dragon (Revelation 12:3). This theory attempts to revive a head of the wrong beast!

A revival theory based on the premise that the Antichrist's kingdom must exist as the Roman Empire is that of Dave Hunt who writes:

> Since the Roman Empire was never ruled by ten kings at one time as foreseen in the image's ten toes and the fourth beast's ten horns ("ten kings that shall arise" - Dan 7:24), it must be revived…accountable to Antichrist.[135]

A look at the image with the ten toes he speaks of would reveal that the kingdom of the feet and toes, which are part of iron and part of clay, is a distinct kingdom separate from the kingdom of the legs of iron, just as the kingdom of the legs of iron is a separate kingdom from the kingdom of the belly and thighs of brass. The Bible does not say the legs of iron were "divided," but it does say the feet were.[136] The concept of two separate and distinct kingdoms portrayed in this image with ten toes also applies to Daniel's fourth beast seen with ten horns. Therefore, the "ten kings that shall arise" that are "accountable to Antichrist" are not of the legs of iron but of the feet and toes that are part of iron and part of clay. The Roman Empire never was nor ever will be accountable to the Antichrist.

Another revival theory is based on the premise that the Antichrist's kingdom must exist as the Roman Empire so that the ancient Roman Empire can be destroyed suddenly as were the preceding empires of Greece, Medo-Persia, and Babylon. Mark Hitchcock writes:

> We know from history that the Roman Empire never existed in a ten-king form as required by both Daniel 2 and 7. Moreover, according to Daniel 2 and 7, the final form of the Roman Empire will experience complete, sudden destruction. Note that the image in Daniel 2 will suddenly be smashed to pieces, and then the dust will be blown away....
>
> The fact that the Roman Empire declined slowly over a long period of time tells us that the sudden destruction prophesied in Daniel 2 has yet to be fulfilled....We must conclude that there is yet to come a revived Roman Empire that will experience a swift and total destruction.[137]

The Roman Empire never needs to exist in a ten-king form to experience "complete, sudden destruction" as required by this theory. Here is what Daniel had to say of this coming destruction:

> [34]*You saw till that a stone was cut out without hands, which smote the image upon his feet that were of iron and clay, and broke them to pieces.*
>
> [35]*Then was the iron, the clay, the brass, the silver, and the gold, broken to pieces together, and became like the chaff of the summer threshing floors; and the wind carried them away, that no place was found for them: and the stone that smote the image became a great mountain, and filled the whole earth.*
>
> [44]*And in the days of these kings shall the God of heaven set up a kingdom, which shall never be destroyed: and the kingdom shall not be left to other people, but it shall break in pieces and consume all these kingdoms, and it shall stand for ever.*
>
> *(Daniel 2:34–35, 44)*

Verse 35 tells us that the kingdom of iron will be destroyed in the same manner and at the same time (*broken to pieces together*) as the kingdoms of brass, silver, and gold will be destroyed. Verse 34 tells us when all these kingdoms will be destroyed—at the time the kingdom of iron and clay will be destroyed.

The ancient Roman Empire will therefore not need to be revived any more than will the empires of Greece, Medo-Persia, or Babylon for the fulfillment of this prophecy. These verses are simply saying that when Jesus comes to establish his kingdom, he will dissolve all nations that man has created.

Another theory, based upon a Roman Empire that was never destroyed in the same manner as its predecessors, is one where the empire divided into ten nations which, it is claimed, have already brought about the kingdom of the Antichrist.

This list of ten nations into which the ancient Roman Empire supposedly divided varies marginally from author to author as each selects his own ten from out of a fairly large pool of nations borne out of the territory that was Rome. A typical example of such a list includes the "Anglo-Saxons (England), Alamanrii (Germany), Burgundians (Switzerland), Franks (France), Lombards (Italy), Suevi (Portugal), Visigoths (Spain), Vandals, Ostrogoths, and Heruli."[138] This theory always morphs the ancient Roman Empire via some set or another of ten nations into the Roman Catholic Church of today as the kingdom of the Antichrist. (In this case, the three horns that were "uprooted" by the pope were the Vandals, Ostrogoths, and Heruli.)

What is most telling about such lists of nations is that this Revived Roman Empire is exclusively European. What is absent from every list are those nations of the eastern portion of what was the Roman Empire. The exclusion of the lands of the Grecian, Medo-Persian, and Babylonian Empires as the origin of the ten nations of the kingdom of the Antichrist in itself invalidates this theory.

The problem continues with "Roman" as to be Roman quickly gravitates to being European:

A reconstituted Roman Empire - that means Europe. It can only mean Rome and its environs: Italy, Germany, France, Holland, Belgium, and England; all of which and more were a part of the original Roman Empire.139

Labeling the kingdom of the Antichrist "Roman" has led our thinking in the wrong direction geographically. The nations of Egypt, Israel, Syria, and Iraq are just as "Roman" as are England, France, Germany, and Spain. John had said, *"The beast which I saw was like unto a leopard, and his feet were as the feet of a bear, and his mouth as the mouth of a lion"* (Revelation 13:2). This territory is not Europe!

Labeling the kingdom of the Antichrist "Roman" has not only led in the wrong direction geographically but in reason as well. The depiction of the European Union coming to power as the world empire of the Antichrist has seduced the minds of the scholars, even to the point of the necessity of creating a new math to defend it as truth. Jack Van Impe proclaims:

> Belgium, the Netherlands, and Luxembourg [are] the first three horns on the terrible fourth beast, and the first three nations of what presently comprises the European Union…France, Italy, and Germany joined the confederation, making it six…Britain, Ireland, and Denmark joined the group to make it ten in number…However, in Daniel 7:8, 20, and 24 we read that the confederation will grow to thirteen…This has already taken place: Numbers eleven and twelve who joined the EU were Spain and Portugal…Then with the arrival of Austria into the movement…the EU grew to thirteen…But this is only the beginning. Eventually the fourth beast becomes a world empire.[140]

By referencing Daniel 7:8, 20, and 24 as the basis of his reasoning, Van Impe proclaims, 10 minus 3 equals 13. But what does God say in these verses that is used to justify this theory and the new math needed to support it? Daniel 7:8 states, *"I considered the horns, and, behold, there came up among them another little horn, before whom there were three of the first horns plucked up by the roots."* What does God mean by being *plucked up by the roots?* Daniel 7:20 said they *"fell."* And, how did they fall? Daniel 7:24 stated that this little horn *"shall subdue three kings."* Is the demise of three nations of the union really a growth spurt in membership numbers? John had said of this kingdom of the Antichrist, *"I stood upon the sand of the sea, and saw a beast rise up out of the sea, having seven heads and ten horns, and upon his horns ten crowns"* (Revelation 13:1). The *ten horns* with *ten crowns* are the ten kings of Daniel 7:8. The *seven heads* are the remaining nations of those ten kings after the three kings were *plucked up by the roots* and their lands incorporated into the nation in which the Antichrist is king. There is nothing in these verses that implies there will ever be more than ten kings or ten nations in this kingdom.

And, where is Israel in all of this? We must take into account that, with the exception of that portion of the Scripture dealing exclusively with the church, every mention of a Gentile nation in the Bible from the time of Jacob to the return of Jesus is in reference to its interaction with Israel. Have we forgotten that God's focus in the last days is again on the nation of Israel? The king of Israel has to be one of those horns of this beast that shall rise up out of the sea.

The label "empire" brings about as much confusion to the Antichrist's rise to power as does the rest of the erroneous title of Revived Roman Empire. I must state emphatically here that there will be an empire over which the Antichrist will rule. The issue is not if there will be an empire, but how and when it will arise. The "how and when" we have seen throughout the preceding chapters with a confederacy consisting of ten sovereign nations rising first at the start of the Tribulation Period, the rise of the Antichrist shortly thereafter as the king of one of those nations, and then the formation of an empire from this confederation by the Antichrist sometime around the midpoint of the Tribulation.

An Impossibility

But is it even reasonable to postulate a Revived Roman Empire that would include every nation of the world? Daniel 7 verse 23 tells us that *"The fourth beast shall be the fourth kingdom upon earth."* Verse 24 tells us that "the ten horns out of this kingdom are ten kings that shall arise."

Now, let's put these two verses together. *The fourth beast, the fourth kingdom upon earth,* is the ancient Roman Empire. *The ten horns are ten kings that shall arise.* To be a king, one must rule a kingdom. Therefore, we can be assured that it will be ten kingdoms *that shall arise.* These ten kingdoms are to rise *out of this kingdom* that is the ancient Roman Empire.

Now, if the Antichrist is to rule the world, it must be that all nations of the world are then to be within the ten kingdoms that are to rise *out of this kingdom* that was the ancient Roman Empire. Whether the number 10 is symbolic, as some claim, or literal, as the visions of the Beast portray, this theory of a world rule still requires that all nations of the world are to arise *out of this kingdom* that was the ancient Roman Empire. If out of this kingdom means that all the nations of the world are to rise "*out of* the territory *of this kingdom,*" the theory of a world rule fails; the Roman Empire simply did not contain all the territory occupied by the nations of the world today. If to rise *out of this kingdom* means that all the nations of the world are to rise "*out of* some esoteric characteristic *of this kingdom*" such as bloodline, ethnicity, culture, system of law, or manor of rule rather than territory, the theory of a world rule also fails for the same reason.

Postscript

Just a few comments on some of the fallacies prevalent in the theories of this revived "empire" that have not been addressed elsewhere:

●The Antichrist will select the ten kings of the empire.

First, at the time this confederacy of ten sovereign nations will be formed, the Antichrist will still be *the prince* that shall come of Daniel 9:26. As a prince, he will not have the authority to select the king of any sovereign nation. Second, there will be only seven ruling kings in the empire of the Antichrist.

●The Antichrist will rule over the ten kings of the empire.

This implies eleven kings—the Antichrist and the ten over which he rules. Daniel 7:8 states the Antichrist will come *up among them,* referring to the ten kings of verse 7 that are the ten sovereign kings of a confederacy, so there remain only ten kings in this union. Nowhere in the Bible do we ever see more than ten kings in this union, whether a confederacy or an empire. Therefore, the Antichrist will come into this union by replacing one of the ten kings already in place. He will, in time, create his empire from this confederacy. Since the Antichrist is one of the ten kings of the confederacy, he will rule over only nine other kings as he creates his empire, three by force, six apparently by consent.

●The empire will be in existence when the Antichrist *shall arise.*

When the Antichrist does rise to a position of authority as king, he *shall arise* as one of ten kings of a confederation of ten sovereign nations. This cannot be stressed enough as the Bible states that the Beast (the kingdom of the Antichrist) will have but *"ten horns"* (Revelation 13:1) when it comes on the prophetic scene and *"upon his horns ten crowns,"* meaning they are kings of sovereign nations. A nation cannot be sovereign and yet be in an empire. Therefore, there will be no "empire" at the time the Antichrist *shall arise.*

What Then of the European Union?

It is oft said that the European Union (EU) is the Revived Roman Empire, the last Gentile empire to rule the world. The EU does have some of the earmarks of the League of Ten in that it is a confederation of sovereign nations. And, seventeen of its twenty-seven current member nations are of the territory of the Roman Empire, in whole or in part. That there are already twenty-seven nations in this confederacy is in itself contrary to every prophecy that describes the confederacy of which the Antichrist will become a part. All prophecy portrays the coming confederation as arising with ten nations; there is nothing in Scripture that would imply that the union of these ten will come about by an expansion of a smaller union of nations as did the European Union. Neither is there Scripture that implies this confederation of ten nations will expand into a union with a greater number of nations, as is the case with the European Union. On the contrary, prophecy portrays the demise of this confederation of ten nations into an empire having only seven nations.

But first and foremost is the fact that Israel is not in the EU's confederation of nations! This union of nations is European, nations only of the western territories of the old Roman Empire. One could argue that nations from its eastern territories will join the EU, and that Israel will eventually join. But the certain failure of this theory according to Scripture is that Israel is to be one of the founding nations of this coming confederacy. Where was the nation of Israel when the European confederation was formed? Further, the formation of the European Union is history—this league of nations already exists! The *covenant with many* that is the authorizing document forming the League of Ten is yet to be signed. The ten nations that will sign on that dotted line may exist, but that signed *covenant* does not!

What then of the European Union? The EU may not be the League of Ten, but it is still of considerable value for us to consider. God has given us an example via the European Union that it is possible for ten nations historically at war with one another to voluntarily come together in a union for mutual benefit.

The EU formed in a time and place where nations had been at war with one another for centuries. After the social and economic devastation of two World Wars initiated in Europe within a thirty-year period came the recognition within the European community that they could not continue to war amongst themselves—that there was a need for unity. In Europe's case, the need for economic survivability became as important a factor for a united Europe as was their desire for peace. As the world grew smaller with advancements in communication and transportation, international trade became commonplace and then expanded into a global economy. The desire for peace and the need of a stable economy brought the European Union into being.

What we see today began when France and Germany agreed to form a coalition to combine their resources and centrally manage their production of coal and steel in order to compete in the international market. This brought about the European Coal and Steel Community (ECSC), formed by the six Western European nations of France, Germany, Belgium, Italy, Luxembourg, and the Netherlands. The ECSC was the predecessor of the European Economic Community and of today's European Union. The economic success of the ECSC in unifying their competing coal and steel industries encouraged similar cooperation in other areas of trade until today when the EU has integrated nearly all aspects of commerce, finance, law, politics, foreign relations, and even some aspects of the military.

It's important to note that the European Union emerged from amongst many other alliances of the time. It was almost as if one did not know what to look for, for you could not see the forest for the trees. In today's global climate, there is any number of alliances of nations, from the political, to the financial, to the military. But I find it interesting that one of those alliances, the League of Arab States, which includes ten nations of which all or in part are of the territory of the old Roman Empire, has escaped attention in this theory of a Revived Roman Empire.

Will the League of Ten come about in the same manner as the European Union? We see many of the earmarks of Europe in the Middle East, nations (supposedly) desiring peace after years of war, nations wanting economic prosperity after years of destruction, but I can't venture to say what will unite these ten nations. But if we don't know in which direction to look for that proverbial forest, we will not see it because of the trees.

A Conundrum of Ten

It has finally begun to dawn on some that the kingdom of the Antichrist will really consist of just ten nations. But that has left a problem having only a conjectural answer: how can there be only ten sovereign nations under a world government? That answer came when it was observed that "many organizations connected with the coming world government have divided the world into "Ten

Kingdoms," as Daniel revealed in Nebuchadnezzar's vision of world empires. The Club of Rome, the Trilateral Commission, and the Council on Foreign Relations each use a "ten kingdom" administration model in their plans for the coming world government."[141] This is not an unreasonable assumption (at least to a point) while Daniel 11:40 (the introduction of the coming war between the king of the north and the king of the south) remains a mystery. But can this theory of a world comprised of just ten sovereign kingdoms be squared with Scripture as that mystery is now revealed?

There are a myriad of variations of this theory, but they all have the commonality of the world being ruled by ten kingdoms of one sort or another. So let's look as this theory in the light of Scripture.

Daniel 7:24 tells us of these ten kings and also foretells the elimination of three of the ten: *"And the ten horns out of this kingdom are ten kings that shall arise: and another shall rise after them; and he shall be diverse from the first, and he shall subdue three kings." Revelation 13:1* also shows us that these ten kings are sovereign, for each has a crown: *"I stood upon the sand of the sea, and saw a beast rise up out of the sea, having seven heads and ten horns, and upon his horns ten crowns. "*To be sovereign kings, each must be the ruler of a sovereign kingdom of some sort. The elimination of three kings is therefore the elimination of three of the ten kingdoms; thus, the seven heads of the empire as we see in this verse.

Daniel 11 verses 40 through 43 describe the elimination of these three sovereign kingdoms. As we have seen, it is a given that two of the three kingdoms are the nations of Israel and Egypt. By this theory of a world divided into just ten sovereign kingdoms, Israel would in and of itself be one of those kingdoms; Egypt would be another of those kingdoms. It is unreasonable to believe that Israel would be one of those ten kingdoms, and Egypt another with all the rest of the world's nations being divided amongst the remaining eight kingdoms. This theory is even more untenable if the Palestinian state, potentially the third of the three kingdoms to be eliminated, was the third kingdom of this ten-kingdom world. Since *"Edom, and Moab, and the chief of the children of Ammon"* are to *"escape out of his hand"* (v. 41), it would be just plain ridiculous if Jordan was the fourth kingdom of the ten. The rest of the world's nations would then have to be divided among just six kingdoms!

If we were to imagine a scenario where "Egypt" is meant to represent the African Economic Kingdom (the name is for example only) rather than just the nation of Egypt, Jordan, the Asian Economic Kingdom, and Syria (or Iraq), the origin of the king of the north, the Asia Minor/Balkan Economic Kingdom, Israel then would be surrounded by three of the world's economic kingdoms. Israel would then, by necessity of Scripture and geography, be the fourth, the Israeli Economic Kingdom. Now we have a conundrum: why would Israel be a world economic kingdom unto itself? And, where is the third world economic kingdom that is to be "uprooted" on the Antichrist's path from the north of Israel down to Egypt?

It makes no difference whether these ten kingdoms of a divided world are called nations, economic regions, or administrative units. By any name, each by Scripture would be required to be a sovereign entity with a sovereign ruler. Because these ten kingdoms would be sovereign, they, as a unit, could be a confederation, but not an empire.

This theory of a world comprised of just ten kingdoms by any name cannot be squared with the Bible.

There is a way which seems right unto a man, but the end thereof are the ways of [fairy tales].

—Proverbs 14:12

127 Hal Lindsey, *Planet Earth: The Final Chapter* (Beverly Hills, CA: Western Front Limited, 1998), 81.

128 Ibid., 85.

129 Tim LaHay, *Revelation-Illustrated and Made Plain* (Grand Rapids: Zondervan Publishing House, 1980), 178.

130 David Breese, "Europe and the Prince That Shall Come," http://www.raptureme.com/terry/james4.html 6/1 3/2003.

131 Jeffrey, *Prince of Darkness,* 214.

132 Dave Hunt, "Mystery Babylon Identified," http://www.pre-trib.org/articles/view/mystery-babylon-identified, accessed 12/19/10.

133 Walid Shoebat, *God's War on Terror: Islam, Prophecy and the Bible* (Top Executive Media, 2010), 81.

134 Lindsey, *Planet Earth,* 88.

135 Dave Hunt, "Mystery Babylon Identified," http://www.pre-trib.org/articles/view/mystery-babylon-identified, accessed 12/19/10.

136 The theory that the ten kings of Revelation 13:1 must arise from both the western and the eastern halves of the Roman Empire is based on Nebuchadnezzar's image having two legs of iron that is said to portray this dividing of the Roman Empire. This "dividing," however, is first seen in the dividing of the thighs of brass of the Grecian Empire. If this "dividing" theory is a correct interpretation, then the brass should have divided into four appendages, as that would portray history correctly. This theory is invalid; Daniel 2 only indicates that the toes are to be considered as divided.

137 Hitchcock, *Who is the Antichrist?,* 74–75.

138 Andrew Power, "The Prophecies of Daniel & the Revelation," http://www.angelfire.com/bc/bibleprophecies/index.html 8/3/00.

139 David Breese, "Europe and the Prince That Shall Come," http://www.raptureme.com/terry/james4.html, accessed 6/13/2003.

140 Jack Van Impe, *Final Mysteries Revealed* (Thomas Nelson Publishers, USA: 1998), 124–25.

141 Jeffrey, *Prince of Darkness,* 80.

CHAPTER FIFTEEN
The Death of the Antichrist and Other Fairy Tales

I decided to address a few of the more outlandish tales told of the Antichrist after reading one too many glorified accounts of just how great and wonderful he will be. What I have seen written of late is akin to the proverbial fisherman's tale where each time the tale is told about his catch, the size of the fish gets bigger. In so doing, the accounts of the exploits of the Antichrist have become more and more fanciful as if we are paying homage to this man! Here are just a few of those tales:

The Death of the Antichrist

> *[1]And I stood upon the sand of the sea, and saw a beast rise up out of the sea, having seven heads and ten horns, and upon his horns ten crowns, and upon his heads the name of blasphemy. [2]And the beast which I saw was like unto a leopard, and his feet were as the feet of a bear, and his mouth as the mouth of a lion: and the dragon gave him his power, and his seat, and great authority. [3]And I saw one of his heads as it were wounded to death; and his deadly wound was healed: and all the world wondered after the beast.*
>
> *(Revelation 13:1–3)*

I start with this because it is the prime example of how even a fragment of a single verse is used to create a tale that has become "gospel." From the phrase *I saw one of his heads as it were wounded to death* comes the tale that is universally told of the Antichrist being shot in the head and dying.

The phrase *one of his heads* is interpreted to be literally that of a head of a man. But Scripture does not say *his head;* the Scripture *says one of his heads.* The phrase *one of his heads* is without doubt a statement of a plurality of heads. If the phrase *I saw one of his heads as it were wounded to death* applies literally to a head of a man, this man must literally have more than one head! Just how many heads does he have? John said he saw him as *having seven heads.* If it is true that the phrase *I saw one of his heads* applies to a man, then that man must literally have seven heads. If the Antichrist is alive today, as many of the tellers of this tale say they believe, he should be easily identifiable. What then of 2 Thessalonians 2:3, which describes a precondition of some event that must occur before he can be revealed? A man with seven heads is just hard to miss.

Further, the head that appeared *as it were wounded to death* clearly is one of the heads of the *beast* that John saw *rise up out of the sea.* If the phrase *one of his heads* is to be taken literally as the head of the Antichrist, then it follows that this *beast* is itself very literally the Antichrist. Thus, the Antichrist must also have ten horns sprouting from those seven heads (and I won't even bring up the fact that he looks like a leopard with the feet of a bear).

I can hear the wheels turning— "But you can't take all of these words literally!" Then, which words of the phrase I saw one of his heads as it were wounded to death can't be taken literally?

The Bible is very definitive in its use of symbols to describe this beast. A horn is a man of authority. A crown on the horn shows that his authority is sovereign—he is a king. The ten horns with crowns are the ten kings of this beast; the Antichrist is one of those ten kings. The Antichrist is therefore symbolized by a horn with a crown. The kingdom of a king is symbolized by a head of this beast. It is a head that is wounded by the sword, not a horn.

The Resurrection of the Antichrist

> *And I saw one of his heads as it were wounded to death; and his deadly wound was healed: and all the world wondered after the beast.*

(Revelation 13:3)

To show how the fish of this proverbial tale gets bigger, now that the Antichrist is dead, we have to come up with a tale of how he comes back to life. Thus, the tale that is also told as "gospel" is that the Antichrist, who will die from this wound to his head, will be raised from the dead. Tim LaHaye states, "As far as I know, this will be the first time that Satan has ever been able to raise the dead. His power and control of man is limited by God, but according to His wise providence He will permit Satan on this one occasion to have the power to raise the dead."[142] What brings LaHaye to come to such a conclusion? Is it that the Bible tells us that God gives others the keys to death in sundry times and places? Or is it that we have to spawn another tale because we claim that someone will shoot one of the heads of this man?

Postscript

To embellish this tale even further, we are now given the identity of this assassin, for Jack Van Impe boldly proclaims, "The Antichrist is killed by Gog of Russia."143

He Will Be a Pleasure to Behold

The world will go delirious with delight at his manifestation.[144] And just what does God say this man will do at his "manifestation" that inspires this author to give such worthy note?

At the time the *"man of sin be revealed," he will "sit in the temple of God, showing himself that he is God" (2 Thessalonians 2:3–4)*. This occurs at the time spoken of as the *"midst of the week"* when *"he shall cause the sacrifice and the oblation to cease"* making the Temple *"desolate" (Daniel 9:27)*.

Thus, his "manifestation" comes at the time when he invades Israel (Daniel 11:41) and conquers Jerusalem (Luke 21:20), just for a start. Continuing from there, he goes forth *"with great fury to destroy, and utterly to make away many" (Daniel 11:44)*.

Will the world really go delirious with delight as the Antichrist goes on this bloody rampage?

He will be the seeming answer to all its [the world's] needs…A genius, superbly at home in all the scientific descriptions…a brilliant conversationalist in a score of tongues…he will be the idol of all mankiAnd.[145]

Where in Scripture are we told of these superb attributes of the Antichrist?

Daniel did say of him that he had *"a mouth speaking great things"* *(Daniel 7:8)*, but does the Scripture tell us that these *great things* will be praiseworthy? What the Scripture does say of his words is that *"He shall speak great words against the most High"* *(Daniel 7:25)*. Will his great words against God fall into the realm of this brilliant conversation?

Benevolence, prudence, integrity, and principle mark his circumspect public behavior.[146]

This man will *"oppose and exalt himself above all that is called God"* *(2 Thessalonians 2:4)*. How is this circumspect public behavior?

He will be the consummate unifier and diplomat. Everyone will love him.[147]

Daniel spoke of this "consummate unifier" when he said this man will come to power by conquering three of his allied kings (Daniel 7:24). I suppose overpowering others by brute force is one way to unify.

We are also told of his diplomacy that *"he shall go forth with great fury to destroy, and utterly to make away many"* *(Daniel 11:44)*. I'm sure everyone who feels his great fury will love this diplomat.

He appears to be the most wonderfully benevolent leader of all time.[148]

Let's take a look at what the Bible says of the benevolence of this most wonderful leader:

He had power to give life unto the image of the beast, that the image of the beast should both speak, and cause that as many as would not worship the image of the beast should be killed.

(Revelation 13:15)

> *I saw the souls of them that were beheaded for the witness of Jesus, and for the word of God, and which had not worshipped the beast, neither his image, neither had received his mark upon their foreheads, or in their hands.*

(Revelation 20:4)

Would beheading those who will not worship him really make the Antichrist "the most wonderfully benevolent leader of all time"?

He Will Be an Economic Genius

The initial rise of Antichrist to world power and prominence will result in dramatic changes throughout the world! One of these changes will be creation of a world-economy so prosperous it will seem as if a golden age of prosperity has arrived for all humanity![149]

God said of this world economy that is to come at the rise of the Antichrist, *"A measure of wheat for a [denarius], and three measures of barley for a [denarius]"* (Revelation 6:6). Just a day's supply of food for one person in exchange for a day's labor—and the Antichrist is glorified for this prosperity?

The Antichrist will be Satan's CEO of the world's economy. He will set interest rates, prices, stock values, and supply levels…the world will turn to the Antichrist in search of answers for the crushing problems the world faces.[150]

And where are these specifics found in the Bible? Scripture does, however, speak of his monetary policy in that *"16He causes all, both small and great, rich and poor, free and bond, to receive a mark in their right hand, or in their foreheads: 17And that no man might buy or sell, save he that had the mark, or the name of the beast, or the number of his name"* (Revelation 13:16–17). How would this be the answer for the economic problems of the world? Daniel's words that he "shall prosper, and practice" indicate that the Antichrist will bring about tremendous economic prosperity, at least initially. His brilliant economic policies will transform and enhance world wealth as "through his policy also he shall cause craft (the economy) to prosper in his hand."[151]

These "words" come from Daniel 8, which speaks of Antiochus IV Epiphanies, not the Antichrist.

As we have previously seen, it was Antiochus who was the one who "shall prosper, and practice" in that he was to *"destroy wonderfully…the mighty and the holy people"* (v. 24) of Judah. Antiochus did not bring "economic prosperity" but rather the looting of the temples of his empire to prop up his failing economy. That *"through his policy also he shall cause craft to prosper in his hand"* (v. 25) speaks to the deceit (*craft*) wrought by Antiochus, not to his "economy."

This picture of Antiochus gives us a view of the Antichrist in that the Antichrist will also bring economic disaster, not prosperity worthy of acclaim.

His military conquests will produce massive amounts of captured treasures. "He shall have power over the treasures of gold and silver, and over all the precious things of Egypt." [152]

If this fairy tale is to come true, Egypt's economy will have to improve considerably from what it has been these last thousand years.

He Will be Another Robin Hood

It will be a Robin Hood scenario where he takes from the rich and gives to the poor - an activity for which he will receive uncritical, rave reviews. He will heap masses of money and an abundance of material things upon the have-nots of the world.[153]

The Antichrist *"shall divide the land for gain"* (Daniel 11:39), but this is only for his gain, for the land he shall divide is Jerusalem (Zechariah 14:1–2) and Israel (Joel 3:1–2). He shall also sell the Jews into slavery for his gain (Luke 21:24; Zechariah 14:2; Joel 3:2–3).

And, the only thing we see in Scripture of the generosity of the Antichrist is that *"a god whom his fathers knew not shall he honor with gold, and silver, and with precious stones, and pleasant things"* (Daniel 11:38).

Again, we see vain imaginings used to glorify the Antichrist.

The Antichrist is the Mastermind of His Covenant with Israel

"He shall confirm the covenant with many for one week" (Daniel 9:27). By this verse alone, the Antichrist is elevated to the great mastermind of diplomacy. He is portrayed not only as the originator of the covenant but also the sole force behind its accomplishments. And, he is proclaimed the only one to sign this covenant with Israel as if this covenant is his and his alone:

The Antichrist will apparently have the power and skill to initiate, formulate, and impose a peace treaty on Israel and possibly her neighbors.[154]

But what does the Bible really tell us? Daniel 9:27 states, *"He shall confirm the covenant."* As previously explained, *confirm* is the Hebrew verb *gabar,* meaning to strengthen. More specifically, as used here it means *he caused to strengthen.* To confirm does not mean he creates the document but rather *he caused to strengthen* an already existing document provided by another. Therefore, his signature adds strength to this covenant only because it adds the assets and the support of the nation he represents to those of the other nine nations also confirming this covenant.

We are only told that *the prince that shall come* will *confirm the covenant;* beyond that, it's all one's fertile imagination as to his influence on the creation and enforcement of this covenant.

The Antichrist "All by Himself"

The Antichrist composes his infamous forthcoming covenant destined for Israel's seal of approval.[155]

The Tribulation will commence when the Antichrist forges his peace treaty with Israel.[156]

Antichrist, "the prince that shall come," will personally guarantee that covenant.[157]

The Antichrist breaks his peace treaty with Israel.[158]

The Scripture states that he shall confirm the covenant *with many.* The Antichrist is not the Lone Ranger in this process—there are *many* involved in the confirming of this covenant.

Although it's not specifically stated in Scripture, it is generally accepted that Israel will also be one of the signatories of the covenant. With that, it is often said that it is the Jewish leadership who are the *many* that will sign this covenant with the Antichrist.[159] It is inconceivable that a document of this import between sovereign nations would be signed by a single representative (an underling at that) of one nation and by a covey of high administrative officials from the other. It is more conceivable that the *many* are representatives of other nations that also *confirm the covenant*. It is also conceivable that these nations will also have something to say about this *covenant*. Why then give such great acclaim to the Antichrist?

The Details of the Covenant

Apparently, someone has already leaked the text of this covenant:

This pact will tie Israel so tightly to the Antichrist that Israel will, for all practical purposes, be an "arm" of this revived Roman ruler in the Middle East.[160]

The Jews will make this ungodly league with the Antichrist, permitting them to take the city of Jerusalem from the hands of the Arabs.[161]

When a Gentile ruler over the ten nations imposes a peace treaty on Israel....It will include the fixing of Israel's borders, [and] the establishment of trade relations with her neighbors.[162]

Israel will pin its hopes for protection on one man, the one we call the anti-Christ...he'll enforce a seven-year treaty that includes provisions for building a Temple in Israel.[163]

In return for certain concessions from the Jews, he will guarantee protection for them so that they can rebuild their Temple and reinstate animal sacrifice.[164]

The tales told here are portrayed as the conditions imposed upon Israel that are detailed in the *covenant*. But these tales are nothing more than vain conjecture glorifying the Antichrist's great works; the Scripture is totally silent on the content of this *covenant with many*.

Postscript

A side note on Walvoord's statement that "when a Gentile ruler over the ten nations imposes a peace treaty on Israel…" The manner in which this covenant is said to be confirmed is often portrayed more as Israel's surrender to the Antichrist than anything else. Phrases such as "imposes a peace treaty" portray Israel as having nothing to say about this agreement. There is nothing in Scripture that implies there will be any authority of this neighborhood underling over the nation of Israel at the time of the signing of this covenant that would subvert Israel's will.

The Greatest Peacemaker Ever

"And he shall confirm the covenant with many for one week" *(Daniel 9:27)*. From this, the Antichrist is also elevated to the greatest peacemaker ever, as if he single-handedly brings about this agreement:

This leader - the Antichrist - will seemingly accomplish the impossible, solving the Middle East peace puzzle. And, indeed, if he is able to bring peace…he will be hailed the greatest peacemaker ever.[165]

The Bible says nothing of the Antichrist bringing peace to the Middle East. On the contrary, the Bible tells us that he will not only bring death and destruction upon the Middle East but war to the world.

The Antichrist Has All the Answers
to the World's Problems

Under the Antichrist…it will appear that the world's economic, social, and ecological problems have been solved.[166]

And where in Scripture do we find the Antichrist accomplishing such glorious wonders?

Jesus said of this very time that *"there shall be famines, and pestilences, and earthquakes, in divers places"* *(Matthew 24:7)*, and these will be just the beginning of sorrows. As for the Antichrist's solution to the world's social ills, *"they [will] deliver you up to be afflicted, and shall kill you" (v. 9)*, and many will *"be offended, and shall betray one another, and shall hate one another" (v. 10)*. As for his solving the world's ecological problems, *"the third part of trees was burnt up, and all green grass was burnt up…the third part of the sea became blood…the third part of the creatures which were in the sea, and had life, died" (Revelation 8:7–9)*.

He uses Satan's super-human wisdom to solve (temporarily) earth's overwhelming crises - poverty, hunger, and war.[167]

Another glimpse of how well this earth will be doing under the reign of the Antichrist: *"There went out another horse that was red: and power was given to him that sat thereon to take peace from the earth, and that they should kill one another…⁸and behold a pale horse: and his name that sat on him was Death, and Hell followed with him. And power was given unto them over the fourth part of the earth, to kill with sword, and with hunger" (Revelation 6:4, 8)*.

"For nation shall rise against nation, and kingdom against kingdom" (Matthew 24:7).

The Antichrist, energized by Satan (Daniel 8:24), will seem to have all the answers to the world's problems.[168]

Daniel 8:24 speaks not of the Antichrist but of Antiochus IV. But Scripture does say of the Antichrist in 2 Thessalonians 2:9: *"Even him, whose coming is after the working of Satan with all power and signs and lying wonders."* And, Jesus said of Satan, who will indwell the Antichrist, *"He was a murderer from the beginning, and abode not in the truth, because there is no truth in him. When he speaks a lie, he speaks of his own: for he is a liar, and the father of it" (John 8:44)*.

Who, then, has seen great and honorable deeds done by Satan? His track record has been one of problem-creation, not one of problem-solving. Are we to expect any different from the man possessed of Satan?

He Will Save the World

He will begin his rise to power as a dynamic, charismatic, insightful, visionary leader who will astound the world with the cleverness of his solutions to world problems. He will appear to be the savior of the world.[169]

When the time has come for his ascension to power - it will be in the midst of an unprecedented global crisis - he will be hailed as the world's savior, and so he will appear to be.[170]

Scripture states of the works of this visionary leader: *"No marvel; for Satan himself is transformed into an angel of light. Therefore it is no great thing if his ministers also be transformed as the ministers of righteousness;"* but their *"end shall be according to their works"* (2 Corinthians 11:14–15). This speaks to the deceitfulness of Satan and of the Antichrist, for they are incapable of good works, which is confirmed by their end. And what is Antichrist's end according to his works? He will be cast alive into the lake of fire (Revelation 19:20).By God's accounting, the solutions for the world's problems achieved by the Antichrist will not be worthy of such accolades as proclaimed here.

The Antichrist will rise to power on a wave of world euphoria, as he temporarily saves the world from its desperate economic, military & political problems with a brilliant 7-year plan for world peace, economic stability & religious freedom.[171]

An agreement between the Antichrist and Israel that is to save the entire world from all its problems! Is Israel really the cause of every problem in the world? This may take the trophy for the tallest tale.

He Will Talk the World into Surrender

We can be sure that the Antichrist will not have to shoot his way into power. Rather, he will be accepted by a grateful people as the proper custodian of the future.[172]

During the first part of the Tribulation his satanic backing will assure him eventual domination of the whole world population without a fight.[173]

But Scripture describes the Antichrist's rise to power quite differently:

> *I considered the horns, and, behold, there came up among them another little horn, before whom there were three of the first horns plucked up by the roots.*
>
> *(Daniel 7:8)*

> *I beheld, and the same horn made war with the saints, and prevailed against them.*
>
> *(Daniel 7:21)*

> *He shall enter also into the glorious land, and many countries shall be overthrown.*
>
> *(Daniel 11:41)*

> *He shall go forth with great fury to destroy, and utterly to make away many.*
>
> *(Daniel 11:44)*

> *[20]And when you shall see Jerusalem compassed with armies, then know that the desolation thereof is nigh…[24]they shall fall by the edge of the sword, and shall be led away captive into all nations: and Jerusalem shall be trodden down of the Gentiles.*
>
> *(Luke 21:20, 24)*

I doubt if those who will be staring into the barrel of his gun will be a grateful people or will consider him as the proper custodian of their future.

He Will Even Defeat Gog of the Land of Magog

Jack Van Impe writes of Daniel 11:40: "When Russia heads south to do battle, she will be a mighty force as she comes against the Antichrist's army with chariots, horsemen, and many ships….Ezekiel 38:16 says, "And thou shall come up against my people of Israel, as a cloud to cover the land." …Once Russia has made her move, the

Antichrist will be furious…When he hears that Russia and the Arab federation are invading the region, he moves at breakneck speed and puts an end to the militaristic activity of Russia, Egypt, and her hoards…the Antichrist has subdued and driven back the first wave of Russian and Arab invaders. At this point Russia has fled to Siberia."[174]

Hal Lindsey adds, "Jerusalem was first besieged by an onslaught of the Russian-led Muslim alliance which included units from North and Black Africa. The Gog-Magog attack took the world leader by surprise, and it took him some time to muster the Western armies under his direct command for a counterattack."[175]

Why is the Antichrist magnified for the defeat of Gog? It was God who said of this coming victory over Gog, *"I will plead against him with pestilence and with blood; and I will rain upon him, and upon his bands, and upon the many people that are with him, an overflowing rain, and great hailstones, fire, and brimstone"* (Ezekiel 38:22).

It was God who said of this victory, *"I will turn you back, and leave but the sixth part of you…. I will smite your bow out of your left hand, and will cause your arrows to fall out of your right hand"* (Ezekiel 39:2–3).

It was God who said where he will fall: *"You shall fall upon the mountains of Israel, you, and all your bands, and the people that is with you"* (Ezekiel 39:4).

It was God who said what his end would be: *"I will give you unto the ravenous birds of every sort, and to the beasts of the field to be devoured"* (Ezekiel 39:4).

It was God who said, ***"Thus will I magnify myself,*** *and sanctify myself"* with this victory (Ezekiel 38:23).

This victory is God's and God's alone. Does not God say He would do this so the world would know that He is God? Did God not say He would do these things to *magnify myself, and sanctify myself?*

Why then magnify the Antichrist and sanctify the Antichrist for what God said He will do?

Postscript

Read Ezekiel 38 and 39. Egypt is not allied with Gog, nor is the name of Egypt even found in the account of this attack on Israel.

Seventy weeks are determined upon your people and upon your holy city.

—Daniel 9:24

142 LaHaye, *Revelation-Illustrated and Made Plain,* 180.

143 Van Impe, *Final Mysteries Unsealed,* 207.

144 John Phillips, *Exploring Revelation* (Neptune, NJ: Loizeaux Brothers, 1991), 166, as quoted in *Who is the Antichrist?* by Mark Hitchcock (Harvest House Publishers, Eugene, Oregon: 2011), 52.

145 John Phillips, *Exploring Revelation* (Neptune, NJ: Loizeaux Brothers, 1991), 166 as quoted in *Who is the Antichrist?* by Mark Hitchcock (Harvest House Publishers, Eugene, Oregon: 2011), 52.

146 Dave Hunt, *Global Peace and the Rise of the Antichrist* (Eugene Oregon: Harvest House Publishers, 1990), 5.

147 Hitchcock, *Who is the Antichrist?,* 54.

148 Hal Lindsey, *There's a New World Coming* (Eugene, Oregon: Harvest House Publishers, 1984), 173.

149 Frank L. Caw, Jr., *The Ultimate Deception* (Bloomington, Indiana: 1stBooks, 2005), 110.

150 Hitchcock, *Who is the Antichrist?,* 54.

151 Jeffrey, *Countdown to the Apocalypse,* 61.

152 Jeffrey, *Prince of Darkness,* 223.

153 Van Impe, *Final Mysteries Revealed,* 202.

154 Tomas Ice and Timothy Demy, *Prophecy Watch* (Harvest House: Eugene, OR, 1998), 150, found in Mark Hitchcock, *Who is the Antichrist?,* 122.

155 Bill Salus, "Antichrist Treaty with Israel No Mideast Peace-Pact," http://www.raptureready.com/soap/salus8.html accessed 12/6/2011.

156 Hitchcock, *Who is the Antichrist?,* 134.

157 Terry James and Todd Strandberg, "European Union in Prophecy," http://www.raptureready.com/rr-eu.html 12/29/09.

158 Lindsey, *Planet Earth,* 219.

159 Bill Salus, "Antichrist Treaty with Israel No Mideast Peace-Pact," http://www.raptureready.com/soap/salus8.html, 12/6/2011. 160 Van Impe, *Final Mysteries Unsealed,* 202.

161 LaHaye, *Revelation Unveiled,* 185.

162 John F. Walvoord, *Major Bible Prophecies: 27 Crucial Prophecies That Affect You Today* (Grand Rapids: Zondervan, 1993), 329; Who is the Antichrist? by Mark Hitchcock, 122.

[163] Jack Kelly, "A Covenant With Death," http://www.raptureready.com/featured/kelley/jack185.html Accessed 12/6/2011.

[164] Lindsey, *There's a New World Coming*, 150.

[165] Ron Rhodes, *Northern Storm Rising* (Eugene, Oregon: Harvest House Publishers, 2008), 172.

[166] Hunt, *Global Peace and the Rise of the Antichrist*, 13–14.

[167] Lindsey, There's a New World Coming, 178.

[168] Dr. David R. Reagan, *"The Rise and Fall of the Antichrist,"* http://www.lamblion.com/articles/articles_tribulation7.php, accessed 2/298/12.

[169] Ibid.

[170] Hunt, *Global Peace and the Rise of the Antichrist*, 6.

[171] "The Antichrist," an article in Countdown to Armageddon, http://countdown.org/armageddon/antichrist.htm, 4/26/2002.

[172] David Breese, "The Roman Empire's Greatest Caesar," http://www.raptureme.com/terry/james23.htm, 6/13/2003.

[173] p. 178 (note that "world domination" will be by Satan by spiritual means) Lindsey, *There's a New World Coming*.

[174] Van Impe, *Final Mysteries Unsealed*, 206–07.

[175] Lindsey, *Planet Earth: The Final Chapter*, 270.

CHAPTER SIXTEEN
The Seventy Sevens of Daniel

The vision of the Seventy Sevens told in the ninth chapter of Daniel sets forth the most important schedule of events ever recorded in the history of mankind. To the Jew, it identifies the time of the redemption of his people and the coming of his Messiah. To the Christian watching for the blessed hope, it is a time schedule sought to be understood for the return of Jesus to rule this earth. To the one seeking to know God's prophetic word, it is the cornerstone to the understanding of the events of the end of this age. To the world, it is a useless tale that will soon become impossible for them to ignore. For these reasons, we will spend some measure of time considering the prophecy of the Seventy Sevens of Daniel.

The Prophecy

[24]Seventy weeks are determined upon your people and upon your holy city, to finish the transgression, and to make an end of sins, and to make reconciliation for iniquity, and to bring in everlasting righteousness and to seal up the vision and prophecy, and to anoint, the most Holy.

[25]Know therefore and understand, that from the going forth of the commandment to restore and to build Jerusalem unto the Messiah the Prince shall be seven weeks, and threescore and two weeks: the street shall be built again, and the wall, even in troublous times. [26]And after threescore and two weeks shall Messiah be cut off, but not for himself: and the people of the prince that shall come shall destroy the city and the sanctuary; and the end thereof shall be with a flood, and unto the end of the war desolations are determined.

> *[27]And he shall confirm the covenant with many for one week: and in the midst of the week he shall cause the sacrifice and the oblation to cease, and for the overspreading of abominations he shall make it desolate, even unto the consummation, and that determined shall be poured upon the desolate.*
>
> *(Daniel 9:24–27)*

The Number Seven

I have titled this chapter "The Seventy Sevens of Daniel" rather than the traditional *Seventy Weeks of Daniel* to keep our focus on the number 7 as we study this prophecy. The word that translated as *week* in the telling of this prophecy is the Hebrew *shabua*, meaning *a seven*. *Shabua* can be used for any group of seven, just as we use the word *dozen* as meaning a group of twelve. *Shabua* in Daniel's prophecy is a group of seven, thus, properly, a *week* in Old English. However, to use the phrase *seventy weeks* rather than the original *seventy sevens* loses an important point of God's message.

The number 7 is used throughout Scripture to indicate completeness, or to bring about a completion. Through the use of the number 7 applied strategically in the fulfilling of this prophecy, God is telling us that these events will bring about a completion. There is finality in God's plan—there will be no straggling days here or there to throw in an afterthought or an uncompleted task. This concept of completion needs to be kept in mind to receive the fullness of God's message through Daniel.

Daniel's Question

The understanding of the prophecy of the Seventy Sevens begins with a question Daniel asked of God. Reading the books of the prophet Jeremiah, Daniel *"understood by the books the number of the years, whereof the word of the Lord came to Jeremiah the prophet, that he would accomplish seventy years in the desolations of Jerusalem"* (Daniel 9:2). The seventy years of the desolations of Jerusalem were about to come to an end—but would they?

In 606 BC, in the third year of King Jehoiakim, God had brought the Babylonian Empire against Judah and the city of Jerusalem. For her sins, Judah was to serve Babylon: *"And now have I given all these lands into the hand of Nebuchadnezzar the king of Babylon, my servant; and the beasts of the field have I given him also to serve him"* (Jeremiah 27:6). During this time of servitude, Judah retained its kings and its autonomy. Nebuchadnezzar withdrew with no spoil except the holy vessels of the Temple and some of the young men of the royal families who were taken to Babylon to serve in the Persian court. Daniel was among those taken. This era of the Servitude was to last seventy years.

The seventy years of the punishment of the Servitude had hardly begun when Jehoiakim revolted. This rebellion had been against God as much as it was against Babylon, for God had told the Jews that *"the nation and the kingdom which will not serve the same Nebuchadnezzar the king of Babylon, and that will not put their neck under the yoke of the king of Babylon, that nation will I punish, says the Lord, with the sword, and with the famine, and with the pestilence, until I have consumed them by his hand"* (Jeremiah 27:8).

Thus, in 598 BC, Nebuchadnezzar came against Judah and Jerusalem a second time. To the world, it would have appeared that this act had been due to the rebellion of Jehoiakim, but *"³surely at the commandment of the Lord came this upon Judah, to remove them out of his sight, for the sins of Manasseh, according to all that he did; ⁴And also for the innocent blood that he shed: for he filled Jerusalem with innocent blood; which the Lord would not pardon"* (2 Kings 24:3–4). This time, Nebuchadnezzar took all the treasures of the Temple (the nation's bank) and of the king's house and took many more of the people of Jerusalem captive to Babylon. He also took King Jehoiakim to Babylon and replaced him with Zedekiah, a king of his own choosing. The severity of this punishment for the Jew's continued rebellion against God had increased several fold from that of the punishment of the Servitude. This era of the Captivity was to run concurrently with that of the era of the Servitude.

The era of the Captivity had not run its course before Zedekiah *"¹⁹did that which was evil in the sight of the Lord, according to all that Jehoiakim had done. ²⁰For through the anger of the Lord it came to pass in Jerusalem and Judah, until he had cast them out from his presence, that Zedekiah rebelled against the king of Babylon"* (2 Kings 24:19–20).

Thus, Nebuchadnezzar came against Judah and Jerusalem a third time because they did provoke God *to anger with the works of [their] hands.* In 589 BC, *"Nebuchadnezzar king of Babylon came, he, and all his host, against Jerusalem, and pitched against it; and they built forts against it round about"* (2 Kings 25:1). The city fell eighteen months later, not by the sword, but by famine. Nebuchadnezzar *"slew their young men with the sword in the house of their sanctuary, and had no compassion upon young man or maiden, old man, or him that stooped for age"* (2 Chronicles 36:17). *"And they slew the sons of Zedekiah before his eyes, and put out the eyes of Zedekiah, and bound him with fetters of brass, and carried him to Babylon"* (2 Kings 25:7).

Nebuchadnezzar stripped the Temple of all its wealth, *"⁹and he burnt the house of the Lord, and the king's house, and all the houses of Jerusalem, and every great man's house burnt he with fire...*[10] *[and] brake down the walls of Jerusalem round about"* (2 Kings 25:9–10). All those who escaped the sword were taken captive to Babylon, leaving only the poor of the land as vinedressers and husbandmen. *"So Judah was carried away out of their land"* (2 Kings 25:21), fulfilling the words of Jeremiah that *"this whole land shall be a desolation, and shall serve the king of Babylon seventy years"* (Jeremiah 25:11). Thus began the era of the seventy years of the Desolations of Jerusalem. The severity of this punishment for the Jews' continued rebellion against God had again increased several fold the punishment of the Captivity.

Daniel had been a witness to all of this. The land that God had promised to Abraham, Isaac, and Jacob as a possession forever now lay desolate before him. With this punishment of his people in mind, Daniel said:

> [3]*I set my face unto the Lord God, to seek by prayer and supplications, with fasting, and sackcloth, and ashes:* [4]*And I prayed unto the Lord my God, and made my confession....* [11]*Yea, all Israel have transgressed your law, even by departing, that they might not obey your voice; therefore the curse is poured upon us, and the oath that is written in the law of Moses the servant of God, because we have sinned against him....* [13]*As it is written in the law of Moses, all this evil is come upon us: yet made we not our prayer before the Lord our God, that we might turn from our iniquities, and understand your truth.*

> *(Daniel 9:3–4, 11, 13)*

Daniel was confessing to God that even though Israel was being severely punished for her disobedience to God, she still continued her disobedience. Daniel knew the Law of Moses, and he knew that law surely applied in this case. The Law of Moses was this: If the people were obedient to God, He would bless them (Leviticus 26:3–13). If they were disobedient, He would punish them (Leviticus 26:14–17). And, if after being punished, they continued in their disobedience, He would punish them seven times more (Leviticus 26:18–40).

For their disobedience, God had put Israel under servitude to the Babylonian Empire. But the people continued in their disobedience. For this continued disobedience, the Law of Moses was applied, and the great majority of her people were taken captive to Babylon—a sevenfold punishment of the Servitude. But the remnant of the population of Judah yet continued in their disobedience. For this God destroyed the city of

Jerusalem, burned the Temple, and made the Promised Land a desolation—certainly a sevenfold punishment of the Captivity.

This series of sevenfold punishments of the Law was what was on Daniel's mind as he sought the Lord.

His people were already held captive in a foreign land because of their corporate sin, a great many of his countrymen lay dead, and his country, his holy city, and the temple of his God lay in ruins as further punishment, all because his people had continued in *the sins of their fathers.* Even after all that God had brought against the Jews as a rod of punishment, Daniel still said of his people, *"⁶We have sinned, and have committed iniquity, and have done wickedly, and have rebelled…. ¹¹Yea, all Israel have transgressed thy law, even by departing, that they might not obey your voice; therefore the curse is poured upon us, and the oath that is written in the law of Moses the servant of God, because we have sinned against him"* (Daniel 9:5, 11).

With the Law in mind, Daniel was asking, "Lord, what about the seventy years of the desolations of Jerusalem—will they really come to an end?"

God's Answer

God answered Daniel with these words: *Seventy sevens are determined upon your people and upon your holy city.*

These *seventy sevens* are therefore in reality *seven seventies*—a sevenfold punishment of the seventy years of the Desolations of Jerusalem. God was telling Daniel that the Law of Moses was to be applied yet again because of Israel's continued disobedience.

The Number of the Years

Daniel had *"understood by the books the number of the years…that [God] would accomplish seventy years in the desolations of Jerusalem"* (Daniel 9:2). And, it was specific to these seventy years that Daniel asked his question. Thus, it is the length of these seventy years that is critical to the chronology of events of the last days of this age.

Nebuchadnezzar came to Jerusalem to lay siege against the city on Tebeth 10, 589 BC. This is the event that marks the start of the era of the Desolations. The event marking the end of the era was the laying of the foundation of the second Temple in Jerusalem on Chisleu 24, 520 BC. From Tebeth 10, 589 BC to Chisleu 24, 520 BC is a period of 25,202 days, if both Tebeth 10 and Chisleu 24 where to be included. However, Chisleu 24 must be excluded from this number of days because of that which God had said of this day: *"¹⁸Consider now from this day and upward, from the four and twentieth day of the ninth month, even from the day that the foundation of the Lord's temple was laid, consider it…¹⁹from this day will I bless you"* (Haggai 2:18–19). Chisleu 24 was a day of blessing—that day therefore can not be counted as a day of the era of the Desolations; thus the era ended on Chisleu 23. Scripture is silent on Tebeth 10; we do not know if Jerusalem fell on that day or the next. That leaves at the maximum 25,201 days for the era. Now, 70 years of 360 days per year contain exactly 25,200 days. We may conclude, therefore, that the era of the Desolations was a period of 70 years of 360 days per year, which began the day after the Babylonian army invested Jerusalem and ended the day before the foundation of the second Temple was laid.

Daniel's question was specific to the seventy years in the Desolations of Jerusalem. So also was God's answer—seven times those seventy years by the Law of Moses. Seven times seventy years would be 490 years. But further, seven times the seventy years of the Desolations of Jerusalem require the length of those years also to be 360 days. The Seventy Sevens of Daniel would therefore be 7 times 70 years times 360 days per year—exactly 176,400 days.

The Prophetic Year

The 360-day year seen in the vision of the Seventy Sevens was not the Hebrew year. The Hebrew year at the time of Daniel was lunisolar. The months began at the first sighting of the new moon and were thus twenty-nine or thirty days long. The year was then normally 354 days in length. The start of a new year, however, was corrected to align with the sun's cycle by periodically adding an intercalary month of thirty days.

The 360-day year is called a prophetic year and is not unique to Daniel's vision of the Seventy Sevens. We have already seen the 360-day year in the time period of the Desolations of Jerusalem. We have another example in the account of Noah, which tells us that the rain came in the second month, in the seventeenth day of the month and abated 150 days later as the ark came to rest in the seventh month, on the seventeenth day of the month (Genesis 7:11, 8:3–4). Five months of any lunisolar year would yield less than 150 days. However, five months of 30 days gives us the 150 days, indicating that the account of Noah is recorded in years of 360 days. We see the prophetic year again in the twelfth chapter of Revelation. Verse 14 states that *"to the woman were given two wings of a great eagle, that she might fly into the wilderness, into her place, where she is nourished for a time, and times, and half a time, from the face of the serpent."* This flight into the wilderness is spoken of again in verse 6 in terms of days: *"And the woman fled into the wilderness, where she hath a place prepared of God, that they should feed her there a thousand two hundred and threescore days."* The *"time, and times, and half a time"* of verse 14 is a year, two years, and half a year and is the *"thousand two hundred and threescore days"* of verse 6. This 3 ½ years is 1,260 days long, the years having 360 days.

The Seventy Sevens

The time period of the Seventy Sevens was determined, according to Daniel 9:24, to complete seven issues concerning the Jews: to finish the transgression, to make an end of sins, to make reconciliation for iniquity, to bring in everlasting righteousness, to seal up the vision, to seal up prophecy, and to anoint the most holy.

This period of seventy sevens allotted to the Jews was divided into two significant periods: a period of sixty-nine sevens and a period of one seven. The period of the sixty-nine sevens was to begin at the commandment to restore the city of Jerusalem that had been destroyed by Nebuchadnezzar in 486 BC. The end of this period was marked by the coming of the Messiah the Prince. This Messiah was to be "cut off," that is, to die the death of a criminal. His death was to be sometime after the end of the sixty-ninth seven. The period of the seventieth seven was to begin at the confirming of a covenant. This seventieth seven, and thus the Seventy Sevens, was to end when the seven requirements determined by God were completed.

The Sixty-Nine Sevens

The period of the sixty-nine sevens were secondarily divided into a period of seven sevens and a period of sixty-two sevens. There was no explicit explanation for this secondary division. However, there is reference to two events concerning the period of the sixty-nine sevens, the building of the city of Jerusalem, and the coming of the Messiah the Prince (Daniel 9:25). The coming of the Messiah ends the period of the seven sevens plus the sixty-two sevens. Thus, only the reference to the building of the city remains. The period of the seven sevens must, therefore, refer to the time of the rebuilding of the city. Since the start of the period of the seven sevens is the commandment to go forth to begin the building of the city and its walls, it is logical that the end of these seven sevens was to be the completion of that task. There is no date given in the Scriptures for completion of the restoration of Jerusalem. There is, however, a date that appears reasonable to apply. This date will be addressed later.

From the Commandment

The Seventy Sevens were to begin *"from the going forth of the commandment to restore and to build Jerusalem"* (Daniel 9:25). The Bible records the issuing of five commandments[176] by Persian kings concerning authorization for the Jews for the building and the furnishing of the Temple and for the building of the city, its walls and its gates.

The first commandment was issued by Cyrus the Great in 538 BC, in the first year of his reign over Babylon and the Jews, in which he proclaimed, *"²The Lord God of heaven has given me all the kingdoms of the earth; and he has charged me to build him an house at Jerusalem, which is in Judah. ³Who is there among you of all his people? his God be with him, and let him go up to Jerusalem, which is in Judah, and build the house of the Lord God of Israel, (he is the God,) which is in Jerusalem…. ⁵Then rose up the chief of the fathers of Judah and Benjamin, and the priests, and the Levites, with all them whose spirit God had raised, to go up to build the house of the lord which is in Jerusalem"* (Ezra 1:2–3, 5).

The rebuilding of the Temple in Jerusalem that had been destroyed by Nebuchadnezzar fifty years earlier began under this commandment. But this could not have been the commandment of Daniel's vision, for it spoke only to the building of the Temple, making no mention of building the city of Jerusalem, its wall or its gates.

"¹Now when the adversaries of Judah and Benjamin heard that the children of the captivity builded the temple unto the Lord God of Israel… ⁴the people of the land weakened the hands of the people of Judah, and troubled them in building, ⁵And hired counsellors against them, to frustrate their purpose, all the days of Cyrus king of Persia, even until the reign of Darius king of Persia" (Ezra 4:1, 4–5).

At the beginning of the reign of Cambyses,[177] the Persian king between Cyrus and Darius, these same adversaries wrote a letter to the king in accusation against the inhabitants of Judah and Jerusalem claiming that *"the Jews which came up from you to us are come unto Jerusalem, building the rebellious and the bad city, and have set up the walls thereof, and joined the foundations"* (Ezra 4:12), adding, *"if this city be builded again, and the walls thereof set up, by this means you shall have no portion on this side the river"* (Ezra 4:16). Further, they requested of the king *"That search may be made in the book of the records of your fathers: so shall you find in the book of the records, and know that this city is a rebellious city, and hurtful unto kings and provinces, and that they have moved sedition within the same of old time: for which cause was this city destroyed"* (Ezra 4:15).

"⁷Then sent the king an answer.…¹⁹I commanded, and search has been made, and it is found that this city of old time has made insurrection against kings, and that rebellion and sedition have been made therein.… ²1 Give you now commandment to cause these men to cease, and that this city be not builded, until another commandment shall be given from me" (Ezra 4:17, 19, 21). With this, the adversaries of Judah went *"in haste toward Jerusalem with a troop of horsemen and a multitude of people in battle array, began to hinder the builders; and the building of the temple in Jerusalem ceased until the second year of the reign of Darius king of the Persians"* (1 Esdras 2:30).

This commandment issued by Cambyses, the second commandment given to the Jews returning from exile, speaks only to the building of the city of Jerusalem; no reference to the building of the Temple was made either in the accusation to the king or in the king's response to that accusation. The importance of this in our search for the commandment *to restore and to build Jerusalem* is that Cambyses ordered the building of the city of Jerusalem to cease. Since a Persian king could not countermand his own word, much less the word of a previous king,[178] his order to cease work on the restoration of the city of Jerusalem confirms that the commandment of Cyrus had not authorized the rebuilding of the city. (This commandment issued by Cambyses applies not only to the commandment of Cyrus to *"build the house of the Lord God of Israel, (he is the God,) which is in Jerusalem"* (Ezra 1:3), which was the command in question but applies also to the statement of Cyrus recorded in Isaiah 44:28, which states *"That said of Cyrus, He is my shepherd, and shall perform all my pleasure: even saying to Jerusalem, You shall be built; and to the temple, Your foundation shall be laid"* that is erroneously claimed to be a command by Cyrus to build the city of Jerusalem.)

Note that even though Cyrus had authorized the restoration of the Temple, the adversaries of Judah still used the commandment of Cambyses for their purpose to stop the work on the Temple. *"Then ceased the work of the house of God which is at Jerusalem. So it ceased unto the second year of the reign of Darius king of Persia"* (Ezra 4:25).

In 421 BC, Zerubbabel again *"began to build the house of God which is at Jerusalem"* (Ezra 5:2). When the work on the Temple began again, the authority to build the Temple was challenged by a letter to King Darius from the adversaries of Judah. The content of that letter is given to us in Ezra 5:3–17. This letter speaks only to the building of the Temple; no mention is made of the city, its walls or its gates. In response to the letter, *"Darius the king made a decree and search was made in the house of the rolls, where the treasures were laid up in Babylon. ²And there was found at Achmetha, in the place that is in the province of the Medes, a roll, and therein was a record thus written: 3In the first year of Cyrus the king the same Cyrus the king made a decree concerning the house of God at Jerusalem, Let the house be built, the place where they offered sacrifices" (Ezra 6:1–3).*

With the finding of the decree of Cyrus (note, there was only one decree issued by Cyrus, that of Ezra 1:2–5), Darius issued another commandment, the third concerning restoration work in Jerusalem, which stated in part, *"Let the work of this house of God alone; let the governor of the Jews and the elders of the Jews build this house of God in his place. ⁸Moreover I make a decree what you shall do to the elders of these Jews for the building of this house of God: that of the king's goods even of tribute beyond the river, forthwith expenses be given unto these men, that they be not hindered…¹⁰that they may offer sacrifices of sweet savors unto the God of heaven" (Ezra 6:7–8, 10).* Thus, Darius not only confirmed the authority the Jews had been given to build the Temple in Jerusalem but also reinforced that authority by providing the means for the Jews to obtain sacrifices to be offered in that Temple. Again, only the Temple was spoken of in the letter from Judah's adversaries, and only the Temple was spoken of in the king's response; there was no authority given in this decree to rebuild the city, its walls or its gates.

In the seventh year of the reign of Artaxerxes I Longimanus, who followed Xerxes the son of Darius to the throne, others of the captivity were allowed to go up from Babylon to Jerusalem. This group was led by Ezra. Ezra was granted *"all his request"* of the king *"according to the hand of the Lord his God upon him" (Ezra 7:6).* *"Now this is the copy of the letter that the king Artaxerxes gave unto Ezra…. I make a decree, that all they of the people of Israel, and of his priests and Levites, in my realm, which are minded of their own free will to go up to Jerusalem, go with you…. And to carry the silver and gold…for the house of their God which is in Jerusalem…. That you may buy…offerings…and offer them upon the altar of the house of your God which is in Jerusalem…. And whatsoever more shall be needful for the house of your God…. Whatsoever is commanded by the God of Heaven, let it be diligently done for the house of the God of heaven" (Ezra 7:11–23).* This was the fourth commandment concerning this issue, given in the year of 458 BC.

This decree of Artaxerxes I provided a means for supplying sacrifices for the altar in the house of God, which was in Jerusalem. No mention was made in this decree of restoring the city of Jerusalem, its walls or its gates. To reinforce that thought, we see that Ezra, when he praised the Lord for this decree, said, *"Blessed be the Lord God of our fathers, which has put such a thing as this in the king's heart, to beautify the house of the Lord which is in Jerusalem" (Ezra 7:27).* The text states that Ezra was granted all that he had requested of the king. If Ezra had requested authority to rebuild the city of Jerusalem, it is not probable that he would have forgotten about this great gift in this praise to the Lord God. Thus, even by Ezra's words, this commandment did not include the authority for the rebuilding of the city.

Further, it is important to note that Ezra made this request to the king *"according to the hand of the Lord his God upon him" (Ezra 7:6),* and the king granted *"all his request."* Since there was no authorization given by this decree to rebuild the city, God must not have asked Ezra, and Ezra must not have asked the king, for such authority. It is obvious that it was not yet God's time to bring forth the commandment *to restore and to build Jerusalem.*

Another commandment was issued by Artaxerxes I in the twentieth year of his reign concerning the situation in Jerusalem. This was in response to a request of Nehemiah to return to Jerusalem to rebuild the city, it walls and its gates:

> *¹And it came to pass in the month Nisan, in the twentieth year of Artaxerxes the king, that wine was before him: and I took up the wine, and gave it unto the king. Now I had not been beforetime sad in his presence. ²Wherefore the king said unto me, Why is your countenance sad, seeing you are not sick? This is nothing else but sorrow of heart. Then I was very sore afraid, ³And I said unto the king…why should my countenance be sad, when the city, the place of my fathers' sepulchers, lays waste, and the gates thereof are consumed with fire? ⁴Then the king said unto me, For what do you make request? So I prayed to the God of heaven. ⁵And I said unto the king, If it please the king, and thy servant have found favor in your sight, that you would send me unto Judah, unto the city of my fathers' that I may build it.*
>
> *(Nehemiah 2:1–5)*

We see here a specific request by Nehemiah to the king that he *would send me…unto the city…that I may build it.*

There was nothing in this request concerning the Temple. To reinforce the fact that it is indeed the city that is in view here, we have Nehemiah's request for the king to write a letter to the keeper of the king's forest *"that he may give me timber…for the wall of the city"* (Nehemiah 2:8).

It is clear that Nehemiah asked the king to allow him go to Judah and to build the city of Jerusalem (v. 5). It is also clear that it pleased the king to send Nehemiah to do so (v. 6). Nehemiah then states, *"So I came to Jerusalem"* (v. 11).

He could have done so only by the authority of the king, for he was a captive returning to a captive land, not only to rebuild its capital city but also to rebuild the walls of its capital city. Such an act was of extreme significance not only for the Jews and the nations that were neighbor to the land of Judah but also for the Medo-Persian Empire, for it returned a significant degree of autonomy to the state of Judah. This could only have been done with the authority of the king.

Some have made the claim that the action taken by Artaxerxes I in this account could not have been the fulfillment of Daniel's prophecy of the *going forth of the commandment to restore and to build Jerusalem* because there is no mention in the Biblical record of a decree, meaning a written document, having been issued. However, there was no requirement by God for a written document. The word translated as *commandment* in Daniel's prophecy is the Hebrew dabar, which literally means a word. The *going forth of the commandment* could refer to a "command" or a "decree" as it depicts an official authorization, but only a word need be spoken to *restore and to build Jerusalem*. This was the fifth, and last, commandment recorded concerning this issue.

Lastly, note what Nehemiah did when he went to Jerusalem. He took survey of the city and then drew the rulers, the priests, and the nobles together. To these, he said, *"You see the distress that we are in, how Jerusalem lies waste, and the gates thereof are burned with fire: come, and let us build up the walls of Jerusalem, that we be no more a reproach"* (Nehemiah 2: 17). Nehemiah spoke nothing of the building of the Temple, only of building the city, its walls and its gates.

From these Scriptures, it is most reasonable to conclude that the commandment *to restore and to build Jerusalem* could only have been that which was issued *in the month Nisan, in the twentieth year of Artaxerxes the king*.

The Twentieth Year of Artaxerxes

The date of the twentieth year of the reign of Artaxerxes as used by Nehemiah needs to be clarified as there are several potential ways by which to date his reign.

The death of King Xerxes, the father of Artaxerxes, occurred "shortly after a partial lunar eclipse which can be dated to 5 June 465 BC (corresponding to the third month of Xerxes' year 21)."[179]
More specifically, the date of his death as recorded on a clay tablet known as a Babylonian Astronomical Text was the 14?-18? day of the fifth month of the twenty-first year of his reign, which was dated to August 4?-8? 465 BC. The day is uncertain as the day number of the text is imperfectly preserved. All day numbers from 4 to 8 are possible.[180]

Xerxes was assassinated by Artabanus, the commander of the royal bodyguard and the most powerful official in the Persian court.[181] Greek historians give contradicting accounts of the full story, but it is certain that Darius, Xerxes's eldest son and crown prince, was also killed at that time, putting Artaxerxes in line for the throne.[182] But at the death of Xerxes, the real power of the throne came into the hands of Artabanus, who put his seven sons in key positions in an apparent attempt to take the throne.[183] Some seven months later, as he attempted to assassinate Artaxerxes, presumably to ascend to the throne himself, he was killed by Artaxerxes who then took full control of the government.[184]

Some accounts of the transfer of the Achaemenid throne from Xerxes to Artaxerxes regard Artabanus as a king with a seven-month reign, thereby reckoning Artaxerxes's reign as beginning only at the death of Artabanus. Classical Greek historians, however, refer to Artabanus only as a high official, never as king.[185] The question then is, when did Artaxerxes become king?

The time of Artaxerxes's reign is found through a number of archeological documents which we will consider. To apply the chronological information given in these documents, we must first be familiar with the calendars and customs of the people from which the documents originate. The Aramaic Papyri used in this analysis are court records of a Persian military outpost at Elephantine, a Jewish community in Egypt, which at the time was a part of the Persian Empire. Thus, the calendars and customs of the Hebrews, the Egyptians, and the Persians must be considered.

The Hebrew and Babylonian calendars were lunisolar. They were the same calendar, except for a different day for the start of a new year. The Persians used the Babylonian calendar so the Babylonian calendar will be referenced in this analysis. The months of these calendars began at the first sighting of the crescent new moon, making the length of the year typically 354 days.

Being short of the solar year, the calendar was adjusted to the sun by adding an intercalary month according to defined rules every two or three years for a total of seven times throughout a nineteen-year cycle. The Egyptian year was 365 days in length consisting of twelve months of thirty days, each with a five day epagomenal (extra) month added at the end of the year to celebrate religious festivities and the birthdays of the gods. The Egyptian calendar was not correlated to either the moon or the sun. The Egyptians thus had a "wandering year" with the beginning of the new year wandering throughout the seasons. A given Hebrew or Babylonian day would thus align with a given Egyptian day only once every 1,460 years. Therefore, a document doubled-dated with a given Hebrew day and month and a given Egyptian day and month can be used to identify the date of the document.

The accession-year system was used by all three cultures to count the years of a king's reign. In this system, the portion of the year from the accession of the new king to the end of the calendar year was treated as the new king's "accession year" but was credited toward the expiring king's last regnal year. The new king's "year 1" or first regnal year, therefore, began with the new calendar year and was accounted as a complete year. However, each culture observed the start of a new calendar year at a different time of the year.

After the death of Xerxes in August of 465 BC, the Hebrews observed the start of the new civil year on the following Tishri 1, October 17, 465 BC.186 Thus, by the Hebrew calendar (and assuming that Artaxerxes ascended to the throne upon Xerxes's death), the ascension year of Artaxerxes would have been approximately two months in length, from early August of 465 BC to October 16, 465 BC. The start of the new year by the Egyptian calendar occurred on the following Thoth 1, December 17, 465 BC. By the Egyptian calendar, the ascension year would have been four months in length, from August to December of 465 BC. The start of the Babylonian new year occurred on the following Nisanu 1, April 13, 464 BC. By the Babylonian calendar, used by the Medo-Persian Empire, the ascension year lasted eight months, from August of 465 BC to April 12, 464 BC. These ascension periods are shown schematically in figure 16.1.

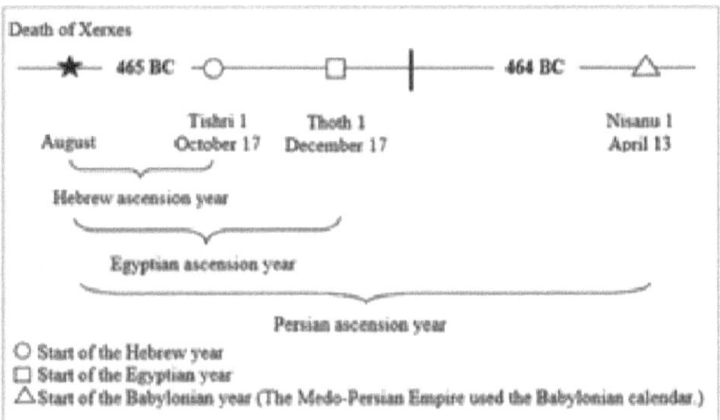

Figure 16.1. A king's ascension
year by cultural customs. The
ascension year would end the day
before the new year dates shown.

To determine the time Artaxerxes ascended to the throne, we begin with Aramaic Papyrus No. 6 (AP 6). AP6 is a court record from Elephantine of a landownership dispute. It reads, "On the 18th of Chisleu, that is the [?] day of Thoth, in year 21, the beginning of the reign when King Artaxerxes sat on his throne…"[187] AP 6 is double-dated with a Babylonian date Chisleu 18 (Kislev) and an Egyptian date with an unreadable day in the month of Thoth.[188] Because the court documents are double-dated by day and month, and the year of the king's reign given, the Egyptian day can be determined. The Egyptian date is most likely Thoth 9, as determined from the Julian date Chisleu 18, as follows:

- The year is 465 BC because the court record states the time is "year 21," meaning the twenty-first year of the reign of Xerxes and "the beginning of the reign when King Artaxerxes sat on his throne," meaning the ascension period of Artaxerxes.
- Chisleu 18 is then determined by the first sighting of the New Moon, which establishes Chisleu 1 in 465 BC. The time of the Astronomical New Moon on which Chisleu 1 was determined was December 7, 465 BC at 7:21 A.M.[189] However, the phrase Astronomical New Moon as used today is not quite the same as the ancient Hebrew and Babylonian Observed or Crescent New Moon. The dates and times referenced here for a "new

moon" are from astronomical charts and are Astronomical New Moons, meaning the exact times of the conjunction of the sun and the moon.

The Astronomical New Moon can not be seen by the naked eye for one and a half to three and a half days after its conjunction with the sun, as its position does not initially reflect sufficient light to be seen from earth. The Observed New Moon of the Hebrews and the Babylonians was the first visible sight of the crescent of the Moon. Since the Astronomical New Moon occurred about sunrise on December 7, the first sighting of the Crescent New Moon may have been on December 8 at its earliest. Chisleu 18 would then occur eighteen days later on the evening of December 25.

- December 25, 465 BC can then be converted from the Julian calendar to the Egyptian calendar by published charts of the dates of Thoth 1, the first day of the new Egyptian year. Thoth 1 occurred on December 17.[190] December 25 would then be Thoth 9, Chisleu 18.[191]

The importance of AP 6 is that it speaks of both "year 21" of Xerxes and "the beginning of the reign when King Artaxerxes sat on his throne" as in force at the same time. From this we can deduce that "the beginning of the reign when King Artaxerxes sat on his throne" is reference to the accession year of Artaxerxes and that "the beginning of the reign" began in 465 BC. How this is determined is best understood by laying these dates out schematically as shown in figure 16.2.

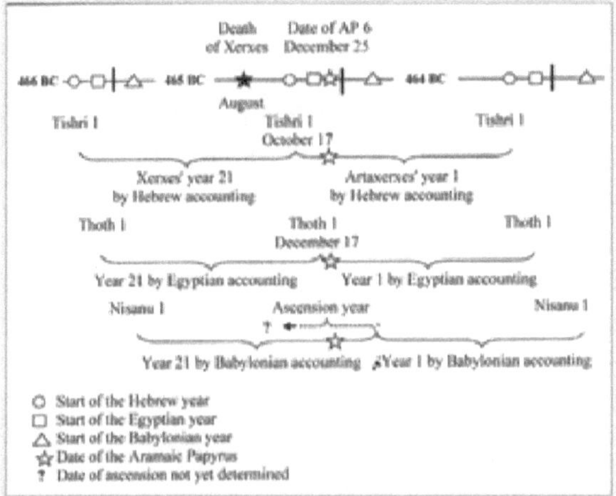

Figure 16.2. Time lines for
understanding Aramaic Papyrus No. 6.

AP 6 effectively states that "year 21" of the reign of Xerxes
and "the beginning of the reign" of Artaxerxes were both in force on
December 25, 465 BC. By Hebrew accounting, year twenty-one of
Xerxes ended on October 16, and by Egyptian accounting on
December 16, both prior to the date of AP 6. Since AP 6 was dated
within the period of "year 21" of Xerxes, the court record could not
have been dated by either Hebrew or Egyptian accounting. Only by
Babylonian accounting does year 21 of Xerxes extend beyond
December 25, the date of AP 6.

AP 6 does not identify the starting date of "the beginning of
the reign" of Artaxerxes, but other court records do. Aramaic Papyrus
No. 8 (AP 8) is the court record of the transfer of the land that was
in dispute in the record of AP 6. The record begins, "On the 21st of
Chisleu, that is the 1st day of Mesore, the 6th year of Artaxerxes, the
king…"[122] In this case, we know the Hebrew and Egyptian days of
the document, but we do not know the year, only that it is the sixth
year of Artaxerxes's reign. We can determine the year by essentially
the same process we determined the Egyptian day of AP 6. The
difference here with AP 8 is that we need to determine the year by the
new moon that was seen twenty-one days prior to Chisleu 21.

The month of Mesore was the twelfth month of the Egyptian
year. Thus, counting back in time five days for the epagomenal month
and thirty days for Mesore from the start of the next new Egyptian

year we can determine the date of the first day of Mesore. The first day of the Egyptian new year was December 16 in the years of 461, 460, and 459 BC, the years in which "the 6th year of Artaxerxes, the king" could possibly occur.[123] Thirty-five days back from December 16 would be November 11, the day of Mesore 1. Since the document is double-dated, Chisleu 21 has to be the same day as Mesore 1, that of November 11. Therefore, the Observed New Moon starting the month Chisleu would occur about twenty-one days prior to November 11, on or about October 20.

We can then determine the year of AP 8 by the Observed New Moon that would begin the month of Chisleu on or about October 20. The dates for the Astronomical New Moons are listed in table 16.1. Note that the new Crescent Moon would have been seen on October 22 at the earliest.

Table 16.1

Year	Astronomical New Moon	Observed New Moon[124]	Date of Chisleu 21
461 BC	October 31	November 2	November 23
460 BC	October 21	October 22	November 11
459 BC	October 10	October 12	November 1

Dates of Astronomical New Moons[124]
for Aramaic Papyrus No. 8

As shown in table 16.1, the Astronomical New Moon in the year 460 BC would result in Chisleu 21 occurring on November 11. By Egyptian and Babylonian accounting, AP 8 would have been dated in year 5 of Artaxerxes's reign, as shown in figure 16.3. By Hebrew accounting, the date of AP 8 falls in "year 6" as stated in the court record. (It's a bit disconcerting for a court recorder of a Persian military court to record the date of the proceedings by the regnal year of reign of the Persian king by Hebrew accounting. The names of the months of the dates in the record are, however, given in Egyptian and Hebrew, not Babylonian. Assuredly, there is no year other than 460 BC that could contain that double-dated date.) For year 6 of Artaxerxes's reign to begin on Tishri 1 of 460 BC, year 1 of his reign had to have begun on Tishri 1 of 465 BC. The ascension year of

Artaxerxes therefore began prior to October 17, 465 BC and could have extended back to the death of Xerxes. This is confirmed by other Persian court records.

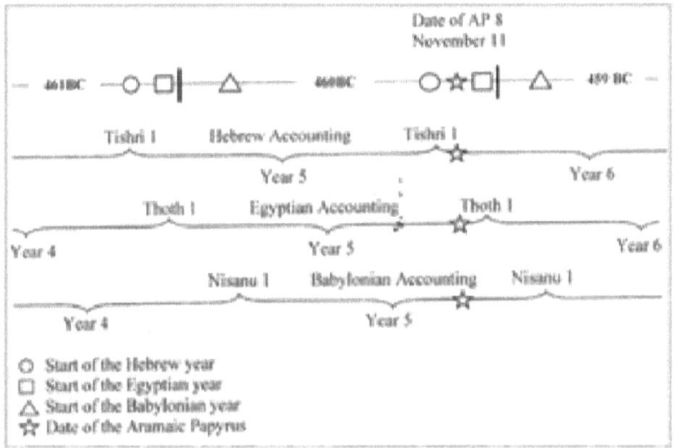

Figure 16.3. Time lines for understanding
Aramaic Papyrus No. 8.

Aramaic Papyrus No. 14 (AP 14) is a court record of a divorce. The record begins, "On the 14th of Ab, that is the 19th day of Pahons, year 25 of Artaxerxes the king…"[195] This document is also double-dated. The month of Ab (Av) is the eleventh month of the Hebrew civil calendar and the month of Pahons (Pachon) is the ninth month of the Egyptian calendar. To determine the date of AP 14, we again start with the known date of the first day of the Egyptian new year in the possible years of "year 25" of Artaxerxes. Thoth 1 in the years of 441, 440, and 439 BC all began on December 11.[196] Counting the days back from December 11 to the nineteenth day of Pachon in any of these years would bring us to August 28. Because AP 14 is double-dated Av 14 would have to be August 28 in one of those years. We can then determine the year by the Observed New Moon that would begin the month of Av fourteen days prior to August 28, which would be on or about August 14. The dates for the Astronomical New Moons are listed in table 16.2.

Table 16.2
Dates of Astronomical New Moons[197]
for Aramaic Papyrus No. 14[198]

Year	Astronomical New Moon	Observed New Moon[198]	Date of Av 14
441 BC	August 23	August 24	September 7
440 BC	August 12	August 13	August 28
439 BC	August 2	August 3	August 17

As shown in table 16.2, the Astronomical New Moon in the year 440 BC would result in Av 14 occurring on August 28. By Hebrew, Egyptian, and Babylonian accounting, AP 14 was dated in year 25 of Artaxerxes's reign, as shown in figure 16.4.

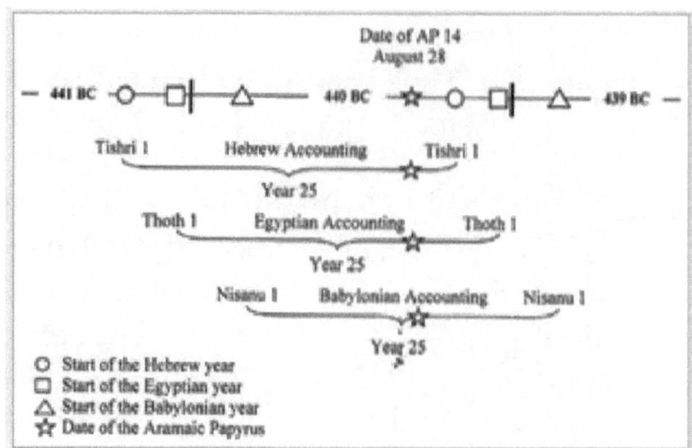

Figure 16.4. Time lines
for understanding Aramaic Papyrus No. 14.

From the dates and the given years of Artaxerxes's reign recorded in these Aramaic Papyri, the twentieth regnal year of his reign would begin on Tishri 1, 446 BC by Hebrew accounting, on Thoth 1, 446 BC by Egyptian accounting, and on Nisanu 1, 445 BC by Babylonian accounting. The next question is, what accounting did Nehemiah use when he said the commandment to restore and to build Jerusalem was given him *"in the month Nisan, in the twentieth year of Artaxerxes the king"* (Nehemiah 2:1)?

"In the month Chisleu, in the twentieth year" (Nehemiah 1:1) of the reign of Artaxerxes, Nehemiah spoke to some Jews who had come from Judah

concerning conditions in Jerusalem. He was told that *"the remnant that are left of the captivity there in the province are in great affliction and reproach: the wall of Jerusalem also is broken down, and the gates thereof are burned with fire" (v. 3).* Nehemiah was yet grieved by these words when in *"the month Nisan, in the twentieth year of Artaxerxes the king"* he came before the king. Artaxerxes, seeing the unusual sad countenance of Nehemiah, asked him of his sadness. Nehemiah answered, *"Why should not my countenance be sad, when the city, the place of my fathers' sepulchers, lay waste, and the gates thereof are consumed with fire?" (v. 3).* When then asked of his request, Nehemiah *"said unto the king, If it please the king, and if your servant have found favor in your sight, that you would send me unto Judah, unto the city of my fathers' sepulchers, that I may build it" (v. 5).*

For the month Chisleu (November) to precede the month of Nisan (April) in any regnal year of Artaxerxes's reign, the accounting could only have been by the Hebrew calendar as shown in figure 16.5.

Artaxerxes's twentieth year by Hebrew accounting began on September 18, 446 BC. However, the month Nisan of his twentieth year, the time of the commandment to *restore and to build Jerusalem,* was the next spring, in the year 445 BC.

To close the subject of Artaxerxes's reign, year 1 of his reign began on Tishri 1 (October 17) of 465 BC with his ascension year appearing to extend back to the death of Xerxes in early August of 465 BC.

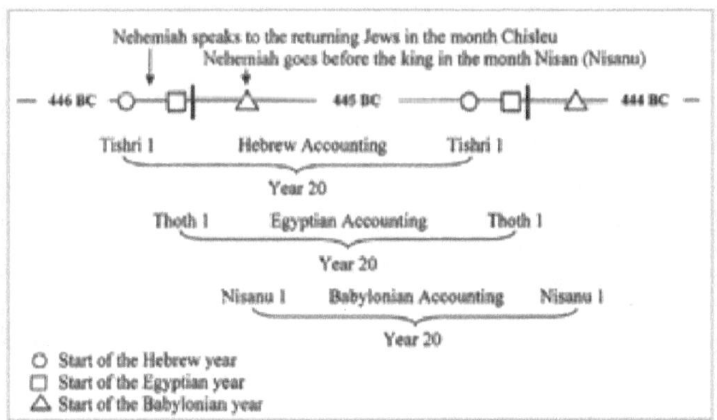

Figure 16.5. Nehemiah's accounting of the 20th year of the reign of Artaxerxes.

Completing the Restoration of Jerusalem

Daniel was told that seventy sevens were determined not only on his people but also upon his holy city, Jerusalem. From this we see that Jerusalem was to play an important role in the fulfillment of the prophecy. The city therefore had to be rebuilt. The time to completion of the rebuilding of the city is given in Daniel 9:25: *"From the going forth of the commandment to restore and to build Jerusalem unto the Messiah the Prince shall be seven weeks, and threescore and two weeks: the street shall be built again, and the wall, even in troublous times."* It is the first seven weeks referenced within this verse that is the allotted time to rebuild the city, its walls and its gates. Based on the date of Nisan 8, 445 BC for *the going forth of the commandment,* the city was to be rebuilt by Tammuz 17, 397 BC.[199]

Tammuz 17 is mentioned in the book of Zechariah as *"the fast of the fourth month."* According to the Mishnah (Taanit 4:6), five calamities befell the Jewish people on this day. However, only two of these calamitous events had occurred by the time of Nehemiah: It was the date on which Moses broke the first set of Ten Commandments upon seeing the people sinning with the Golden Calf. It was also the day on which Nebuchadnezzar and his Babylonian forces breached the walls of Jerusalem on their way to destroying the Temple.

Prayers on this day include special *selichot* prayers that mourn their losses and ask for forgiveness. Excerpts from the *selichot* of Tammuz 17 state "We rebelled against Him Who dwells in heaven, therefore we were scattered in all directions…. We acted rebelliously before Thee with slandering tongues, therefore our tongues were made to learn to utter lamentation."[200]

I see a sign in this act of rebuilding the city of Jerusalem of the nation of Israel moving toward finishing their transgression and making reconciliation for the iniquity that had brought about this destruction of Jerusalem. Thus, I do not believe it is coincidental that the rebuilding of Jerusalem, its walls and its gates, was to be completed on the same day that the wall was first breached. Such a time schedule is not unlike God's workings.

Unto the Messiah the Prince

From the commandment to restore and to build Jerusalem *unto the Messiah the Prince was to be seven weeks, and threescore and two weeks.* The one who is the *Messiah the prince* is Jesus. The use of prince in reference to Jesus in verse 25 was not as a title as was *Messiah* but as a proper description of the status of his earthly reign at that point in the chronology of the vision. The intent is to contrast his coming as a servant at the end of the sixty-ninth seven with his coming as a ruler at the end of the seventieth seven. Whatever event that was to fulfill the words *unto the Messiah the Prince* therefore had to occur before the crucifixion of Jesus, since after threescore and two weeks shall Messiah be cut off, referring to his death on the cross.

There are several events recorded in Scripture that would appear to mark the coming of Jesus in some manner as the Messiah. The first would have been the birth of Jesus when he was proclaimed *"Christ the Lord" (Luke 2:11)*. Another would have been the time when Jesus was recognized as the Messiah by Andrew, recorded in John 1:41. Also at the start of his ministry would have been the baptism of Jesus by John. The last event would have been at the end of his ministry when, as he rode into Jerusalem, the people proclaimed him king (Luke 19:37–38).

To determine which event was to bring to a close the first sixty-nine sevens, we first must determine the general time frame of the end of these 483 years. Since there are several sets of dates used by scholars to start and to end this 483-year period, we will consider the time of occurrence of several historical events to eventually identify the specific event and its date that fulfills Daniel's prophecy.

The Birth of Jesus

We start our search for the event that fulfills the phrase *unto the Messiah the prince* with the birth of Jesus, since there is considerable information on the time of his birth, limiting this date to a quite narrow period in time. From this we can determine the start of his ministry, as we know that *"Jesus himself began to be about thirty years of age" (Luke 3:23)* when he began his ministry.

Tertullian, born about AD 160, was one of the earliest Christian historians. He states that Jesus was born the forty-first year of the reign of Augustus [Octavianus Caesar], and that Augustus reigned fifteen years after the birth of Jesus.[201] There were three ways in which the years of the reign of Augustus could be reckoned: (1) from the death of Julius Caesar on March 15, 44 BC; (2) from the establishment of the Second Triumvirate on November 27, 43 BC[202];

or (3) from the defeat and death of Marcus Antonius (Mark Antony) and Cleopatra in August of 30 BC when Augustus became supreme over all of the Roman world.

It is apparent that Tertullian reckoned the start of the reign of Augustus from 43 BC as he assigns a rule of fifty-six years, forty-one years prior to the birth of Jesus and fifteen years following. From the establishment of the Second Triumvirate on November 27, 43 BC until his death on August 19, AD 14 is just three months short of that fifty-six-year period of reign. (Tertullian apparently used regnal years for the length of reign.) Based on this, it might be assumed that Jesus was born about the end of the forty-one-year period and the start of the fifteen-year period, thus about the end of November, 2 BC.

Eusebius (ca. AD 263–339), another early historian and a native of Palestine, wrote, "It was in the forty-second year of the reign of Augustus…that our Saviour and Lord Jesus Christ was born."[203] As did Tertullian, Eusebius begins the reign of Augustus from 43 BC.

That Eusebius gives the date as the forty-second year rather than the forty-first year, as given by Tertullian, would appear to be a contradiction. However, Irenaeus (ca. AD 120–203), yet another early Christian writer, states of the birth of Jesus that "our Lord was born about the forty-first year of the reign of Augustus."[204] As did Tertullian and Eusebius, he also begins the reign of Augustus from the fall of 43 BC.

Irenaeus gives us the solution to the contradiction in years with the phrase "about the forty-first year." Adam Rutherford, in his *Treatise on Bible Chronology*, makes the point that "at that period of literature, the word 'about', applied to chronological numbers, was often used not in the sense of *roughly, vaguely, or approximately*, but with the meaning of with close proximately to or almost exactly."[205] Thus, according to the language of the day, when Irenaeus says "about the forty-first year" of the rule of Augustus, he means within only a few days of the start or of the end of the forty-first year. If the birth of Jesus occurred during the period of the last days of the forty-first year or first days of the forty-second year of the reign of Augustus, all three writers would be referring to the same narrow time period. This points to the conclusion that Jesus was born in late November or early December of 2 BC.

Tertullian also tells us that Jesus was born twenty-eight years after the death of Cleopatra[206] who died on August 12, 30 BC.[207] Twenty-eight complete years after Cleopatra's death would come to an end on August 11, 2 BC. A birth date of November/December of 2 BC well fits this time span.

Further, Eusebius tells us that Jesus was born twenty-eight years after the subjugation of Egypt and the death of Antony and Cleopatra.[208] The naval forces of Augustus severely defeated Antony at the battle of Actium in Greece on September 2, 31 BC.[209] Less than a year later, Antony committed suicide when defeated by Augustus at Alexandra. After Antony's death, Cleopatra was taken to Augustus, where she too committed suicide, bringing all of Egypt under the rule of Rome. Thus, the date of the birth of Jesus given to us by Eusebius was no earlier than August of 2 BC, which agrees with the time given by Tertullian.

The conclusion from these dates is that Jesus was born in late November or early December of 2 BC.

These date comparisons are laid out graphically in Table 16.3, "Chronology of Events Dating the Birth and Death of Jesus."

The Death of Herod

Another measure of the time of the birth of Jesus is the time of the death of Herod the Great, the king of Judea, for Matthew 2 indicates that his birth was before Herod's death. We can identify the approximate time of Herod's death from Josephus who records an eclipse of the moon a short time before his death, the only mention Josephus makes of an eclipse in any of his writings.[210] History also records Herod's death shortly before the Jew's Passover.

It has been universally accepted that this eclipse occurred on March 13, 4 BC. The Passover of that year began on the evening of April 9. However, Rutherford, in his *Treatise on Bible Chronology,* makes a strong argument for the premise of Herod's death in 4 BC to be entirely wrong.[211] The eclipse of the moon cited to justify the 4 BC date for the death of Herod preceded the Passover of that year by only twenty-eight days. He claims the events that took place between the burning of "the other Matthias" on the day of the eclipse and the following Passover required a considerable longer period of time than those twenty-eight days.

Table 16.3
Chronology of Events Dating the
Birth and Death of Jesus

BC 43	November 27 Second Triumvirate					
BC 42	November 27 End of year 1					
BC 41	2					
BC 40	3					
BC 39	4			185th Olympiad		
BC 38	5			185th Olympiad		
BC 37	6			185th Olympiad	1	
BC 36	7			185th Olympiad	2	
BC 35	8				3	
BC 34	9				4	
BC 33	10				5	
BC 32	11				6	
BC 31	12			September 2 Battle of Actium	7th year of Herod's reign	
BC 30	13		August 12 Death of Cleopatra	September 1 End of year 1	8	
BC 29	14		August 11 End of year 1	2	9	
BC 28	15		2	3	10	
BC 27	16		3	4	11	
BC 26	17		4	5	12	
BC 25	18		5	6	13	

Table 16.3

BC 24	19		6	7	14	
BC 23	20		7	8	15	
BC 22	21		8	9	16	
BC 21	22		9	10	17	
BC 20	23		10	11	18	
BC 19	24		11	12	19	
BC 18	25		12	13	20	
BC 17	26		13	14	21	
BC 16	27		14	15	22	
BC 15	28		15	16	23	
BC 14	29		16	17	24	
BC 13	30		17	18	25	
BC 12	31		18	19	26	
BC 11	32		19	20	27	
BC 10	33		20	21	28	
BC 9	34		21	22	29	
BC 8	35		22	23	30	
BC 7	36		23	24	31	
BC 6	37		24	25	32	
BC 5	38		25	26	33	
BC 4	39		26	27	34	

Table 16.3 continued
Chronology of Events Dating the
Birth and Death of Jesus

BC 3	40		27	28	35	
BC 2	November 27 End of year 41	Reign of Augustus after birth of Jesus	August 11 End of year 28	29	36	November/December Birth of Jesus
BC 1	42	November 27 End of year 1		30	37th year of Herod Dec 29, moon's eclipse	November/December Jesus 1 year old
AD 1	43	2		31	January, Herod's death	2
AD 2	44	3		32		3
AD 3	45	4		33		4
AD 4	46	5		34		5
AD 5	47	6		35		6
AD 6	48	7		36		7
AD 7	49	8		37		8
AD 8	50	9		38		9
AD 9	51	10		39		10
AD 10	52	11		40		11
AD 11	53	12		41		12
AD 12	54	13		42		13
AD 13	55	14		43		14
AD 14	56th year, Aug 19 Death of Augustus	56th year, Aug 19 Death of Augustus	September 17 Tiberius begins reign	44		15
AD 15			September 16 End of year 1	September 1 End of year 45		16
AD 16			2	46		17
AD 17			3	47		18

AD 18		4			19
AD 19		5			20
AD 20		6			21
AD 21		7			22
AD 22		8			23
AD 23		9			24
AD 24		10			25
AD 25		11			26
AD 26		12			27
AD 27		13			28
AD 28		14			29
AD 29		September End of year 15		May/June John turns 30	November/December Jesus turns 30
AD 30		16			Passover of April 5, 30 AD
AD 31		17			Passover of March 26, 31AD
AD 32		September End of year 18			Passover of April 13, 32 AD

Herod had been ill for some while prior to this time, but it appears from the words of Josephus that Herod's illness greatly increased at the time of this eclipse.[212] His physicians thus recommended he go beyond the Jordan to bathe in the warm baths that were at Callirrhoe on the eastern side of the Dead Sea. Once there, having no hope of recovery, he returned to Jericho where he died. This activity alone must have consumed many days of the period between the night of the eclipse and the day of Passover.

The preparation for Herod's funeral was very elaborate: "It being Archelaus's care that the procession to his father's sepulcher should be very sumptuous."[213] The funeral procession from Jericho to Herodium, where Herod was to be buried, included his numerous relations, his soldiery, distinguished according to their countries and denominations, and behind these the whole army, everyone in their habiliments of war; these were followed by five hundred of his domestics carrying spices. The distance from Jericho to Herodium was a distance of two hundred furlongs, and the procession moved only eight furlongs in a day.[214] This march took twenty-five days in and of itself. Another seven days were consumed in mourning.[215]

The days required for the events described thus far considerably exceed the twenty-eight-day period between the night of the eclipse and the Passover in the year 4 BC. And, there was another problem. Herod's successor, Archelaus, had to deal with another problem that also took place between the time of Herod's death and the Passover. Upon the approach of the Passover, there was an uprising in Jerusalem by those Jews who lamented the death of Judas and Matthias by Herod's hand, who were the leaders of those who had earlier pulled down the golden eagle Herod had placed on the Temple. Archelaus sent a regiment of armed men to suppress the uprising, but the greatest part of the soldiers were stoned by the Jews. Archelaus then "sent out the whole army upon them" to put down the Jew's rebellion.[216] The putting down of this rebellion also consumed many additional days between the time of Herod's death and the Passover.

We have seen that the time required for Herod to travel to Callirrhoe, and then to Jericho where he died, the time for the preparation of his elaborate funeral, the time for mourning, the time to put down the Jew's rebellion, and most likely the time for the lengthy funeral procession from Jericho to Herodium, required far more than the twenty-eight days between the eclipse and the Passover of 4 BC. We must therefore look for a lunar eclipse in another year, and Josephus himself points to that year.

Josephus states that battle for the Roman Empire at Actium between Octavius Caesar and Mark Antony occurred during the seventh year of the reign of Herod.[217] The battle of Actium was fought on September 2, 31 BC. Further, Josephus states that Herod reigned for thirty-seven years.[218] Since we know that the seventh year of Herod's reign overlapped the battle of Actium, his thirty-seventh year would have overlapped September 2, 1 BC. At the extreme, Herod's death would have occurred sometime between September of 2 BC and August of AD 1. That itself puts Herod's death out of the range of 4 BC.

There were no lunar eclipses seen in Jerusalem in 2 BC, but there were two eclipses in 1 BC, the first on January 9/10 that occurred nearly four complete months before the Passover of 1 BC, and the second on December 29 that occurred just over three months before the Passover of AD 1. Matthew's account of Herod's attempt to kill this new "king of the Jews" will help in determining which of these two dates would be the most probable time of his death.

Matthew gives us the story of the wise men from the east who came seeking *"he that is born King of the Jews" (Matthew 2:2)*. From these wise men, Herod learned that he had a threat to his throne. Herod was jealous for his throne, so much so that he had previously killed his own sons so they could not challenge his position. Now Herod had another threat, this one from a newborn "king of the Jews." He also learned of the time the star had appeared that had guided the wise men to this destination.

Sometime after their meeting with Herod, the wise men entered into the house where they saw the young child with Mary his mother. From this text, it appears that some time had elapsed since the birth of Jesus, yet Herod had ascertained the approximate time of the birth of this new rival. Herod had requested the wise men report back to him when they found this king, but being warned of God that they should not return to Herod, *"they departed into their own country another way" (Matthew 2:12)*. Now *"when he saw that he was mocked of the wise men, was exceeding wroth, and sent forth, and slew all the children that were in Bethlehem, Bethlehem,and in all the coasts thereof, from two years old and under, according to the time which he had diligently enquired of the wise men"* (Matthew 2:16).

Now when Herod instructed the wise men, he said to them *"Go and search diligently for the young child"* (Matthew 2:8). The Hebrew word used by Matthew to describe Jesus at this time is *paidion*, meaning *little or young lad*. Herod, therefore, was not looking for an infant when he sent out those to slay the children of Bethlehem. We don't know how long before his death that Herod had met with the wise men or issued the order to slay the children. Therefore, from what is known thus far, I assumed Herod's order to slay the children of Bethlehem, his death and all the proceedings of his burial occurred within two months of the Passover.

The January 9/10, 1 BC eclipse preceded the Passover of April 6, 1 BC by nearly four months. The death of Herod would then have occurred two months earlier in early February of 1 BC. The birth of Jesus in late November or early December of 2 BC would then have Jesus an infant of about two months of age and not the young child being sought. This date is just a little too early.

The eclipse of December 29, 1 BC preceded the Passover of March 27, AD 1 by almost exactly three months. Herod would then have died in late January of AD 1 and Jesus would have been just over a year old. Herod's death at this time would have allowed time for Jesus to become the young child he was seeking.

Cyrenius as Governor of Syria

At some time prior to the birth of Jesus, a decree had gone out that a census was to be taken: *"1And it came to pass in those days, that there went out a decree from Caesar Augustus, that all the world should be taxed. 2(And this taxing was first made when Cyrenius was governor of Syria.) 3And all went to be taxed, every one into his own city"* (Luke 2:1–3). It was this decree that brought Joseph and Mary to Bethlehem.

There is considerable debate about Luke's statement that Cyrenius (Publius Sulpicius Quirinius) conducted a taxation of Judea as the governor of Syria during the time of the birth of Jesus. Even though there are other early writers besides Luke who also claim there was a census in Judea at that time, the claim is still made today that Luke was just plain wrong in his statement about Cyrenius.

A part of this problem of the governorship of Syria is that the focus has been on the wrong historical period, that of 6 to 4 BC, the commonly accepted time of the birth of Jesus.

Roman records show Cyrenius was not the governor of the province of Syria during that period. Therefore, if Jesus was born prior to 3 BC, Luke's critics would be right.

A list of governors of the period typically looks like that of Table 16.4. Various names appear in the space for 3–2 BC depending on the opinion of the chronicler, but I have placed a question mark there, as no records of the governorship of Syria have been found for this time period.

Table 16.4	
Governors of the Province of Syria	
10-9 BC	Marcus Titus
9-6 BC	Sentius Saturninus
6-4 BC	Quinctilius Varus
3-2 BC	?
1 BC-4 AD	Gaius Caesar
4-6 AD	Volusius Saturninus
6-9 AD	Sulpicius Quirinius

Another part of this problem is that Roman records are not clear as to exactly what position Cyrenius held in the government just prior to the birth of Jesus. There are gaps in our knowledge of the career of Cyrenius. We know he was elected consul in 12 BC, which was still the most important office of the empire after that of emperor. Augustus, sometime thereafter, appointed Cyrenius as governor of Galatia and Pamphylia, an imperial province in what is now central Turkey. Between 5 and 3 BC, Cyrenius was in Asia Minor as the military commander charged with quelling the Homanadensian uprising on the northern border of Syria.[219] Even though it was customary for a former consul to stay as proconsul in a territory he had recently conquered, it is not certain that Cyrenius remained as governor of the province of Asia.

In January of 1 BC, he was appointed the advisor to Gaius Caesar, the young grandson and intended successor of Augustus, who was sent to administer the province of Syria. Gaius was wounded in battle in AD 3 and died early in AD 4. Almost immediately, Cyrenius was appointed governor of Syria[220], although his name does not appear as such in table 16.4. From AD 6 to AD 9, he was the imperial legate of Syria-Cicilia, which now officially included Judea. As imperial legate, he was the representative of the governor, since theoretically, the emperor was the actual governor.[221] What is missing in this historical record is the positon held by Cyrenius in 2 BC.

Still another part of this problem of the governorship of Syria is the changing role of government administration during this period in question. Prior to the First Triumvirate in 60 BC, Rome had been a republic where the people elected its leadership. Under the Republic, there was a system of dual administration; the city of Rome and the Roman provinces without military legions were under civilian law administered by the Senate, whereas the provinces with legions (Imperial Provinces) were under military law administered by consuls. Consuls were elected by the military, not the Senate. Under the Republic, administrative careers always followed the same course. However, under the First Triumvirate, an unofficial political alliance of three men who had overwhelming political and military influence, the Republic began to evolve into an emperorship of a single person. The culmination of this was the change, for most intents and purposes, from this dual system of elective administration to a rule by an emperor who appointed administrators. Augustus, who was one of the three who ruled under the Second Triumvirate, became the first of Rome's emperors, and his appointments may also be a key to our answer.

Since our focus here is on the governor of the imperial province of Syria, as it was Luke's claim that Cyrenius was the governor of Syria, it is important to know how Syria was traditionally governed. Because Syria was an imperial province, and thus under military rule, it was administered by a consul. Traditionally, Rome had only two consuls who, between the two, administered several imperial provinces. These two consuls were elected by the army itself for one-year terms, although they could be elected for successive terms. Augustus, who at the time was the civilian head of government, was also elected a consul. In 27 BC, he offered to lay down his consulship. However, the Roman Senate, still retaining some authority, rejected his proposal, charging him instead to not only administer Egypt as consul, but Syria as well. Augustus was reelected consul every year until 23 BC when he did vacate the consulship. However, it is important to note that he was again consul in 2 BC, the time of Luke's census.[222] As consul, it may be that Augustus himself was the governor of Syria at this time, as Syria was one of the two most strategic provinces of the Empire, Egypt being the other. If Augustus did elect himself governor of an imperial province such as Syria, it is quite possible that he did not directly govern the province himself but governed through his appointed representative, an *imperial legate*, as was his custom.

Governance via a representative is what we see in another account by Luke of a later taxing by Cyrenius that may give us some insight as to how his account at the time of the birth of Jesus may have come about. Acts 5:37 refers to a taxing that occurred during the period AD 6 to AD 9 when Cyrenius was the imperial legate of Syria-Cicilia. Josephus states that Cyrenius "came at this time into Syria, with a few others, being sent by Caesar to be a judge of that nation, and to take an account of their substance…. Moreover, Cyrenius came himself into Judea, which was now added to the province of Syria, to take an account of their substance."[223] The governor of an imperial province always had four tasks: responsibility for taxes, accountant, supreme judge, and commander of the army.[224] Here, Cyrenius conducted the taxation, but he did so not as the supreme commander but as an imperial legate, a representative of Caesar Augustus, who was the supreme commander. Thus, we see that he conducted the taxation but did so as a representative of the "governor."

To conclude, we see that at the time of the birth of Jesus in 2 BC, there is a gap in the record of the governance of Syria, and a gap in our knowledge of the career position of Cyrenius. This is a curious juxtaposition of events. We also see that in 2 BC, Caesar Augustus took on the role of consul, the traditional position of governance for an imperial province such as Syria. Although we do not know what role Augustus played in the actual governance of Syria at that time, we do know, and have examples of, his custom to appoint another to govern in his stead. We also see that just prior to the time of the birth of Jesus that Cyrenius was in a position of authority "in the east" and just after the birth of Jesus was appointed by Augustus to govern Syria at the death of the one who, incidentally, is still officially recorded as the governor.

Shortly thereafter, Cyrenius was again appointed to govern Syria as a representative of Augustus. It would appear from this that Cyrenius was capable of governance in Syria in 2 BC. It should be reasonable, then, to accept Luke's statement that *this taxing was first made when Cyrenius was governor of Syria.*

The words of Justin Martyr, who was born in Samaria about 100 AD, confirm this conclusion when he states, "Jesus Christ was born, as you can ascertain also from the registers of the taxing made under Cyrenius, your first procurator in Judea."[225]

The Reign of Tiberius

To put the ministry of Jesus into the context of Daniel's Seventy Sevens, both the time of the start of his ministry and the length of his ministry must be determined.

Luke gives us a starting point for the time of the ministry of Jesus: *"Now in the fifteenth year of the reign of Tiberius Caesar…²the word of God came unto John the son of Zacharias in the wilderness" (Luke 3:1–2).* John, the son of Zacharias, was John the Baptist whom God called out of the wilderness to baptize Jesus, initiating the public ministry of Jesus.

Evidence points to the fact that the reign of Tiberius (Claudius Nero) was reckoned by everyone of the day as beginning after the death of Augustus on August 19, AD 14. The fifteenth year of his reign extended from September 17, AD 28 to September 16, AD 29. Some, however, set the date of the reign of Tiberius Caesar two years earlier when, it is said, he had such powers conferred on him during the last two years of the reign of Augustus. Thus, they reckon the fifteenth year of the reign of Tiberius from AD 26. Which date did Luke use?

Tiberius served in many high administrative positions in his career. He was appointed quaestor in 23 BC, praetor in 16 BC, consul in 13 and again in 7 BC, imperium proconsulare in 11 BC, tribunicia potestas in 6 BC, and imperium maius and tribunicia potestas in 4 BC, which was renewed in AD 13.[226] (Without getting mired in detail, it is sufficient to say that these later offices were of the highest authority but still not that of the supreme authority of *principate,* Augustus's position of emperor.) It appears that it is the renewal of the tribunican power in AD 13 that is taken by modern writers as the authority for the coregency of Tiberius with Augustus. However, whatever power he had as tribunicia potestas in AD 13, he must have also had in 4 BC. By the standard applied by these writers, the reign of Tiberius should have thus begun in 4 BC, not AD 13.

As for the Roman Senate, it appears they did not consider Tiberius to be princeps prior to the death of Augustus.[227] *The New Encyclopedia Britannica* states that "in AD 14, on August 19, Augustus died. Tiberius, now supreme, played politics with the Senate and did not allow it to name him emperor for almost a month, but on September 17 he succeeded to the principate." [228] It appears the Senate did not consider the reign of Tiberius to begin before the death of Augustus.

Further, it appears that even Tiberius himself never claimed that his reign began before the death of Augustus. Shortly after Tiberius began his reign, coins were minted in his honor.[229] These were double-dated as the first year of Tiberius and the forty-fifth year of the battle of Actium, which was fought on September 2, 31 BC.[230] The forty-fifth year of the battle of Actium would extend from September 2, AD 14 to September 1, AD 15. Tiberius succeeded to the principate during this period, on September 17 of AD 14. The forty-fifth year of the battle of Actium and the first year of the reign of Tiberius by this accounting thus began very shortly after the death of Augustus. Later, more coins were minted,
dated as the third year of Tiberius and the forty-seventh year of the Actium Era. These coins are evidence that the reign of Tiberius was officially recognized in his own time as beginning in AD 14.

Josephus, who was born in Jerusalem in AD 37, the very year Tiberius died, appeared to know the details of the reign of Tiberius for he states, "Tiberius died, after he had reigned twenty-two years, and six months, and three days."[231] This brings us right back to AD 14.

If the Roman Senate, Tiberius, and Josephus all reckoned the imperial reign of Tiberius from AD 14, why would Luke do any differently?

The Ministry of Jesus

The fifteenth year of the reign of Tiberius thus began on September 17, AD 28 and ended on September 16, AD 29. From this, we can ascertain the start of the ministry of Jesus.

The text of Luke 3:1 states that it was John the Baptist to whom the word of God came during the fifteenth year of the reign of Tiberius Caesar. But did Jesus begin his ministry during that year? Luke 3:23 states that *"Jesus himself began to be about thirty years of age,"* referring to the time of his baptism. The expression *about thirty years* implies some margin, but only in one direction—*above* his thirtieth birthday. That Jesus was at least thirty years of age when he was baptized by John was of considerable importance, and God makes note of this in His Word. Jesus had come to fulfill the Law of Moses, and everything he did was to that end.[232] Thus, Jesus was fulfilling the Law by his baptism by John the Baptist. This washing of water was the establishment of Jesus as (our Great High) priest, just as under the Law those who were to be priests were washed with water at their consecration. To become a priest, a man had to be at least thirty years of age. Therefore, Jesus was at least thirty when he began to teach.

John the Baptist was of the priestly lineage. Since he was called of God to baptize Jesus, we may correctly assume that he was a righteous man before the eyes of God and that he had the priestly authority to consecrate Jesus as (our Great High) priest.[233] If so, John followed the Mosaic Law as did Jesus. Therefore, he also had to be thirty years of age to become a priest. John, being six months older than Jesus (Luke 1:24–36) must have turned thirty in late May or early June of the fifteenth year of the reign of Tiberius.

Since the fifteenth year of Tiberius began in mid-September AD 28, John turned thirty very near the middle of Tiberius's fifteenth year in AD 29. John thus began to teach after the time of the Passover in AD 29. From Luke's statements about the ministry of John, it appears that John had been preaching for some time prior to baptizing Jesus. This also appears to confirm that John was called out of the wilderness at least six months before the start of the ministry of Jesus. Therefore, at the earliest, Jesus began his ministry in the late fall of AD 29 after the end of the fifteenth year of Tiberius. This timeline is shown in figure 16.7.

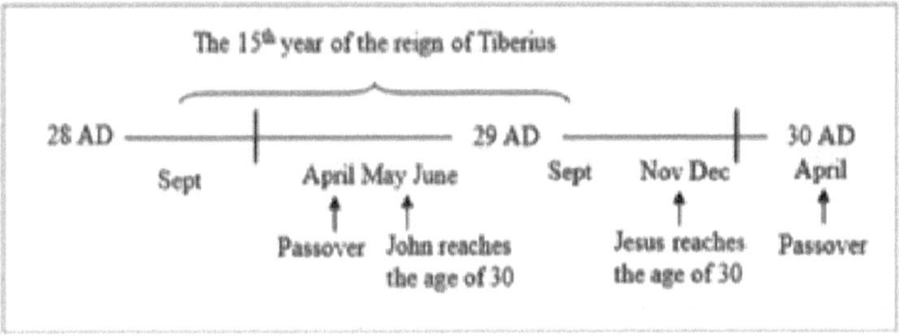

Figure 16.7. The calling of John the Baptist.

Now we must ascertain the date of the end of his ministry. Daniel was told that *"25from the going forth of the commandment to restore and to build Jerusalem unto the Messiah the Prince shall be seven weeks, and threescore and two weeks"* and that *"26after threescore and two weeks shall Messiah be cut off"* *(Daniel 9:25–26).* Since the ministry of Jesus ended at his crucifixion, we must determine the date of the crucifixion.

If Jesus started his ministry in the late fall of AD 29 his first Passover during his ministry would have been on April 5, AD 30. John speaks of three Passovers during the time of the ministry of Jesus: John 1:13, 6:4, and 13:1. With these three, Jesus would have ministered about two and a half years. His third Passover would have been April 13, AD 32, the Passover during which he was crucified.

It has been universally accepted that the Passover of the crucifixion week was the fourth Passover Jesus attended during his ministry, with his ministry lasting sometime above three years. This conclusion is derived from counting the three Passovers John tells us Jesus attended and adding to these the feast of John 5:1 as a Passover feast. However, it has only been assumed that the feast of John 5:1 was a Passover feast—there is no proof that it was. The requirement was that *"three times in a year shall all your males appear before the Lord your God in the place which he shall choose; in the Feast of Unleavened Bread, and in the Feast of Weeks, and in the Feast of Tabernacles"* *(Deuteronomy 16:16).* The feast of John 5:1 could have been any one of these feasts. Therefore, if we go with what we know to be true by John's word, then it would be within reason that the ministry of Jesus ended in AD 32.

Unto the Messiah the Prince

The event we have been searching for that ends the period of the first sixty-nine sevens is defined for us in part by the date of the event itself. The *going forth of the commandment to restore and to build Jerusalem* was issued in the month Nisan in the twentieth year of Artaxerxes I. Selecting any day within the month Nisan 445 BC and adding to it the 483 years as God himself defined the length of those years, we end up in the month of Nisan AD 32 at the time of the Passover. We must therefore seek for some event at the time of the Passover that would satisfy the words *unto the Messiah the Prince*. Any other event such as his birth in 2 BC, his recognition by Andrew as the Messiah or his baptism by John at the beginning of his ministry in AD 29 could not fulfill the words of Daniel's prophecy because these events occur several years prior to the end of the required 483-year period.

The event that ends the first sixty-nine week period is defined in part also by the character of the event. When Jesus came to Jerusalem at the time of the Passover, he came as the *Messiah the Prince*. But when the people saw Jesus coming, they *"went forth to meet him, and cried, Hosanna: Blessed is the King of Israel that comes in the name of the Lord" (John 12:13)*. Note that they called him king, not prince. I say this to focus on the fullness of the phrase *the Messiah the Prince*.

If all Daniel's prophecy intended to do here was to identify the time of the coming of Jesus, simply *unto the Messiah* would have done the job. But we have *the Messiah the Prince,* for there is a purpose, actually two, in the addition of the *Prince*. The use of *Prince* in reference to Jesus in Daniel 9:25 was not as a title as was *Messiah* but as a proper description of the status of his earthly reign at that point in the chronology of the vision. The intent is to contrast his coming as a servant at the end of the sixty-ninth seven with his coming as a ruler at the end of the seventieth seven. The final event in the chronology of this vision, as seen in verse 24, is *to anoint the most Holy*. This is the anointing of Jesus who will rule Israel as their king. The first event of the Passover season was the selection of the sacrificial lamb on the tenth day of Nisan:

> *[3]Speak you unto all the congregation of Israel, saying, In the tenth day of this month they shall take to them every man a lamb, according to the house of their fathers, a lamb for an house …[5]Your lamb shall be without blemish, a male of the first year: you shall take it out from the sheep, or from the goats: [6]And you shall keep it up until the fourteenth day of the same month: and the whole assembly of the congregation of Israel shall kill it.*

(Exodus 12:3, 5–6)

On the day the people were to select a lamb as their sacrifice, Jesus presented himself to the people. Fulfilling the words of Zechariah 9:9, *"Rejoice greatly, O daughter of Zion; shout, O daughter of Jerusalem: behold, your King comes unto you: he is just, and having salvation; lowly, and riding upon an ass, and upon a colt the foal of an ass,"* he presented himself as a sacrifice.

- Just as every household was to take to them a lamb on the tenth day of the month, Jesus presented himself to the people on the tenth day; every person was to take to themselves Jesus.
- Just as the lamb was to be taken from the flock, Jesus was taken from his own people.
- Just as the lamb was to be without blemish, Jesus was without fault.
- Just as the lamb was to be inspected for worthiness, Jesus presented himself to the people for inspection of his worthiness.
- Just as the lamb was to be sacrificed on the fourteenth day of the month, Jesus went to the cross on the fourteenth day of the month.

As Jesus came unto Jerusalem, *"³⁵they cast their garments upon the colt, and they set Jesus thereon. ³⁶And as he went, they spread their cloths in the way. ³⁷And when he was come nigh, even now at the descent of the mount of Olives, the whole multitude of the disciples began to rejoice and praise God with a loud voice for all the mighty works that they had seen; ³⁸Saying, Blessed be the King that comes in the name of the Lord. ³⁹And some of the Pharisees from among the multitude said unto him, Master, rebuke your disciples"* (Luke 19:36–39). Jesus himself then stressed the significance of this event as *"he answered and said unto them, I tell you that, if these should hold their peace, the stones would immediately cry out"* (Luke 19:40). This event fulfills the prophecy of Daniel 9, verse 25, of the coming of *"the Messiah the Prince"* at the end of *"seven weeks, and threescore and two weeks."*

Just as the Passover lamb was sacrificed on the fourteenth of Nisan in remembrance of the lamb's blood that saved the Israelites in Egypt, Jesus shed his blood for the salvation of believers five days after presenting himself as the Messiah the prince.

A Backward Look in Time

It is commonly believed that Jesus was crucified on a Friday. Thus, the attempt to set the year of the crucifixion is most often made by aligning either the Passover Seder of the fourteenth of Nisan or the Feast of Unleavened Bread of the fifteenth to a Friday of a particular year based on the weekly rotation of days of our current calendar as shown on astronomical charts. This is a misleading criterion as nothing guarantees that the weekly rotation of days of the ancient Hebrew calendar matched the weekly rotation of days of our current calendar system. The only event of the crucifixion week where we are assured the day of the week of the event is when Mary Magdalene and Mary, the mother of James, and Salome came to the tomb and found it empty. This morning was the first day of the week, which we know was the day following the weekly Sabbath (Mark 16:1). (The Jews only numbered their days of the week at that time.)

The relationship of this first day of the Jewish week to a named day on the Julian calendar is uncertain. We are, however, certain of the Hebrew date of the selection of the sacrificial lamb as Nisan 10. We are now going to look backward in time from Nisan 10 AD 32 as a check on the validity of the preceding analyses.

To help us visualize the time of these events, the Hebrew calendar and the Julian calendar of AD 32 are first collaborated. The time of the first full moon after the vernal equinox as identified by *Spring Phenomena* of the U.S. Naval Observatory, Astronomical Applications Department, gives us the period of the Passover in any given year. The ancient Hebrew month began at the first sighting of the new moon in the evening sky. The Astronomical New Moon of the month Nisan AD 32 occurred over Jerusalem on March 29 at 10:00 p.m.[234] The first evening the new moon would have been visible in Jerusalem was March 31.[235] Since the Hebrew day begins at 6:00 p.m., Nisan 1 began at 6:00 p.m. on the thirty-first of March.

Jesus entered Jerusalem to present himself to the people on Nisan 10. Nisan 10 began at 6:00 p.m. on April 9, but Jesus did not enter Jerusalem until the daylight hours of the next morning. Therefore, the time of his entry was still Nisan 10 by Hebrew accounting, but now it was April 10 by the Julian calendar. April 10, AD 32 is the day numbered 1,732,845.5 (the .5 signifies noon) in Universal Time.[236] The Julian Date Converter of the U.S. Naval Observatory correlates Universal Time to the Julian calendar and is used here for the accounting of days because of its assured accuracy. Counting 173,880 days (69 × 7 years × 360 days/year) back in time

(April 10 itself being the last day as the days are counted inclusively), the first of these days would have been day 1,558,966.5. This is the Julian day March 21, 445 BC. It is the eighth day of Nisan in the twentieth year of Artaxerxes.

The eighth day in Scripture is the day of new beginnings, a day to begin a covenant with the Lord, whether it be of the first fruits of the harvest (your efforts), the first offspring of livestock (your possessions), or the firstborn of sons (your relationships). God said "on the eighth day you shall give [these] to me" (Exodus 22:30). The Seventy Sevens is a time determined upon the Jews, a covenant instituted by God in which they are to finish the transgression, make and end of sins, make reconciliation for iniquity, bring in everlasting righteousness, seal up the vision and prophecy, and anoint the most Holy. It was no coincidence that this covenant of the Seventy Sevens began on the eighth day of the first month of a new year.

The Crucifixion of Jesus

We have thus come to the end of the first sixty-nine sevens. It was to be *"after [these] threescore and two weeks"* that the Messiah was to be *"cut off" (Daniel 9:26)*. To be *cut off* in the parlance of the day was to die the death of a wrongdoer. To the Jewish authority, Jesus had committed blasphemy and was worthy of death (Matthew 26:63–66). To the Roman authority, Jesus had committed treason and was worthy of death (John 19:12–14). Thus, Jesus was crucified on the fourteenth of Nisan, five days following his entry into Jerusalem as *the Messiah the Prince*.

Jesus did die the death of a wrongdoer, but the price he paid was *"not for himself" (Daniel 9:26)*. He died on the cross to set all mankind free of their spiritual debt of sin.237 But did Jesus fulfill the words of Daniel's prophecy? Did he finish the transgression of the Jewish people? Did he make and end of the sins of the Jews? Did he make reconciliation for the iniquity of Daniel's people? Did he bring everlasting righteousness to the nation of Israel?

Your People

The nation of Israel had transgressed the Law corporately, and God had applied the sevenfold punishment of the Law corporately. Yet, Israel as a nation continued in its transgression. Thus, seventy sevens were determined, and they were determined corporately. The requirement was for the nation of Israel *to finish the transgression, and to make and end of sins, and to make reconciliation for iniquity, and to bring in everlasting righteousness. Transgression* here is the Hebrew word *pesha*, meaning *rebellion*.

To *finish* is *kala*, meaning *to shut* or *restrain*. Because God is dealing with the nation corporately, *to finish the transgression* would be the restraint of rebellion by the turning of the nation to God and the recognition of him as Lord, the only one whom they are to serve.

To make and end of sins refers to acts other than rebellion. *Sin* here is *to miss the mark*.

This speaks to the morality of the nation and to their return to a way of life pleasing to God.

To make reconciliation for iniquity speaks of putting off the old nature and becoming a new creation. The Hebrew word for *reconciliation* is *kaphar*, meaning *to cover, to make atonement*. It means to put right. *Iniquity is avon*, meaning *perversity*, referring to a perverse nature. It is the very nature of the people that must be changed in order to turn away from rebellion and sin.

To bring in everlasting righteousness is to have a permanent, right standing relationship with God. This is the result of putting off the old nature of rebellion and sin and becoming a new creature in Christ.

So, did Jesus finish the transgression of the Jewish people? Did he make and end of the sins of the Jews? Did he make reconciliation for the iniquity of Daniel's people? Did he bring everlasting righteousness to the nation of Israel?

Jesus himself answered that question as he rode into Jerusalem on that ass, for he said of Daniel's people, *"42If you had known, even you, at least in this day, the things which belong unto your peace! But now they are hid from your eyes. 43For the days shall come upon you, that your enemies shall cast a trench about you, and compass you round, and keep you in on every side, 44And shall lay you even with the ground, and your children within you; and they shall not leave in you one stone upon another; because you knew not the time of your visitation" (Luke 19:42–44)*. In AD 70 Daniel's holy city was laid waste, and the Temple of the Jews was leveled, leaving not one stone upon another. In AD 135, the Jews were permanently banned from Jerusalem, and salt plowed into its soil to prevent the growing of crops. And the nation of Israel died by the sword because they did not turn from their transgressions.

Paul, in his letter to the Romans, spoke to the spiritual condition of Israel after the crucifixion. He began by saying, *"¹Brethren, my heart's desire and prayer to God for Israel is, that they might be saved. ²For I bear them record that they have a zeal of God, but not according to knowledge. ³For they being ignorant of God's righteousness, and going about to establish their own righteousness, have not submitted themselves unto the righteousness of God"* (Romans 10:1–3). By Paul's words, Daniel's people were still attempting to establish their righteousness by their own means rather than to submit themselves unto the righteousness of God.

Daniel was told that the requirement of the Seventy Sevens was determined upon his people. The death of Jesus on the cross made the way for their redemption. This redemption was offered freely as a gift, but that gift was of value only if it was willingly received and acted upon by the people. Even though it was, and yet is, by individual choice that this gift is accepted, it was yet expected here of the nation corporately. Israel did not bring in the *everlasting righteousness* of God as is required of Daniel's prophecy. When will the Jews finish the transgression, make an end of sins, make reconciliation for iniquity, and bring in everlasting righteousness? That is the rest of the story of The Mystery of Prophecy.

The Great Parenthesis

Before we continue into the events that are to occur during the last seven-year period we must look at a parenthesis in time between the sixty ninth seven and the seventieth seven that suspends the fulfillment of Daniel's prophecy. While we think it would be natural for the seventieth seven to follow immediately upon the fulfillment of the sixty ninth, yet there has been a break of nearly two thousand years. Unusual, yes, but such a break in the flow of prophetic events is not unique to the prophecy of the Seventy Sevens.

One of the more familiar prophecies with such a parenthesis in fulfillment is Isaiah 61:1–2. Isaiah, prophesying of Jesus coming as the redeemer, said, *"¹The Spirit of the Lord god is upon me; because the lord has anointed me to preach good tidings unto the meek; he has sent me to bind up the brokenhearted, to proclaim liberty to the captives, and the opening of the prison to them that are bound; ²To proclaim the acceptable year of the lord, and the day of vengeance of our God."* Yet, when Jesus came as that redeemer, he said of himself, *"¹⁸The Spirit of the Lord is upon me, because he has anointed me to preach the gospel to the poor; he has sent me to heal the brokenhearted, to preach deliverance to the captives, and recovering of sight to the blind, to set at liberty them that are bruised, ¹⁹to preach the acceptable year of the Lord"* (Luke 4:18, 19). Jesus was quoting the words spoken by Isaiah, but he did not finish Isaiah's words.

When Jesus came to the words of Isaiah which proclaimed *"and the day of vengeance of our God"* Jesus *"closed the book, and he gave it again to the minister, and sat down"* (Luke 4:20) for this part of the prophecy was not to be fulfilled for many a century. The parenthesis in Isaiah's prophecy of Jesus in fact parallels exactly the time of the parenthesis in Daniel's vision of the Seventy Sevens.

There are other allusions to this break in the flow of prophetic events for this time period, which we will see. For the most part, recognition of the existence of such a parenthesis comes not from the author of the prophecy but rather from our looking back at the events of history from our perspective in time. Daniel's vision of the four beasts that were to arise from the sea is just such an example. Daniel unknowingly told of the death and rebirth of the state of Israel in his description of the fourth beast. This beast was diverse from all the others because it was actually two beasts, presented to Daniel as one. From our perspective in time, we know that Israel died by the sword during the time of the Roman Empire, that part of this beast described as having great iron teeth, which devoured and broke in pieces, and that Israel was to be brought back from the sword during the time of the League of Ten, that part of the beast described as having the ten horns. Because Daniel's prophecies are for the nation of Israel, he did not see the age of the church, the time when the nation of Israel would not exist. Thus, he could see the fourth beast only as one beast. But from the events of history, we can now see this fourth beast as two, with a parenthesis in time between the two. This break in the string of seven Gentile empires that were to have mastery over the nation of Israel also parallels quite closely with the parenthesis in Daniel's Seventy Sevens.

Concerning the time line itself of Daniel's prophecy of the Seventy Sevens, the most subtle allusion to this parenthesis is also seen only from our perspective of history, and the recognition that the events of the last seven have not been fulfilled. Verse 26 states, *"After threescore and two weeks shall Messiah be cut off."* Note that we are not told that Jesus was crucified *during* the seventieth seven, but rather, that he was crucified *after* the sixty-ninth seven, an indication that these last two sevens are not connected.

Probably the most important allusion to this great parenthesis is Paul's statement that *"blindness in part is happened to Israel, until the fullness of the Gentiles be come in"* (Romans 11:25). Paul said of Israel that it was his prayer that they might be saved, for the people were spiritually ignorant. And of what were they ignorant? That *"Christ is the end [the fulfillment] of the law for righteousness to everyone that believes"* (Romans 10:1–4). As Jesus rode into Jerusalem on that ass, the people believed Jesus was their king, but they did not believe Jesus was their righteousness. For this, *blindness in part is happened to Israel, until the fullness of the Gentiles be come in.* Paul was speaking here of a spiritual blindness, for he said, *"According as it is written, God has given them the spirit of slumber, eyes that they should not see, and ears that they should not hear"* (Romans 11:8, quoting Isaiah 29:10). And when did this blindness come upon Israel? Jesus said on that fateful day as he rode into Jerusalem, *"If you had known, even you, at least in this day, the things which belong unto your peace! But **now** they are hid from your eyes"* (Luke 19:42). Thus, on the very day the sixty-nine weeks closed, God shut the door on Israel. Corporately, Daniel's people can not finish their transgression, nor make and end of their sins, nor make reconciliation for their iniquity, nor bring in everlasting righteousness until that door is again opened.

Paul said that this blindness was upon Israel until *the fullness of the Gentiles be come in.* What then is this fullness of the Gentiles? Yet speaking of the spiritual condition of Israel, Paul said, *"¹⁹But I say, Did not Israel know? First Moses said, I will provoke you to jealously by them that are no people, and by a foolish nation I will anger you. ²⁰But Esaias is very bold, and said, I was found of them that sought me not: I was made manifest unto them that asked not after me"* (Romans 10:19–20). As that door closed on Israel, it opened to the Gentiles, and the word of God went out unto them that are no people, *"That the blessing of Abraham might come on the Gentiles through Jesus Christ; that [they] might receive the promise of the Spirit through faith"* (Galatians 3:14).

But the time will come when the Gentiles too will not seek God. The line is slowly being drawn between those who believe in

Jesus and those who reject him. When there are none willing to cross that line to Christ, the harvest, *the fullness of the Gentiles,* will be complete, and the door will again open to Israel.

That door will open on the first day of the seventieth week when two witnesses will appear unto Israel (Revelation 11:3). These two may be Enoch and Elijah, two great men of God who were taken up to heaven without seeing death.

It would be reasonable for God to send two from the time of the law and the prophets to tell of Jesus their Messiah, since that is where the spiritual mind of the Jew is still to this day. Thus, on this first day of the last of Daniel's sevens, *"¹there shall be a fountain opened to the house of David and to the inhabitants of Jerusalem for sin and for uncleanness…. ⁸And it shall come to pass, that in all the land, says the Lord, two parts therein shall be cut off and die; but the third shall be left therein. ⁹And I will bring the third part through the fire, and will refine them as silver is refined, and will try them as gold is tried: they shall call on my name, and I will hear them: I will say, It is my people: and they will say, The Lord is my God" (Zechariah 13:1, 8–9).*

In this, we not only see the break between the sixty-ninth and the seventieth seven of this prophecy, but we also see the mighty purpose for it. That purpose, first, is to provoke the Jews to jealousy by the salvation offered to the Gentiles. And, second, it is to offer that salvation to the Gentiles, for Jesus shed his blood for all, Jew and Gentile alike. Those who accept this gift of salvation offered by Jesus during this great parenthesis are called the church.

Hosea, however, did clearly identify this parenthesis in the existence of Israel, for he said, *"⁴The children of Israel shall abide many days without a king, and without a prince, and without a sacrifice, and without an image, and without an ephod, and without teraphim: ⁵**Afterward shall the children of Israel return, and seek the Lord their God,** and David their king: and shall fear the Lord and his goodness in the later days" (Hosea 3:4–5).* It is apparent from Hosea's words that the nation would not only cease to exist, but also that it would be resurrected. And, it is when Israel was to return as a nation that the people were to seek their righteousness. The nation of Israel has returned, but the people have not yet begun to *seek the Lord their God, and David their king* because the seventieth seven has yet to begin.

The Seventieth Seven

The events of the last seven of Daniel's vision of the Seventy Sevens are contained in the last two verses of the prophecy:

> *26The people of the prince that shall come shall destroy the city and the sanctuary; and the end thereof shall be with a flood, and unto the end of the war desolations are determined.*
>
> *27And he shall confirm the covenant with many for one week: and in the midst of the week he shall cause the sacrifice and the oblation to cease, and for the overspreading of abominations he shall make it desolate, even unto the consummation, and that determined shall be poured upon the desolate.*
>
> (Daniel 9:26–27)

Note that this last verse focuses our attention on three points in time: the start of the period of seven years with a confirming of a covenant that is to be in effect for seven years; the stopping of the sacrifices and oblations at the time of the desolation of the Temple at the midpoint of the seven years; and the consummation, the completion, of the seven years. It must be stressed here that this *one week* of time is exactly a period of 7 years of 360 days per year—not a day more, not a day less.

Your Holy City

Up to this point, our focus has been on the first four requirements identified in the vision of the Seventy Sevens that were determined upon Daniel's people; specifically, *"to finish the transgression, and to make an end of sins, and to make reconciliation for iniquity, and to bring in everlasting righteousness" (Daniel 9:24).* These things have to do with the very nature of the people themselves. But Daniel was told that the Seventy Sevens were also determined *"upon your holy city" (Daniel 9:24).* Therefore, there is something required of the city of Jerusalem itself that is apart from that required of the people. What all this may entail, I do not know. However, verse 26 identifies, at least in part, one event determined upon the city in that *the people of the prince that shall come shall destroy the city and the sanctuary.*

This *prince that shall come* and those of his origin, *the people of the prince,* have been addressed in previous chapters. It is sufficient here just to say that this prince who is yet to come upon the scene we call the Antichrist.

Verse 26 continues with the statement that *"the end thereof shall be with a flood." The end thereof* is a reference back to the city of Jerusalem and to the Temple of the Jews. The *flood, sheteph* in Hebrew, is an *overflowing.* This flood is an overflowing of people, *the people of the prince.* Verse 26 continues further:

"And unto the end of the war desolations are determined." This war begins at the invasion of Jerusalem spoken of by Luke wherein he states, *"20When you shall see Jerusalem compassed with armies, then know that the desolation thereof is nigh. 21Then let them which are in Judea flee to the mountains; and let them which are in the midst of it depart out; and let not them that are in the countries enter thereinto. 22For these be the days of vengeance, that all things which are written may be fulfilled"* (Luke 21:20–22). This speaks to the desolation of the city.

Verse 27 expands upon verse 26 with the desolation of the sanctuary: *"And he shall confirm the covenant with many for one week: and in the midst of the week he shall cause the sacrifice and the oblation to cease, and for the overspreading of abominations he shall make it desolate, even unto the consummation, and that determined shall be poured upon the desolate."* Matthew spoke of this wherein he states, *"15When you therefore shall see the abomination of desolation, spoken of by Daniel the prophet, stand in the holy place, (whoso reads, let him understand:) 16Then let them which be in Judea flee into the mountains"* (Matthew 24:15–16). This is the same war that Luke spoke of, just a different focus on what is to be destroyed.

The *he* in verse 27 that *shall confirm the covenant with many* is *the prince that shall come* of verse 26.

To Seal Up the Vision

The fifth element of the vision of the Seventy Sevens that was determined upon Daniel's people and upon his holy city is *"to seal up the vision"* (Daniel 9:24). To seal up is to complete, to make final, just as a scroll was sealed with a wax seal when the writing was complete. *The vision* spoken of here is the vision of the Seventy Sevens itself. Therefore, by the end of the seventieth seven, all elements of the vision will be complete.

To Seal Up Prophecy

The sixth element that was determined is *"to seal up…prophecy" (Daniel 9:24)*. Because the completion of the vision itself is addressed separately, *prophecy* here means prophecies concerning the Israelites beyond those of the vision. There is no reason here to limit the prophecies to be completed to only those uttered during the time of the period of the Seventy Sevens.

It is most reasonable to believe that all prophecies from the time of Abraham to the end of the age are to be completed. And, the vision of the Seventy Sevens is a message to the city of Jerusalem as well as to the people, requiring the completion of the prophecies concerning both. Therefore, God has determined that all prophecies concerning the Israelites as a people and all prophecies concerning the city of Jerusalem will be completed by the end of the period of the Seventy Sevens.

To Anoint the Most Holy

The seventh and last element of the vision of the Seventy Sevens that was determined upon Daniel's people and upon his holy city is *"to anoint the most Holy" (Daniel 9:24)*, the event that completes the period of the Seventy Sevens.

This is the coming of the long-sought anointed one, the Messiah, to the throne of David (Isaiah 9:7). The coming of Jesus on this last day of Daniel's Seventy Sevens is described in Revelation 19:11 through 20:4. There we are told that Jesus will rule all nations of this world as the King Of Kings. To put this into context for the Jews, it means that Jesus will come to rule the nation of Israel as her king. But how could this coming of Jesus to rule Israel be something that could be determined upon Daniel's people or upon his holy city? Jesus will come with all power and authority—who is there of Israel with the authority to put a crown upon his head?

God chose David to be king over all the tribes of Jacob—Who of all the tribes could say differently? Yet, it was the men of Judah who chose to anoint David king over Judah (2 Samuel 2:4), and it was the men of Israel who chose to anoint David king over Israel (2 Samuel 5:3). Even though David was of God's choosing, it was the people of the land who showed their acceptance of David by anointing him their king. Just as it was with David, Daniel's people will anoint their Messiah by a show of their acceptance of Jesus as their king.

And what had been determined upon Daniel's holy city? — From that day on, Jesus will rule from Jerusalem! It is said that what has to be anointed here is the building that is the Temple, or a feature of the building such as "the most holy place" that will be used by the Jews for their sacrifices and oblations as this is the only application of such phraseology in Scripture. But this anointing is of a different type of temple, for Jesus had said, *"Destroy this temple, and in three days I will raise it up…he spoke of the temple of his body" (John 2:19, 21).*

Further, the Temple used by the Jews for their sacrifices will not exist by the end of the Seventy Sevens when the *most Holy* is to be anointed. Of this Temple, *not one stone will be left upon another*—there just will be no Temple to anoint. Nor will the object of this anointing be the Millennium temple described by Ezekiel. If the *people of the prince that shall come* will destroy both the existing Temple and the city of Jerusalem during the reign of the Antichrist, they certainly would never allow the building of Ezekiel's temple before the return of the Messiah.

The Number Seven

I stated at the start of this chapter that I had chosen the title of "The Seventy Sevens of Daniel" rather than the traditional Seventy Weeks of Daniel, so as to keep our focus on the number 7 and the point of God's message in its repeated use throughout this prophecy. The number 7 indicates completion or completeness. It is interesting, therefore, that the English *week* is used in translation of the Hebrew *seven* because the week makes a good illustration to explain this concept of completion.

We have seen the number 7 used in two ways. The first as a cycle of sevens or sevenfold events, as a week is a cycle of seven days. The second use is that of a set of seven, just as a week is a set of seven days; at the end of seven days, the week is finished. Both of these applications in their own way reflect completion or completeness.

An example of the first is the secession of eras in the rule over Judah of the Babylonian Empire for the purpose of bringing about a completion. Babylon was used of God both as a rod of punishment and as a staff of correction to turn His people from the error of their ways. The first era was just a slight wound—one to get the people's attention, so to speak, that they need to turn back to God. When that went unheeded, a second wound was inflicted, a wound seven times more severe. A third wound then was inflicted, a deadly wound yet seven times more severe; the era of the Desolations of Jerusalem. At that point, Daniel said of his people, *"As it is written in the law of Moses, all this evil is come upon us: yet made we not our prayer before the Lord our God, that we might turn from our iniquities, and understand your truth" (Daniel 9:13)*. And because Daniel's people had not turned from their iniquities, God said there was yet to be another era of seven, the time of the Seven Seventies. But these cycles of seven-times greater wrath were not to continue forever; they were to bring about a final result—He was to be their God, and they were to be His people.

We see several examples of the second similarity to a week in that a set of seven makes the objective complete, just as a set of seven days makes a week complete. Seven requirements were determined upon the Jews and upon Jerusalem that addressed the complete social, spiritual, and political condition of the nation of Israel. A set of seven Gentile kingdoms are brought upon Daniel's people and upon his holy city to bring all these things to completion. The time involved to accomplish these seven requirements is a seven (seventies) long, and then the vision is complete. At the anointing of the most Holy, all prophecy concerning Israel will be complete—He will be their God, and they will be His people.

The use of the number 7 is God's message to Daniel's people; the righteous of Israel will occupy the promised land of Abraham. They will anoint their Messiah, and their king will set his rule from the city of Jerusalem, all by the end of the Seventy Sevens of Daniel.

And he shall confirm the covenant with many for one week: and in the midst of the week he shall cause the sacrifice and the oblation to cease, and for the overspreading of abominations he shall make it desolate, even until the consummation.

—Daniel 9:27

[176] Cyrus's statement concerning Jerusalem recorded in Isaiah 44:28, "That said of Cyrus, He is my shepherd, and shall perform all my pleasure: even saying to Jerusalem, You shall be built; and to the temple, Your foundation shall be laid" is just that, a statement of fact that Jerusalem would be built. It was not a commandment to build Jerusalem. [177] Cambyses, who reigned from 530 to 522 BC, is identified as Ahasuerus in Ezra 4:6 and as Artaxerxes in Ezra 4:7. These two verses are confusing in that two different names for this king are given in successive verses while the name Cambyses is not found anywhere in Ezra. These two successive verses with differing names came about when the portion of Ezra from chapter 2:1 through chapter 4:6 was inserted from Nehemiah when the combined works of Ezra and Nehemiah were divided into separate works. Evidence of this is seen in an early version of Ezra, 1 Esdras 2, which does not contain this portion of Ezra as we now have it. Nehemiah used Ahasuerus, Ezra used Artaxerxes, both in reference to Cambyses. Ahasuerus and Artaxerxes were used historically both as a title and as a name. Daniel 9:1 is an example of Cambyses named as Ahasuerus: *"In the first year of Darius the son of Ahasuerus, of the seed of the Medes, which was made king over the realm of the Chaldeans…"* Several Persian kings used the name Artaxerxes, meaning Great King, but are today identified by other names. [178] We have two examples of this custom in the Bible. In the book of Esther, we find the account of Haman's attempt to destroy the Jews by deceiving the king into issuing a commandment *"that they may be destroyed" (Esther 3:9)*. But the king favored Esther, a Jew, so when he learned of the deception, he attempted to reverse the results of his commandment. Since the king could not reverse his own word (8:8) and withdraw his earlier commandment,a second commandment was written (8:10), which gave the Jews authority to rise up against those who would have destroyed them. We see an account of a similar attempt to destroy Daniel through an ill-advised commandment issued by Darius that landed

Daniel in the lion's den. In this account, we are told in Daniel 6:8, in 6:12, and again in 6:15 "that the law of the Medes and Persians is, That no degree nor statute which the king establishes may be changed."

[179] Christopher Walker, Achaemenid Chronology and the Babylonian Sources (British Museum Press, 1997) 21. http://www.caeno.org/_Nabonassar/pdf/Walker_Grand%20Saros.pdf, accessed 7/2/12.

[180] Richard A. Parker and Waldo H. Dubberstein, Babylonian Chronology: 626 BC - AD 75 (Eugene, Oregon: Wipf and Stock Publishers, 2007), 17.

[181] Diodorus Siculus xi 69 [Diodorus Siculus. Diodorus of Sicily in Twelve Volumes with an English Translation by C. H. Oldfather. Vol. 4–8 (Cambridge: Harvard University Press; London: William Heinemann,Ltd.1989) [http://www.perseus.tufts.edu/hopper/text?doc=Perseus%3Atext%3A1999.01.0084%3Abook%3D11%3Achapter%3D69%3Asection%3D1 7/30/12].

[182] M. A. Dandamaev, A Political History of the Achaemenid Empire, translated into English by W. J. Vogelsang, E. J. Brill (Leiden: The Netherlands, 1989), 234.

[183] Iran-e-Bastan/Pirnia book 1 p. 873 [http://en.wikipedia.org/wiki/Xerxes_I_of_Persia]

[184] The Chronology of Ezra 7. A Report of the Historical Research Committee of the General Conference of Seventh-Day Adventists 1953. Prepared for the Committee by Siegfried H. Horn, PhD, professor of archeology, Seventh-day Adventist Theological Seminary, and Lynn H. Wood, PhD, sometime professor of archeology, Seventh-day Adventist Theological Seminary Review and Herald Publishing Association, Washington, DC. Footnote 17: Diodorus Siculus xi. 69 (Loeb ed., volume 4, pp. 305, 307). Also Justinus iii.1. source: http://www.scribd.com/doc/3084145/THE- CHRONOLOGY-OF-EZRA-7-Siegried-H-Horn 5/30/12.

[185] Ibid.

[186] Nehemiah reckoned regnal years by the civil calendar years beginning Tishri 1 and ending Elul 29.

[187] Aramaic Papyri of the Fifth Century B.C. Edited, with Translations and Notes by A. Cowley (Oxford at The Clarendon Press, Printed in England, 1923).

[188] A. Cowley, in his Aramaic Papyri of the Fifth Century B.C states, "The number in the Egyptian month is broken, and the space requires something before \|||, most probably III, but it might be ~> (making 14). Gutesmann and Hontheim calculate that it should be 17, but there is hardly room for Ml -»."

[189] Herman H. Goldstine, New and Full Moons, 1001 BC to AD 1651 (The American Philosophical Society, Independence Square, Philadelphia, 1973), 45.

[190] Chronology of the Ancient World by Bickerman, 117.

[191] The day Thoth 9 is approximate, as the sighting of the new moon could vary by a day, and there was a difference in the start of the day by culture, which was at sunset by Hebrew practice and sunrise by Egyptian practice.

[192] Aramaic Papyri of the Fifth Century BC.

[193] Chronology of the Ancient World, 117.

[194] Herman H. Goldstine, New and Full Moons, 1001 BC to AD 1651, © 1973 by The American Philosophical Society, Independence Square, Philadelphia, copyright 1973, p 45

[195] Aramaic Papyri of the Fifth Century B.C.

[196] Chronology of the Ancient World, 117.

[197] Herman H. Goldstine, New and Full Moons, 1001 BC to AD 1651, © 1973 by The American Philosophical Society, Independence Square, Philadelphia, copyright 1973, p 45

[198] Earliest possible sighting.

[199] The specific date of Nisan 8, 445 BC for the going forth of the commandment to rebuild Jerusalem will be confirmed later in the chapter.

[200] http://www.israelnationalnews.com, November, 17, 2009.

[201] Tertullian, Adversus Judaeos, volume III, chapter 8.

[202] Garrett G. Fagan, "De Imperatoribus Romanis," An Online Ecyclopedia of Roman Emperors, Pennsylvania State University, 1 Mar. 2004http://www.roman-emperors.org/auggie.htm.

[203] Eusebius, History of the Church, book I, chapter V.

[204] Irenaeus, Refutation & Overthrow of what is wrongly called Knowledge, book III, chapter 25.

[205] Adam Rutherford, Treatise on Bible Chronology (Liverpool, London and Prescot: C. Tinling & Co. Ltd, 1957), 414.

[206] Tertullian, chapter 8.

[207] Cleopatra VII, Ptolemaic Dynasty, 29 Dec. 2003. http://interoz.com/egypt/cleopatar.htm

[208] Eusebius, chapter V.

[209] Cleopatra VIII.

[210] Josephus, Antiquities of the Jews, book XVIII, chapter 6.4.

[211] Rutherford 417.

[212] Josephus, book XVII, chapter 6:5.

[213] Ibid., chapter 8.3.

[214] Ibid.

[215] Ibid., chapter 8.4.

[216] Ibid., chapter 9.3.

[217] Ibid., chapter 8.1. [Footnote to this date: "It is here to be noticed, that this seventh year of the reign of Herod, and all the other years of his reign, in Josephus, are dated from the death of Antigonus, and never from his first obtaining the kingdom at Rome, above three years before." The Works of Josephus, trans. William Whiston A.M. (Massachusetts: Hendrickson Publishers, Peabody, 1985)].

[218] Josephus, book XV, chapter 5.2.

[219] http://www.livius.org/su-sz/sulpicius/quirinius.html, June 23, 2008.

[220] Ibid.

[221] http://www.unrv.com/government/provincialgovernment.php, September 5, 2008.

[222] http://www.britannica.com/EBchecked/topic/507905/ancient/Rome, July 15, 2008.

[223] Josephus, book XVIII, chapter 1.1.

[224] http://www.livius.org/gi-gr/governor/governor.html, June 23, 2008

[225] Justin Martyr, The First Apology of Justin, chapter 34.

[226] Augustus and the Succession, 21 Nov. 2003, http://www.csun.edu/~hcfll004/seccession.html.

[227] Princeps – The term's original meaning was "first among equals" which was applied to Augustus and to later emperors. There is no Latin word which wholly corresponds to what "emperor" signifies in English.

[228] "Tiberius," The New Encyclopaedia Britannica, vol 11, 2002 ed.

[229] Rutherford, 452–53.

[230] Cleopatra VII.

[231] Josephus, Wars of the Jews, book II, chapter 9.5.

[232] The Old Testament is the shadow of the Law; the New Testament is the substance of the Law. What this means is that the Old Testament showed the way to the spiritual application of the Law by a physical example, while the New Testament is the actual spiritual application.

[233] The consecration of Jesus as priest was not into the order of Aaron but into the order of Melchisedec.

[234] Spring Phenomena of the U.S. Naval Observatory, Astronomical Applications Department, http://www.usno.navy.mil/USNO/astronomical-applications/data-services/spring-phenom.

[235] http://www.judaismvschristianity.com/Passover_dates.htm, accessed January 11, 2011.

[236] Universal Time (UT) refers to a time scale called "Coordinated Universal Time," which is the basis for the worldwide system of civil time. The times of various events, particularly astronomical phenomena, are often given in Universal Time, which is sometimes referred to as Greenwich Mean Time. Universal Time is simply a continuous count of days and fractions thereof since noon on January 1, 4713 BCE, which is O.5 UT.

[237] We often think of the symbolism of the shed blood of the innocent lamb at Passover as the symbol of Jesus, the Lamb of God, who shed his blood to pay the price for the sins of man. This symbolism is certainly worthy of our attention. There is equally striking symbolism in the relationship of Barabbas to Jesus also worthy of our attention. Barabbas was a man guilty of the crimes for which he was charged, and the price of his crimes was death. An investigation of the events of the Passover week shows us that Barabbas was freed of his debt in exchange for the life of Jesus during the late evening hours of the fourteenth but was not freed from his bonds. The point I want to make is the timing of his release from bondage. Barabbas was truly set free during the Feast of Unleavened Bread, which was eaten late afternoon on the fifteenth.

In this we are shown that ***Jesus had to die before guilty men could be set free!***

CHAPTER SEVENTEEN
First? Or Last?

The last seven years, or week, of the Seventy Sevens of Daniel must consist of years of 360 days because the first sixty-nine weeks of the vision were fulfilled with years of 360 days. This week is therefore 2,520 days, or 84 months, in length with the months consisting of 30 days. Daniel's vision focuses on three events of that week; the signing of the covenant at the start of the week, the stopping of the sacrifices at its midpoint, and the anointing of the most Holy at the end of the week. From the wording of the text, we see that this last week is divided *"in the midst"* (Daniel 9:27) into two equal parts. Both parts of this last week would therefore be of the same length: 1,260 days or 42 months. In the book of Revelation, we find two references to events that are 1,260 days long, and two references to events that are 42 months long that begin to fill the voids between Daniel's three events of that week. Now, the purpose of bringing all this together is to determine the proper application of the time period of the 1,260 days and the time period of the 42 months to the prophecies of the last days.

A Little Bit of Logic

If the period of 1,260 days is exactly the same length of time as the period of 42 months, why would God speak of some events in terms of 1,260 days and others in terms of 42 months? The answer is found when we look closely at the events defined by these two time designations. When we do, we find that God did not use these two different numbering schemes just to add variety to the words of the text but rather to bring understanding of the sequence in which these prophecies are to occur. By applying logic to the events that take place during each time period, we can see that even though the 1,260-day period and the 42-month period are equal in length of time, they are not the same time period. Also, we can see that the two time period designations are not interchangeable. One time period applies strictly to one half of Daniel's seventieth week, the other time period applies strictly to the opposite half of the week. By applying logic to the events that take place during each time period, we can also determine which time period, the 1,260 days or the 42 months, to apply to each half of Daniel's last week.

42 Months; The Last Half of the Tribulation Period?

We will start first with the 42-month period because this period is the easiest to envision. As previously stated, there are two events of 42-months duration described in Scripture. Both involve the reign of the Antichrist, with one account focusing on the actions of the man and the other focusing on the actions of his empire. The two events are separated here for ease of discussion, but it must be kept in mind that these two events are in reality one set of actions led by the Antichrist.

One event describes the reign of the Antichrist:

¹And I stood upon the sand of the sea, and saw a beast rise up out of the sea, having seven heads and ten horns, and upon his horns ten crowns, and upon his heads, the name of blasphemy. ²And the beast which I saw was like unto a leopard, and his feet were as the feet of a bear, and his mouth as the mouth of a lion: and the dragon gave him his power, and his seat, and great authority… ⁵And there was given unto him a mouth speaking great things and blasphemies; and **power was given unto him to continue forty and two months.**

⁶And he opened his mouth in blasphemy against God, to blaspheme his name, and his tabernacle, and them that dwell in heaven. ⁷And it was given unto him to make war with the saints, and to overcome them: and power was given him over all kindreds, and tongues, and nations.

(Revelation 13:1-2, 5-7)

The beast with seven heads and ten horns that arises from the sea we know as the empire of the Antichrist, but the one who was given *a mouth speaking great things and blasphemies* is the ruler of this empire. This king who speaks blasphemies is *"that man of sin…the son of perdition; Who opposes and exalts himself above all that is called God, or that is worshipped,"* the one who enters the Temple *"so that he as God sits in the temple of God, showing himself that he is God" (2 Thessalonians 2:1–4).* This is the act of abomination that Daniel is speaking of in 9:27 where at the midpoint of the week, the Antichrist will make the Temple desolate by his presence and will stop the sacrifices and oblations of the Jews.

Revelation 13:5 states that power was given unto this king *"to continue forty and two months."* This *course of action* for which the Antichrist is given power to perform is to *"make war with the saints, and to overcome them" (Revelation 13:7).* There are several accounts of the Antichrist that confirm his time of rule over Israel within the confines of Daniel's seventieth week; four are given here.

Daniel 9:27 states that the Temple is made desolate *"even until the consummation." Consummation* here is *kalah,* which means *completion.* Therefore, the Temple will be made desolate from the midpoint of the week until the completion of all things spoken of in Daniel 9:24 at the end of the week.

The reign of the Antichrist is also spoken of in Daniel 11 and 12. This account starts in Daniel 11:36: *"And the king [of the north] shall do according to his will; and he shall exalt himself, and magnify himself above every god, and shall speak marvelous things against the God of Gods, and shall prosper till the indignation be accomplished."* There are many things that the Antichrist *shall do according to his will* during his reign, but the words *he shall exalt himself, and magnify himself above every god* repeats the words of 2 Thessalonians 2:1–4, strongly implying a reference to his act of desolating the Temple. The statement that *he shall prosper till the indignation be accomplished* identifies the time when he *shall do according to his will, for Daniel asks, "How long shall it be to the end of these wonders?" (Daniel 12:6).* The answer: *"It shall be for a time, times, and an half; and when he shall have accomplished to scatter the power of the holy people, all these things shall be finished" (Daniel 12:7).* The time, times, and a half is a year, two years, and a half a year. Again, we are told that the Antichrist rules for only three and a half years. And, again, we have a reference back to the end of the Seventy Sevens of Daniel when *all these things shall be finished.*

Another account of the reign of the Antichrist is Daniel 7:25: *"And he shall speak great words against the most High, and shall wear out the saints of the most High, and think to change times and laws: and they shall be given into his hand until a time and times and the dividing of time";* again, a rule of three and one half years. We are told further in verses 21 and 22 that this rule ends *when "the Ancient of days"* comes, and the saints possess the kingdom.

At the time of *the consummation,* at the end of *the indignation,* when *the Ancient of days* will come to rule the nations with a rod of iron

(Revelation 19:15), Jesus will cast the Antichrist into a lake of fire burning with brimstone (19:20), ending his rule of *forty and two months.*

From this we see that the 42-month rule of the Antichrist over the nation of Israel begins at the time of the abomination of desolation at the midpoint of the seventieth week and extends to the end of the week.

The other event of 42 months' duration is described in Revelation 11:2: *"But the court which is without the temple leave out, and measure it not; for it is given unto the Gentiles: and the* **holy city shall they tread under foot forty and two months."** The holy city is Jerusalem. They that rule Jerusalem are other Gentile nations of the League of Ten.

From Daniel 9:27, we know that the abomination of desolation spoken of in Matthew 24 occurs at the midpoint of Daniel's seventieth week. Jesus said of this time:

> *"15When you therefore shall see the abomination of desolation, spoken of by Daniel the prophet, stand in the holy place, (whoso reads, let him understand:) 16Then let them which be in Judea flee into the mountains: 17Let him which is on the housetop not come down to take any thing out of his house: 18Neither let him which is in the field return back to take his cloths. 19And woe to them that are with child, and to them that give suck in those days! 20But pray you that your flight be not in the winter, neither on the sabbath day: 21For then shall be great tribulation, such as was not since the beginning of the world to this time, no, nor ever shall be.*
>
> *(Matthew 24:15–21)*

This time of *great tribulation* that is to come upon the nation of Israel is spoken of elsewhere in Scripture. Zechariah describes it this way: *"Behold, the day of the Lord comes, and your spoil shall be divided in the midst of you. 2For I will gather all nations against Jerusalem to battle; and the city shall be taken, and the houses rifled, and the women ravished; and half of the city shall go forth into captivity, and the residue of the people shall not be cut off from the city"* (Zechariah 14:1–2). Zechariah does not give us the length of this period of tribulation, but he does give us the time of the end of this Gentile invasion, for he states, *"3Then shall the Lord go forth, and fight against those nations, as when he fought in the day of battle. 4And his feet shall stand in that day upon the mount of Olives"* (Zechariah 14:3–4). Verse 4 defines the endpoint of this Gentile rule as the day Jesus returns to the earth. Daniel, however, does define the duration of this *great tribulation* for he states, *"At that time shall Michael stand up, the great prince which stands for the children of your people: and there shall be a time of trouble, such as never was since there was a nation even to that same time; and at that time your people shall be delivered, every one that shall be found written in the book"* (Daniel 12:1). *This time of trouble* will last *"for a time, times, and an half; and when he shall have accomplished to scatter the power of the holy people, all these things shall be finished"* (Daniel 12:7). This *time* of trouble is three and a half years—but is it the *forty and two months?*

Luke gives us the starting time for the period of Jerusalem's captivity by the Gentiles. Jesus states in Luke 21 that *"²⁰when you shall see Jerusalem compassed with armies, then know that the desolation thereof is nigh. ²¹Then let them which are in Judea flee to the mountains: let them which are in the midst of it depart out; and let not them that are in the countries enter thereinto. ²²For these be the days of vengeance, that all things which are written may be fulfilled… ²⁴and Jerusalem shall be trodden down of the Gentiles, until the time of the Gentiles be fulfilled"* (Luke 21:20–24).

The nearly identical descriptions given by Matthew and Luke tell us that they are describing the same event, the only difference being that one speaks of the abomination of desolation, the other of the invasion of Jerusalem. The abomination of desolation must therefore occur on the very day of the invasion. Jerusalem therefore comes under Gentile rule at the midpoint of the seventieth week. This we should expect, for the leader of this Gentile invasion is the Antichrist.

Note also the words of Jesus in Luke 21:22 that states that in this 42-month time period following the invasion of Jerusalem, *"all things which are written may be fulfilled."* This confirms what was said of Daniel's vision of the Seventy Sevens, that by the end of the seventieth week all prophecy concerning the nation of Israel and the city of Jerusalem will be completed.

Both events of 42 months' duration, the power of the Antichrist over the Jews and the captivity of the city of Jerusalem by the Gentiles, begin at the midpoint of the seventieth week and end at the return of Jesus. The 42-month period is therefore the last half of the Tribulation Period.

1,260 Days; The First Half of the Tribulation Period?

One of the two events that will occur over a time period of 1,260 days is the appearance and testimony of two men spoken of as the two witnesses:

> *³And I will give power unto my two witnesses, and **they shall prophesy a thousand two hundred and threescore days,** clothed in sackcloth. ⁴These are the two olive trees, and the two candlesticks standing before the God of the earth.*
>
> *⁵And if any man will hurt them, fire proceeds out of their mouth, and devours their enemies: and if any man will hurt them, he must in this manner be killed. ⁶These have power to shut heaven, that it rain not in the days of their prophecy: and have power over waters to turn them to blood, and to smite the earth with all plagues, as often as they will.*
>
> *⁷And when they shall have finished their testimony, the beast that ascends out of the bottomless pit shall make war on them, and shall overcome them, and kill them. ⁸And their dead bodies shall lie in the street of the great city, which spiritually is called Sodom and Egypt, where also our Lord was crucified. ⁹And they of the people and kindreds and tongues and nations shall see their dead bodies three days and an half, and shall not suffer their dead bodies to be put in graves. ¹⁰And they that dwell upon the earth shall rejoice over them, and make merry, and shall send gifts one to another; because these two prophets tormented them that dwell on the earth.*
>
> *¹¹And after three days and an half the Spirit of life from God entered into them, and they stood upon their feet; and great fear fell upon them which saw them. ¹²And they heard a great voice from heaven saying unto them, Come up here. And they ascended up to heaven in a cloud; and their enemies beheld them.*
>
> *(Revelation 11:3–12)*

Logic insists that the 1,260-day period in which these Two Witnesses appear must be the first half of the Tribulation Period, for at the end of their ministry, *when they shall have finished their testimony,* they are killed.[238] Their dead bodies will then be left on the streets of

Jerusalem for three and a half days while *people and kindreds and tongues and nations celebrate* their death. This will be some celebration, *as they that dwell upon the earth* shall even *send gifts one to another* in their elation. Such a celebration of the death of God's Two Witnesses could only happen under the Antichrist's administration, meaning sometime during his 42-month reign. To apply this 1,260-day period of the Two Witnesses to the last half of the seventieth week would mean that they would be killed on the very day that Jesus returns to earth to reign. That would also mean that these Two Witnesses would lie in the streets of Jerusalem, now under the reign of Jesus, as a wicked world celebrated their death. Would Jesus allow such a thing? Never!

From this alone, we could conclude that the 1,260-day period could only be the first half of the Tribulation Period. But we can further confirm this conclusion by the requirements of Daniel's vision of the Seventy Sevens. These Two Witnesses are in all probability Israelites, and when they are killed, they lie in the streets of Jerusalem. This prophecy of the Two Witnesses therefore applies to *"thy people"* and to *"thy holy city" (Daniel 9:24)*, referring to Daniel's people and to Jerusalem. The death and resurrection of these Two Witnesses, therefore, has to be complete prior to the end of the period of the seventy sevens, prior to the *anointing of the most Holy*.

To extend the death and resurrection of these Two Witnesses past the end of the last half of the Tribulation Period simply would not meet the requirements of the allotted time to fulfill the prophecy of the Seventy Sevens.

Applying the 1,260-day period to the first half of the Tribulation Period would have the Two Witnesses coming on the scene the day the covenant is confirmed. They would then be killed at the time of the Antichrist's invasion of Jerusalem and would lie in the streets of Jerusalem for three and a half days during the time of the rule of the Antichrist. The conclusion here is that the 1,260 days is the first half of the Tribulation Period.

Another Bit of Logic

This brings us to the fourth event described in Scripture that has a duration equal to one half of the seventieth week. In Revelation 12, John tells us of a vision in which he first sees *"a woman clothed with the sun, and the moon under her feet, and upon her head a crown of twelve stars"* (v.

1). Then appears *"a great red dragon, having seven heads and ten horns, and seven crowns upon his heads" (v. 3).* As the scene unfolds, the dragon confronts the woman, intending to do harm. The Red Dragon is Satan's empire; the Woman is the nation of Israel. Although this scene is seen in heaven, it is a picture of actual events that are to take place on the earth. This is a picture of the last conflict between the Red Dragon and the nation of Israel.

Verse 6 states that in this conflict *"the woman fled into the wilderness, where she has a place prepared of God, that they should feed her there a thousand two hundred and threescore days."* The phrase *that they should feed her there* speaks of the protection provided to the nation of Israel. Note that this time of 1,260 days applies not to the length of time that the Woman is in the wilderness but to the length of time that she is protected from the dragon while in the wilderness.

Logic would tell us that the time of this 1,260-day period would follow the pattern established by God, as we have just seen defined. Therefore, this 1,260-day period of protection of Israel is to occur during the first half of the Tribulation Period! This will become quite evident in the following chapter, "The (non)Flight of the Woman."

And to the woman were given two wings of a great eagle, that she might fly into the wilderness, into her place, where she is nourished for a time, and times, and half a time, from the face of the serpent.

—Revelation 12:14

[238] The Woman, Israel, is protected from the Dragon (Revelation 12:6, 14). The Dragon here is Satan himself. At the end of their testimony, the Two Witnesses to Israel are killed by Satan, *"the beast that ascends out of the bottomless pit" (Revelation 11:7, Revelation 17:8)*. It is a reasonable expectation that these witnesses could only be killed by the hand of Satan as these two witnesses will come on assignment from *"before the God of the earth" (Revelation 11:4)* with His power and authority.

CHAPTER EIGHTEEN
The (non)Flight of the Woman

In the twelfth chapter of Revelation we saw the conflict between Satan and Israel told in a vision shown to John. John wrote of this vision that he saw a great red dragon standing before a woman who was about to give birth, ready to destroy the child as soon as it was born. But the Woman was given the wings of a great eagle to enable her to flee from the Dragon into a wilderness where she was to be kept safe for a period of three and a half years.

This conflict between the Dragon and the Woman has traditionally been taken to be the attempt of Satan to destroy the Jews during the last half of the Tribulation Period. It is said of this time that the flight of the Woman is the fleeing of the people of Israel into the desert east of the Jordan River to a place where they will be protected from the Antichrist. Since the Antichrist has not yet come, it is envisioned that this flight into the wilderness is to be a future event.

I have titled this chapter "The (non)Flight of the Woman" to draw your attention to a very different conclusion—the Woman **will not** flee!

How can I proclaim such an outlandish thing when the Scripture clearly states that she will? The answer lies in the perspective of time.

The Woman will not flee (future tense) because she has already fled (past tense). The Woman is now in that wilderness. The time that she is to be protected from the Dragon while in this wilderness is, however, yet future. God tells us exactly where this wilderness is into which she has fled, and it's not where we have been looking.

The Vision

[1]And there appeared a great wonder in heaven; a woman clothed with the sun, and the moon under her feet, and upon her head a crown of twelve stars: [2]And she being with child cried, travailing in birth, and pained to be delivered.

[3]And there appeared another wonder in heaven; and behold a great red dragon, having seven heads and ten horns, and seven crowns upon his heads. [4]And his tail drew the third part of the stars of heaven, and did cast them to the earth: and the dragon stood before the woman which was ready to be delivered, for to devour her child as soon as it was born. [5]And she brought forth a man child, who was to rule all nations with a rod of iron: and her child was caught up unto God, and to his throne.

[6]And the woman fled into the wilderness, where she has a place prepared of God, that they should feed her there a thousand two hundred and threescore days.

[7]And there was war in heaven; Michael and his angels fought against the dragon; and the dragon fought and his angels. [8]And prevailed not; neither was there place found any more in heaven. [9]And the great dragon was cast out, that old serpent, called the Devil, and Satan, which deceives the whole world: he was cast out into the earth, and his angels were cast out with him. [10]And I heard a loud voice saying in heaven, Now is come salvation, and strength, and the kingdom of our God, and the power of his Christ: for the accuser of our brethren is cast down, which accused them before our God day and night. [11]And they overcame him by the blood of the Lamb, and by the word of their testimony; and they loved not their lives unto the death. [12]Therefore rejoice, you heavens, and you that dwell in them. Woe to the inhibitors of the earth and of the sea! For the devil is come down unto you, having great wrath, because he knows that he has but a short time.

[13]And when the dragon saw that he was cast unto the earth, he persecuted the woman which brought forth the man (child). [14]And to the woman were given two wings of a great eagle, that she might fly into the wilderness, into her place, where she is nourished for a time, and times, and half a time, from the face of the serpent. [15]And the serpent cast out of his mouth water as a flood after the woman, that he might cause her to be carried away of the flood. [16]And the earth helped the woman, and the earth opened her mouth, and swallowed up the flood which the dragon cast out of his mouth.

[17]And the dragon was wroth with the woman, and went to make war with the remnant of her seed, which keep the commandments of God, and have the testimony of Jesus Christ.

(Revelation 12)

This vision of the confrontation between the Red Dragon and the Woman tells a portion of three separable stories that are woven together into our story of the wrath of the Lamb upon Israel and of his redemption of her people. The first story as we have seen is of the age-old conflict between our series of seven Gentile empires and the nation of Israel. This was done with the introduction of the Red Dragon with its seven heads and ten horns. The second story is shown through the flight of the Woman into the wilderness and her protection there, which tells of the political confrontation between the seventh Gentile empire and the nation of Israel during the days preceding the return of Christ. The third story is the spiritual conflict between Satan and the remnant of the seed of the Woman, a personal conflict of those of Israel who will return to God.

The Woman Identified

The understanding of the identity of the Woman began with a dream of Joseph recorded in Genesis 37. Joseph had told his father and brothers of his dream in which he saw the sun and the moon and eleven stars made obedient to him. His father, Jacob, had *"rebuked him, and said unto him, What is this dream that you have dreamed? Shall I and your mother and your brethren indeed come to bow down ourselves to you to the earth?"* (v. 10). From Jacob's response when hearing of the dream, we saw that Jacob had understood the symbols of the sun and the moon to be the father and mother of Joseph, and the eleven stars to be Joseph's eleven brothers. Joseph's dream was fulfilled when his father, mother, and eleven brothers, and all their families (the whole house of Israel), bowed before him in Egypt.

God had used the symbols of Joseph's dream in John's vision of the Woman. The interpretation of Joseph's dream then became a guide to us in the identification of the Woman. The twelve stars in the crown worn by the Woman represented the twelve sons of Jacob. Joseph was the twelfth star in the crown as he was one of the twelve sons. These twelve became the twelve tribes of Israel, which became the nation of Israel. The crown of twelve stars on the head of the Woman would therefore have represented the twelve tribes of Israel, and the sun that clothed the Woman and the moon that was under her feet would have represented the father and mother of the twelve tribes if we had viewed these symbols as individuals. However, the sun, moon, and stars in John's vision were not taken to be specific individuals, as in Joseph's dream, but rather were taken collectively to be the whole house of Israel. Just as the sun, moon, and eleven stars of Joseph's dream represented the people of Israel, then the same symbols were used in John's vision to identify the people of Israel today. The composite symbolism of the sun, moon, and stars therefore represented the nation of Israel.

The Woman is the source of the man child, which the vision spoke of, who was to rule all nations with a rod of iron (v. 5). John was given a glimpse of this one who will come to rule, for he later stated, *"⁴¹I saw heaven opened, and behold a white horse; and he that sat upon him was called Faithful and True, and in righteousness he does judge and make war. ¹²His eyes were as a flame of fire, and on his head were many crowns; and he had a name written, that no man knew, but he himself. ¹³And he was clothed with a vesture dipped in blood: and his name is called The Word of God. ¹⁴And the armies which were in heaven followed him upon white horses, clothed in fine linen, white and clean. ¹⁵And out of his mouth goes a sharp sword, that with it he should smite the nations: and he shall rule them with a rod of iron"* (Revelation 19:11–15).

This one who is to rule all nations with a rod of iron can only be Jesus. The Woman seen as being with child therefore gave birth to Jesus. The text showing that Jesus was to come out from this Woman was also given as an aid to her identification. Jesus was born physically of Mary, but the text of the vision simply will not support this Woman being Mary—this Woman has to very literally exist during the Tribulation Period.

Neither can this Woman be the church since Jesus did not come out of the church—he brought forth the church. But Jesus was born a Jew, of the tribe of Judah, so he did come out of the nation of Israel.

The statement that *the dragon stood before the Woman which was ready to be delivered, for to devour her child as soon as it was born* spoke simply of Satan's attempts to destroy not only Jesus, but Israel also.

The one who is *to rule all nations with a rod of iron* was also *caught up unto God, and to His thrown* (v. 5). This was a reference to the ascension of Jesus after his crucifixion and to his location during the time period of these three stories.

Either one of these last two references to Jesus would have been sufficient to identify the Woman as Israel, but there was a purpose for the inclusion of both references. With the Woman seen as *being with child* and later the child being *brought forth*, and with a reference to both the past (*was caught up*) and the future (*is yet to rule*), there was a picture of extended time within the vision. With this picture, we began to see conformation that the confrontation between the Woman and the Red Dragon was not just some singular event of the Last Days but is rather a long-standing conflict.

The Woman clothed with the sun, with the moon under her feet, and wearing a crown of twelve stars is in its broadest sense the nation of Israel consisting of both the people and the land they occupy. This is shown graphically in figure 18.1. With that said, it must be noted that John at times spoke as if the symbol of the Woman applied only to the people, such as when the Woman is said to flee into the wilderness. (It is logical to believe that it is just the people that flee into the wilderness as the land can go nowhere.) At other times, John's reference to the Woman applied more directly to the corporate state of Israel, meaning that some action was directed more toward the state and its government than toward the people as individuals.

Figure 18.1. The Woman
as the Nation of Esrael.

The Red Dragon Identified

It was stated in verse 9 that this dragon is *"that old serpent, called the Devil, and Satan, which deceives the whole world."* But John saw this dragon as a beast *having seven heads and ten horns, and seven crowns upon his heads,* which we know is not a description of Satan himself but rather a description of his empire. The seven heads are our seven Gentile kingdoms with the crowns signifying their sovereignty. The seventh head of this beast with its ten horns includes yet another beast, the beast that is the empire of the Antichrist. The *third part of the stars of heaven* that were drawn by the Dragon's tail are the rebellious angels (demons) that follow Satan.

The Historical Conflict

Portraying Satan as a beast with seven heads and ten horns, and with seven crowns upon its heads, introduced the seven Gentile empires of the first story told in this vision—that of the Dragon's adversarial relationship with Israel throughout a defined period of history. As we have seen through this period of time, there was to be a series of seven confrontations between the Red Dragon and Israel.

The first six have resulted in Israel being made a part of the invading empire. The first confrontation was with the Assyrian Empire. The second confrontation was with the Egyptian Empire, portrayed in figure 18.2, and so forth unto the sixth, which was with the Roman Empire.

With these events occurring over many centuries, we got a sense of extended time in the symbolism of the Red Dragon just as we did with the symbolism of the Woman.

Figure 18.2. The conflict between the
Egyptian Empire and the nation of Esrael.

The Last Conflict Between the Red Dragon and the Woman

The second of the three stories told in John's vision is of the seventh, and last, confrontation between the Red Dragon and the Woman. This last confrontation starts with a war, but not between the Dragon and the Woman, but between Satan and God:

> *[7] And there was war in heaven: Michael and his angels fought against the dragon; and the dragon fought and his angels, [8] and prevailed not; neither was their place found any more in heaven.*

[9]And the great dragon was cast out, that old serpent, called the Devil, and Satan, which deceives the whole world: he was cast out into the earth, and his angels were cast out with him…

[13]And when the dragon saw that he was cast unto the earth, he persecuted the woman which brought forth the man (child). [14]And to the woman were given two wings of a great eagle, that she might fly into the wilderness, into her place, where she is nourished for a time, and times, and half a time, from the face of the serpent.

(Revelation 12:7–14)

This war ended with Michael and his angels throwing Satan and his demons out of heaven and casting them to the earth. When the Dragon saw that he was cast to the earth, he persecuted the Woman. In verse 6, we see that when the Woman was persecuted, *she fled into the wilderness…[where] they should feed her there a thousand two hundred and threescore days.* Again, in verse 14, we see that when the Woman was persecuted, she was given *two wings of a great eagle, that she might fly into the wilderness…where she is nourished for a time, and times, and half a time, from the face of the serpent.* So, twice we are told that while the Woman is in this wilderness, she is fed, or nourished, for a period of 1,260 days. The repetitiveness of the text stresses the importance of this flight from persecution and of the 1,260-day period when sustenance is given to the Woman.

The sustenance given speaks of protection from the Dragon—*she is nourished…from the face of the serpent.* The symbolism of feeding the Woman to say that the Woman is protected may have come from another flight of Israel, their flight from Egypt. Manna, quail, and water were provided by God to nourish the people while they were in the Sinai Desert. With this provision of nourishment, the people were provided for, or protected, while in their wilderness.

The three and a half years of verse 14 is the same time period identified as 1,260 days in verse 6. Therefore, the length of time the Woman is protected from the Dragon is a period of 1,260 days. It is critical to understand that this 1,260-day period is the period of protection. There is no requirement to limit the time that the Woman is in this wilderness to 1,260 days. Neither is there a requirement that the flight of the Woman was to begin the period of the 1,260 days. What the Scripture does state is that while the Woman is in the wilderness, she will be protected *from the face of the serpent* for a period of 1,260 days. Thus, the

Woman could be in the wilderness for many years but is protected from aggression for only a period of 1,260 days during those years.

At this point, it is of help in seeing the focus of this story to divide the Red Dragon and the Woman into their component parts. The Woman is said to be protected from the face of the serpent, meaning from the Red Dragon, from Satan. Thus the focus of this vision is on the conflict between one of the heads of the Dragon as the agent of Satan and the corporate state of Israel, the land that is *Judah, Israel, and Jerusalem.* In other words, this story is the story of the political and military conflicts between the League of Ten and Israel, as depicted in figure 18.3.

Figure 18.3. The conflict
between the League of Ten
and the nation of Esrael.

To say that the League of Ten will be in political and military conflicts with Israel when Israel itself is a member of the League appears to be contradictory. Israel will voluntarily join this confederation of sovereign nations when the League is formed. However, Daniel, describing this last empire of Nebuchadnezzar's image, said of them, *"⁴¹Whereas you saw the feet and toes, part of potters' clay, and part of iron, the kingdom shall be divided.... ⁴³And whereas you saw iron mixed with miry clay, they shall mingle themselves with the seed of men: but they shall not cleave one to another, even as iron is not mixed with clay (Daniel 2:41, 43).* During the 1,260-day period, these words of Daniel will manifest themselves when *"the serpent [shall] cast out of his mouth water as a flood after the woman, that he might cause her to be carried away of the flood"* (Revelation 11:15). The agent of Satan is therefore an Arab contingency of the League that will first come into political conflict (out of his mouth) with Israel. This contingency, led by the king of the north, will later invade Israel at the midpoint of the Tribulation Period as the empire of the Antichrist comes into being. Thus, Israel will in one way be a part of the League of Ten but yet will be in conflict with it.

As the seventieth week of Daniel opens, Israel will have just signed *"the covenant" (Daniel 9:27)* along with nine of its Arab neighbors to form the confederacy of the League of Ten. Israel will feel secure under the protection of this covenant; there would be no reason for the people to flee.

At the time of the signing of the covenant, the man who will become the Antichrist is yet a prince, *"the prince that shall come" (Daniel 9:26)*. During this time of protection, this *prince* will rise to the position of king of his country. Then, sudden destruction will come upon Israel, and Israel will not escape as this newly risen king invades Israel, breaking the covenant (Daniel 9:27). He now stands in the temple of God, *"showing himself that he is God" (2 Thessalonians 2:4)*. We are now at day 1,260 + 1.

Thus, what John's vision is now showing us is the period of 1,260 days when the Dragon will be kept from the Woman; the time when the Antichrist will be kept from militarily invading Israel. During this 1,260-day period of protection, the Dragon will *"cast out of his mouth water as a flood after the Woman, that he might cause her to be carried away of the flood" (v. 15)*. This *flood* that is to come *out of his mouth,* meaning out of the mouth of this *prince*, now king, will be a stream of words intended to stir up those who would *carry away* or eliminate the state of Israel.

Now, this is the protection given the Woman: *the earth helped the Woman, and the earth opened her mouth, and swallowed up the flood which the dragon cast out of his mouth.* The earth, (gē, also meaning *land* or that which is on the land) is the nations of the world who, through political pressure, force the League to honor the covenant. Therefore, the Woman (the state of Israel) is kept safe from the Red Dragon (the League of Ten) for the 1,260 days of the first half of the Tribulation Period.

Day 1,260 + 1 of this seventieth week of Daniel is the first day of the 42-month reign of the Antichrist (Revelation 13:5). The protection given the Woman during the first half of the Tribulation is now in marked contrast to the events of the second half, which begins with the invasion of Israel: *"[20]And when you shall see Jerusalem compassed with armies, then know that the desolation thereof is nigh. [21]Then let them which are in Judea flee to the mountains; and let them which are in the midst of it depart out; and let not them that are in the countries enter thereinto. [22]For these be the days of vengeance, that all things which are written may be fulfilled" (Luke 21:20–22)*. Special note should be taken of this last sentence.

Matthew also speaks of this invasion of Jerusalem. Because he is writing to the Jews, his focus is more on the Temple than on the city, as was Luke's, whose message is for the Gentiles.

But the degree of tribulation to come upon the people at this time is still clearly stated by Matthew: *"[15]When you therefore shall see the abomination of desolation, spoken of by Daniel the prophet, stand in the holy place…[21]then shall be great tribulation, such as was not since the beginning of the world to this time, no, nor ever shall be"* (Matthew 24: 15, 21).

When Jesus spoke of the invasion of Jerusalem and of the concurrent abomination of desolation, he said that when you see these things, *"[16]then let them which be in Judea flee into the mountains: [17]Let him which is on the housetop not come down to take anything out of his house: [18]Neither let him which is in the field return back to take his clothes"* (Matthew 24:16–18). The words he used to describe the fleeing of the people at this time are more to tell the people of the type of invasion this one will be more than to warn the people to flee quickly. We saw earlier where the words used to describe an invasion where *they shall not leave in you one stone upon another* helped us to separate and identify the two very different invasions of Jerusalem, the one that occurred in AD 70 and the one spoken of here. This invasion will be very different than the former; this invasion will be said and done in an instant.

From the words Jesus uses to describe this invasion, it sounds as if this would be the time for the Woman to flee into the wilderness. Some may be able to flee this invasion, but the Woman will not. When we look at *"all things which are written"* (Luke 21:22), it becomes obvious that during the last half of the Tribulation, the Woman will not be protected from the Dragon. Just the opposite will occur; she will come under the destroying hand of the other nations of the League of Ten led by the Antichrist. Zechariah gives us more details of this invasion and some description of the terror to come upon her people: *"[1]Behold, The day of the Lord comes, and your spoil shall be divided in the midst of you. [2]For I will gather all nations against Jerusalem to battle; and the city shall be taken, and houses rifled, and the women ravished; and half the city shall go forth into captivity, and the residue of the people shall not be cut off from the city"* (Zechariah 14:1–2). This is not a time of safety for the Jews, for *"it shall come to pass, that in all the land, says the Lord, two parts therein shall be cut off and die"* (Zechariah 13:8).

But could not these verses of Zachariah apply to only those Jews who do not escape into the wilderness? Jeremiah describes what is to come upon the entire nation, not just to those who may be slow in taking heed of the warning:

³For, lo, the days come, says the Lord, that I will bring again the captivity of my people Israel and Judah, says the Lord: and I will cause them to return to the land that I gave to their fathers, and they shall possess it. ⁴And these are the words that the Lord spoke concerning Israel and concerning Judah. ⁵For thus says the Lord; We have heard a voice of trembling and fear, and not of peace. ⁶Ask you now, and see whether a man does travail with child? Wherefore do I see every man with his hands on his loins, as a woman in travail, and all faces are turned into paleness? ⁷Alas! For that day is great, so that none is like it: it is even the time of Jacobs's trouble; but he shall be saved out of it.

(Jeremiah 30:3–7)

This is the time of Jacob's trouble concerning Israel and concerning Judah, the entire nation, where every man, all faces, all are turned into paleness, not just those who were too slow to flee.

Could not the phrase *but he shall be saved out of it* mean that those who fled into the wilderness are protected from the Antichrist?

Jeremiah is speaking here of spiritual salvation, not of physical safety. This is confirmed by Daniel who also spoke of this same time:

And at that time shall Michael stand up, the great prince which stands for the children of your people: and there shall be a time of trouble, such as never was since there was a nation even to that same time: and at that time your people shall be delivered, everyone that shall be found written in the book.

(Daniel 12:1)

Those names found written in the book of life are those who have received Jesus as Lord and Savior (Revelation 20:12). Their safety is spiritual, not physical, as we shall see.

As previously stated, Zechariah had said of this time, *"It shall come to pass, that in all the land, says the Lord, two parts therein shall be cut off and die"* (Zechariah 13:8). To be *cut off* is to die the death of a transgressor.

Zechariah is speaking here of the death of those Jews who will refuse to turn to God during this time of great tribulation. To God, they are transgressors of His law. He still sees their sin, for they reject the salvation found only in Jesus. But Zechariah also said, *"⁸The third shall be left therein. ⁹And I will bring the third part through the fire, and will refine them as silver is refined, and will try them as gold is tried: they shall call on my name, and I will hear them: I will say, It is my people: and they shall say, The Lord is my God"* (Zechariah 13:8–9). Zechariah's refining fire is the 42-month Gentile rule over Israel (Revelation 11:2). The *third* part is those Jews who will accept Jesus as the Christ. This is the Israel that will be saved.

But, can those who accept Jesus at this time flee to the wilderness for protection? Daniel said of this time, *"I beheld, and the same horn made war with the saints, and prevailed against them"* (Daniel 7:21). John repeated Daniel's words when he said, *"It was given unto him to make war with the saints and to overcome them"* (Revelation 13:7). Neither does it sound, then, as if the saints will find protection in another wilderness.

Those Jews who accept Jesus during this time will not take the mark of the Beast, nor will they worship the image of the Beast. John says of these, *"As many as would not worship the image of the beast should be killed"* (Revelation 13:15). Reason would tell us then that the *third part* of the Jews will also die. Now, the mark and the image of the Beast exist for the Jews only during the 42-month reign of the Antichrist. Certainly then, the Woman is not protected from the Dragon during the last half of the Tribulation Period.

Jesus said of the reign of the Antichrist, *"¹⁵When you therefore shall see the abomination of desolation, spoken of by Daniel the prophet, stand in the holy place...²¹then shall be great tribulation, such as was not since the beginning of the world to this time, no, nor ever shall be"* (Matthew 24:15, 21). How great is this time of tribulation for Israel? It must be greater than that of the siege by Titus when over one million Jews died, and it must be greater than the time of the Holocaust when over six million Jews died, for it shall be *such as was not since the beginning of the world to this time, no, nor ever shall be.* We have seen from the previous verses that no Jew *in all the land* will be left alive. The people will not be fleeing to a place of safety during the reign of the Antichrist. The 1,260-day period of protection of the Woman therefore cannot be the last half of the Tribulation Period.

The Wilderness Identified

From the scene depicted in the twelfth chapter of Revelation, we know that the flight of the Woman into the wilderness was a direct result of persecution from the Dragon after the Dragon was cast to the earth. We also know that the Woman is to be protected from the Dragon for a period of 1,260 days, and that the 1,260 days are the first half of the Tribulation Period. Therefore, the flight of the Woman must occur before the start of the Tribulation Period.

God was speaking of the Jews of the Diaspora when he proclaimed, *"[34]I will gather you out of the countries wherein you are scattered...[35]and will bring you into the wilderness of the people"* (Ezekiel 20:34–35). To make sure we get that point, God again proclaims in verses 41 and 42, *"[41]I [will] bring you out from the people, and gather you out of the countries wherein you have been scattered.... [41]I shall bring you into the land of Israel, into the country the which I lifted up my hand to give it to your fathers."*

[I] will gather you out of the countries wherein you are scattered—this is the gathering of all the tribes of Jacob, the whole nation of Israel, from all the countries where they had been scattered. This is the gathering of Israel the world has witnessed these last one hundred or so years and continues to this day. And, when they were gathered, they were brought into **the wilderness...into the land of Israel,** meaning the land **of the people...into the country the which I lifted up my hand to give it to your fathers.** The land into which they have gathered is the present state of Israel—the Woman has already fled into that wilderness!

We typically do not think of the state of Israel as a wilderness. Today, the land flourishes in many ways. But when the people were brought back into the land, that land was a physical and a spiritual wilderness.

The physical nature of the wilderness into which the people were to flee is described by Ezekiel: *"[33]Thus says the Lord God; In the day that I shall have cleansed you from all your iniquities I will also cause you to dwell in the cities, and the wastes shall be builded. [34]And the desolate land shall be tilled, whereas it lay desolate in the sight of all that passed by. [35]And they shall say, This land that was desolate is become like the garden of Eden; and the waste and desolate and ruined cities are become fenced, and are inhabited"* (Ezekiel 36:33–35). Ezekiel implies a span of time in these words—the desolate land shall be tilled and become like the garden of Eden,
the waste places shall be rebuilt, and the cities made inhabitable—as if to say the Woman was to be in this wilderness for some time.

The spiritual nature of this land is also as much a wilderness to the people of the second Exodus as was the wilderness of the Sinai to the people of the first Exodus. God said of this land into which they were to flee, *"[35][I] will bring you into the wilderness of the people, people, and there will I plead with you face to face.... [37]And I will cause you to pass under the rod, and I will bring you into the bond of the covenant"* (Ezekiel 20:35, 37). It is here, in this modern wilderness, that His people will again come face-to-face with God, just as they did in the wilderness of the Sinai—but I'm getting into the third story.

This second story, the last conflict between the Red Dragon and the Woman, is thus the telling of the conflict between a contingency within the League of Ten and the state of Israel. The conflict, while still a spiritual battle, manifests itself as a political and military conflict between nations. The story begins with the Israelites fleeing into a wilderness, being driven by persecution out of the countries in which they had earlier been scattered. After having fled into the wilderness, the state of Israel will be protected for a period of 1,260 days from the nations that are intent on destroying her. Those nations are of the very nations that had joined with Israel to form the League of Ten. When this period of protection ends, Israel will be destroyed as a nation, and the Jews will be destroyed as a people.

The Last Conflict Between Satan and the People

The third separable story told in the vision of Revelation 12 is a different type of spiritual battle between the Dragon and the Woman. John tells us in verse 17 that after the Woman has fled into the wilderness, it is then that *the dragon was wroth with the woman, and went to make war with the remnant of her seed, which keep the commandments of God, and have testimony of Jesus Christ.* This conflict is fought at an individual, personal level in contrast to the corporate level conflicts seen in the other stories of the vision. Thus, this story is of the conflict between Satan and each individual; it is the battle for the soul.

In Ezekiel's vision of the second exodus, God had said He would yet rule over this rebellious people, that there would come a time in which He would personally intervene in the affairs of men to bring about His desires.

There, God told the Jews, *"I will bring you out from the people, and will gather you out of the countries wherein you are scattered" (Ezekiel 20:34).* This verse speaks of two different events, two different separations. The gathering *out of the countries wherein [they] are scattered* is the physical separation of the people within the world. This is the physical rebirth of the nation of Israel. To be brought *out from the people* is the spiritual separation of the people from the world. This is the spiritual rebirth of the people of Israel, the *"remnant of her seed"* that is spoken of in Revelation 12:17.

From history, we have seen that the physical rebirth of the nation has come about before the spiritual rebirth of the people. This is in fact the order of events God had foretold, for He said of His people, *"[85]I will bring you into the wilderness of the people, **and there** will I plead with you face to* *face.... ³⁷And I will cause you to pass under the rod, and I will bring you into the bond of the covenant" (Ezekiel 20:35, 37).*

Again, we go back to Daniel 9:24 to see the nation's spiritual condition, and God's plan for His people: *Seventy weeks are determined upon your people and upon your holy city, to finish the transgression, and to make and end of sins, and to make reconciliation for iniquity, and to bring in everlasting righteousness. We know that "blindness in part is happened to Israel, until the fullness of the Gentiles be come in" (Romans 11:25).* This condition of blindness is a spiritual blindness as explained in Ephesians 4:18: *"Having the understanding darkened, being alienated from the life of God through the ignorance that is in them, because of the blindness of their heart."* But this spiritual blindness is to be removed, for God has also said of this people:

> *²⁷When I have brought them again from the people, and gathered them out of their enemies' lands, and am sanctified in them in the sight of many nations; ²⁸Then shall they know that I am the Lord their God, which caused them to be led into captivity among the heathen: but I have gathered them unto their own land, and have left none of them anymore there. ²⁹Neither will I hide my face any more from them: for I have poured out my spirit upon the house of Israel, says the Lord God.*
>
> *(Ezekiel 39:27–29)*

> *¹In that day there shall be a fountain opened to the house of David and to the inhabitants of Jerusalem for sin and for uncleanness...⁹and I will bring the third part through the fire, and will refine them as silver is refined, and will try them as gold is tried: they shall call on my name, and I will hear them: I will say, It is my people: and they shall say, The Lord is my God.*
>
> *(Zechariah 13:1, 9)*

The *remnant of her seed* on whom Satan *makes war* are the people of Israel, but only a part of the people. Those that are in this conflict between the Dragon and the Woman are only those *"which keep the commandments of God, and have testimony of Jesus Christ"* (v. 17), who will overcome Satan *"by the blood of the Lamb, and by the word of their testimony; and [love] not their lives unto the death"* (v. 11). There will be no need for the Dragon to make war on all the seed of the Woman, for two-thirds of her seed will never accept Jesus; they are already defeated.

From the Wilderness into the Promised Land

There is another part of Ezekiel's account of the second exodus that would appear to contradict what has just been stated as the location of the wilderness into which the Woman was to flee. According to Ezekiel 20, God said of His people, *"[34][I] will gather you out of the countries wherein you are scattered…[35] and will bring you into the wilderness of the people…[42] into the land of Israel"* (vv. 34, 35, 42). Yet in verse 38, God said of this same event, *"I will bring them forth out of the country where they sojourn, and **they shall not enter** the land of Israel."*

I purposely quoted only a portion of verse 38 to magnify this point to bring our full attention to these next verses:

> [33] *As I live, says the Lord God, surly with a stretched out arm, and with fury poured out, will I rule over you:* [34] *And I will bring you out from the people, and will gather you out of the countries wherein you are scattered, with a mighty hand, and with a stretched out arm, and with fury poured out.* [35] *And I will bring you into the wilderness of the people, and there will I plead with you face to face.* [36] *Like as I pleaded with your fathers in the wilderness of the land of Egypt, so will I plead with you, says the Lord God.* [37] *And I will cause you to pass under the rod, and I will bring you into the bond of the covenant:*
>
> [38] *And I will purge out from among you the rebels, and them that transgress against me: I will bring them fourth out of the country where they sojourn, and they shall not enter into the land of Israel: and you shall know that I am the Lord.*
>
> *(Ezekiel 20:33–38)*

In these verses, we see a separation in the *wilderness of the people* of those who continue in their rebellion from those who choose to turn to God in repentance, just as there was a separation of those in the wilderness of the Sinai who rebelled against God. Only two of those who entered the wilderness of the Sinai came out of that wilderness and entered into the promised land of Israel; the others died in that wilderness. God is telling the people of Israel that when He has brought them into the wilderness of the people, He will plead with them face-to-face, just as He did with their forefathers before them, and He will purge out from among them those who will not turn from their rebellion and their disobedience, and they shall not enter the promised land. This separation of those who transgress against God comes to completion during the Tribulation Period:

> *¹On that day there shall be a fountain opened for the house of David and the inhabitants of Jerusalem to cleanse them from sin and uncleanness....⁷And I will turn my hand upon the little ones. ⁸And it shall come to pass, that in all the land, says the Lord, two parts therein shall be cut off and die; but the third shall be left therein. ⁹And I will bring the third part through the fire, and will refine them as silver is refined, and will try them as gold is tried: they shall call on my name, and I will hear them: I will say, It is my people: and they shall say, The Lord is my God.*

> *(Zechariah 13:1, 7–9)*

There are two Israels spoken of in these verses. Each is the land of Israel, but they are separated in time. The first Israel is the wilderness in which the people will come face-to-face with a personal decision, to accept the redemption offered by Jesus or to continue in their rebellion. Those who reject Jesus *shall be cut off and die,* dying the death of the transgressor. They shall be resurrected unto death, forever separated from the presence of God. They will never inhabit the land as God intended for His people—*they shall not enter the land of Israel* that is the promised land of milk and honey. But those who *call on my name* will God hear, and will say of them, *It is my people.* Even if these die, they will be resurrected unto life. They will return with Jesus to rule, and thus shall they inhabit the promised land of Israel.

And there was war in heaven: Michael and his angels fought against the Dragon; and the Dragon fought and his angels, and prevailed not; neither was their place found any more in heaven.

—Revelation 12:7–8

CHAPTER NINETEEN
Heavenly Wars

The claim was made in the previous chapter that the flight of the Woman into the wilderness was the recent flight of the Jews out of all nations of the world into Israel. According to Scripture, this flight of the Woman was due to Satan having been cast to the earth after losing a war in heaven between the Red Dragon and the archangel Michael. Since the validity of the claim that the flight of the woman is the return of the Jews to their homeland is dependent upon the time of this war, we must see what the Scriptures have to say about the time of this heavenly war.

Historically, there have been two interpretations of the time of the war between Michael and the Dragon. One interpretation is that this war is yet future, to occur sometime during the Tribulation Period. The other is that this war occurred in ages long past, when Satan first rebelled against God. We need to see if either of these two theories could be possible.

The War

> *⁷And there was war in heaven: Michael and his angels fought against the Dragon; and the Dragon fought and his angles, ⁸and prevailed not; neither was their place found any more in heaven. ⁹And the great Dragon was cast out, that old serpent, called the Devil, and Satan, which deceived the whole world: he was cast out into the earth, and his angles were cast out with him.*
>
> *¹⁰And I heard a loud voice saying in heaven, Now is come salvation, and strength, and the kingdom of our God, and the power of his Christ: for the accuser of our brethren is cast down, which accused them before our God day and night. ¹¹And they over came him by the blood of the Lamb, and by the word of their testimony; and they loved not their lives unto the death.*

¹²Therefore rejoice, you heavens, and you that dwell in them. Woe to the inhabiters of the earth and of the sea! For the devil is come down unto you, having great wrath, because he knows that he has but a short time.

¹³And when the Dragon saw that he was cast unto the earth, he persecuted the woman which brought forth the man child. 14And to the woman were given two wings of a great eagle, that she might fly into the wilderness, into her place.

(Revelation 12:7–14)

A Future War?

The theory of a future war proposes that the war between Michael and the Dragon is to occur sometime near the start of or during the Tribulation Period. At that time, Satan, with angels that also rebelled against God, will be cast to the earth after losing this war. When Satan is restrained to the earth, he will persecute the Jews through the agency of the Antichrist. The Jews will then flee from Israel into the Jordanian wilderness where they will be protected from the Antichrist for the 1,260-day period of the last half of the Tribulation. This theory fails on every point:

- The 1,260-day period of protection of the Woman is the first half of the Tribulation Period, not the last half. Therefore, the Woman must flee *into the wilderness, into her place* prior to the start of the Tribulation Period.
- Further, the persecution of the Woman is the reason for the Woman to flee into the wilderness. The period of persecution of the Woman must then also occur prior to the start of the Tribulation.
  Therefore, the root source of this persecution of the Jews is Satan, not the Antichrist.
- The *wilderness* into which the Woman was to flee is *her place,* her homeland, the land of Israel not the Jordanian wilderness.
- The Jews will not escape the hand of the Antichrist. Just the opposite is to occur, as the Antichrist will have complete authority over the Jews during his 42-month reign of the last half of the Tribulation Period.

If the period in which the Woman is to be protected is the 1,260 days of the first half of the Tribulation Period, then the war between Michael and the Dragon must take place prior to the Tribulation Period.

A Long Past War?

The second theory historically taught of the time of the war between Michael and the Dragon is that this war took place at the time of Satan's first rebellion against God. So let's see what the Scriptures say about this rebellion.

First, the time of Satan's rebellion. The story of Adam and Eve shows that Satan was in rebellion against God at the time of the creation of man. Genesis 2:7–8 tells us *"⁷the Lord God formed man of the dust of the ground, and breathed into his nostrils the breath of life; and man became a living sole. ⁸And the Lord God planted a garden eastward in Eden; and there he put the man whom he had formed."* God also planted a tree in that garden, the fruit of which Adam and Eve were forbidden to eat. In Genesis 3:1–4, we see Satan using this in rebellion against God:

> *¹Now the serpent was more subtle than any beast of the field which the Lord God had made. ²And he said unto the woman, Yea, has God said, You shall not eat of every tree in the garden? And the woman said unto the serpent, We may eat of the fruit of the trees of the garden: ³But the fruit of the tree which is in the midst of the garden, God has said, You shall not eat of it, neither shall you touch it, lest you die. ⁴And the serpent said unto the woman, You shall not surely die*

and thus tempted Eve to disobey God. From this, we know that Satan's rebellion against God occurred before, or at least during, the time of Adam and that Satan was present on the earth at the time of Adam and Eve. But had he been *cast out into the earth* at that time?

The King of Tyrus

An account of the rebellion of Satan in Ezekiel 28 gives us a little more information. Here Satan is called the king of Tyrus (Tyre), a rich, seafaring city-state on the Mediterranean Sea coast. This account first speaks of the prince of Tyrus, who is the physical king. We see from the text of Ezekiel how this physical king reflected the arrogant, proud attitude of Satan, who is the spiritual king of Tyrus. Then the text speaks of the spiritual king:

> *¹²Son of man, take up a lamentation upon the king of Tyrus, and say unto him, Thus says the Lord God; You seal up the sum, full of wisdom, and perfect in beauty. ¹³You have been in Eden the garden of God; every precious*

stone was your covering, the sardius, topaz, and the diamond, the beryl, the onyx, and the jasper, the sapphire, the emerald, and the carbuncle, and gold: the workmanship of your tabrets and of your pipes was prepared in you in the day that you were created. [14]You are the anointed cherub that covers; and I have set you so: you were upon the holy mountain of God; you have walked up and down in the midst of the stones of fire. [15]You were perfect in your ways from the day that you were created, till iniquity was found in you.

[16]By the multitude of your merchandise they have filled the midst of you with violence, and you have sinned: therefore I will cast you as profane out of the mountain of God: and I will destroy you, O covering cherub, from the midst of the stones of fire. [17]Your heart was lifted up because of your beauty, you have corrupted your wisdom by reason of your brightness: I will cast you to the ground, I will lay you before kings, that they may behold you. [18]You have defiled your sanctuaries by the multitude of your iniquities, by the iniquity of your traffic; therefore will I bring forth a fire from the midst of you, it shall devour you, and I will bring you to ashes upon the earth in the sight of all them that behold you. [19]All they that know you among the people shall be astonished at you: you shall be a terror, and never shall you be any more.

(Ezekiel 28:12–19)

This king of Tyrus is *the anointed cherub that covers* (v. 14); therefore, we know this king is an angel, not a man.

The king was *in Eden, the garden of God* (v. 13). The only angel recorded to be in Eden was Satan.

This angel is also an angel in rebellion against God, for he is described as having iniquity (v. 15). This confirms the spiritual king of Tyrus to be Satan.

The Holy Mountain of God

Verse 14 says of Satan, *you were upon the holy mountain of God.* The identification of this *mountain* is required to determine the whereabouts of Satan through time. *The holy mountain of God* may be a specific place in heaven, such as the place of government, possibly even the throne room of God, or it may be the entirety of heaven.

The concept of a mountain representing the government or administration of God is seen elsewhere in Scripture. It's a natural word picture of the day when kings built their centers of government on mountaintops, hilltops, or high places because it was the best place of defense against their enemies. We also see elsewhere in Scripture that angels appear to have assigned positions or duties within the administration of God. Michael, the chief warrior, and Gabriel, the chief messenger, are examples. In this scenario, an angel in an administrative position could be said to be *upon the holy mountain of God.*

Satan is addressed as the *anointed cherub that covers,* set as so by God Himself. With this, and the glorious description of him given in the text, we could well assume that he was quite special. It could be that because of *the multitude of [his] merchandise* (his abilities) that he held a high position in the administration of God before his rebellion. It was because of his beauty, his ability, and possibly his position, that he became proud, and in his pride, rebelled against God. If Satan was in a position of authority in God's administration, his removal from authority would have come swiftly after his rebellion. To consider otherwise would challenge God's intolerance of sin. God told Satan, *you have sinned: therefore I will cast you as profane out of the mountain of God.* This may mean Satan was thrown out of the administration of God at the time of his rebellion. But does it mean that he was also *cast out into the earth* at that time?

This *lamentation upon the king of Tyrus* was given to Ezekiel to, in turn, tell Satan of God's pronouncement of judgment: *You are the anointed cherub… you were upon the holy mountain of God…. You were perfect in your ways…till iniquity was found in you…you have sinned: therefore I will cast you as profane out of the mountain of God.* The statement *"I will cast you as profane out of the mountain of God"* would then be an act of God, yet future from the time of Ezekiel. Since Satan would have been thrown out of any position of authority at the time of his rebellion, *the holy mountain of God* would appear to be heaven itself rather than just the administration of God.

Because the time when Satan is to be *cast out into the earth* was yet future at the time of Ezekiel, the second theory of the time of the war between Michael and the Dragon as occurring at the time of Satan's first rebellion against God is also incorrect.

So, Where Has Satan Been?

As Michael defeats Satan in this heavenly war, a voice is heard, saying, *"Now is come salvation, and strength, and the kingdom of our God, and the power of his Christ: for the accuser of our brethren is cast down, which accused them before our God day and night" (Revelation 12:10).* At the time of this war, Satan must have been in heaven, before God, as an accuser of *our brethren. Our brethren are men, not angels, for "they overcame him [Satan] by the blood of the Lamb, and by the word of their testimony"* (v. 11), something an angel cannot do. Satan is therefore an accuser of man, not angels. The speaker whose voice was heard by John was thus also a man and not an angel. Therefore, the time of this war has to be after the time of the disobedience of Adam and Eve in the Garden of Eden, for before that time, there was no sinner for Satan to accuse. So, Satan was back in heaven, before God, as our accuser, after he was on the earth to tempt Eve.

We see Satan again, both on earth and in heaven, in Job: *"There was a man in the land of Uz, whose name was Job; and that man was perfect and upright, and one that feared God, and eschewed evil"* (Job 1:1). Job's righteousness before God was about to be proven to Satan as God would allow Satan to come against Job:

> *6Now there was a day when the sons of God came to present themselves before the Lord, and Satan came also among them. 7And the Lord said unto Satan, Whence come you? Then Satan answered the Lord, and said, From going to and fro in the earth, and from walking up and down in it. 8And the lord said unto Satan, Have you considered my servant Job, that there is none like him in the earth, a perfect and upright man, one that fears God, and eschews evil? 9Then Satan answered the Lord, and said, Does Job fear God for naught? 10Have not you made a hedge about him, and about his house, and about all that he has on every side? You have blessed the work of his hands, and his substance is increased in the land. 11But put forth your hand now, and touch all that he has, and he will curse you to your face. 12And the lord said unto Satan, Behold, all that he has is in your power; only upon himself put not forth your hand. So Satan went forth from the presence of the Lord.*
>
> *(Job 1:6–12)*

In this passage, we see that Satan is in heaven standing before God. Therefore, he still had access to heaven and to the throne at the time of Job. Satan also claimed to have been chasing around on the earth before coming before God.

We see Satan on the earth again long after the time of Job. Matthew records the account of Satan confronting Jesus:

¹Then was Jesus led up of the Spirit into the wilderness to be tempted of the devil. ²And when he had fasted forty days and forty nights, he was afterward an hungered. ³And when the tempter came to him, he said, If you are the Son of God, command that these stones be made bread… ⁵ Then the devil took him up into the holy city, and set him on a pinnacle of the temple… ⁸Again, the devil took him up into an exceeding high mountain, and showed him all the kingdoms of the world, and the glory of them… ¹⁰Then said Jesus unto him, Get thee hence, Satan… ¹¹Then the devil left him.

(Matthew 4:1–11)

From these passages, it is clear that Satan was here on the earth at the time Jesus began his ministry.

Satan has thus gone back and forth between earth and heaven throughout time. He has also had access to heaven after his rebellion and was there *"before our God day and night" (Revelation 12:10)*. God is omnipresent, but Satan is not. For Satan to be *before our God day and night*, he has had to have access to heaven after his rebellion.

This war in which Satan was to be cast out of heaven could not have been fought at the time of the initial rebellion.

One more point about this account of Satan's rebellion: God said, *"²⁷I will cast you to the ground, I will lay you before kings, that they may behold you…. ²⁸I will bring you to ashes upon the earth in the sight of all them that behold you" (Ezekiel 28:17–18). Satan has not yet been lay[ed] before kings, that they may behold [him].* Neither has he been brought to ashes [destroyed] upon the earth in the sight of all them that [beheld him]. These things have not yet occurred: they are still future, for they speak of his defeat at the return of Christ when he is revealed for just what he is. God is saying that His response to Satan's iniquity was not completed at the time of the rebellion, but more consequences were yet to come. So, it's not out of order to consider Satan's ejection from heaven at a time other than at the time of the rebellion.

The Time of the War

We know the war between Michael and the Red Dragon did not occur at the time of Satan's initial rebellion against God, as Satan has had access to heaven and to the throne of God after his rebellion. At this point, there seems to be reason to believe that Satan has stood before

God as our accuser through the ages from the time of the rebellion and stands there as our accuser until this war with Michael occurs.

The flight of the Woman into the wilderness is a result of Satan losing this war and being cast to the earth where he persecutes the Woman. The time of protection of the Woman while she is in this wilderness is the 1,260-day period of the first half of the Tribulation, so the flight of the Woman into the wilderness must be prior to the start of the Tribulation. Thus, we know that the war in heaven can not take place during the Tribulation Period. So when could this war take place?

The account of the war in heaven between Michael and his angels and the Dragon and his angels states that as the result of this war, *"neither was their place found any more in heaven" (Revelation 12:8). Place here is topos,* the word from which we get our word *topography.* Topos has to do with physical location, not administerial position. This verse clearly states that after this war, Satan could no longer return to heaven—his *place,* his physical location, could not be found any more in heaven. As a result of this war, Satan is cast to the earth and bound there, never to return.

As the war is won by Michael, a voice warns, *"Woe to the inhibitors of the earth and of the sea! For the devil is come down unto you, having great wrath, because he knows that he has but a short time" (Revelation 12:12).* Man measures time; God does not. A day and a thousand years are the same to God (2 Peter 3:8).

If Satan measures time, he must then measure time by man's measure. Therefore, if Satan counts a short time from this war to his defeat at the Battle of Armageddon, it is a short time as we would consider a short time to be. The battle of Armageddon is not too far ahead of us, so it is plausible that this heavenly war could have been recently fought.

It is the war between Michael and the Dragon that precipitates the events that leads to the flight of the Woman. Revelation 12 thus states:

The Woman flees into the wilderness
because
the Woman is being persecuted
by the Dragon
because
the Dragon is enraged
because
the Dragon was cast to the earth
because
the Dragon was thrown out of heaven
because
the Dragon lost the war with Michael.

In short, the Woman flees into the wilderness as a direct result of Satan losing the war. The Woman is protected for 1,260 days while in the wilderness, but there is no requirement that the length of the time she is in this wilderness is limited to 1,260 days. The flight of the Woman also has to be prior to the Tribulation Period. Since it is plausible that the war in heaven has recently occurred, it is also plausible that the flight of the Woman into the wilderness has also recently occurred.

Our generation has seen the flight of the Woman as the Jews have fled from the persecution of the countries wherein they were scattered and have fled into the wilderness of the people, the land of Israel. It is reasonable to believe that the war that resulted in the flight of the Woman did not precede her flight by any great measure of time. The war, then, has been recently fought.

All this means that Satan has been cast to the earth…and is now confined to our world. He has come with great wrath having lost the war. He knows that he has but a short time to work before his defeat at the battle of Armageddon. Is it any wonder then why the world is in such chaos?

I make known the end from the beginning, from ancient times what is still to come.

—Isaiah 46:10 (NIV)

CHAPTER TWENTY
A Resolution of Times

We have considered several prophecies in which specific time periods have been given concerning the days just prior to the return of Jesus. Most notable was the period of the Seventy Sevens of Daniel where the last seven is a time period of 1,260 days plus a period of 42 months. While we have these times fresh in our mind, there are two more time periods that must be addressed, a time period of 1,290 days of Daniel 12:11 and a period in time identified by the days of 1335 of Daniel 12:12. The applications of these two verses to the Last Days have been sorely maligned with the book of Daniel sealed. What is presented here are resolutions to the application of these times as the understanding of his words is now revealed.

The 1,290 Days

> *"And from the time that the daily (sacrifice) shall be taken away, and the abomination that makes desolate set up[239], there shall be a thousand two hundred and ninety days."*
>
> *(Daniel 12:11)*

This verse states that there are 1,290 days from the time that the *daily (sacrifice) is taken away* until the occurrence of the *abomination that makes desolate*. This verse can not be correctly understood until it is contrasted with that of Daniel 9:27, which states in part, *"In the midst of the week he shall cause the sacrifice and the oblation to cease, and for the overspreading of abominations he shall make it desolate."* Both of these verses speak of the abomination of desolation that is spoken of by Jesus in

Matthew 24:15: *"When you therefore shall see the abomination of desolation, spoken of by Daniel the prophet, stand in the holy place…"* Therefore, the abomination of desolation is the time anchor in both of these verses.

Verse 9:27 states that both *the sacrifice and the oblation will cease,* and the *overspreading of abominations* that will *make it [the Temple] desolate* will occur at the same time—*in the midst of the week.* Verse 12:11, however, states *the daily (sacrifice) shall be taken away* 1,290 days apart from the time of *the abomination that makes desolate.* But this *abomination that makes desolate* is the very same event that is the *overspreading of abominations* that *shall make it desolate,* so it too must occur *in the midst of the week.*

In short, one verse states that the *sacrifice and the oblation* will *cease in the midst of the week,* and the other states that the *daily (sacrifice) shall be taken away* 1,290 days prior to *the midst of the week.*240 Thus, these two verses appear to contradict one another. Therein lies the mystery; either the Bible is in error or the *sacrifice and the oblation* that will *cease* is not the *daily (sacrifice)* that *shall be taken away.*

Space does not allow me to dwell long on this subject, so I will make the resolution to the period of the 1,290 days brief. The Bible is not in error. Daniel 9:27 is to be taken literally and at face value; *in the midst of the week he* [the Antichrist] *shall cause the sacrifice and the oblation* [the historic sacrifices practiced by the Jews] *to cease.* Daniel 12:11 is also to be taken literally, including the concept that the *daily (sacrifice)* will be taken away. However, the *daily (sacrifice)* here is not to be taken at face value for it is of another type of sacrifice, one offered daily by believers in Jesus. *This daily (sacrifice)* is that of Romans 12:1: *"I beseech you therefore, brethren, by the mercies of God, that you present your bodies a living sacrifice, holy, acceptable unto God, which is your reasonable service."*

This *living sacrifice* is the *daily (sacrifice)* that will be *taken away* fulfilling the prophecy of 1 Thessalonians 4:16–17: *"16For the Lord himself shall descend from heaven with a shout, with the voice of the archangel, and with the trump of God: and the dead in Christ shall rise first: 17Then we which are alive and remain shall be caught up together with them in the clouds, to meet the Lord in the air: and so shall we ever be with the Lord."*

The Rapture therefore occurs 1,290 days before the abomination of desolation, 30 days prior to the start of the Tribulation Period.

The Days of 1335

"Blessed is he that waits, and comes to the thousand three hundred and five and thirty days."

(Daniel 12:12)

To begin to understand what this verse is saying, one must first recognize that this verse does not say "Blessed is he that waits and comes to the 1,335th day." This verse is not saying that one is blessed at the end of a period that is 1,335 days in length. The *thousand three hundred and five and thirty days* is itself singular. In other words, this verse is saying "Blessed is he that waits and comes to the days of 1335." The *thousand three hundred and five and thirty* is a year—the year 1335. Thus, this verse is saying, "Blessed is he that waits, and comes to the days of this time in history." To be *blessed* in the context of this verse was to receive joy and hope. To wait was to live in earnest expectation. This prophecy of Daniel was for the Jews; thus it was the Jews who had lived in earnest expectation, who had come to the year 1335, who were joyous and filled with hope.

Earnest expectation of what? The year 1335 must also be put into the perspective of the people and the land that was Israel. In AD 135, what was left of the Jews were driven from Jerusalem, and what was left of the great nation that was Israel ceased to exist. For nearly two thousand years, the Jews had looked with hope and expectation of returning to the homeland of their fathers. This hope and expectation of returning came to fruition in 1917 when a letter was written by Britain's Foreign Secretary Arthur James Balfour to Baron Rothschild, the leader of the British Jewish community who was advocating a permanent homeland for the Jews. This letter, called the Balfour Declaration, was considered a formal statement of policy that the British government would "view with favour the establishment in Palestine of a national home for the Jewish people."[241]

This letter had great weight because of Britain's status within the world community.

Great Britain soon thereafter became the administrator of Palestinian territories under a mandate system established in 1919 under Article 22 of the Covenant of the League of Nations. Article 22, which stated, in part, that "the Mandatory should be responsible for putting into effect the declaration originally made on November

2nd, 1917, by the Government of His Britannic Majesty, and adopted by the said Powers, in favor of the establishment in Palestine of a national home for the Jewish people....Whereas recognition has thereby been given to the historical connection of the Jewish people with Palestine and to the grounds for reconstituting their national home in that country."

In 1947, Great Britain turned its mandate over to the United Nations, which then divided Palestine into Arab and Jewish lands. On May 14, 1948, on the day in which the British Mandate over Palestine expired, the Jewish People's Council declared the establishment of the State of Israel.

What does all this have to do with the year 1335? At the time of the signing of the Balfour Declaration in 1917, the land that was Israel was a part of the Ottoman Empire, and the calendar of the empire was the Islamic calendar. Thus, the year 1917 in the rest of the world was the year 1335 in the land that was Israel. The prophecy of Daniel 12:12 had been given from the perspective of the disposition of Israel's land at the time of the fulfillment of the prophecy. Jerusalem never reached the year of 1336. From 1335, Jerusalem used the calendar of Anno Domini (the year of our Lord).[242]

When the fullness of the time was come, God sent forth his Son, made of a woman, made under the law, to redeem them that were under the law.

—Galatians 4:4–5

Appendix

The Old Testament
Believers Join the Church

A question arises. How, and when, do the Old Testament saints get to heaven, those who, like Abraham, are righteous before God because of their faith but yet were not redeemed by the blood of Jesus?

The righteousness of the Old Testament saints is conformity to the will of God expressed in the Mosaic Law, the covenant between Yahweh and the people of Israel. This covenant of the Law given to the people by Moses at Mount Sinai *"was added because of transgressions"* *(Galatians 3:19). "For until the law sin was in the world: but sin is not imputed when there is no law" (Romans 5:13) "for by the law is the knowledge of sin" (Romans 3:20).* Thus, the essential element of this covenant was dealing with sin. This brings us to the situation of the Old Testament saints.

Paul, in his letter to the church in Galatia, was warning those who, having been born of the spirit of Jesus, were returning to the Mosaic Law, of the failure of that very covenant. Now Paul was speaking to the New Testament believers, but his message spoke to the very issue that pertained to the Old Testament saints. He spoke of two covenants, the one from Mount Sinai which begot bondage, and the one from Jerusalem which brings freedom (Galatians 4:24–26; 5:1). His reference to Jerusalem was to the new covenant in the blood of Jesus that brings that freedom. In essence, the old covenant just covered over the sins of the people by the shed blood of sacrificed animals. But the sins of the people were still there, and they demanded a price be paid for their remittance, *"For the wages of sin is death" (Romans 6:23).* This speaks of a spiritual death. The new covenant, on the other hand, washes away all evidence of one's sins by the price paid by the shed blood of Jesus on the cross.

Now, concerning the disposition of the Old Testament saints. They were righteous before God because of their faith, but they were still held in bondage by the old covenant of the Law for their sins still demanded a price be paid: *"⁴But when the fullness of the time was come, God sent forth his Son, made of a woman, made under the law, ⁵To redeem them that were under the law"* (Galatians 4:4–5). To be righteous before God was one thing, but to be redeemed by the blood of Jesus was quite another. *To redeem* here is *to acquire out of the forum,* the forum in this case being the old covenant of the Law. In simpler terms, *to be freed at a price.*

Jesus had said, *"I am the way, the truth, and the life: no man comes unto the Father, but by me" (John 14:6).* There is but one way to heaven—redemption by the blood of Jesus as encapsulated in the new covenant just hours before he was hung on that cross: *"²⁷And he took the cup, and gave thanks, and gave it to them, saying, Drink you all of it; ²⁸For this is my blood of the new testament, which is shed for many for the remission of sins"* (Matthew 26:27–28). But how can this apply to the Old Testament believers? They never knew of Jesus, or of the new covenant! How then could Jesus *redeem them that were under the law?*

Jesus, after his death, *"⁸when he ascended up on high, he led captivity captive… ⁹(Now that he ascended, what is it but that he also descended first into the lower parts of the earth?)" (Ephesians 4:8–9).* Peter said of this descent of Jesus, *"¹⁸being put to death in the flesh, but quickened by the Spirit,"* Jesus *"¹⁹went and preached unto the spirits in prison" (1 Peter 3:18–19).* So where is this prison that is in the lower parts of the earth? The writer of Acts, speaking of David's prophecy of the death and resurrection of Jesus, states:

²⁵For David spoke concerning him, I foresaw the Lord always before my face, for he is on my right hand, that I should not be moved: ²⁶Therefore did my heart rejoice, and my tongue was glad; moreover also my flesh shall rest in hope: ²⁷Because you will not leave my soul in hell, neither will you suffer your Holy One to see corruption… ³⁰Therefore being a prophet, and knowing that God had sworn with an oath to him, that of the fruit of his loins, according to the flesh, he would raise up Christ to sit on his throne; ³¹He seeing this before spoke of the resurrection of Christ, that his soul was not left in hell.

(Acts 2:25–31)

Hell, *Sheol—the unseen state* in David's prophecy, *Hades—the unseen world* in Acts, *the prison* of Peter's account, and *the lower parts of the earth* of Ephesians 4, are all the same place.

The *spirits in prison* and the *soul in hell* are both in that place when Jesus *descended into the lower parts of the earth.*

Paul, still speaking to those of the new covenant, wrote, *"For as many as are of the works of the law are under the curse"* (Galatians 3: 10), but *"Christ has redeemed us from the curse of the law, being made a curse for us"* (Galatians 3:13). As Jesus hung on the cross, the Old Testament believers were still under that curse, held prisoner, held captive by the Law. Upon his death, Jesus descended into hell and presented himself to those held captive by the old covenant of the Law. The Old Testament saints had been righteous before God because of their faith but now are offered the gift of redemption through the blood of Jesus by their faith in him as their Lord and savior; the same offer Jesus presents to the world today. We can believe that these saints accepted his offer of the new covenant of grace. By this act, Jesus took *captivity captive.* Therefore, *when he ascended up on high, he led captivity captive.* What was thus *led captive,* taken away, was the *captivity* of the old covenant Law that restrained the Old Testament saints.

The Old Testament saints are still in hell (or Sheol, if you prefer) awaiting resurrection, but through Jesus, they have joined the church. Thus, when *"the Lord himself shall descend from heaven with a shout, with the voice of the archangel, and with the trump of God,"* these Old Testament saints shall also rise as those who are *"dead in Christ"* (Thessalonians 4:16).

239 "Set up" here is *nathan,* meaning *to give up,* or *give forth.*

240 "Prior to" is based on two facts: (1) The time period is given in days, not months, matching the pattern (1,260 days vs. 42 months) set by the time's notation of the two halves of the seventieth seven; (2) the time period of 1,290 days can not extend from the "midst of the week" beyond the end of the seventieth seven, as all Israelite prophecies are complete by the end of the last period of seven years. Thus, the time period of 1,290 days must extend back in time from the "midst of the week" to some point prior to the start of the period of 1,260 days.

[241] Letter from Foreign Secretary Arthur James Balfour to Lord Rothschild, dated November 2, 1917. 242 An Egyptian coin of 1917 bearing the Muslim 1335 date is shown at www.cai.org/bible-studies/coin-daniel-1212.

Contents

Why Did God Seal Up Daniel's Words?

— *The Red Dragon, the Beast, and the False Prophet* —

The Empires of the Red Dragon,
the Beast, and the False Prophet

Deciphering the Symbols that
Define These Three Beasts

A Man Just Like His Boss

Revealing the Identity of Babylon
the Great, the Mother of Harlots

Israel's Place in the Empire
of the Antichrist

Putting the Story of These Three
Beasts into Perspective

— *The City of Jerusalem and the Nation of Israel* —

The Resurrection of the Nation of Israel

History with a Message

Adding the Tenth Nation
to the League of Ten

The Time of the Annihilation of Israel

Are They in Town to Destroy
the Temple?

— *The Rule of the Antichrist* —

When Israel's Cup of
Iniquity Overflowed

The Misconception of a World Rule

Why Do We Glorify the Antichrist?

— *Daniel's People and His Holy City* —

A Time Schedule Like No Other

There Really Is a Difference Between 1,260 days and 42 months

It's a Done Deal, Folks

The Devil's on Your Doorstep

Discerning the Numbers 1,290
and 1335 of Daniel